PROTECTION OF BEAUTY

PROTECTION OF BEAUTY

BOOK ONE OF THE ARMOR SERIES

BY KATARINA KYDE

Flying Squid Leaf Media

Printed in the United States of America

Second Edition: 2025
Paperback ISBN: 979-8-9918929-1-9
Ebook ISBN: 979-8-9918929-0-2

First Printing: 2014

For Phoebe

A NOTE FOR MY READERS:

The Armor Series, at its core, is a contemporary low fantasy about the walls we put up and the armor we all don when we're scared, uncomfortable, or insecure, and moving forward through these times as best we can with self-love and self-acceptance. This central theme is woven into the backdrop of heart-pumping action. Be aware that some scenes within the series are emotionally charged and/or highly action-oriented.

This book specifically, *Protection of Beauty*, contains scenes depicting fear, anxiety, violence, emotional, verbal, and physical abuse, blood, death, sexual situations, and profanity.

Prologue

DON'T BE WEAK

Wednesday, May 30, 2012

I f only he'd sold that goddamn ring when he'd had the chance.

As Richard Woods stared at the ring his wife had placed into his hand, he shivered, unable to shake how creepy it felt. He wondered why it elicited such a visceral reaction in him. It was just an orange stone in a bronze-colored setting. How can something so precious and priceless—according to his mother, anyway—bring on such a foreboding feeling? Its mere presence in his hand made goosebumps cover his arms. Maybe it was haunted. Or cursed. Or...

You're ridiculous, he told his imagination and locked the ring in the safe in their bedroom closet. But did it really need to be in the safe? If no appraiser was able to give him a reliable value, and no one remembered its history, was it actually as valuable as his mother had claimed it to be? His guess was no. That's why he'd offered it to his wife to wear as costume jewelry that evening. It had looked beautiful on her hand. It'd made her smile. It'd made him shiver.

All thoughts of the ring dissipated like fog in the rising sun as he noticed his wife undressing.

"You like what you see?" Marilyn asked him with a smirk as she stood naked in front of him.

"Very much," he gushed, his head bobbing up and down. He swept her up in an embrace, twirling her around until they fell on the bed together, laughing. *This is exactly how love should feel. Dizzy and exciting and happy and comfortable all at the same time.*

It was pitch black when Richard awoke later that night with a jolt, his heart beating in his ears. *What was that sound?*

"Are you okay, Rich?" asked Marilyn sleepily, as she reached over and turned on the bedside lamp.

In the low-wattage light, Richard saw a gun aimed at his face and three strangers wearing ski masks.

Marilyn screamed.

"It'll be okay," the tall and fit one said to Marilyn in a masculine voice that might've been calming in any other situation.

"Where's the ring?" the short one hissed at Richard in an elderly woman's voice, her brown eyes wild.

They reminded Richard of pirates. The small woman's voice sounded mean like the famous pirate Anne Bonny. The ocean could be viewed in the eyes of the tall, fit man, tumultuous and blue. The third one was a shorter, rounder man who had red facial hair poking through his mask—Red Beard. And they were here to pillage and plunder. A warm puddle of urine surrounded Richard's legs.

Marilyn screamed again.

Ocean View silenced Marilyn with a chloroform rag. Richard looked at his unresponsive wife with a sick stomach as Ocean View placed her head on her pillow with a surprising tenderness. Richard put his arms around his unconscious wife, wishing he could get to his gun under the bed. "What...what are you talking about?" he stammered, sweat running into his eyes.

"The ring! You candy-ass! Where is it?" screeched Anne Bonny.

Richard looked more closely at her and recognized her eyes through the mask. "Wait a minute! I know you!" he said, his voice wavering. "You're the one who offered to buy that old ring tonight." His stomach clenched. She'd just been an old lady at the restaurant who'd come across as somewhat odd, offering him a blank check while grabbing Marilyn's hand and trying to remove the ring. If he'd known refusing her would lead to this, he'd have thrown it at her and ran.

Red Beard waved his gun around, getting as impatient as Anne Bonny. "The ring—where is it? Tell us *now!*"

"In the...the safe in the closet." Richard pointed to it with a trembling hand.

Anne Bonny twisted the dial as Richard gave her the combination. "It's here!" she announced. "I have it!"

Now that the pirates had the ring, would they leave? Or would they... "Look, I'm sorry I didn't sell it to you before," babbled Richard as he fought to take in a full breath. Tears cascaded down his face. "Please don't hurt us!" His arm tightened around his wife.

"It's far too late to beg for your life!" Anne Bonny pointed her gun at him.

"This isn't necessary," Ocean View said, grabbing Anne Bonny by the arm. "You have the ring. Let's go."

"Don't be weak!" she snarled at him. "It *is* necessary. He recognized me!"

Being completely certain he was about to die if he didn't escape, Richard threw off the blankets and pulled Marilyn toward the edge of the bed.

"No! He can't prove anything!" Ocean View declared and tackled the old woman.

"Mother!" Red Beard yelled and tried to pull Ocean View off of her.

The old woman pressed a spot on Ocean View's neck that made him yell out in pain and release her.

Richard picked Marilyn up and ran for the bedroom door. Two sparks flashed like lightning while the accompanying muffled echoes rang out. He heard himself scream. Anne Bonny's aim had been perfect; Richard saw Marilyn's skull shatter a split second before feeling a bullet rip through his side.

Richard fell and watched Marilyn's body crumple on the floor next to his own, her brain matter splattered above their heads on the wall next to them. He tried to push himself to his feet but only managed to roll over onto his back. Richard saw Red Beard turn green as his eyes focused on Marilyn's inside body parts that were now outside.

"You're next, you weak, worthless piece of shit!" Anne Bonny said, turning the gun on Ocean View. "Are you trying to get us caught? I should've killed you years ago like I wanted to!"

"No, mother, please!" begged Red Beard. "We're going to need him, and you know it."

Without a word, she put her gun in the holster under her jacket and tossed her keys to Ocean View. "Go make yourself useful and bring the car around."

With a glare, Ocean View did as he was told.

Richard couldn't help but groan from the pain in his side as he stared up at the two remaining pirates.

"Mother!" Red Beard exclaimed. He pointed a shaking hand at Richard. "He's still alive!"

"I know," she agreed, stepping over to Richard. "If I wanted him dead, he'd be gone by now."

"What are you going to do?" Richard asked, struggling to catch his breath.

"I'm going to make sure this ring is the real thing," she told him. She knelt next to him on the floor and held the ring between her thumb and index finger. "What time did you and your wife leave the house tonight?" she demanded.

The pain from the bullet in his side was so great, Richard struggled to remember. "Uh...six, I think."

"Good." She looked at Red Beard who knelt next to her. "That means the sun was still up." She put the ring on her finger, grabbed the setting with the fingers of her other hand, and twisted it counter-clockwise.

To Richard's surprise, the setting turned easily. The twisting motion triggered a mechanism inside the ring that flipped the stone over. The other side of the orange stone had bands of yellow and red running through it. *What the hell?* Richard stared at it in disbelief. He'd never known it could do that.

The woman pirate touched the orange, red, and yellow side of the stone to Richard's arm for a brief moment. Richard's arm felt a pinprick from the touch. *How can that be? It's just a stone.*

"Now watch this," Anne Bonny told her son.

As terrible as Richard already felt from the bullet in his side, it was nothing in comparison to the hot, sick feeling that began pulsing through his stomach and bowels. Strangely, his fear was fading, and he surrendered to his exhaustion and let himself relax on the floor. He didn't even worry when the intense trembling began.

"Mother, what's happening?" Red Beard asked with a wavering voice as Richard convulsed.

Anne Bonny twisted the setting of the ring clockwise which flipped the stone back into its original position. Only the orange side was still showing, and it sat on her finger, innocent-as-you-please. "This is the real thing," she said, a delighted smirk oozing across her face. "The poison ring." She stood up.

"The what?" Red Beard stood up too. "What kind of poison? A stone can't do that."

"It's more than the stone. It's ancient magic."

Richard finally understood why that ring had creeped him out so much—it was poisonous. But ancient magic? Not a real thing. Right? He knew he had no time left to wonder about it, no time to even grieve for Marilyn.

Anne Bonny stepped over him on her way out of the room. "Are you coming?!" she demanded of her son. "It's time for step two." She smirked and waved at Richard right before shooting him in the head.

Part 1

FATE AND DESTINY

Chapter 1

At least death would've been a good excuse for not being there. But no one had died, and it only *felt* like a cemetery to Anise Viston as she stood just inside the front door of her mother's lonely house with bereft tears, mourning the dearly non-departed.

Instead of happy words of congratulations, the *tick-tick-tick* of the clock on the mantle was the only sound to be heard. It reminded her that she needed to leave soon so she wouldn't be late. Kicking aside a musty pile of wrinkled clothes that had taken up residence in the middle of the foyer, she grimaced when Miller moths flew out of them and headed straight for her face to protest the disturbance of their nap. Her arms waved to shoo away the annoying, dusty pests.

Grabbing a tissue from the nearby powder room, Anise dabbed away the tears that were still falling. *Thank god for waterproof mascara.* Looking in the mirror, she paused to let the sight of the pencil that sat behind her ear comfort her and wished she had some time to sketch to calm her nerves. But that would have to wait.

Stepping back into the foyer, she noticed the painting she'd made for her mother's birthday had been removed from its place on the wall. A lonely nail jutted from the stud, looking embarrassed for having its one purpose denied. Somehow, it made the house seem even quieter. She wasn't surprised no one was home, but she had hoped. It was the damn hope that tore her heart to shreds every time.

Dropping her mortarboard hat on the table in the foyer, Anise pulled her phone out of her tote bag, brought up her list of contacts, and hovered her finger over the "Mom" button. She wanted to touch it as much as she didn't. The phone went back in the bag. Anise closed her eyes and took a deep breath. She grabbed her phone again, and her finger hovered over "Mom," a little closer this time. The hesitation made her pace, her clicking heels on the tile floor keeping time with the ticking clock.

If her mother could see her now, she'd roll her eyes and tell Anise she's overreacting.

It's just a silly ceremony, her mother would say.

"Not to me," Anise replied out loud to the imagined statement. She hung her head and looked at her shoes. Her mother would also say she hated her silver pumps.

Who are you trying to impress?

"Well, *I* like them," came Anise's defiant reply. She never actually responded to her mother's hurtful comments when they happened in real life. She figured the fight that would inevitably follow wouldn't be worth it.

Anise reread the text messages she'd received from her parents a few moments before. Mom wasn't coming to her graduation because Dad *was* coming, and her nerves were so shot, she needed to go to the spa for a massage. But Dad wasn't coming either now because some girlfriend he'd never mentioned before—another floozie du jour as Mom liked to call them no matter how many times Anise asked her not to—had a scheduling conflict. But it wasn't just that. It was everything.

Against her better judgment, Anise's finger pressed

the "Mom" button. The butterflies in her stomach flapped harder with every ring.

"What?" Deborah's voice demanded through the phone. "I'm about to go in for my massage."

"Dad's not coming now, so you can still make it." Anise knew better than to wish for a positive response, but she couldn't help it.

"My schedule does not revolve around your father's whims," Deborah spat.

"What about your daughter's major life accomplishments?" Anise threw back.

"My daughter *betrayed* me by inviting her *father* to this life accomplishment when she *knew* I didn't want to see him."

"How could you call me inviting my father to my graduation a betrayal to *you*?" Tears began to flow again. "I have two parents that I love, and it's not fair of you to make me pick one."

"Don't talk to *me* about not fair! You know what your father did to me," came Deborah's wailing voice. "My nerves are *so* on edge! I won't be able to *function* without a massage!"

Anise began to speak again but realized her mother had hung up. That had gone pretty much how she'd expected, and she wondered why she even bothered to try. She dialed her father's phone next, her stomach in a knot again because she already knew how the conversation would go. But something in her had a need to try anyway. It was that damn, evil hope.

"Hey, kiddo!"

"Dad, in your text you said you had to go back home. Does that mean you're in town? Are you at the airport?"

"No, I'm still in New York. My girlfriend has a scheduling conflict. We couldn't make it."

"You could've come alone, Dad. Or at least let me know earlier. Mom isn't coming because she thought you were coming. Now neither of my parents will be there."

"Sorry, kiddo. Next time." Ben didn't sound sorry at all.

"You never even booked a flight, did you?" Anise's chest hurt.

"Like I said, next time." His voice sounded distracted, and Anise could hear the changing radio stations in his car.

"What do you mean, 'next time?' There is no next time! This is my college graduation. It happens once."

"This is for your college graduation? Aw, if I'd known that..."

"You knew! I told you in the email. And the text. And the last time we talked."

"I'll call you tomorrow, kiddo, and you can tell me all about it. I just got to Katie's. Good luck tonight!" He hung up.

Anise attempted to relax her clenched jaw. He wouldn't call tomorrow. They only spoke when *she* called. She wondered why she kept trying to have a normal relationship with either of them. It'd never been normal.

"You can't control the actions of others, only your reaction to them," Anise read aloud from the handwritten 3x5 note card she'd brought with her and dropped it back in her vintage floral tote bag with the others. Sometimes the affirmations helped, and other times, like today, they simply weren't enough. It was times like these when she didn't know what to do that her own mind felt like a stranger. She'd been an adult for a few years now and wished she had a more solid sense of herself. *Who do I want to be in this situation?* Anise asked herself. Actually, *that* was a good one. She took out a blank note card, grabbed the yellow Ticonderoga pencil from behind her ear, and wrote down the inspiring question. It would help anytime she didn't know how to handle herself. It might help her answer the big question of who she wanted to be in *any* given situation—in life in general. She promised herself she'd think hard about it as she walked out the front door.

Her silver high heels announced each step as she descended the concrete stairs toward the street, and her wavy, brown hair rippled past her shoulder blades and danced to the rhythm of the breeze. She brushed her bangs to the side as she spotted a man who looked to be in his early forties walking up the sidewalk. He had brown hair cut short and a face that made her wonder if she'd seen him somewhere before.

"Hi," he called out. "I'm looking for Deborah Viston. Do I have the right house?"

"You do," Anise replied, "but she's not home. Can I take a message?"

"Please," he said, nodding. "My name is Les Wilkins. If you could have her call me..." He handed her a scrap of paper with his name and a phone number and nothing more.

"Sure, does she know you?"

"Yes. Well, sort of. It's a long story." He paused, a serious expression washing over his face. "It's really important that I get in touch with her."

"Don't worry," she assured him. "I'm Anise, her daughter. I'll make sure she gets this."

Les's hazel eyes lit up. "Her daughter! It's good to meet you." He motioned to her outfit. "It looks like congratulations are in order."

"Thank you! It's my college graduation. Finally. I've been looking forward to this night for years."

"That's great! I remember mine. Lots of celebrating."

"Yes!" she said, her excitement for the evening ahead making her smile. "After the ceremony, my friends are taking me out for dinner and then they have some kind of surprise planned."

He smiled back at her. "That sounds fun. Enjoy your special night. And thank you for your help."

"No problem."

Les turned to leave but stopped and faced her again.

"Anise, has your mother ever...mentioned me?"

She shook her head. "No, not that I recall." She paused, feeling like there must be a lot more to Les's story than he was letting on. "How did you say she knows you?"

"I didn't," he replied slowly, grabbing on to a nearby tree and squeezing his eyes shut.

"Are you okay?"

"Yeah, just dizzy. It'll pass. Anyway, I got a strange letter a long time ago and didn't think of it again until recently. It's from someone named Thomas-something. I don't know him and never heard of him, but his letter mentioned your mother. I'm not sure what it all means, and I was hoping she could shed some light on the mystery."

"What did it say?" Anise asked him, intrigued.

Les hesitated before speaking. "I'm wondering if someone is trying to play a joke on me. It talks about some ancient jewelry that has healing power. It can make you stronger, protects you..." Les's eyes rolled into the back of his head, and he collapsed in a ball on the front lawn.

Anise knelt over him and touched his shoulder. "Les? Les?"

ANISE SAT IN THE HOSPITAL ROOM brushing off the worried calls from her friends with a quick text message. She texted her boyfriend, Brian, as well, not that he was even thinking about her that evening. *Whatever.* He didn't matter right now.

Les's phone was locked, so she rooted through the bag he'd brought to see if she could find anything to give her a clue as to who to call on his behalf. It contained a hoodie, a mechanical pencil, three puzzle books of crosswords, Sudoku, and logic puzzles, and the letter he'd mentioned. Her curiosity buzzed in her fingertips as she held the letter, but she'd never read someone else's personal correspondence. When he woke up, she'd ask him about it. She tucked all of it back in the bag. A search through Les's wallet left her with little knowledge except that he was from Philadelphia. *Halfway across the country is a long flight for someone who's sick.*

Anise couldn't help but wonder about Les. Why did he want to see her mother, and who was he to her? Was a strange letter really the reason he came all the way from Philadelphia? She stared at him as he remained still as a stone, his chest barely moving with his breath. She made up her mind to stay put until she could find a relative of his. Regardless of whether or not she got her answers, no one should have to be alone when they're not well and far from home. After an online search on her phone, she started calling every listing for anyone named Wilkins in the Philadelphia area.

Her anxiety was high as her worry for him grew. It'd been a couple hours. He hadn't woken up, and since she wasn't family, the doctors wouldn't tell her anything else. As she made her phone calls with her left hand, her right hand pulled her sketchbook out of her tote bag, grabbed the pencil from behind her ear, and drew his motionless form in the stark, white bed. The scratching noises of the pencil on paper soothed her as she focused on her drawing.

"What are you still doing here, hun?" a nurse asked her. "You don't even know him."

"I won't leave him alone," Anise insisted. "Not until I find someone who does know him."

Saturday, June 2, 2012

THE SUN HAD SET AND RISEN again by the time Anise found a relative of Les's. She shifted in her plastic chair next to his bed and stifled a yawn as she pressed the phone to her ear.

"He's where?" his mother screeched. "I'm booking a flight right now! What was he doing with you anyway?"

"I don't know, ma'am. He came to my mother's house looking for her when he collapsed. Is there anything else I can do to help?"

The woman began sobbing. "No one can help him! The doctors are useless."

"I'm so sorry."

"He's had every medical test they can think of, and they've found nothing wrong with him!"

"That's good news at least."

"There's nothing good about any of this," the woman scoffed.

"I'm sorry, that's not how I meant it."

"Whatever. Thank you for calling, but you tell your mother to stay away from him! And you do the same!" the woman yelled before hanging up.

"What?" Anise asked no one in particular. Her sketchbook was still open in her lap. The drawing was done, but an unconscious man in a hospital bed was too sad. The picture needed a ray of positivity. In an oval acting as a border for the drawing, she added the words: "Someone who loves you is rushing to be by your side for when you wake."

Her eyes drooped, and she bought a coffee before climbing on to the bus to go home to shower and change before work. Leaning back in her seat, she tried to decompress as the bus plodded along down the city streets. Reaching into her tote bag, she pulled out a list of goals she'd made several months earlier.

Have a job that will make my parents proud

Marry Brian by age 25

Graduate college

She put a satisfying checkmark by the third item on the list before looking over the rest of it. The first one made her scowl, and she crossed it out with a definitive stroke of her pencil. She frowned as she wondered if she even wanted the second goal on the list anymore. And was that it? Three goals? There had to be more to life. She pulled out a note card from her bag and stared at its message. *Who do I want to be in this situation?*

As soon as she walked through the door and heard the little bell above it ring, Anise felt at home. The donations to Doreen's Thrift Shoppe had been piling up for weeks, and as this morning would be busy soon enough, now was the time to at least start sifting through the community's unwanted treasures. Anise had worked at the thrift shop since she'd turned sixteen and was still happily employed there, even as a twenty-four year old who had just earned her bachelor's degree. Often, she'd find an item of clothing or an accessory in the donation piles that perfectly complimented her vintage-inspired style of dress. The customers were usually a joy to help. And the owner, Doreen, was the best boss she could ask for.

"There you are; I was so worried!" Doreen embraced Anise in a bear hug when she walked in the shop.

"I'm sorry." Anise dropped her tote bag on the colored concrete floor behind the counter. Weaving her way through the clothes racks and tables of bygone treasures, she grabbed a few plastic bags containing donations and carried them to a large empty table near Doreen's office in the back of the shop.

Doreen followed her. "What happened last night? I was already at the ceremony when I got your text saying you weren't coming."

Anise felt herself frown as she thought about Les's curious visit. "You've known my mom for a long time."

Doreen nodded. "Ever since our junior high days."

"Did she ever mention someone named Les Wilkins to you?"

Doreen shook her head, and her shiny black hair swept back and forth over her broad shoulders. "No." After Anise told her about Les and the hospital, Doreen smiled. "I'm proud of you, dear. You and your big heart."

"I just hope he'll be okay. I'm going to swing by the hospital before I go home tonight." She grabbed a pile of hangers and pulled out moth-ball scented clothes from one of the donation bags.

"I'm sure he'd appreciate that. But now I want to congratulate you on your graduation! I'm so very proud of you. I just can't say it enough." She enveloped Anise in another embrace.

"Okay, stop! You don't have to make a fuss," laughed Anise.

"I most certainly do!" Doreen protested. "And I never got to give you your gift." She handed Anise a small but beautifully wrapped package. "Open it!"

"Thank you!" Anise looked at her friend with a smile which quickly turned into a frown of concern. "Are you crying, Doreen?"

"Oh, no, dear, it's my contacts again. Open the box!"

The delight and anticipation bubbled up inside her as Anise tore off the brown paper. She opened the tea box Doreen had recycled into a gift box and peered inside. Anise took in a deep breath. "Oh, it's stunning! And so unique! I love it. Where did you find it?"

"Believe it or not, it was in one of the donations we received. A nice lady brought it in and commented on how it would make a great gift for a vibrant young woman. When I saw it, I had to agree with her. I, of course, thought of you." Doreen touched Anise's face with a loving hand.

The large pendant was square-shaped but with rounded corners, about three inches on each side, and made of out a reddish-golden metal she couldn't quite place. In the center was a large, round, black stone with white bands randomly running through it. The black stone was surrounded by a circle of five smaller stones evenly placed around it, each orange and white. It hung on a simple chain of the same metal.

"It looks like an amulet someone may have worn in the Middle Ages! It's amazing! Thank you so much!" Anise gave her friend a hug, put the amulet around her neck, and lifted her wavy, brown hair from under the chain. Her fingers traced the gemstones as she wondered what the amulet's story might be. She couldn't wait until she had time to sketch it—maybe around the neck of a fourteenth century sorceress. And what caption would she pair with it? Maybe something like: Magic exists for those who seek it.

"You're very welcome," said Doreen. "I'm sorry that it's late. I tried calling you last night..."

"I know, I'm sorry," Anise said, picking up another hanger. "I spent the entire night trying to find a family member for Les."

"Of course. I was just worried and so were your friends. Was Brian with you at least?"

Anise almost scoffed but held it back. "He was...sick yesterday."

A scowl took over Doreen's expression. "And by sick you mean drunk?"

Anise said nothing. She unfolded a blouse with a

swift, angry shake.

Doreen took her hand and in a soft, gentle tone asked, "Why do you keep making excuses for him?"

A sigh escaped Anise's lips. "I don't know. I guess because he never used to get drunk this often. He wasn't always like this. I keep hoping things will go back to how they used to be. We had such a cute meeting. Did I ever tell you about it?"

Doreen shook her head. She poured them each a cup of tea from the vintage teapot that sat on a silver tray at the end of the table.

"I was late for the rom-com movie I'd been wanting to see ever since the trailer came out. I ran to the theater through the rain, found the last empty seat, and that's when the explosions and killings started. I said, 'This isn't a rom-com!' I didn't think I said it that loudly, but Brian was sitting next to me and started laughing. He gave me his jacket because I was cold and drenched. He walked me down the hall to the movie I actually wanted to see and watched it with me. We've been together ever since."

"That is cute," Doreen agreed.

"Since then I dreamed about how romantic it would be if we got married and were together forever. But he was never that charming again. Not even close. I was just kidding myself."

"You don't need to feel bad for having dreams," Doreen said kindly. "But you shouldn't feel the need to lie to cover up his bad behavior like you used to do all the time for Deb and Ben. I didn't see them at the ceremony either. Did *they* ever contact you yesterday?"

"Yeah, they sent texts. I called each of them, but neither wanted to show up."

Doreen touched Anise's hand. "I'm so sorry. You know you deserve better than that, don't you? You know you deserve people who adore you and respect you and love you to pieces like I do?"

Anise nodded. "I do know." She thought about her promise to herself to discover who she wants to be. Once she figured that out, she'd know what to do about all her life messes. But how does one know who they want to be?

Doreen changed the subject after Anise's eyes filled with tears. "Now tell me, sweetie, what's next for you? I know you've had a few job interviews, right? Don't get me wrong, I'd love to keep you here forever, but I knew the day would come when you'd have to spread your wings and fly."

Anise shifted her weight from one foot to the other and felt her cheeks grow warm. "Well, it's been really difficult, actually. I've had a few interviews so far, but I get so nervous that I completely screw up my answers. I'm ashamed to say I skipped my last one because I was embarrassed and afraid."

"You skipped it?!"

Anise hung her head. "Brian's sister Corinne is a psychologist, and she's told me that I keep letting fear make my decisions for me. I think she's right or else I wouldn't have skipped my interview. In fact, the only interview I aced was the one for the job I really don't want."

"So your stage fright was acting up. Were you hearing your mother in your head again?"

Anise nodded. "Every time."

"What was she saying?"

"Same old. She likes to tell me I make bad decisions. Or that I'm not going to be good at something which makes me not want to even try." She emptied a bag of shoes on the table, finding catharsis in the satisfying thumps they made upon landing.

"Remember that self-help book we both read last year?" Doreen asked. "The one that was called 'The Things You Tell Yourself,' or something like that? It said that you need to be mindful of not adopting other people's words as your own. And your mother's *past* words have become your *current* inner monologue."

"Yeah. And I know I shouldn't listen to that, and I try to push her out of my head, but then self-doubt sneaks in..."

"You need a new inner monologue."

Anise stood a little straighter, proud of what she was about to say. "I have one! I was thinking about that book, and I'm following its advice. I ask myself who I want to be in a situation, and then I act accordingly. It lets me set aside my fear and self-doubt and consider who I'd be otherwise or who I'd like to practice becoming."

"That's fantastic! So, what job did you end up getting?" Doreen asked, taking a sip of Earl Gray.

"You know those annoying market research survey takers in the mall? The ones that run after you while you're shopping and try to ask you questions? That'll be me starting Monday. It's only a part-time job, so I'll be staying on here, too, with the same schedule you have for me now. I didn't mention it earlier because I'm a little embarrassed about it."

"If you don't want to do it, why did you take it?"

"It's the only thing I could get that had something to do with my marketing degree. Plus, I need the extra money. Brian's still in a lot of pain from his accident and can't work."

Doreen narrowed her eyebrows. "That boy is taking advantage of you. Who do you want to be in your situation with him?"

Anise hung her head and looked at her floral flats. "That's a good question."

"Maybe come at it from a different angle. Close your eyes and picture your perfect dream man. What's he like?"

Anise complied and smiled dreamily as her imagination brought him to life. "He's handsome and exciting. Romantic. Daring and bold and brilliant. He plays by his own rules. We show each other new things and travel the world together. He's encouraging of my dreams and my art. We teach each other things. He's powerful—he knows how to do things that most other people can't. He's serious and thoughtful when I need him to be, but he's also not afraid to be silly and playful at the right times. He makes me laugh, somehow makes anything fun, and he dances with me in the rain. He fights for me and stands up for me in every sense of the phrase. He makes me feel safe, like I could say or do anything and he'd love me regardless." She loved him already. If only he actually existed.

"And how many of those boxes does Brian check?"

Anise's eyes opened. Brian was good-looking when he bothered to shower and comb his hair. Otherwise... "I think we have some customers waiting for the store to open," she said, no longer wanting to talk about it. She checked the clock on the wall. "And it *is* already 10:02."

Doreen frowned but kept quiet. Anise was grateful that her friend said nothing and let in the customers that had lined up outside instead.

A few minutes later, a small, elderly woman wandered in. Her clothes were stylish, but her pure white hair looked like it had been through a hurricane. Her eyes darted around the store. "Good morning, can I help you find anything?" Anise greeted her. At 5'5", Anise towered over the woman who looked to be no more than five feet tall.

"Oh my, what a stunning necklace," the woman replied, running her finger over the black center stone of Anise's amulet.

Anise took a step back, surprised and uncomfortable with the lack of personal space. "Thank you. It was a graduation gift from a friend."

"Well, congratulations, uh..." The woman looked at Anise's nametag. "Ann-niss? Like the herb?"

Sometimes Anise wished she had a more common name like her friends Vanessa, Erin, and Joy, so she wouldn't have to keep pronouncing it for people. "It's spelled like the herb but pronounced Uh-neese."

"I see, as in a nephew and *a niece.*" The elderly woman flashed what seemed to be a forced smile at her own joke.

"Yes, ma'am." As if she hadn't heard that gem a thousand times before. Internally, Anise's eyes were rolling. "So, what can I help you find?"

"Well, Anise, I can't keep my eyes off your lovely necklace. How much will you take for it?"

"Oh, ma'am, like I said, this was a gift from a dear friend. I couldn't possibly sell it."

"Don't be silly, child. I'll make it worth your while. How about $200? 300?"

Anise began to protest again, but the elderly woman stopped her. "500?"

"Ma'am, this was a donation item here at the store; I'm sure it's not worth that much."

"Then recognize a good bargain when you see it. $1000. And that's my final offer." She opened her small leather purse and took out her checkbook. "What's your last name, Anise?"

"No, really, it's not for sale. But we have some other jewelry items in the display case over here," Anise started to say.

"Well, this is getting ridiculous!" sputtered the woman. "I'm sure your friend will understand. Just tell me what you want for it!" she exclaimed, her voice getting loud enough for the other customers to turn around to see what the commotion was about.

Doreen rushed over, and Anise could tell by her quick but heavy footsteps that she was getting her mother hen feathers ruffled. "Ma'am," Doreen said firmly, "this necklace is not for sale."

"BULLSHIT!" the woman yelled. One hand grasped her wild, white hair while the other pointed a finger in Anise's face. "Everyone has a price! Just name yours!"

"Ok, it's time for you to leave," said Doreen firmly, as she grabbed the old woman's arm and ushered her toward the door. Doreen had a large, strong frame, but the small, elderly woman somehow was able to wriggle free from Doreen's grasp. "Get out, or I'll call the police," Doreen warned.

The older woman grasped her own hair with one hand and pulled. "I will end you!" she declared to them both. She reached for the amulet.

"Stop!" Anise raised her forearm to block the old woman's reach. The snarl she received back was unsettling.

"Give it to me! That necklace is mine!" The woman tried to grab the amulet, faster this time.

"No! Stop it!" Anise once again blocked her with a forearm. She looked in the woman's brown eyes and saw nothing but determination and hatred.

To Anise's surprise, the woman grabbed her hand instead of reaching for the amulet again. Anise felt an intense pain between her thumb and index finger and let out a cry as she jumped back.

The woman clutched the amulet with both hands and tried to yank the chain from Anise's neck. Anise put her arms between the woman's and opened them with a swift push outward. "Leave me alone!"

The woman grabbed an iron figurine of a horse and cart from a nearby table full of toys from the 1940's and hurled it at Anise's head. Anise ducked and barely missed being hit. The horse and cart crashed into a glass curio cabinet filled with collectible coins and was followed by a slinky and a die-cast metal Buick. Anise caught the slinky but was sideswiped by the Buick. Her hand went to her ribs as she cringed.

"I'm calling the police," Doreen announced and headed toward the phone at the front counter.

"I wouldn't do that if I were you," the old woman said, pulling a small knife out of her pocket. Opening the blade, she pointed it at Anise. "You don't know who you're dealing with, little girl!"

"Neither do you," Anise shot back, trying to sound more confident than she felt and hoping that this woman couldn't see her shaking. Pivoting on one foot, the other foot kicked the old woman's legs out from under her. As she fell, the woman's arms flailed and grabbed the tablecloth of one of the nearby displays. The tablecloth slid down, dragging everything on top of it with them. Antique china shattered on the floor as the woman landed with a thud in a seated position. The knife she'd dropped skidded across the floor and was retrieved by a middle-aged man, his face mostly hidden under the bill of his baseball cap. "Sorry about Mother," he mumbled. "Please, no cops. She's not well. Here. For the china." He pushed some cash into Doreen's hand.

"Where were you a few minutes ago?" Doreen demanded of him. "My friend could've been seriously hurt!"

Ignoring Doreen, he pulled the old woman toward the front door. "You're going to get yourself arrested," he hissed.

"Shut up!" she screeched at him as they walked out the door. "I was this close."

"What was that?!" Doreen asked Anise, her mouth hanging open in shock.

"I don't know." Anise pursed her lips and let out a slow breath in an attempt to get out some of the nervous energy. Her heart was still pounding in her ears. "Maybe the amulet reminded her of something she once had."

"No, I mean you!" Doreen laughed in disbelief. "You looked like an expert fighter the way you took control of that situation. What have you been hiding from me?" She laughed again, holding her hands out with her palms facing up as if an answer might fall out of the sky and she'd need to catch it.

"It was...instinct," Anise replied softly, not looking Doreen in the eyes. "I'll get the broom."

✳✳✳

AFTER WORK, ANISE CHANGED INTO HER sneakers, stepped out of the shop, and half expected the violent old woman to still be there. The sidewalk was clear, however, except for the pigeons fighting over a scrap of what looked to be peanut butter and jelly on wheat. She let out a sigh of relief and hoped the old woman was somewhere nice getting the help she needed. Having to fight her had been terrible. Anise hated violence with a passion, and even though she was grateful she'd been able to hold her own, she hoped she'd never have to fight anyone ever again.

"I'll be home soon, Brian," Anise said into her phone as she unlocked her bicycle chain outside of Doreen's. "I just have to...um, stop by the market. And...run a few other errands." She rolled her eyes when he began speaking. Reaching into her tote bag, she pulled out the affirmation card she wanted. *I do not have to please everyone.* "No, Brian. Get your own beer. I have to go." She hid herself under a cap, sunglasses, and an oversized sweat jacket. It was way too warm outside for the jacket, but she wouldn't go without the disguise. She didn't want anyone to know where she was headed next or why.

Climbing on her bike, she pedaled furiously through the downtown streets of the medium-sized city she loved. It was big enough for everything she wanted to do, but not so big that the traffic would slow her down this afternoon. Parks, statues, sculptures, murals, and tall brick buildings lined her path, and she knew every one of them. Mountains loomed in the background, this being the only time of year when they weren't snowcapped.

Today was one of the rare days when she ignored the scenery, however. Her mind kept going to Les, and she was eager to see how he was doing. She just had to make one stop first, and she'd been looking forward to it all day. Rounding the corner, she flew past the market and continued on for a few more blocks, coasting down a hill. Finally reaching her destination, she put on the brake and looked around. When she was sure she didn't see anyone she knew, she slid off the seat. In a trot, she wheeled her bike past the bike rack and into the alley-way, chaining it to a metal pipe that ran up the side of the building where no one would see it. She breezed into the side door, down a narrow hallway, and into a room where people were waiting for her. She removed the cap, sunglasses, and jacket, and took her place in front of the crowd.

"Is everyone ready?" she asked, her voice command-ing undivided attention.

The room reverberated with ardent yeses.

Anise grinned at them and put on some upbeat music. "We're going to have a great workout today!" she prom-ised her class. She led her students through the warm-up exercises and then had them each claim a free-standing punching bag. As she demonstrated the kickboxing drills, she took a moment to feel gratitude for where she was. Every Saturday and Tuesday she got to come here, teach this class, and feel safer and stronger. It had become an important part of her life, and she liked that no one knew a damn thing about it.

Chapter 2

Anise poked her head into the hospital room to find Les sitting up on the edge of the bed, staring at the floor. "Hey, you're awake!"

His head rose at the sound of her voice. "Anise, hi! Yeah, I'm being released."

"I'm so glad you're okay!"

"Thanks! And thank you for helping me yesterday."

"Of course. So...all's good now?" She didn't want to pry into a stranger's medical issues but couldn't help but wonder why an otherwise healthy-looking person would pass out.

Les shrugged. "This has been happening for the last five years. I get dizzy, sometimes lose consciousness, and wake up sometime later."

She sat on a plastic chair across from his bed. "That sounds awful. When I talked to your mom on the phone, she said the doctors didn't know what was going on."

"They have no clue," Les confirmed. "Everything they thought it might be, it's not."

"Have they tried to offer a prognosis?" she asked.

He shrugged. "They tell me it could be stress, or that it's all in my head, or else it's something new and they don't know how to help me."

"You know your body best," Anise said. "What do you

think?"

"I wish it was just stress. But the unconscious spells are generally getting longer. They used to be for only a few minutes at a time. Now they last for hours or days. I was told they could keep increasing in length until eventually one day I won't wake up."

Anise couldn't help but tear up and grabbed a tissue out of her tote bag. "I'm so sorry. I can't imagine how much that must disrupt your life."

"Yeah. I'd give anything to find a way to treat this. I had to quit my job and do something else. I'm not allowed to use a stove or power tools without supervision. I can't drive anymore." His eyes twinkled with a hint of rebellion. "Not supposed to travel by myself."

"That sucks. Have your doctors found anything that helps?"

"They've tried, but no luck." He shook his head.

Her eyes spilled over and she pressed them with the tissue.

"I should say no luck *so far*. I have hope," he added.

Anise nodded at him. *Please, hope, don't be as bitchy to him as you've been to me.* During the silence that followed, Anise stood. "I should go. I'm glad you're feeling better."

Les rose too. "It was really nice to meet you, Anise. And I'd still like a call from your mom if she doesn't mind."

"Oh...I think I may have lost your number," Anise cringed. "During everything that happened yesterday..."

"No worries," Les replied, rooting through his wallet. He handed her a business card.

Anise glanced at it. "Oh, wow. You're a survival instructor?"

He shrugged. "I used to be."

"Ready to go?" A woman who looked a few years younger than Les walked into the room. Her brunette bob was razor sharp, and her expression looked relieved and sad at the same time.

"This is my wife, Olivia," Les told Anise. He turned to his wife and gave her a kiss. "This is Anise. She's the one who called my mother."

Anise stuck out her hand. "It's nice to meet you."

"Oh, Anise! Hi!" Olivia enveloped her in a surprise hug. "Thank you for helping him! I heard you stayed with him all night."

"I didn't want him to wake up alone and not have his family know where he is," Anise replied once Olivia let her go.

"Who are you?" growled another voice from the doorway.

"This is my mother, Patricia," Les said. "Anise is the one who called you, Mom."

Patricia wore a sweat suit and a scowl. "I thought I made it clear on the phone that you should stay away! Is your mother here, too?"

"No, it's just me," Anise said. The older woman's glower made her feel as if she were on trial. "I'm sorry for intruding, I just wanted to make sure Les was okay."

"No, he's not okay! He hasn't been okay for a long time! And this is none of your business! You need to leave!"

"Stop," Les commanded his mother with a glare. He turned to Anise. "I'm sorry about her. You're welcome to stay. Thank you again for everything you've done."

"I'm glad I could help," Anise said, feeling Patricia's eyes grinding a hole in the side of her head. "But I should get going anyway. It was nice meeting you all."

"I'll walk you out," Olivia offered. "Les isn't supposed to travel by himself," she said when they reached the hallway, "but he's pretty sick of staying at home and being baby-sat all the time. If this ever happens again, could you please call me instead of Pat? I'm sure you've noticed she's more than a little overprotective. It's easier on the both of us if we don't tell her everything."

"I completely understand," Anise agreed. "Of course." She entered the number Olivia gave her into her phone. "And are *you* okay?" she added, seeing the drooping eyes and hunched shoulders of the other woman.

Olivia's eyes welled up. "Some of his doctors think he might only have a few years left because his spells have been happening more often and lasting longer each time." She crossed her arms and sighed. "The restrictions this puts on him has been really frustrating for him. Did he tell you he used to be a survival trainer?"

Anise nodded. "Yes."

"He misses it so much. He works at home doing transcription for doctors and lawyers now, and it's excruciatingly boring for him. He loses himself in puzzles a lot, and he loves them, but that's not enough for him. He's so independent but can't do anything alone. It's draining away the joy he used to have for life. And when I imagine having to go on without him..." She dabbed her eyes with a tissue. "Sorry. I don't mean to put all this on you."

"It's okay," Anise assured her.

Patricia stuck her head out the door. "Liv, find that nurse with the wheelchair. We're ready to leave!"

Olivia nodded her agreement to her mother-in-law. "Thank you again," she said to Anise.

"Have a safe trip home," Anise told her and headed out of the hospital.

As she weaved through the streets on her bicycle, Anise realized she'd forgotten to ask Les about the strange letter he'd talked about at their first meeting. Why would it have mentioned her mother? And protective, healing jewelry as if it were an actual thing? The nearer she got to home, the more she brushed it out of her mind. Les was probably right. Someone had tried to play a joke on him.

✳✳✳

ANISE WHEELED HER ORANGE SCHWINN DOWN the concrete hallway, unlocked her door, and stepped into her apartment. The late afternoon light beamed through the open blinds, lighting up the small space. Anise's landscape paintings she'd made after taking an oil-on-canvas class dotted the walls, bringing some color to the room that otherwise had neutral, second-hand furnishings. She'd tidied up the day before, but somehow her boyfriend Brian's clothes, shoes, receipts, and take-out containers covered the table, chairs, and couch.

"Hey! I'm home!" she called out over the sound of electronic gunfire. She slipped out of her shoes and hung up her light jacket in the closet.

"Hey," a deep, distracted voice replied. "Have you been at the market this whole time? Did you pick up my beer like I asked?"

"I told you I wouldn't. I can't carry it on my bike."

"Then what took you so long?"

She didn't feel like talking about Les. Not with him. She thought about the one thing about her day that she was willing to share with him. "You won't believe what happened at the thrift store today!" She began telling Brian about the irate old lady as she picked up his sweatshirt and baseball cap that he'd dropped on the closet floor. "She kept insisting that I give her my necklace that Doreen gave me today. She wouldn't leave! She wanted it so badly that she even—"

He never took his eyes off his video game. "That shop is full of crazy, old people."

"Don't call them that," Anise scolded.

"Well, they are, and I don't need to hear you ramble on about every single one of them." He was sitting on the floor with his legs crossed and leaned against the lumpy, brown couch that stood sadly against the wall. It groaned a little from the pressure of his wide frame and tall, bulky build every time Brian moved.

"Sorry." She hung her head and threw his jacket and

cap back on the closet floor. She hadn't even gotten to the part of her story where she'd had to fight the old lady. Coming home to him was getting more and more unsatisfying. This was her first long-term relationship. Were they all like this or was hers especially unhappy? It would be nice if they could reconnect. She should be able to tell him about her kickboxing fitness class, but she doubted he'd be supportive. "I was thinking I might want to teach," she said, wondering if he might surprise her and be supportive after all.

"Teach what?" he asked with a doubtful expression that never left the television. "Drawing or something?"

"Maybe! I think I'd enjoy it." She placed her tote bag on the floor, making sure to lean the opening toward the wall so he wouldn't be able to see her sweatshirt or cap inside it.

Brian laughed. "You get stage fright. You'd suck at teaching."

That reaction right there was why she'd never tell him about the class she taught or anything else he'd put her down for. Was the sweet guy she'd met at the movie theater still in there, or was this how it would be from now on? "It stinks in here," she complained, raising the blinds and opening their two windows and balcony door. "I've asked you not to smoke that shit inside."

"It's medicinal. I need it to make it through the day," Brian snapped back. "So lay off."

"The balcony is literally five steps away from you. Smoke outside." No response. "Did you hear me?"

"Yeah, hey, throw me a beer."

"No. You've had enough," she said, picking up the empty cans that littered the floor wherever Brian had happened to drop them. "There are eight beer cans on the floor, Brian!"

"So? What are you? My mother?"

"I certainly feel like it when I have to pick up after you. At least throw your empty cans in the garbage. One of them leaked on the carpet!"

A grunt from Brian while still engrossed in his game was the best possible response she could hope for. She stepped out on their small balcony to water the petunias. She'd bought some for herself after falling in love with the way they'd grown so hardily at her mother's.

"I'm outside," Brian said with a joint in his hand as he joined her. "Are you happy now?"

She sighed. "Can you wait until I'm done out here, please? The point was for me to not have to smell it. And when you do smoke out here, could you not put it out in the dirt? I don't want to have to keep picking them out of the flowers."

He was watching people walk by on the downtown street below. "Uh huh."

"Did you know petunias symbolize hope?" she asked as she grabbed the watering can and gave the flowers a drink. "I have a love-hate relationship with hope, but these flowers are so strong and grow so easily; it makes me think that maybe if I hold on to hope, I can be the same way."

"Uh huh." Brian went back inside and sat back down on the floor. He picked up the joystick and the gunfire sounds continued.

Anise followed him inside and nudged his arm with her leg as she stood over him. "Look. This is the necklace Doreen got me for my graduation. The one that the old lady wanted so badly. I think it looks like an amulet from the Middle Ages, don't you?" She held out her amulet.

He glanced at it and recoiled. "It's big. And fugly. Where the hell would you ever wear that?"

She sighed again. "I'm going to take a nap before I start making dinner. Remember, we're meeting my friends tonight at Club Lava." She stared at him as he ignored her. "To celebrate my graduation. Remember?"

"Oh, shit, is that tonight?"

"Yes, Brian." Anise hoped he heard the annoyance in

her voice. "I texted you last night, and I reminded you again this morning."

"I thought you had a big party last night at one of your friend's places."

"It got canceled. I told you that in the text. I had to take someone to the hospital."

"Is it one of those stuck-up places where I have to dress up, or can I just go like this?"

She cringed at the thought of him wearing his Budweiser t-shirt, carpenter shorts, and flip flops to the club. "It's not a pretentious crowd, but it is a little more upscale. Just wear slacks and a nice shirt. And your nice shoes, please, not black sneakers."

After her nap and dinner, Anise opened the closet door in the bedroom. On Brian's side, most of his clothes were on the floor or threatening to jump from their precarious positions on hangers. She tried to ignore the weird smell coming from under the pile of his jeans. Someday she'd make enough money to have a house with his-and-hers closets. Anise's side had her clothes neatly organized by category. Dresses, skirts, pants, tops with long sleeves, tops with short sleeves, tops without sleeves. She was excited to put on her new retro-printed tank dress paired with necklaces, a belt, and Mary-Jane heels that she'd found at the thrift store. She drew on a cat eye with her new black liquid eyeliner, just like her friend Erin had taught her. "How do I look?" she asked, twirling around for Brian, whose eyes were still glued to his video game. With a sigh, he hit the pause button.

"Holy shit, you look too hot to leave the apartment," he replied.

She grinned. "Thanks! Now go change; we have to leave in five minutes."

"Yeah, about that. Do you mind if I skip it?"

Anise stepped closer to him and glared down at the matted brown hair on top of his head. "What?!"

"I feel like staying in. I'll go next time."

Next time. Ugh. "You sound just like my dad."

"My back is really hurting today. And I'm about to level up."

"But this is my celebration for a milestone event in my life. And anyone's back would hurt from sitting on the floor all day. It'll do you good to get up and move around a little."

Brian looked up at her. "Exactly. It's *your* celebration. You should go and have fun. I just don't feel like going out tonight." He ran a hand up her leg and under the short, colorful dress while his eyes devoured her slender form. "But why don't you show me what's under here first?"

She smacked his hand away. "No, Brian! I have to leave. And besides, I thought your back hurt."

"It's been so *long*, Anise," he complained. "If you're worried about my injury, I'll lay back and relax, and you can do the work."

With her mind not finding the words she wanted at that moment, she shook her head at him with disgust, turned on her heel, and stormed toward the door.

"Well, fine!" he yelled. "But make sure you wipe off that makeup first and put a longer dress on. I don't want you going out alone looking like a..." He stopped talking and looked at his lap.

"Like a what?" Anise challenged him.

Brian ignored her and unpaused his video game.

Anise could feel her face burning with rage and disappointment. Instead of exploding, she decided to just walk out. Club Lava was only three blocks away from her downtown apartment. As she made her way down the bustling city sidewalk, she told herself she would have an amazing evening and didn't need him there. Her three friends since grade school, Vanessa, Erin, and Joy, would be there. Brian would only have sat there, complained that he wanted to leave, gotten too intoxicated to stand (much less walk home), and tried to flirt with Joy. This way, at least she'd be spared the embarrassment.

When she got to the club, it was almost 10 o'clock. She saw Vanessa waving at her from a small table she had managed to claim. "Hey girl, congratulations," Vanessa exclaimed, hugging her friend. "I'm so proud of you!" Vanessa's raven hair shined, and her gold-colored dress made her complexion glow. "Wait before you sit," she added. "It's not as clean in here as it was last time." She wiped the chairs and table with a napkin. "How's that guy that you took to the hospital?"

Anise shrugged. "He was awake at least. The doctors don't know why he keeps passing out though."

"Oh, no! I hope they figure it out."

"Me too." Anise sat across from Vanessa. "How was your day?"

"Dull. I had to go into the office for a couple hours."

Vanessa had graduated two years before with a computer science degree and gotten a job right away with a defense contractor. Anise had always been impressed by her friend's intelligence and drive. "On a Saturday?"

"Yeah, sucks," Vanessa agreed. "But I'm excited to be here now. We haven't been to a club in so long!"

"Cherry mojitos, bitches!" shouted Joy over the crowd and heavy bass, as she and Erin came up to the table, carrying pitchers. "All your drinks are on me tonight, babe! Congrats!"

"Thank you!" Anise replied, grinning. She stood up to hug Joy.

"Just tell me you didn't bring your sketchbook with you tonight," Joy commanded with a smirk.

Anise laughed. "Not this time, you'll be happy to know."

"Or your affirmation cards."

"All I have is my license and a debit card, I swear."

Joy's light blonde hair played around her beautiful face, and she wore the paw print necklace that Anise had given her when she'd gotten her veterinary technician job at the zoo. Her smile and high-energy personality would make her the center of attention tonight as always, Anise assumed.

"You did your cat eye perfectly! It really brings out the hazel color of your eyes even more. You look great!" exclaimed Erin to Anise as she gave her friend a hug.

"You're a great teacher," Anise grinned. "I will take any make-up tips you have."

A makeup artist and esthetician, Erin always looked perfectly done up, while her bronzy, golden highlighted locks framed her pretty, freckled face. Crystals hung from her ears and neck, and Anise could smell the rose and jasmine essential oils she'd chosen instead of perfume for the evening. Her strapless dress allowed her to show off the phases-of-the-moon tattoo on her shoulder.

"This is pretty," Anise commented as they all sat at the table, pointing to the light pink crystal around Erin's neck. "What is it?"

"Rose quartz," Erin replied. "To attract true love in our direction."

"Awesome!" said Joy, pulling on Erin's chair. "Bring that thing closer to *me*."

"You guys, what happened to this place?" Vanessa asked, frowning at the empty glasses that littered almost every table. "It used to be so upscale."

"I noticed that too," Anise agreed. The sophisticated look and feel of the club was gone. The décor had changed from modern lighting and long, plush sofas to flickering florescent bulbs and cheap tables and chairs constructed from something that sort of looked like wood and wobbled at the slightest touch.

"Yeah, I had to hop over beer puddles on my way to the table," Erin piped up.

"I asked the bouncer about that when I got here," Joy said. "New management. These tables give people more places to sit and drink and also free up some more room to dance. They're also having contests and theme nights to appeal to a younger crowd since it's near the college. Eighteen to party, twenty-one to drink."

"That's a shame," said Anise, making a face. "This place was so nice."

"Does this mean we have very discerning tastes, or are we just getting old?" Joy asked with a snicker.

"We can go somewhere else if you guys want." Vanessa turned to Anise. "It's your night, you decide."

"No," Anise said with a smile. "It's fine. The drinks are good, and I have amazing company."

"Speaking of contests, we should all find some guys and enter that Sexiest Couple Dance Contest," Erin joked with a smirk, pointing to a banner that hung over a small stage.

"I'm going to need three or four more pitchers if you really want that amount of tacky to happen," Vanessa laughed.

"So, what's up with your aura?" asked Erin, her finger pointing to either side of Anise. "I see two black spots."

"One of them is probably Brian," Anise replied, making a face at the thought of him.

"Oh, yeah. Where is he?" Vanessa demanded. "He better have a good reason for not showing up again."

"Oh, you know, his lifestyle is just too busy, what with his video games, beer, and weed," said Anise through gritted teeth. A collective groan echoed around the table. "Whatever, I'm kinda glad he's not here. He's been saying asshole things lately, and I'm sick of it."

"Did something happen?" Vanessa asked with concern.

"I think he's mad at me. I haven't slept with him since Valentine's Day."

"Whoa, four months?!" Joy exclaimed.

Anise nodded. "I just haven't been in the mood. Like at all. I hope there's nothing physically wrong with me."

"Have you been to the doctor?" Vanessa asked.

"Oh, there's nothing wrong with her!" Joy interjected. "Brian won't work, clean, grocery shop, pay any bills...he does nothing but play video games. I wouldn't want to fuck a guy like that either."

"Things used to be so much better..." Anise lamented. "I don't know how to fix this."

"Take tonight off from thinking about him," Erin suggested.

"Yes! Forget him tonight, babe," huffed Joy. "Have you looked around yet? There are so many hot guys here! Plus, we have the rose quartz working for us." She pointed at Erin's necklace. "You could find an upgrade so easily!"

Anise laughed. "I'm not looking for a guy, Joy. I just want to hang out with you fabulous women."

"Whatevs. Either way, he's a loser and doesn't deserve you."

"You're right, let's change the subject," Anise said. "I don't want to think about Brian tonight."

"Great," Joy agreed. "What are you all wearing next weekend to Lundville?"

"Lundville?" Anise asked.

Joy slapped a hand over her mouth.

"Joy!" Erin and Vanessa scolded her in unison.

"I'm sorry, I'm sorry!" came Joy's muffled apology from behind her hand.

Vanessa turned to Anise. "We *were* going to surprise you next weekend with a trip to the art fair in Lundville as a present for your graduation."

"Really? I've been wanting to go to that forever!" Anise exclaimed. "You guys are the best!"

"We were going to kidnap you Saturday morning," Erin told her with a glare in Joy's direction.

"Don't look at me like that!" Joy protested. "It's partly your fault for telling me. You know I can't keep my big mouth shut." She looked at Anise with an expression of regret. "But I tried; I really did."

"It's okay!" Anise laughed, reached over, and squeezed Joy's hand to comfort her.

"So what's the other black spot in your aura about?" Erin wanted to know.

"Well..." Anise thought for a moment. "Maybe it's because I'm nervous about starting my new job on Monday."

"What time does work start?" Erin asked.

"Not until ten."

"Come over about eight-thirty that morning for some Reiki," Erin offered.

"Reiki?" Vanessa asked.

"It's an energy treatment."

"Will it help?" Anise asked.

"It works on the nervous system, so yes, it should."

All four heads swiveled when they heard someone interrupt them. "Excuse me, ladies; my buddies are waiting on me, but I need to get your opinion on something really quick." A man of about their age who'd emerged out of the crowd was pulling up a chair and joining their table.

"Oh, fuck yeah," Joy whispered to Anise. "You know my opinion about him." Her eyes sparkled with lust as they moved over him.

Anise laughed at her friend's reaction. She took another look at the man and then ripped her eyes away as if it were forbidden to behold him. Taking a breath, she suppressed the growing warmth before it reached her cheeks. She didn't want to gawk at him like Joy was, but... Her eyes ambled back toward him, trying to avoid a replay of the initial attraction that almost made her blush, but it didn't work. He was tall and fit, his almost-black hair was cut into a professional but modern style, and he looked at each of them with striking, cobalt blue eyes. They reminded Anise of the vibrant color she'd specifically mixed to get the mood right for the darkening evening sky in her last landscape painting—deep and soothing, almost transcendental. The outer edge of his right eye ended in a scar that was small but prominent enough to make her wonder how it got there. She noticed his nice shoes and appreciated that his dark clothes were more classic than trendy. Hints of tattoos jutted from his collar and the edge of his slightly rolled up right sleeve. His handsome face wore the perfect amount of well-groomed stubble and a mischievous sideways smile that she could've stared at all night. His movements seemed purposeful and confident when he dragged his chair around the table to place it next to Anise. He sat down with them looking as comfortable as if they'd been expecting him. Being so close, Anise caught faint suggestions of his cologne. It made her imagine that he'd showered under a summer rain cloud in the middle of a cedar and pine forest.

"Sure," said Erin, smiling at him. "What's up?"

"So this buddy of mine has been married for a couple years now, and his wife is always saying how unromantic he is. He wants to surprise her with some big romantic gesture or gift, but he doesn't know what to do. Do you ladies have any suggestions for him?" He looked straight at Erin.

"Any girl would love to go on a picnic," she said.

"That's not bad," he replied, nodding. He looked at Vanessa next.

She looked thoughtful for a few seconds. "He should surprise her at work with flowers, then dinner, and Shakespeare in the Park."

"Yeah, I think she'd like that. What do you think?" he asked Anise.

"Oh, I don't know," she hesitated, feeling uncomfortable at being put on the spot. She tried to think of something romantic Brian had done for her, but nothing was coming to mind. She looked down at her hand and remembered that he'd given her jewelry for her birthday once—a garnet ring that she never took off. She then thought of her amulet and how happy she would have been if Brian had been the one to give it to her. "Maybe jewelry? See, this is my birthstone..." Distracted by her thoughts, she lifted her hand to show him the ring and accidentally knocked her drink into his lap. She watched in horror for a moment as his pants soaked up some of the sticky liquid while the rest dripped onto his chair and down to the floor.

He grabbed half of the napkins Vanessa had brought to the table and began dabbing his pant leg.

"Oh, shit! I'm so sorry!" Anise grabbed more napkins and helped him dry his pants.

"So is this how you typically pick up guys?" he asked her.

"What?"

"You try to get guys out of their pants by ruining them?" The left side of his mouth teased her with a smile.

"Oh, yeah," she replied with a smirk, pushing a napkin into his thigh. "It was all part of my evil plan to grope you and leave you with a stiff...dry cleaning bill."

Anise's friends snickered.

He grinned at her. "Interesting method. Points for originality. You might have more game than I do. I'll have to find you again later and ask you for tips."

Joy cleared her throat. "You haven't asked me for my opinion yet," she said to the man.

He turned to face her. "You're right. What do you think my friend should do?"

"Definitely buy her sexy lingerie," Joy purred at him and flipped her blonde hair over her shoulder. "What's your name?"

"I'm Nate."

She introduced him to the rest of the table. "And I'm Joy. By name *and* reputation."

He gave her a devilish smirk. "I bet you are."

"And I bet you have some incredible tattoos," she replied, grabbing his wrist and pushing up his sleeve. She furrowed her eyebrows and squinted at his arm. "What is it?"

Nate pulled his sleeve back down. "Something I regret deeply."

"Well, now I have to know what it is!" Joy reached for his arm again, but he ignored her demand and stood up.

"I need to get back to my friends." He grinned at them. "Ladies, it was a pleasure. Thanks for the advice."

"Really?" complained Joy to Anise once Nate had left. "He had to flirt with *you*, the only one of us who isn't single?"

"Aren't you dating multiple people right now?" Erin asked Joy.

"Only two, and only casually," Joy informed her with a pout. "And I could handle one more if it were him."

Vanessa laughed. "Come on, let's go dance. You'll feel better when you hook another one in like two seconds."

"That's true," said Joy, giving her friends a grin.

✳ ✳ ✳

BRIAN SWALLOWED THE LAST FEW DROPS of beer in the can and let out a belch that could've won a contest. Yawning, he rubbed his eyes that were dry from staring at the television screen for most of the day and headed to the small bedroom. It was too hot to sleep under the covers, so he lay down on top of the comforter without bothering to remove his clothes. He was tired but couldn't sleep. Getting out of bed, he picked up Anise's amulet that she'd placed next to her jewelry box on the dresser.

So goddamn fugly.

He inspected it and wondered about its worth as he grabbed another beer and turned his video game back on in the living room. Dropping her jewelry in the pocket of his shorts, he turned up the volume and engrossed himself in his game.

Not long after, he turned the game back off. *I really need to get laid!* If he got dressed now, he'd have plenty of time to join Anise at the club. Maybe she'd show her appreciation. Besides, he felt a little guilty for canceling on the plans she'd made again. He got up and opened the closet door. Maybe Joy would be there. Maybe he could get them drunk enough to get Joy to come home with them. He imagined Anise riding him with Joy sitting on his face.

I have to make that happen tonight.

He pulled out a shirt Anise had once told him was nice. Would Joy like it too? Did he have enough cash to buy her all the drinks she'd want? He pulled out his wallet and checked. No, not enough. But since the girls had been there for a while already...maybe it could be.

On the other hand, maybe Anise would make him dance.

Dancing makes dudes look like ass-hats. Fuck that.

He put the shirt back in the closet. Maybe Anise was dancing with some other guy right now. Scowling at the thought, his mind pictured it until the jealousy burned his cheeks. Two could play at that game. He grabbed his phone and scrolled through his contacts until he found the one he wanted. He hadn't talked to this girl for months, but before he went on medical leave they'd had conversations when he came into the office and she'd smile at him from behind the front desk. They texted on and off when he was at the construction sites. There'd been a vibe. He sent a text.

Brian: U up?

In just a few minutes, he got the response he was hoping for. Grabbing his keys, he hurried out the door.

Chapter 3

Anise sat at the table with her friends finishing a large glass of water and listening to Vanessa describe with disgust how some guy's hand had wandered too low when she'd danced with him.

"I'm not taking his side or anything," Joy projected over the music, "but you do have a really nice ass."

"Thank you, but that's not an excuse," Vanessa insisted.

"Hey," Erin said to Anise in a teasing tone and pointed a finger. "Look who's coming back."

Anise saw Nate and couldn't help but stare at him as he approached. He walked with his chest pushed out, shoulders back, and eyes scanning his surroundings, taking care not to bump into anyone as he weaved through the dancing patrons.

"We all knew he'd be back for you," Vanessa said to Anise with a grin.

"At least the rose quartz is working for one of us," Erin sighed, looking down at her necklace.

"Yeah. Why won't it work for *me*?" Joy demanded.

"Because I told it that it was pretty," Anise explained with a smirk.

"Hi again," Nate said as he stepped up to their table.

"Hi!" Anise chirped with more enthusiasm than she'd meant to. They both turned to look at Joy who'd put her face near Erin's chest to caress the rose quartz with a finger, offering it sweet nothings.

Nate raised his eyebrows. "Should I ask?"

Anise laughed and shook her head. "Probably best not to."

"Okay." He grinned and gave a slight nod. "Would you like to dance?"

His offer made her smile as she imagined being close to him, staring into those bright blue eyes... And then Brian invaded her mind, making her feel guilty for even considering it. "Thank you, but I'm only dancing with my friends tonight."

"In that case, I'm really going to need those tips on upping my game," he replied, pulling up a chair and sitting next to her.

"I just saw you dancing with several women," Anise said. "It didn't look like you needed any help."

"Except that the woman I *really* want to dance with just told me no." He gave her sad, puppy-dog eyes.

She laughed. "Aw, well, you can't take that personally. Sometimes a 'no' has nothing to do with you."

He nodded. "You're right. I think I know what's going on here."

"Oh, you do?" she challenged him.

"If you saw me dancing, then you know how good I am, and you're worried you can't keep up with me."

She laughed again. "No, that's not it. Besides, you were in a crowd, I really didn't see anything."

"I'm convinced that's it. You're a bad dancer. But don't worry about that. Once I start dancing, no one's even going to be looking at you." His eyes smiled teasingly at her.

Anise opened her mouth in disbelief. "You're so full of shit! I can dance circles around you."

"That's a big claim. You're going to have to prove it," he said, grinning.

"I see what you're trying to do!" she informed him,

failing at her attempts not to smile.

"Is it working?" He gave her a sideways smirk that was equal parts playful, cocky, and ridiculously charming.

She felt an urge to bite into that smirk and wondered how he'd react if she did. Instead, she shrugged. "Maybe a little," she admitted with a kittenish frown.

"Good." He stood and offered her his hand.

"But it's not working enough!" she declared with finality.

Joy leaned over and whispered to her, "You better dance with him, or I will be so disappointed in you."

Anise wrinkled her nose. "I don't think so."

Joy gave her a look of disbelief. "Why?! Don't you think he's hot?"

Anise shrugged and made a face of indifference.

Erin gave her a knowing look. "Seriously?"

Her friends knew her too well. "Okay, *fine*. He's probably the hottest guy I've ever seen," Anise conceded.

"So what's the problem?" Joy asked. "He's confident and sexy. What more could you want?"

"I'd love to dance with him, but I'd feel guilty. Brian..." Anise said softly.

"Dancing is not cheating," Vanessa insisted.

"Besides," Joy added, "it's not like you're going to fall in love with him. Just dance. Flirt. If you give him a chance, you might have some fun which you *deserve* after the shit couple of days you've had."

Nate was still standing there with an outstretched arm and an amused expression. Anise looked at his gorgeous face. *Who do I want to be in this situation?* The question made her realize she wanted to give in to her intense desire to prove him wrong about her dancing skills, even though he'd only been kidding. "Okay," Anise said to Nate and took his hand, allowing him to lead her out to the dance floor. Anise wasn't sure what to expect from Nate's dancing and was delighted when she saw that he had some impressive moves. Not to be outdone, Anise made sure to use all of her best moves as well.

Whenever she was with Brian, his eyes would wander to other women in the room, but every time she looked up at Nate's face, he was looking back at her. She wasn't used to a man's full attention, and she enjoyed the ego boost, pushing encroaching thoughts of Brian out of her mind. Soon, the music and her movements began to relax her, and she smiled at Nate to let him know she was having a great time.

During one of her turns, she flashed him a flirty glance over her shoulder. "So what do you think? Have I humbled you?" she teased.

He took hold of her moving hips and put his mouth by her ear. "Yes, I was completely wrong," he admitted. "You *can* dance circles around me." He put his arms around her from behind.

She gave him a victorious smirk at his admission of defeat, and without thinking, she let her body melt against his as they moved together. He felt strong, and she let herself enjoy the heat from their friction. Soon though, his breath on her ear and his body against hers made a wave of guilt surge through her. She shouldn't be dancing with him like this. And she certainly shouldn't be loving it. "I should really get back to my friends," she told him, but continued to lean against him as they moved together. She tried to step away from him but found herself pressing up against him instead. She enjoyed the sense of being surrounded by his arms, and wondered what it would feel like if his hand grabbed her hips again and where it might go if she allowed it to wander.

"Sure. After one more song?"

Another wave of guilt slapped her in the face. This time, she stopped dancing and turned to face him. "No, I should really be getting back."

He grinned at her. "If you don't dance with me for one more song, I'm afraid I'll have to take drastic measures."

"Um, like what?"

"I'll have to follow you around all night dancing like this." Nate started moving like his clothes were on fire and mixing it up with the Cabbage Patch and the Robot.

"Stop!" said Anise, laughing at him and smacking him on the arm. "Everyone's looking!"

"Dance with me and I'll stop."

"Okay, okay, one more song." She saw Vanessa watching her from their table and gave her a thumbs up to let her know everything was good.

One more song turned into several, and she didn't want to stop. Brian always refused to dance with her, and he got upset when she danced with other men. Nate, on the other hand, seemed to enjoy dancing with her, and unlike Brian, he could actually dance.

When a popular dance craze started playing, Anise stopped. "I never learned how to do this," she said.

"Me neither," said Nate. "Let's see if we can pick it up."

They cracked each other up trying to emulate the moves of the surrounding club patrons and bumping into each other again and again. Anise had never felt clumsier and couldn't remember the last time she'd laughed so much.

"Nailed it!" Nate told her, puffing his chest out with pride when the song ended which made her burst out laughing again. He laughed along with her.

Once she calmed herself down, she realized her feet had started to ache in her high heels. "I need a break."

"Let's get a drink," Nate responded, putting an arm around her shoulders and leading her to the bar.

"I've already had more than I usually do," she told him. "Just a Coke for me."

"Two Cokes," Nate ordered. He paid for their drinks, tipping the bartender well.

Anise thanked him for the dance and the drink. "Now

I should really find my friends again," she said. "We're having a little celebration tonight."

"They're out on the dance floor," Nate replied, pointing them out as they waved. He and Anise waved back. "I think they can spare you for another few minutes. Sit with me," he said, finding a small empty bench seat.

"Okay!" She sat next to him, looking forward to learning more about him.

"What are you celebrating?"

"My college graduation," she said proudly.

"Nice! Congratulations! What's your major?"

"Thanks. It's marketing."

"Job market is pretty rough," Nate said. "Have you found anything yet?"

She frowned. "Not really. The only thing I could find related to my major was a market research survey taker."

"Not those people at the mall with clipboards," he teased.

"Yes. That'll be me starting Monday. This is so embarrassing. I can't believe I'm telling you this." She looked down at the ground.

"Hey, that's not a bad entry-level job. Sounds like it might be fun."

"Fun?" She laughed. "I don't know about that. Maybe I'm just nervous, but walking up to random strangers and asking them to take a survey doesn't sound like something I'd be good at."

His eyebrows narrowed in an expression of disbelief. "Why not? From the way you speak, it's obvious you're smart. You're probably someone who's good at everything she tries. You should have all the confidence in the world."

Anise gave him a half-smile and twisted her garnet ring around her finger, a little embarrassed by the compliment.

"Well, except for that dance craze we just tried," he continued with a grin. "You were terrible. That was hard to watch."

She laughed and smacked him on the arm. "Like you were any better!" she shot back.

He grinned again and looked at her, and their mutual gaze held for a few moments. She couldn't put her finger on it, but there was something about him that she found incredible, and it was far more than just his handsome face. He hadn't done or said anything specific, but there was an undefinable quality behind those eyes, like they'd seen a lot. She found herself longing to know him better.

Her long bangs had fallen in her eyes, and with a soft touch that grazed her forehead, he pushed them to the side behind her ear. A look of surprise washed over his face when a short pencil fell into his hand. "Oh. What else do you have hidden in there?"

She laughed. "Nothing. Just that. I always have a pencil behind my ear."

"What's the story with that?" he asked, handing the pencil back to her.

"Sometimes I think of something that I want to write down, and I don't want to have to root through my bag to find a pencil first, or I might forget exactly how I want to word it. I usually have a sketchbook with me too, in case there's something I need to draw."

"I'm guessing that happens a lot?"

"Yeah," she said. "Keeping the pencil there really comes in handy." She put it back behind her ear and covered it with her hair. It felt weird when it wasn't there.

"It'll come in handy tonight, too."

"For what?" she asked him.

He grabbed a napkin off a nearby table and handed it to her. "For when you write down your phone number."

Anise smiled at him but shook her head. "No. I have a boyfriend."

He gave her a small frown, looking disappointed. "A boyfriend? Where is *he* tonight?"

She shrugged. "At home, I'm sure."

"Why isn't he here for your celebration?"

"Oh...he just wasn't feeling that great."

"I see. Well, at least give me your e-mail address, and I'll give you mine. I have a friend who works in marketing. Maybe he has some job leads that I can forward to you. And you can write *me* when this boyfriend situation changes," he said, as if he already knew her situation.

And how did he know? Was it that obvious? Her jaw dropped as a bubble of anger began to form in her stomach. She'd been right—his eyes saw a lot. In this case, too much. "You're very presumptuous!" she huffed, standing up to leave.

"Am I wrong?" he asked calmly, standing up next to her.

She frowned at him but said nothing.

"I can see you're conflicted. I think we should let fate decide."

Anise's intrigue popped the anger bubble. "You believe in fate and destiny and all that kind of thing?"

"Absolutely. Don't you?"

She couldn't stop her delight. "I do! It's just that most guys I know..." She shook her head. "What did you have in mind?"

He pointed at the banner over the stage. "There's a dance contest."

"Oh, don't remind me," she groaned with an eye roll.

"Yeah, it's tacky," he agreed. "But so what? We should enter."

Anise gave him an incredulous and disgusted look. "No way! What does that have to do with fate anyway?"

"Hear me out. If we win, you can keep all the prize money, but I get your email."

"There's prize money?" Anise took another look at the banner. "Whoa, five hundred dollars?"

"If we lose, I'll pay the cover charge for you and your friends at the new club across the street. I think it'd be more your speed than this dump. You let fate decide, and either way you have nothing to lose."

"Just my dignity."

"That grows back. I promise."

She laughed.

"So, what do you say?"

"Well, the prize money would help with bills. But I don't know..."

"It's up to you," Nate said with a shrug. "But the way I see it, this is what you *really* have to choose between—this can either be the night your boyfriend stood you up for your celebration, or it can be the night you won a dance contest with the hottest guy you've ever seen."

"Oh my god, you heard that?" Her cheeks burned.

He flashed her his mischievous sideways smile again. "So what do you say?"

"Um..." She'd had more fun with him tonight than with anyone else in a long time, and now he'd found another way to ask who she wanted to be in this situation which made her like him even more. "I hate to admit it, but your argument was good. I can't believe I'm going to agree to this."

"Great! I'll go sign us up."

I'M TOO GODDAMN OLD FOR THIS.

At 77, she knew there was a good possibility that her legs would ache when she crouched under a staircase in an apartment building that smelled like the dinner of every single resident that lived there. Not to mention the stiffness in her back. But she didn't have a choice. The two men—who were *far* younger than her—hadn't been any help in retrieving the amulet so far, and if she'd brought them with her tonight, they'd have found a way to screw everything up. *The candy-asses.* Her whole reason for being was tied up in that amulet, and she would get it or die trying.

She hadn't planned to crouch under the staircase. The girl, Anise, had gone out for the evening, and the plan was to simply pick the lock, enter the apartment, find the amulet, and go home. However, on her way there, she encountered the boy that lived there as he stumbled in his drunken stupor into the building and looked up the stairs like he was about to tackle Mount Everest. That's when she'd had to duck underneath the staircase.

He must be six-and-a-half feet tall! The giant, out-of-shape candy-ass looked like a tree whose roots had grown into feet and was just learning how to walk. He took his sweet time lumbering up the stairs to the third floor and took at least five minutes to manage to put his key in the door.

She thought about pushing him down the stairs to be rid of him, but someone that tall and large would make too much noise falling to his death. Why did these annoyances always have to happen to *her*?

She waited a few minutes after he'd entered before pushing on his front door that he hadn't closed all the way. The door opened slowly with a cre-ee-ee-eak. Her aging brown eyes peered inside the apartment and focused on the young man asleep on the floor in front of a blaring television. She entered and creaked the door closed behind her. Her flying hands searched every drawer, cabinet, container, and closet. They reached into the pocket of every jacket and pair of pants. They felt in between couch cushions and underneath the mattress.

"Where the hell is the amulet?!" she whispered to herself, pulling on her white hair.

"Hey!" came a loud, slurred protest. "What are you... doing here?"

She sighed and pulled on her hair again. "Nothing. Go back to sleep." She rooted through the front closet by the door.

"Get the hell out!" the ridiculously large man cried

holding his hands out in confusion.

"Shut up!" she snapped. "I'll leave when I'm good and ready!"

The giant began to giggle furiously. "Are you senile or something?"

She grabbed each pair of shoes, shook them to see if anything would fall out, and then threw them back on the closet floor. "Go sleep it off, you candy-ass." She headed to the bathroom and opened the medicine cabinet.

"You crazy, old bitch!" the boy slurred and grabbed her arm. "You're leaving now." He pulled her toward the front door.

She pressed a spot on his hand that made him cry out and double over in pain. Happy that she could now more easily reach his shoulder, she pressed her fingers into it. He sunk to his knees with an "aaaahhhhhnnnoooaaahhh" or something equally unintelligible, crying real tears. She found another sensitive spot on his massive frame and dug her fingers into it until he fell unconscious to the floor. "Sleep, little boy!"

She continued her search for the amulet. But the damn thing was nowhere. She pulled on her hair in frustration, and stepping over the large sleeping man, she let herself out. This wasn't over. She'd been searching for the amulet for nearly her entire life, and she wasn't about to give up now. It had to be somewhere, and wherever it was, she'd find it.

✳ ✳ ✳

ANISE'S HANDS BECAME FIDGETY AND SHE twisted her garnet ring around her finger as she and Nate waited for their turn on stage.

"Are you okay?" he asked her.

She frowned. "Just some stage fright."

"We don't have to do this," he said.

"You already paid the entrance fee."

"Don't worry about that."

She wanted to say something more—anything—but felt frozen in her fear. The right words weren't coming to mind, and she was afraid if she tried to speak she'd say something embarrassing like when she got nervous in her job interviews.

After a moment of silence, Nate added, "Hey, if you get nervous, just focus right here." He pointed at his eyes. "It's just you and me having fun out there. Right now, no one else, nothing else matters."

Anise was surprised at how genuine he seemed and how comforting his words were. She'd have to write that down on a blank card later. "But what if I screw up?"

He shrugged. "So what if you do?"

That right there. That was who she wanted to be in this situation. No judgment, no pressure. Her butterflies settled, bringing on a surge of confidence. Smiling at him, she grabbed his hand and led him on stage when their names were called. She focused on him, let her body move, and basked in the flashing lights, loud music, and the energy of her performance. Before she knew it, five one hundred dollar bills were being counted into her outstretched hand in front of the cheering crowd.

"That was incredible!" she exclaimed, throwing her arms around Nate's neck. Her heart was racing, and for once, the adrenaline rush had felt exciting instead of scary. He squeezed her back, and when she loosened her grip and pulled back, their faces paused inches from each other as their eyes connected. She could feel a tension buzzing in their locked stare, and for a moment, he was all she could see. The pleasure of it all made her guilt overtake her, and peeling her gaze from his face, she forced her arms to drop and headed toward her friends.

"You guys were so great up there!" Joy squealed, giving Anise a happy hug as she stepped off the stage. Vanessa and Erin excitedly joined in with their congratulations.

"Thanks!" Anise told them, returning their hugs. She turned to Nate, grabbed her pencil from behind her ear, and started scribbling on a napkin she grabbed off the bar.

"I can't believe you got her up on a stage," Vanessa said to Nate. "You're a miracle worker."

"She owned it," he replied.

"This is for you," Anise said, handing Nate the napkin. She'd written her name, email address, and had felt bold enough to include a note that said, "Thank you for a night I'll never forget."

He took it and read it. "Same to you," he told her with a smile. He wrote his email and phone number on a napkin for her. "Until later."

"You're leaving?" Joy asked him.

He nodded. "You ladies have a good night."

"Nothing wrong with that," Erin said in approval as they watched Nate disappear into the crowd.

"Nothing at all," Anise agreed, biting her lower lip.

Joy looked at her friends with her mouth hanging open in disbelief. "Understatement of the year! How glad are you that we stayed here tonight?"

"It was fate," Anise replied, unable to control the big smile spreading across her face.

"What happened with your stage fright?" Erin asked.

Anise shrugged. "I don't know. He made me feel really comfortable."

"That's awesome!" said Joy. "You've never said that about anyone before. And I have to know. You were dancing really close. Does his body feel as good as it looks?"

Anise felt herself blush. "Yes," she admitted. "He's muscular, but lean."

"I'm jealous!" Joy cried. "I need to find someone that ridiculously hot."

Anise laughed. "He *is* hot, but there's so much more to him. He's smart and intuitive. He knew things about me that I didn't have to tell him. And he said something that was close to one of my new affirmation cards, so I know he can prioritize the important things. And when I was starting to get anxious backstage, he calmed me down so quickly and made me feel like nothing was important except for us having fun up there. He didn't care if I screwed anything up, and knowing that got me to relax." She couldn't keep the smile off her face. She'd been smiling so much that her cheeks were starting to ache.

"Uh oh," Erin said with a grin. "You really like him."

"Is that why you gave him your number?" asked Vanessa.

"Oh my god, are you going to see him again?" Joy demanded.

"No! It was just my email address," said Anise. "And I can't see him again. Maybe if I were single..."

"You could be," teased Joy.

"But right now I'm not. And I shouldn't have given him my email; it's just that we made this deal...I'll tell you about it later. He probably won't even write. And I won't respond if he does."

"I've never had a guy that hot work so hard for just my email address," Erin told her. "I kind of hate you right now."

"Aw, thank you," Anise told her with a big grin.

AFTER THE THREE-BLOCK WALK HOME, ANISE opened the door to her apartment a little after 2 o'clock in the morning, cursing Brian for forgetting to lock it again. She grunted with disgust. Brian was sleeping on the floor where she'd left him, television still on with the volume up, and several more beer cans surrounding him. Shaking her head, she turned off the TV, went to the bedroom, and closed the door.

Exhausted, she crawled in bed and closed her eyes thinking sleep would find her quickly. Her mind had other ideas. It wouldn't stop replaying scenes at the club. She was back on the dance floor, in between Nate's arms. But this time, she didn't hold back. She faced him and pressed herself against him as they moved, wanting to feel what she'd missed out on. His hands traced her body, starting at her face and taking their time as they moved lower. She got a chill as his fingers softly touched her neck and reached her cleavage. Then they were on her hips, pulling her closer to him as she gently bit into his sexy smirk like she'd wanted to earlier. Then he kissed her and...

She opened her eyes and kicked off the covers which were getting too warm. Staring at the ceiling, she knew there was no way she'd be able to fall asleep just yet. She tiptoed to her dresser, opened a drawer, and fumbled through it in the dark until her hand closed on her vibrator.

Chapter 4

Sunday, June 3, 2012

Rays of sun shone through the curtains to awaken Anise the next morning. She stayed still for a few moments, smiling, thinking about the adventure of the night before. Then, yawning and stretching, she rolled out of bed and padded into the kitchen to make breakfast. She looked over and saw that Brian was still passed out in the same place on the floor. She rolled her eyes and walked around the kitchen, purposely slamming cupboards and drawers while grabbing the eggs, milk, and pancake mix.

Brian woke up while she was cooking, and he trudged over to their apartment-sized kitchen table, stepping on beer cans and cursing from the pain on his way.

"Could you not slam shit?" he mumbled, groggily. "I have a headache."

Anise ignored him and turned on the TV. A young woman from Canada was crying on the news. "My mother and my stepfather were killed *in cold blood*, but the only thing that was missing as far as I could tell was a ring. It had meant a lot to my stepfather; it was a family heirloom, and he'd want me to try to get it back. It was a carnelian stone in an electrum setting, and—"

Brian switched off the TV.

"Hey, I was watching that!" Anise protested.

"I need quiet!" Brian complained gruffly.

"What are you doing with my amulet?" she asked as he pulled it out of a pocket in his shorts and put it on the table.

"I was just looking at it. I accidentally slept on it last night. It fucking hurts." He rubbed his hip. "I dreamed of that crazy old lady you told me about. You know, the one that came into the thrift store?"

Anise gave him no response. She'd asked him a thousand times to stop insulting her customers. He never listened.

"She was here in the living room and wouldn't leave. It was funny." Brian snorted a laugh. "Then I dreamed some guy was here looking through the drawers. But I knew it was just a dream so I ignored him. I closed my eyes and a different dream started."

Anise put butter and maple syrup on the table and sat down to devour her pancakes and coffee.

"Don't I get any pancakes?" Brian asked.

"Sure. If you make them yourself."

"Come on, Anise. Can we not fight for once?" He slumped back in his chair and rubbed his forehead with his hand.

"I would love to not fight." She felt her jaw tighten as she couldn't help but glare at him.

"Great. Can you tell that to your face?"

"Fine. It's a beautiful day," she sighed, ignoring the fact that she was still upset with him. "Would you like to do something?"

"I have errands to run," he answered dismissively.

"All day?"

"No," he said with a sigh. "What did you want to do?"

"I have to go check on my mom and hit some shops."

"I don't wanna shop, and I definitely don't wanna

visit your mom," he replied. "But you can come with me to the dispensary if you want."

Anise's nose wrinkled in disgust. "No, you know I hate the way that place smells. But why don't you at least meet me for lunch on the way home?"

"Okay. Where?"

"That Greek place around the corner."

"Yeah. Okay."

"Oh, I meant to ask you—were you able to get the tickets?"

Brian looked confused. "What tickets?"

"Brian," she replied, unable to hide the disappointment in her voice. "The tickets to the Concert in the Park on Tuesday. You said you'd get them as a graduation gift for me."

"Oh, shit, I spaced it. Sorry."

"I was really looking forward to it," she said with a frown. "They have some great local bands in the lineup."

"I thought it was next week."

She stared at him. "It's always on the first Tuesday in June. Every year. You know that."

Brian looked at her with an expression of regret. "I don't really have the money for tickets anyway. My workman's comp checks aren't that big."

"You told me you'd buy less beer last week so you could get the tickets."

"I just forgot, okay?" he said, irritation evident in his voice.

"Okay," she replied, backing down. "I'll call now and see if I can get some." She grabbed her phone and called the ticket office, who informed her that the tickets had sold out the week before.

"So, what are you shopping for?" he asked as soon as she put her phone down.

She frowned. He didn't care what she was shopping for. He was obviously trying to change the subject. "I could use some work clothes. I start my new job tomorrow."

"Oh, yeah, I forgot. Well, have fun. I'll see you later." He got up from the table. "Hey, where's your ring?"

Anise looked at her hand. The garnet ring Brian had given her wasn't on her finger. "I don't know," she replied, surprised. She looked at the floor around her but saw nothing. "I guess it must've fallen off."

"I'll help you look for it later," he said as he stood up and headed toward the bathroom.

"Let's look now," Anise requested. "I had it yesterday. It's gotta be here somewhere."

"I said later." He continued walking away.

"Why are you in such a hurry?"

"I have shit to do!" he replied in annoyance. "We'll look later."

She was going to say nothing so as not to start another fight but then thought about her favorite affirmation card. *Who do I want to be in this situation?* "Brian, what's happening here?"

"I'm going to take a shower," he replied, as if it were obvious.

"No, I mean, what's happening with us? Are we ever going to get back to how we used to be?"

He sighed and rejoined her at the table. "I don't have time for this. Why don't you just tell me what I did wrong so I can apologize?"

She closed her eyes for a moment and centered herself so she wouldn't explode. "That right there. You have no interest in talking to me. You have no interest in maintaining our relationship. You skipped my graduation, and you didn't come to the club with me either. You forget everything I tell you, probably because you weren't listening in the first place."

He looked at his watch and shrugged. "You're right. I'm sorry. It won't happen again. We good?" He stood up.

"No! But you do get the award for the most insincere apology ever!"

He groaned and sat again.

"It's not just that. You get drunk every night. I think you're developing a problem."

"Now you sound just like my sister." He leaned back in his chair with a huff.

"And you still haven't gone back to work."

"I'm still in pain!" he yelled.

"I didn't say you weren't, and you don't have to go back to construction. But you sit on the floor all day. You could get a job in an office and sit in a comfortable padded chair. It would be better for your back. And I really need you to contribute to our finances again."

"Well, I'm still in pain and can't work yet," he replied. "I could use some support from you about that."

"I've been nothing but supportive of you, but now I'm running out of money, and I don't make enough to support the both of us!"

"You'll find a better job soon," Brian told her and took her hand.

She angrily pulled her hand from his grip. "Do you remember how we first met?" She reminded him of the details. "That Brian was sweet, supportive, romantic, fun. What happened to him?"

He'd been staring at the part of her thighs just under the hem of her pajama shorts. "That Brian stopped getting laid. It's been months, Anise. Come on, let's stop fighting and go make up in the bedroom."

She glared at him. "So you have time for that but none to help me find my ring?"

Brian glared back but said nothing.

"You always smell like beer or weed and you hardly shower anymore. All you do is sit around and play video games and forget things I tell you. What about that is supposed to make me want to rip your clothes off? You're not the guy I met at that movie theater."

He laughed and shook his head. "Everyone's on their best behavior when they first meet. I was romantic so I could land the hot, flakey girl who sat next to me at that movie theater. But no one's like that all the time. That's not reality and everyone knows it."

Condescending jerk. "I don't believe that for a second. And I was in a hurry that day. I made a mistake by walking into the wrong theater. That doesn't make me a flake! And calling me hot and flakey makes me sound like I'm nothing more than a biscuit."

"Fine. You're not a flake. Are we done here?"

"No! Not even close!"

"I think you need to calm down before we talk more. I'll see you at lunch." He got up and walked away, ignoring her protests.

While he was in the bathroom, Anise checked her e-mail on her phone. Only spam and advertisements. Nothing from Nate.

✳✳✳

"Mom?" Anise called out as she let herself into Deborah's house. "I have the groceries. I brought in your mail. You have overdue notices again...Mom?" After receiving no answer, Anise grew worried. She darted up the stairs and burst into her mother's bedroom.

"Go away," Deborah mumbled from under the covers. "It's the middle of the night."

Anise rolled her eyes. "It's almost eleven in the morning. How was the spa?"

Deborah didn't move. "Awful. They couldn't give a good massage if their lives depended on it."

"Are you okay?" Anise pulled the blankets off of her mother's face.

"No, I'm sick. Leave me alone."

Anise felt her mother's forehead. "You don't have a fever. What hurts?"

"Everything. Why are you here?"

Anise sighed and waited to see if her mother would ask about her night.

"Sometime today," Deborah said with annoyance.

"Aren't you going to ask about the graduation ceremony?"

Deborah snorted and rolled over. "I never got to go to college. Other people were too busy deciding my life for me. You think you're a big shot now with your fancy degree? Why don't you use it to find a better job? Working at the mall at age twenty-four. How embarrassing for us both."

Anise felt her eyes well up. The tone of this conversation with her mother was typical, but it still hurt.

"Anise, I need to sleep. Shut the door on your way out." Deborah pulled the covers over her head.

"Not yet. I need to ask you something."

"What?" Deborah groaned.

"Who is Les Wilkins?"

Deborah paused before answering. "How should I know?"

"He came here the other day looking for you."

"I don't know what you're talking about. Now are you going to let me sleep?"

Anise frowned at the futility of their conversation. "Yeah." She went back downstairs and into the kitchen. The sink was overflowing with dirty dishes, and a stack of bills had fallen off the table and onto the tile floor. She put away the groceries, picked up the mail from the floor, and then started on the dishes. Thinking about the things her mother had said to her, Anise's stomach cramped up. Every weekend the same thing.

"No sponge?" she said aloud, her eyes scanning the counter and underneath the sink. She dug through the supply closet in the garage and found the new sponges on the top shelf. Standing on her tiptoes on a step stool, she reached as far as she could to grab a packet of yellow sponges. Losing her balance, she grabbed whatever her hands found and landed hard in a seated position on the garage floor, a cardboard box falling on her head. Envelopes scattered everywhere.

Anise groaned and rubbed her tailbone. Crawling around the garage floor, she grabbed the envelopes and put them back in the box. She was about to stand up to put the box back in the closet when she looked at the last envelope. "What?" She dug through the box. Each unopened envelope had a red "Return to Sender" stamp and was addressed to Les Wilkins with her mother's name on the return label—except one. This one was addressed to Deborah Viston. The postmark was over thirty years old. As the envelope had already been opened, Anise removed the letter and read it.

Deborah,

As I've reminded you many, many times, it was a closed adoption. You have no further legal rights as far as Les is concerned. If you continue to harass us and attempt contact with him, we will have no choice but to pursue legal action. I beg of you, do the right thing and leave us alone. I assure you he is happy and wants for nothing.

Patricia Wilkins

"I have a brother." Anise stayed seated on the filthy concrete for several moments, letting the shock settle in her mind. That's why Les's eyes—his hazel eyes, the same color as her own—had lit up when she'd introduced herself. That's why he asked her if Deb had mentioned him—he knew the truth. A few tears rolled down her cheeks while thoughts raced through her head about Les, his mysterious fainting issue, and her own pain for being kept in the dark and having a sibling whom she never got to know. She'd always wanted a sibling. Someone to be on her side when her mother told her she wasn't good enough to be cast in the high school play so she shouldn't even try. Someone to hang her kindergarten art on the fridge instead of watching it be crumpled up and thrown in the trash when they thought she wasn't looking. A family member to openly share her child-like joy with instead of keeping it to herself because she knew it would illicit an eye roll from her parents.

Anxiety and anger grew in her chest, and it tempted her to run upstairs and scream at her mother. But then she wondered how her mother must've felt keeping this secret. Obviously missing her son and reaching out to him so many times only to have her letters returned unopened must've been devastating. Anise wondered if that's what may have led to her mother's perpetual anger and her father's desire to leave. A wave of compassion filled her, but as strong as it was, it didn't wash away the hurt at having been lied to and made to deal with her parents' emotions that they weren't dealing with themselves.

Anise let herself sob on the cold and dirty garage floor until the tears wouldn't come anymore. She gathered her things and walked out of her mother's house. She paused on the porch to water the petunias that were wilting from thirst, wondering what she should do next.

Brian's older sister Corinne, a psychologist, had tried to talk to Anise about her relationship with her parents a few times before, but Anise hadn't wanted to listen. "They've had the same patterns of behavior throughout your whole life," Corinne had said. "I think you should stand up to them."

Anise had been horrified. "No. They're my parents.

I could never disrespect them like that. They're just... stressed out."

"And what about demanding the respect that *you* deserve?" Corinne had asked her. "What you think is the moral high ground is actually a self-betrayal."

Anise hadn't wanted to believe it at the time but was starting to see now.

Who do I want to be in this situation? she asked herself, willing the self-knowledge to manifest in her mind. The water droplets on the petals sparkled in the sun, reflecting a light that hadn't been there a moment ago. "Inspiration blooms," Anise said, looking at the petunias, "but still needs water." A smile made its way across her face as she grabbed another blank note card and wrote down her newest affirmation. Something so simple and obvious, but so often forgotten or overlooked. It's not enough to be inspired by affirmations; one must use them to take action, and *that's* who she wanted to be. It was at that moment Anise Viston decided to change her life.

Her mother was only a flight of stairs away, but Anise didn't want to lose her nerve by attempting this in person. Not yet. Baby steps. She started a text message to both of her parents. Her thumbs flew over the keyboard on her phone, and for once, she didn't carefully go over what she wrote to correct typos. Mom could say what she wanted about it.

Anise: Mom & Dad, Our relationship needs to change. Right now, I'm expected to be fine with you not showing up for me, talking down to me, ignoring me, and criticizing my choices. This ends now. If you want to continue to have contact with me, you will need to treat me like an adult and with the respect that I deserve.

Never in her twenty-four years had Anise spoken to her parents like that. Even she was surprised with her forcefulness and conviction, and damn, it felt good.

After speaking her truth, it was so much easier to breathe. But the happiness and strength she felt was soon replaced by images of her brother popping into her mind. When thoughts were especially insistent on creating difficult emotions, it always helped to draw them. She sat on her mother's front porch steps next to the petunias and pulled her sketchbook out of her bag. She grabbed the pencil from behind her ear and turned to the next blank page. An image of Les emerged on the paper. How long had he known about her? Had he maybe always wanted a sibling, too? Was there still time for them to get to know each other? Her falling tears smudged his face, and she wanted a distraction from the overwhelming sadness. She texted her friends.

Anise: Shopping, anyone?

Hopping on her bike, she pedaled furiously downtown.

Joy was the only one able to join her. Anise considered confiding in her friend, but her mind was still reeling from the shock of her discovery. She'd let it settle for a while first. They met at their favorite clothing store, and Joy helped Anise pick out flattering blouses, skirts, and trousers for her new work wardrobe.

"Thanks so much for your help," Anise told Joy. "I'm supposed to meet Brian for lunch across the street in five minutes. Will you join us?"

"Okay, sure!"

They grabbed a table on the patio of the Greek restaurant and ordered strawberry lemonades while waiting for Brian.

"So what's new with you?" Anise asked.

"I haven't told you much about Adam and Mindy yet!" Joy gushed about the two new people she'd started dating.

"They both sound really fun! Any relationship potential for either of them?"

"Maybe?" Joy wondered out loud. "I know they're both dating other people too, so we'll see how it goes. I've only seen Adam the one time, and we were at a noisy party so it was hard to talk. I've been out with Mindy twice, and she asked me out again for Thursday!"

"I'm excited for you! Let me know how it goes!"

"I'll tell you all about it on the drive to Lundville on Saturday!"

"Can't wait!" Anise made a mental note to find another instructor to cover for her kickboxing class on Saturday morning.

"So, what about *your* relationship?" Joy asked. "I know it's only been a day since we talked about him, but are things any better for you and Brian?" Joy asked. "Tell me he apologized or cleaned up the apartment or went down on you or *something!*"

Anise shook her head. "No. When I got home last night, he was sacked out on the floor, shit-faced. His video game was still on, and it looked like he hadn't moved at all except to get more beer from the fridge. He also forgot to get the tickets to the concert like he promised, and he spaced that I start my new job tomorrow. He didn't even ask if I had fun at the club last night. It seems like he doesn't think about me at all anymore."

"Ugh! What the hell?" Joy's face crinkled in disgust.

Anise shrugged. "He's getting really drunk just about every night. And his doctor says he's better now and can go back to work, but he insists he's still in pain and refuses to look for a job. He says he can barely move and that picking his clothes up off the floor hurts too much, but he has no problem carrying several cases of beer up the stairs or sitting on the hard floor all day. What he says he can't do and what he does is inconsistent."

"Have you tried confronting him? Telling him you don't believe him?"

Anise shook her head. "I've tried reasoning with him. Telling him to get a job that doesn't involve physical labor. But as far as telling him I don't believe he's still in pain, no."

"Seriously?! Why not?"

"Because he's the only one who knows how he actually feels. And he's my boyfriend. If we don't have trust..." Anise paused for a moment, letting the details of a memory fill her mind. "I was in fifth grade when my panic attacks started. I'd feel dizzy, faint, nauseated, sweaty, and my arms would go numb. I didn't know what was happening, and I was so scared. I thought I was really sick or dying. I went to the school nurse so many times that she didn't believe me anymore. She shamed me for trying to get out of class. My mother didn't believe me either. She accused me of trying to make her life harder on purpose. After I begged and begged for her to take me to the doctor, she finally did, but he found nothing physically wrong with me and told me that if I didn't stop lying, he'd recommend that my parents send me to a boot camp for delinquent kids. On the car ride home, my mother let me know how much I'd humiliated her in front of the doctor."

Joy grabbed Anise's hand as her eyes flooded.

"So, I know what it's like to feel horrible and have no one believe you," Anise continued. "I promised myself I'd never make anyone feel the way I felt. I will always give people the benefit of the doubt." She checked the time on her phone. "Where is Brian, anyway?" Anise wondered aloud. "He was supposed to be here twenty minutes ago. I'll text him."

Anise: Where are you?

Brian: Sorry I forgot. I can come now.

Anise: Don't bother. I have Joy here with me. See you later.

Brian: K.

Anise rolled her eyes. "Sorry about that. He's not coming."

"What happened?"

"I'm guessing he's still at the dispensary. He usually gets to talking to someone there. This isn't the first time he's stood me up because he lost track of time there."

"Really? What an ass!"

"To put it mildly."

"If he's not coming, let's order. I'm starving!" Joy picked up her menu.

Anise wanted to continue to show Brian compassion for his pain but couldn't ignore her growing doubt about her love for him. "Do you think we're a good couple?" Anise asked her friend.

Joy put her menu back on the table and looked at Anise. "You already know what I think of him and that it isn't good. But it doesn't matter what anyone thinks except for you and Brian. Do *you* think you're a good couple?"

"I used to," replied Anise, as she checked her e-mail with her phone under the table.

"Did Nate write?!" Joy squealed, leaning over to see Anise's screen.

Anise put her phone back on the table. "No, but that's a good thing."

Joy laughed.

"What?" Anise asked her curiously.

"Nothing," Joy responded. "It's just that sometimes—especially when it's about a guy you're interested in—you do this thing where you lie to yourself about how you're really feeling when you don't want to feel that way. Like that one guy you refused to admit you liked back in high school."

"He had a girlfriend. I was trying not to like him," Anise explained.

"And that professor you had a crush on in college..."

"He was my professor! So not appropriate!"

"So you agree with me?"

"You're not the first one to tell me that I'm not always completely honest with myself," Anise admitted with a guilty glance.

"Really? Who else told you that?"

"I used to do therapy sessions with Brian's sister, Corinne. She's a psychologist."

"So what did she say exactly?" Joy wanted to know.

"That when you feel something you don't want to, you can feel guilty or ashamed or confused because it's threatening your sense of identity. I believe I'm a loyal person. But if I start thinking about a man who isn't my boyfriend...that doesn't fit with how I think of myself. And when you lie to yourself, it's because you're getting something from the lie."

"What do you mean? Like when you say you're glad Nate didn't write, that means you're still loyal?"

"I guess," Anise agreed with a shrug. "That's probably what Corinne would say anyway."

Joy pulled her mouth to the side like she did every time she was thinking. "What about when you keep trying to make things work with Brian, even though you just admitted that you don't think you're a good couple anymore?"

Anise shrugged. "I don't know. I keep hoping things

will change for the better."

"I know that," Joy said. "I mean what would Corinne say?"

"I'd never talk to Corinne about Brian like that. He's her baby brother, and she's too biased. But we did talk about my parents and how I'd make up excuses for them when they lied to me or told me negative things about myself that aren't even true. Corinne made me see that they said things that made me feel incapable of handling my own life, and I started to not trust myself. Even after all that, I didn't want to set any boundaries with them. I'd lie to myself about my relationship with them because it was easier than dealing with the fallout if I tried to confront them about it."

Joy nodded. "I get that. I just want you to know it's okay to feel what you feel, even if it's disappointment because Nate didn't write. True, it's not always okay to act on a feeling, but it's okay to admit you feel it."

"Yeah," Anise agreed. "But I acted on it. I gave Nate my email address. I feel guilty. I never acted on my feelings for that guy in high school or my professor."

"Maybe that's a good thing!" Joy exclaimed. "Maybe it's different this time because it's your way of telling yourself you're ready to move on from Brian."

Anise shrugged slightly. "Yeah...maybe."

"Loyalty is a good thing, but being loyal to yourself is important too," Joy said matter-of-factly. "I think you're depriving yourself of knowing someone who might be great so you can stay with someone we already know isn't."

"I have a lot to think about when it comes to Brian," Anise admitted in a mumble. Could they still fix things? And why was she so intent on fixing a relationship with a man she wasn't sure she loved anymore?

"Right. So about Nate...don't be so hard on yourself," Joy demanded. "And may I remind you that it's only been half a day. If he wrote already, he'd seem too eager."

"Maybe," Anise shrugged. "I kinda like it when the guy calls the next day though. Or in this case writes. But it *is* a good thing that he didn't. I know after this conversation you won't believe me, but I really am glad I haven't heard from him. Like I said, I'm not single. And as much as I said I liked him...that was probably just the mojitos talking. He seems so worldly and confident..." Anise felt herself frown.

"That's a bad thing?" Joy laughed.

"I just mean I doubt we'd actually have anything in common." Something about saying those words made her stomach clench up. Corinne had once told her that she'd gotten really good at believing her own lies as a protective mechanism to deal with her parents, and a way to overcome that was to trust her own intuition. Once she did that, she could use the truth about her situations to make decisions that actually made her happy. Did the stomach clench come from her intuition trying to tell her something? Was she lying to herself about her feelings surrounding her current relationship as well as her feelings about the possibility of seeing someone else? She wondered what would happen if she broke up with Brian. She'd threatened to leave him a couple weeks ago after a big fight, and he'd threatened to destroy everything she owned before apologizing and begging on his knees for her to stay. *Am I just afraid of what he'll do if I leave him?* Anise pushed the uncomfortable and confusing thoughts aside. Or was Corinne full of shit? Maybe her stomach clenched because she was hungry and they hadn't ordered yet.

"I think you belong with someone worldly and confident," Joy declared. "Not someone like Brian who runs on beer and only wears clothes that were shot out of a t-shirt cannon."

They both laughed so hard, they got weird looks from people walking by on the street.

"So how is everything else?" Joy asked once they

regained composure.

"I do have some good news!" Anise chirped, happy to change the subject. "It's interesting timing that we talked about my parents and setting boundaries because as of this morning, I've decided to overhaul my life, starting with my relationship with my parents. I texted them that things need to change. I told them that if they don't start treating me with the respect I deserve, I want no further contact."

"Really?" asked Joy with a look of shock on her face. "That's great! What did they say?"

Anise shrugged. "Nothing yet. So we'll see."

"I'm proud of you!" Joy said, leaning over and giving Anise a hug. "Something had to happen there. I'm glad you took that step."

"Thank you! I'm a little nervous about what they'll say, but I'm glad I did it, too."

"Something has to happen with Brian also," Joy continued, giving Anise a firm look.

Anise nodded. "It does. But one thing at a time."

AFTER TEXTING WITH ANISE, BRIAN DECIDED to visit his older sister Corinne instead of going home. He was sorry for disappointing Anise again but was somewhat glad he missed their lunch. They really didn't have much to say to each other these days that didn't revolve around her trying to convince him get a job, or her nagging him about his behavior at home.

Corinne Kellin was eight years older than Brian, and she worked as a psychologist at an inpatient facility downtown. Despite their age difference, they had always been very close, and Brian felt like he could tell her anything. "Hey, kid!" she greeted him, when he got to her house.

"Hey," he said, giving her a hug. He was almost a foot taller than her, but he'd always think of her as his big sister. "Where's Ray?" Brian asked, referring to Corinne's husband.

"He took your nephews to the park. Come in! Sit!"

Brian walked through the living room of the small but impeccable house and took a seat at her kitchen table. "What's new with you?" he asked.

Corinne sat next to him. "Congratulate me because I just got that new job I interviewed for!"

"Awesome. Congrats. What is it again?"

"Psychologist for that big correctional facility, remember? I'll be doing initial inmate assessments, individual and group therapy, emergency counseling, and any court-ordered assessments."

"You'll be working in a prison? Is that safe?" Brian's brow wrinkled with concern.

"Perfectly. Don't worry; I'll be fine! I'm so excited! I find the criminal mind to be so fascinating, don't you?" she asked him, smiling.

"Not really," Brian replied, his voice flat.

"What's the matter with you today, Bri?"

"Sorry. I'm happy for you if you're happy. I really am."

"But...?"

He shrugged. "I don't know."

"Okay," Corinne said. "So, how's Anise?"

"Fine," Brian replied. He picked up his phone when he received a text. "She got a job at the mall taking surveys because she bombed her other job interviews."

"Oh, that's too bad." Corinne cleared her throat.

He was smiling at his phone when he remembered how annoyed his sister got when she didn't have his full attention. "Sorry," he said, putting his phone face down on the table.

"Who has you smiling like that? Anise?"

"No, just my friend Hailey. We were hanging out this morning. And last night."

"Who's Hailey?"

"She was one of the admins at J&J Construction."

"...And she's just a friend?"

"Yeah, of course."

"Tell me the truth, Brian. Are you dating her?"

"No." He looked at his sister and saw the disbelief in her eyes. *How can she tell?* "I've slept with her a couple times," he admitted sheepishly.

"Brian!" Corinne exclaimed, in a scolding voice.

"That's all it was, I swear! I'd never date her; she means nothing to me, and I don't even like her very much. I love Anise. But she hasn't wanted anything to do with me for a while. She just nags me and isn't fun anymore. If I try to touch her, she pulls away. What am I supposed to do?" he asked, defeated.

"Not what you're doing! Have you tried talking to Anise about it?"

"I don't know. Sort of, I guess," he replied quietly, remembering the conversation he and Anise had that morning where she'd been nagging him about drinking and not listening to her. "It didn't help."

"Sort of, you guess," his sister repeated, giving him a look. "The two of you need to communicate better. Tell her how you feel, and encourage her to do the same. You can really learn a lot about each other that way, and honestly, it's your only chance to fix things. If you don't, your relationship is doomed. Anise is a great girl; I'd hate to see you lose her."

Brian looked down and didn't say a word. He didn't want to lose Anise, either. He knew Corinne was right, but it was just so hard to talk about these things. Lately, talking always led to fighting, and he was sick of it.

Corinne changed the subject. "So, how are you feeling? Have you been back to the doctor? Are you back at work?"

"No, my doctor's a quack," Brian snorted.

"What do you mean?"

"The physical therapists say I have full use of my body again, but I still have pain, and I told the doctor that. He wants to send me to some specialist, but he said he's not sure it'll help. He doesn't know what else to do for me."

"You could get a second opinion."

"I did; she said the same thing."

"Have you been to the specialist?"

"I've seen enough doctors to last me a lifetime, and they didn't help. I'm done with that shit," Brian proclaimed and went back to looking at the text messages Hailey was sending him.

Corrine got up to pour them glasses of iced tea. She started talking to him about something, but he couldn't concentrate and didn't want to look her in the eye. He'd lied to her, and he hated that. But he couldn't let the truth get back to Anise, and the truth was that he felt fine. He hadn't any pain for the last month and a half, and he was fully ready to return to work. But Anise was keeping something from him, and it was getting harder and harder to control his rage whenever he thought about it. She'd put on a hat and a jacket that hung down to her knees and go to a gym downtown twice a week, and she'd lie every time he asked her where she'd been. He didn't want to break up with her, but he felt he needed to even the score. If she was going to lie about where she'd been, so was he. If she was going to spend money they didn't have on a gym membership, then she could pay for his expenses for a while, too. If she wouldn't sleep with him, he'd meet up with a girl who would. He mentally reminded himself to stop by the dispensary on the way home and let the familiar scent seep into his clothes so that Anise would think he had been there that morning.

Chapter 5

Monday, June 4, 2012

The early morning Reiki session at Erin's apartment relaxed Anise so much, her butterflies disappeared completely, and she felt confident and ready to tackle her first day of work. As she rode her Schwinn to the mall, however, guilt crept back into her mind. Anise scolded herself for how many times she'd checked her email in the last twenty-four hours. She shouldn't have hoped for a message from a man who wasn't her boyfriend. She shouldn't have daydreamed about what he might say. Nate hadn't written to her, and she told herself she was glad. She wouldn't have responded anyway. She shouldn't be giving out her contact information to guys in clubs. Anise secured her bicycle with a chain and smoothed out her skirt, blouse, and bangs. Walking into the mall, she went down a flight of stairs and entered the offices of Bradley Field Services.

"Good morning, Anise!" said her bubbly supervisor Dawn. "Come on into the conference room. I've got a couple of other new hires back there, and I'll train you all together." Her short, blonde curls bounced as she led the way down the hall.

A man of retirement age sat in the conference room along with a bored-looking teenage girl. "This is Victor and Hannah," said Dawn, introducing them, "and this is Anise! Let's get started." Anise sat and Dawn passed out some forms. "These are the qualifier sheets," she explained. "When you're out in the field approaching people to take surveys, you ask them these questions to see if they qualify for the survey."

Dawn droned on while Anise tried her best to focus on the boring directions.

"Questions so far?" asked Dawn.

"No," said Anise and Victor. Hannah's eyes were closed.

"Great!" said Dawn. "So, when they qualify for the survey, you bring them back into the office and go into one of the interview rooms. Each survey has its own packet of questions."

Anise's mind started wandering. It took her back to Saturday night and how much fun she had had with Nate. How he'd made her laugh and how thrilled she'd been when he told her he believed in fate and destiny. His subtle but intoxicating cologne. How his hands on her arms, her hips, her face had given her tingling sensations that came back now as she thought about him. The pleasure she'd gotten by pressing up against him during their embrace and how he'd made the entire club disappear with the way he'd looked at her. She wondered what it would be like to kiss him. But it didn't matter—she couldn't see him again, not as long as she was still with Brian. She forced her attention back to Dawn who unfortunately was still talking.

"For the pasta sauce survey, you need to show them these pictures of the concept sauces, and ask them the questions in the packet. When you're done interviewing them, give them their $10 gift certificate to the mall, which is accepted in any store, and drop the survey off to me at the front desk."

The three trainees were briefed on the other customers' surveys, but Anise couldn't stop thinking about the cobalt color of Nate's eyes. She'd never seen eyes that blue before. Her thoughts were rudely interrupted by Dawn's excited voice letting her newest employees loose in the mall. Anise claimed a busy corridor to stand in and watched the multitude of shoppers walk by. It was overwhelming thinking she'd have to stop them and try to convince them to take a detour from their planned day for her own purposes. Even though her stomach was calmer than she'd expected—Erin's Reiki treatment had helped with her anxiety—she still had a few nervous twinges. She bought herself a Coke before approaching anyone in order to ensure her stomach would settle.

After several futile attempts at talking to shoppers, Anise stood motionless and silent in the middle of the mall hallway, her clipboard hanging sadly from her tenuous grip. She'd never realized how many rude people there were. Many ignored her like she didn't exist. Others told her to go away. Still others just flat out said no before she'd even gotten out a sentence. She understood she shouldn't take it personally but was failing at that. This had to be one of the worst jobs in existence. She was thinking of quitting when she heard someone come up behind her.

"Excuse me, Miss, can I take a survey?"

She turned around. "Nate!" she exclaimed in surprise. She felt her cheeks flush as she looked him over. "What are you doing here?" He wore jeans, navy blue suede sneakers, and a light gray button down shirt with the sleeves rolled up to his mid-forearm. His mouth and eyes smiled, and he looked just as good as he had at the club.

"I came to return this." He dropped something in her hand.

"My ring!" Her eyes widened with delight as she put the garnet back on her finger. "Where did you find it?"

"When you pulled me on stage, it came off in my hand. I put it in my pocket and was going to give it back to you after the contest, but in all the excitement, I forgot I had it."

"Thanks for coming all the way here to return it," she said with gratitude. "That was really nice of you."

"Not a problem. I wanted to see you again anyway." He ran a hand through his almost-black hair. "You know, I couldn't get you off my mind all weekend."

"Really?" Now she had butterflies again, but these felt good.

"Really." He glanced at her clipboard. "So how's your first day going?"

"Honestly, not great. I haven't gotten any respondents yet. People have been really rude, and I'm starting to dread having to approach them."

"I'll be your first respondent," he offered. "Ask me questions."

Grateful again, Anise grabbed her pencil from behind her ear and poised it over the first question on her clipboard. "Do you like pasta sauce?"

"*Hell*, yeah! Who doesn't?" he said dramatically.

Anise giggled. "Okay, great. I need your full name."

"Nathan Brevain." He gave her the correct spelling.

"Your age?"

"Twenty-seven."

"And your address?" He gave it to her.

She qualified him for the survey and led him into an interview room in the office. They sat down, and she handed him the pictures of the pasta sauce, which included a list of ingredients and nutritional information. "Which sauce would you be most likely to buy?"

"This one," he replied, pointing to one of the sauces.

"What do you like about that one?"

"It looks thick."

"What else do you like about it?"

"It has a lot of spices in it. You wouldn't have to add

anything to it."

"It sounds like you cook." *Brian doesn't even know where the kitchen is,* she thought.

"Is that a question on your form?" He grinned at her.

She grinned back. "No, I was just curious."

"If you're asking me to cook for you tonight, that could be arranged."

"I already told you I have a boyfriend," she reminded him, smiling again.

"He's not invited."

"Let's focus on the survey," she said with a laugh.

"Yes, ma'am." His intense blue eyes looked deeply into hers.

Her stomach nervously twinging, she looked back down at her survey form so he wouldn't see the growing warmth in her cheeks. "What else do you like about the pasta sauce?"

A quiet laugh escaped his lips, and his eyes twinkled at her while he dutifully answered the rest of her questions.

After the interview, she handed him his gift certificate.

"You did great," Nate told her, opening his arms to offer her a hug. "You'll be running this place in no time."

She allowed it and squeezed him back, enjoying the feeling of his arms around her and breathing in the faint woodsy scent of his cologne. "Thanks."

"When's your lunch break?" he asked her.

"Half an hour."

"Great. Meet me at the food court upstairs? I'll buy us lunch," he said, holding up his certificate.

She gave him a coy smile. "Okay."

Anise watched Nate walk away as she dropped off the completed survey to Dawn at the front desk.

"Wow," whispered Dawn. "I'm jealous you got to interview him. He's *so* cute!"

"I know, right?" Anise whispered back with a smirk.

***

AT LUNCH, ANISE EYED THE COOKIE on Nate's tray, wishing that she'd gotten one too, but she forgot about it when Nate quickly blew off a work call, saying that he was already in a more important meeting. She returned his playful wink with a grin and curiously asked him questions. She learned that he had a downtown condo, mostly telecommuted for his job in finance, and competed in Motocross competitions for fun.

Her jaw dropped. "Motocross?! That's so bad ass!"

He showed her a few videos of some of his competitions on his phone. The flips and jumps he performed on his dirt bike made her heart leap into her chest. When she told him how impressed she was, he thanked her with humble words but a cocky smile that made her fantasize about his lips on hers.

She told him that she'd been attending college part time and graduated two years behind her friends so she'd have more time to help her mother who hadn't been doing well since her father left. "Besides that, I've been really busy with my job search."

"What about the weekends?" he asked. "Do you usually hit the clubs?"

She shook her head. "No, last Saturday we wanted to do something special. But before then I've been to a club maybe two or three times in my life. Sometimes we'll go to a bar I like downtown. But usually my friends and I will just grab dinner or have a girl's night at one of our apartments. What about you and your friends?"

"The club's not usually our scene either. We like to work on the hot rod in my garage, shoot pool, catch a game." He silently offered her his peanut butter cookie. "So tell me about this boyfriend of yours."

He must've seen her staring at it. Thanking him, she broke off half of the cookie and took a bite. Since he asked, she told him that she started dating Brian two years ago and that they'd been living together for the past year. Brian used to work construction at J&J but had hurt his back when he fell off a one-story roof and had been living off of disability pay until the doctor cleared him to go back to work. However, Brian insisted he was still in a lot of pain and refused to go back to work, not even considering a different kind of job that wouldn't require physical labor.

"He sounds like a loser," said Nate.

Anise looked at the ground, not knowing what to say to that. She wanted to have compassion for Brian, but... what if Brian *was* lying to her?

"Sorry, I shouldn't have said that," Nate apologized immediately. "I just think you deserve better. He's lazy and doesn't seem to care about things that are important to you, like your celebration over the weekend. And if he doesn't work, then why isn't *he* here taking surveys and buying you lunch?"

"That's a really good question," Anise replied with a frown. "It's...complicated." *But is it really?* she asked herself. *Or is it just over?*

"You have to get back," said Nate, looking at his watch. "But I'm going to be at Johnny's Bar tonight – you know where that is?"

She nodded, wondering where he was going with this.

He paused a moment while he looked at her. "I know you don't like when I'm presumptuous, but you don't seem happy with him. If there's any truth to that, meet me at Johnny's. Eight o'clock. Life's too short to be with someone who makes you unhappy."

The thought of meeting Nate out somewhere was exciting, and everything in her wanted to say yes. "Nate, I can't. The fact remains that I'm still with Brian, and I have some things I need to figure out. Sorry."

"It's all good," he told her. "You have my number if

you ever change your mind." He cleared their table and walked her back to her office. At the door, she turned her face toward his, and the way he looked at her almost made her tell him she'd meet him after all. But guilt brought thoughts of Brian to the forefront of her mind.

"Nate, thank you so much for your help today and for lunch. It was really nice getting to know you better. I had a lot of fun."

"So did I. You're an amazing person, Anise. I hope you find the answers you're looking for."

"Thanks. That's really nice of you." It seemed to Anise that Nate wanted to say something more, but all he did was smile at her before walking away.

Chapter 6

Hey, I'm home," Anise called out, as she stepped into her apartment. She looked up after taking off her shoes and saw that Brian wasn't alone. A red-haired man of about fifty was talking to him and holding up Anise's amulet by the chain. He scratched his rounded belly while inspecting the black agate and sardonyx stones.

"Hello, Miss," the man said politely.

"Hi," replied Anise. *Why does he have my amulet?* she wondered, a knot forming in her stomach. There was something familiar about his voice, too, but she didn't recognize his face. "What's going on?" she asked Brian.

"Hey, babe. I was at the dispensary today, and we got to talking. He mentioned he was looking for a unique piece of jewelry for his wife, and I told him about your necklace. We just made a deal for $300!"

Anise couldn't believe it. *This again?* She hoped this man wasn't violent like the old woman at the thrift shop. "There must be some kind of misunderstanding," she told the man. "My necklace is not for sale."

"I already wrote the check," the man protested with annoyance, "and you're getting a really good deal."

"She knows that," Brian said to the man. "Don't be rude," he added, looking at Anise.

"My jewelry is not yours to sell!" she exclaimed to Brian, feeling like she was scolding a small child. She angrily took it out of the man's hands. "Now I'm sorry, but this necklace belongs to me, and I have no intention of selling it!"

"You let her tell you what to do?" laughed the man to Brian.

"Give back the necklace, Anise," demanded Brian.

"No! What part of 'it's not yours' don't you understand?" Anise said in a raised voice, her eyes narrowing.

"Hey, sorry, man, she's not gonna change her mind," apologized Brian to the man.

The man looked perturbed. "I'm willing to pay a little more. How much do you want for it?" he asked Brian in a voice that almost sounded like begging.

Upset at being ignored, Anise stepped directly in front of the man. "It's not for sale. For *any* price," she informed him with a tone of finality.

"If you can talk some sense into her, let me know," the man huffed to Brian. They exchanged phone numbers, and the man left, shaking his head.

"Thanks a lot for embarrassing me like that," snarled Brian.

"Are you kidding me?" yelled back Anise. "You bring some misogynistic asshole into *my* home to sell *my* jewelry without *my* permission, and you think *you* have the right to be upset?"

"Hey, it's my home too, and I don't want to live like this forever! Wouldn't you like to get out of debt? And get a new couch? And some real art?"

She looked at Brian in disbelief. "Now you don't like my paintings?"

"Your paintings are fine, but you're a beginner. Don't you think a real artist's work would be better and make our home look more grown up?"

Anise put her hand to her forehead, not knowing what to say. "Wow, Brian."

"Anyway, don't change the subject. This isn't about your paintings. We need money, and it seems like that fugly necklace could sell for a lot. More than your pearls went for."

"You sold my pearls?!"

"Yeah, last week." He gave her a smug look. "You didn't even notice, did you?"

The sinking feeling in her stomach made her touch her midsection to hold and comfort the ache. "Not yet, but I would have! I don't wear them every day."

"Which is why I picked those to sell. You don't need them."

"That's not the point! My parents gave me those. They weren't yours to sell!"

"Well, we need the money!" Brian stepped closer to her, and she could smell the beer on his breath. She looked around and quickly counted twelve beer cans on the floor. He always had been an emotional and mean drunk. Now was not the time to argue with him, but she couldn't help herself.

"That's because you refuse to work! How would you react if I sold your precious video games behind your back?" she asked. "We need the money after all!"

"Don't you dare touch my shit!" Brian yelled at her.

"Even with the extra money Doreen's giving me, I'm making just enough to take care of the both of us, Brian. If you need money, sell your own shit, or better yet, get a job and help out with the rent once in a while!"

"You know I'm injured, you fucking bitch!"

The name calling had started. *Time to get away from him.* She locked herself in the bathroom and couldn't stop her tears.

"Yeah, go ahead and cry," said Brian through the bathroom door. "You *should* feel bad, goddamn bitch!"

"What happened to us?" Anise whispered to her reflection in the mirror. Her eyes followed her tears down her cheeks. Brian's bulky linebacker build and 6'5" frame gave him an immense presence and had always made her feel safe with him. Now, that same presence frightened her when he got this angry.

When Anise began dating Brian two years prior, she had just moved out of her mother's house and into an apartment—the one they were living in now. It was her place only, but Brian visited every day and stayed over almost every night. They had fun together at first—going out at night, spending time with their friends, or watching a movie at home. He lost his temper every now and then, and sometimes something ended up broken, but he had always apologized and fixed or replaced what he broke. His possessions slowly migrated their way over to her place, until one day last summer when he informed her that his lease had been up three months prior, and he had not renewed. They were living together. Anise was livid that Brian would make such a big decision for them without talking to her about it first, and it had turned into a big fight. However, it had worked out just fine, more or less, until his spinal fracture not six months later. Anise had been so worried about him, but he was strong and assured her everything would be fine. According to the doctors, he'd be able to return to work after about six to twelve weeks. Smoking medicinal marijuana was helping with the pain. But sitting around waiting to heal was boring for him, and Brian got extremely attached to his video games. He claimed his Budweiser dulled the boredom as well, and he was starting to get irritable whenever he ran out of it. He'd been collecting disability pay until his doctor cleared him to return to J&J Construction.

Even after getting a second opinion, which agreed with the first, Brian insisted he couldn't work due to the pain and got extremely annoyed whenever she tried to talk to him about it. Anise lately found herself wondering why Brian was so upset all the time. His anger issues that had seemed mild at first had gotten so much worse.

We used to be happy...or were we? Brian had never

shown much interest in listening to her stories. He had never much respected her likes, possessions, or space. Come to think of it, he was a lot like her parents. Anise wondered why she'd never noticed that before. Maybe it takes new experiences to realize that what felt normal to you your whole life was never actually normal at all. Neither her mother nor Brian were willing to help themselves, and she was starting to see that until they did, there wasn't anything more she could do for them.

She looked at the amulet she clutched in her hand and wondered how old it was. Under the bright lights of her bathroom, she noticed some filth on it she hadn't seen before. Gently, she washed the amulet under running tap water and dried it with a soft towel. She laid it on the window sill, where the sun was still shining in, and left it there while she showered and redid her makeup. She dressed in skinny jeans, high-heeled sandals, and a vintage top she'd found at Doreen's. She added the amulet to her outfit. There was no way she'd leave it in the apartment ever again, not with Brian there. The chain was longer than a regular necklace, she noticed, as the amulet hung underneath the neckline of her low-cut top. *I could wear it over my top*, she thought, but she felt that the black and orange stones clashed with the busy, colorful print. She tucked the amulet underneath her top, walked into the living room, and grabbed her jacket and purse.

"Where the hell are you going?" demanded Brian.

"I'm going out with the girls tonight."

"When will you be home?" he asked more softly.

"Don't know. But when I get home, we need to have a talk," she replied and reached for the door knob. A twinging in her stomach told her that she wasn't completely happy with her decision to delay telling Brian what she felt. *Who do I want to be in this situation?*

She turned back around to face him. "No, you know what? We're going to talk right now. Finding out that you've been selling my stuff behind my back is the final straw. I can't be with someone who doesn't treat me with the respect I deserve. You need to find somewhere else to sleep tonight. You can come back tomorrow to get your shit, but by tomorrow night, you need to be completely moved out." She left him staring at her with his mouth hanging open.

As she walked toward the downtown strip, Anise's newfound freedom caused such a surge of confidence that she couldn't stop strutting, and she reveled in the loudly assertive clicks her heels made on the sidewalk. Feeling so damn good, she wondered why she hadn't broken up with Brian sooner. If she was completely honest with herself, she'd known for a while that Brian wasn't who she wanted. The misplaced hope she'd had for the possibility of their relationship improving had made her hold on to him longer than she should have. *Damn hope.* And if he destroyed her apartment in anger? Let him. She'd take care of it. *Nothing is worth staying with someone who isn't right for you.*

Letting him go made her feel light enough to float. She texted Erin, Vanessa, and Joy, who all broke their plans to meet her for dinner. *How lucky am I*, Anise asked herself, *to have friends like these?* Over burritos at one of her favorite restaurants, she excitedly told them how she'd broken up with Brian.

Vanessa gave her a hug. Joy gave her a high five.

"We need to celebrate!" cried Erin as she squeezed Anise's hand. "We'll do anything you want. Name it!" The others voiced their agreement.

"Let's hit Johnny's tonight," Anise said, decidedly.

"Really?" asked Vanessa, looking surprised. "You mean Johnny's the pool hall? I thought for sure you'd choose The Blue Pineapple."

"I love that bar, but no, let's shoot some pool tonight. It'll be fun!"

"Okay, let's go!" exclaimed Joy.

***

THE SECOND ANISE AND HER FRIENDS walked in the door, she saw Nate waving at them. "You came!" His face lit up.

"Yeah, I changed my mind," Anise said as casually as she could while watching her friends exchange looks of fascination.

"I'm glad. Come on over and join us; what are you ladies drinking tonight?" They told him, and he left to get their drinks.

"Holy shit, what?" said Joy. "Damn girl, you work fast."

Anise laughed. "It's not like that."

"So how...?" Vanessa asked, wide-eyed.

"We need details!" Erin insisted.

Anise told them about Nate's visit to her at the mall and how she'd told him she wouldn't meet him that night.

"But then Brian was being a dickface," interjected Erin.

"Pretty much. And now that Brian and I are done, I can do whatever the hell I want." Anise eyed Nate at the bar. "And this is what I want to do."

Nate brought their drinks and introduced his friends Scott and Peter.

"You two look so much alike!" Vanessa told Nate's friends. Scott looked older than Peter but both had the same sandy hair, brown eyes, and lanky build. "You must be brothers."

"We are," Scott replied.

"How long have you known Nate?" Anise asked them, eager to find out more about him.

"We were neighbors as kids," Peter replied. "Nate and I were in the same kindergarten class and we've been buddies ever since."

"And I had the great pleasure of babysitting for the little punks," Scott piped up with a grin.

"Which of you is better at pool?" Joy asked them, putting money on the table. "Let's make tonight interesting."

The evening seemed to fly by, and during their final game of the night, Anise took her time with the last shot, thoroughly enjoying Nate's attention as he stood bent over her, his hands touching hers on the cue stick, helping her with strategy and a smooth hit. When the 8-ball rolled unswervingly over the field of green and politely hopped into the pocket, Anise let out a cheer and gave Nate a celebratory hug. He wrapped his arms around her and spun her around as she laughed.

Vanessa pulled her aside and out of earshot of the boys. "I'm glad you're having fun tonight," she began. "You deserve it. But I'm concerned. I hope you don't actually believe that Brian is going to leave peacefully." Erin and Joy nodded their agreement.

"I love you all for caring, but can we please not ruin tonight by talking about Brian?" Anise requested. She turned back to Nate and let him help her with her jacket.

"Be ready," Anise barely heard Vanessa whisper to Erin and Joy. "Brian is going to pull some shit. She's going to need us."

As they all left the bar, Anise looked up at Nate and wondered if he'd had as good a time as she did.

He returned her gaze and held it. "It's still early," he said. "Take a walk with me?"

Anise nodded and smiled at him. "I'll see you later," she told her friends who seemed hesitant to leave her.

"I'll get her home safely, I promise," Nate told them.

"You better," Vanessa warned.

Anise and Nate began walking toward the center of downtown. "Want some dessert?" he asked her as they passed an ice cream parlor.

"Sure!" She walked through the door as he held it open for her. Anise ordered a scoop of Rocky Road and Nate got pistachio. "So...what does that taste like?" she asked him once they were back outside. "I've never tried it before."

"Want a taste?"

She hesitated. "I don't know. It's so...green."

He laughed and handed her his cone. "Try it."

She took it and gave it a slight lick. After swallowing, she took another lick, bigger this time. "It's actually really good!" She took another lick and handed it back to him. "Take it back before I eat it all."

"Have as much as you want."

Anise shook her head. "No, I have enough with mine. Want a taste of my Rocky Road?"

He grimaced which made her laugh.

"What's wrong with Rocky Road?" she asked, taking a large, cold bite.

"I don't like chocolate."

"Hmm?!" she said in surprise with her mouth full and swallowed. "Really? You don't like *chocolate*?"

"Yeah, it's too bitter. I never liked it."

"Okay," she replied. Her curiosity about him was piqued by this unexpected revelation. "So tell me something else about you that I don't know," she requested. She eyed his long-sleeved shirt. Maybe he'd tell her about the tattoo on his arm he regretted. Or maybe how he got the scar next to his eye.

He looked at her intensely for a moment. "I'll do one better. I'll show you. But we'll have to go this way instead."

They turned around and headed in the opposite direction. Nate led Anise around the corner from Johnny's Bar, down a wide concrete staircase, and onto a well-lit path leading under and beyond the freeway that marked the edge of town.

"Where are we going?" Anise asked him, holding

on to his arm so as not to trip on the uneven sidewalk. "I bike by here all the time, and I've never noticed that staircase before."

"We're almost there," he told her. "I hope you like it."

For the next few minutes, she allowed herself to enjoy the scent of the nearby flowering trees and the warmth of Nate's arm. Basking in her own giddiness, she smiled at the other couples they passed on their way. A large, wrought iron gate stood prominently ahead and connected two parts of a tall, brick fence. Nate opened the gate for her and they stepped through. Anise drew in a long, slow breath as she looked around in wonder. "It's...magical! What *is* this place?"

She stood on a paved path that looped around a large pond. Soft lights glowed on the ground lining the path as well as on strings above her head. Ripples in the water reflected the lights as fish came to the surface in anticipation of bread crumbs. A small turtle slipped back into the water from the bank by her feet. On the other side of the pond, a couple sat together on one of the several benches along the path. Tall pine trees circled the entire area, and flowers bloomed in planters along the path. She followed Nate onto the arched wooden bridge that connected each side of the pond, and they leaned with their forearms on the railing.

"I used to come here as a kid with my mother almost every day," Nate told her. "Back then it was just a small park with the swings, sandbox, and jungle gym you see over there." He pointed a finger, and she saw the playground equipment in a fenced-in area beyond the edge of the pond. "A few years ago they were going to tear down the park and most of the trees and put up a couple shopping centers. I had too many good memories here to let that happen. So I did what I had to do to stop it, upgraded the playground with new equipment, and had this pond put in. I added the brick fence border and the wrought iron gate last year for ambiance and privacy. It helps to distract from the fact that the freeway is so close."

"Wow, that's a real labor of love," Anise said, enthralled that he gave so much hard-earned money back to the community. "I'm impressed."

Nate smiled at her. "Thanks."

"I wonder why I've never heard of it before."

"It's a well-kept secret by the residents of the area."

"They must really appreciate what you've done. This is absolutely beautiful."

They walked along the path and sat on one of the benches.

"Now tell me something about you that I don't know," Nate said.

The first thing that came to her mind was Les. She hadn't told her friends yet because she didn't feel like answering all the inevitable questions. But she did want to talk to someone about it. "Well, this is something I didn't even know myself until yesterday." She told him about Les's visit, his undiagnosable health issue, his mother, her mother, and the letters she'd found in her mother's garage.

"Wow. A long lost brother. That's a lot. How are you dealing?"

"I'm still in shock about the whole thing." She frowned. "And I'm...so sad. Growing up, I felt alone a lot, and I always wanted a sibling. Now I find out that I actually do have one, but he has a health issue no doctor has ever seen before, and I might lose a brother I never even got to know. And when it comes to my parents, I feel so lied to and betrayed."

Nate's eyes turned downward as if her sadness brought forth some of his own.

"Sorry if this was too heavy to put on someone I've only known for a couple days," Anise apologized.

He shook his head. "Not at all. I think sometimes it's easier to talk to someone you don't know well than someone really close to you."

She sat up taller, excited that he understood. "Exactly! If I had told my friends, I would've had to discuss it to death when all I really wanted was to get it off my chest. And since I haven't told anyone else yet, I'd appreciate it if you could keep this between us."

"Of course. I won't say a word. And if you want to talk more about it, I'm here to listen."

"Thanks. That's so nice of you." She paused and gave him a slight shrug. "Other than that, I don't know that there's much to tell," Anise began and then proceeded to tell him about how she'd broken up with Brian, her job at the thrift shop, her friends, the paintings she'd made and how she wanted to take more art classes, her sketch-book and affirmation cards, and how she had hoped to go to the Concert in the Park but missed out on tickets. When she realized he'd been listening attentively the entire time, she began to feel a little self-conscious. Brian would have interrupted her or fallen asleep by now. But Nate seemed interested in what she was saying and was asking her thoughtful follow-up questions. His blue eyes were so bright in the moonlight, and she found herself fantasizing about him leaning in to kiss her.

"What made you decide to major in marketing?" he asked. "Drawing and painting seem to be your real passions."

"I did want to go to art school," she admitted, "but I let my parents talk me out of it." She thought about how she might explain that better. Her friends never seemed to understand why she hadn't followed her dream.

"It's strange how good parents are at doing that," Nate said before she had a chance to explain further.

"So you understand? No one else I know seems to."

"Very well. I let mine talk me into doing a lot of things I didn't want to do."

"I have something for you." She reached into her bag, pulled out her favorite affirmation card, and handed it to him. She watched as he took it and read her handwritten words. *Who do I want to be in this situation?*

"This is something that's been helping me lately when I'm faced with a decision or at a crossroads of some kind," Anise explained. "I think it might resonate with you too. Keep it and look at it when you need it. I hope it helps."

He was still looking at the card, and Anise wondered what he was thinking. She hoped that it would inspire him as much as it did her.

"Thank you," he told her as he put it in a pocket of the black leather jacket he was carrying. "I think it will."

"I should get going," she told him. "It's late, and I have to work tomorrow. But I want you to know I'm honored that you shared this park with me. Thank you."

"I'm glad you liked it." He stood, and holding out his hand to help her up from the bench, he pulled her into an embrace. "Let's get you home, honey."

Honey? She paused a moment to analyze how she felt about that. Pet names typically made her cringe. The last guy she'd met in a club thought it was fun to call her 'Ani-poo.' So obnoxious. Brian used to call her 'kitten' until she demanded he stop. It sounded so slimy and degrading. But honey...it was generic for sure, but it was also classic, like his good looks and style of dress, so it fit his personality. Therefore, it sounded sincere coming from him. It wasn't drawn-out or sleazy or creepy like every other nickname she'd been given by a man. He said it like he'd say her name. From his lips it sounded sweet, endearing even, and she surprised herself by hoping he'd say it again. Somehow, it increased the intimacy and made her feel closer to him. She made sure their walk back was purposely slow, enjoying holding on to his arm once again.

"That's my bike," he said, nodding toward the street.

Anise looked around for a bicycle before realizing he meant the motorcycle that was parked in front of Johnny's Bar. "Oh! So it's..."

"Harley Davidson Night Rod Special. 1250cc V-Twin."

Anise gave a little laugh. "I have no idea what that means."

"Have you ever ridden on a motorcycle before?" he asked her as they stood in front of the bike.

"No," she replied, a little nervously. The bike looked sleek and powerful. "Are those things safe?"

He grinned at her as he put on his jacket. "Don't worry; I'm an experienced rider."

"Right. Motocross."

"You can wear my helmet for extra protection."

After helping her with the helmet, he got on, and she slipped on behind him. Before they left, he taught her how to lean into the turns. She suppressed the urge to tell him how hot he looked in his black leather jacket as he started the engine.

"Hold on," he said over his shoulder with a mischievous sideways grin that made her even more attracted to him than she already was. She tightened her grip around him, and they took off into the night. He ignored the directions she had given him and began taking the long way toward her home. He made sure she was doing okay and then opened up on a long stretch of highway that was virtually empty that time of night. Anise couldn't believe how fast they were going and held on to Nate as tightly as she could, especially when he blew right through the red lights.

When they got to the front of her apartment building, they got off the bike, and she handed back his helmet.

"So, what did you think?" he asked her.

Anise's eyes were wide and her smile even wider. "I have *never* experienced anything so exhilarating in my whole life! Thank you so much for the ride!" she exclaimed, giving him a big hug around his neck. She squeezed him tightly and pressed herself against him, still feeling tingly from the vibrations of his motorcycle. He put his arms around her torso and squeezed back. She lingered in the moment, not wanting it to end. When she finally did break the embrace, he took both of her hands in his.

"I'm really glad you decided to meet me tonight," said Nate, delivering his intense cobalt gaze that she found almost hypnotizing.

"Me, too. It was fun."

He leaned over, and his lips softly pressed against hers. They were warm and gentle, and then his tongue caressed hers for a moment. "Mmm," she said involuntarily after he pulled away, her eyes still closed. She could still taste him, and the tingling sensation in her abdomen grew. He'd made the outside world disappear once again. She locked her eyes on his mouth, wanting desperately to bite into that delicious cocky smirk. She smirked back, grabbed each side of his unzipped leather jacket, and pulled until their lips met again.

Chapter 7

Nate rode home slowly. His mind couldn't focus on anything but her. Anise's sweet innocence was not a trait he had seen in a woman he'd met in a club before, but there was something else that'd impressed him, too. She was dealing with a lot of personal issues like her job search and her loser ex-boyfriend and her long lost brother, but she was handling everything with ease and positivity, like a flower that could bloom during a hurricane. He found himself becoming more and more intrigued by her.

Before watching her walk into her apartment building, he'd told her he'd call her tomorrow, and she'd given him an adorable, shy look telling him it'd be okay if he stopped by the mall again instead, you know, if he wanted. He'd promised her he'd be there. The smile she'd given him made his night. Parking his bike in the garage, he opened the door to his condo. As he walked up the stairs to the main living area, he found himself actually looking forward to seeing her again. He hadn't expected to like her as much as he did, and it was probably going to get him in trouble.

His thoughts were interrupted by the two uninvited and unwanted guests waiting for him on his couch. "Why are you here?" Nate demanded. "It's late."

"Do you have the amulet?" the white-haired old hag asked him.

"No, I need more time."

"You've had a couple *days*, Nate."

"I just need a little more time. Same as you, I didn't find it when I broke into her place. She must keep it with her, so I need to be there when she takes it off. She's a good girl, but I expect to be invited up soon. The problem is she's got this ex who still lives there," he started.

"I don't give a rat's ass!" the old woman retorted. She slammed her hand down on his coffee table. "You promised you'd get me that amulet!"

Nate glared as he stood over her and her middle-aged son who looked half asleep beside her on the couch. "Relax, Grace. I told you, soon. And if I'm going to do this, you'd better tell me why this old jewelry is so important to you. How is it different from any of the other artifacts?"

"You'd better help me deal with this, Dan," commanded the hag in frustration as she pulled on her hair.

"We don't have to tell you anything," Dan sneered, scratching underneath his red beard. "We made a deal, and telling you anything more wasn't part of it. You have one more day to get that amulet. Don't fail again." He looked at the old woman as if to make sure that he'd pleased her with what he'd said.

Nate shook his head. "No, fuck this; I'm out. I don't want to steal from her, and I won't let you do it either."

"You don't want to steal from her?" the hag repeated in a mocking tone with a look of disgust on her face. "Since when do you have a conscience?"

"I'm not evil like you are. And this isn't the same as stealing from a museum. She's a human being." Nate took his jacket off and dropped it on a chair. His hand reached up to rub the back of his neck. He hadn't seen them in years, but the familiar pains he used to get whenever he was around Grace and Dan were returning.

"You must not want that information we promised

you," Dan said with a shrug.

"You're not getting out of this; we had a deal!" Grace said. "You'll find out about the jewelry sooner or later. Knowing how it works might help you succeed in getting it," she added. She got up and stared at him. "Nate, you'd better sit down for this."

"I don't give a shit about your jewelry. Get the hell out of my apartment!"

"You begged me to let you steal it! I don't think I have to remind you that if you don't get that amulet your way, we'll have to get it my way," warned Grace as her face crinkled into a scowl. "We'll have to use more drastic measures."

"More drastic measures like last time?" Nate fired back. "If I'd known how far you two were willing to go to get that ring, I wouldn't have agreed to help."

"That's why we didn't tell you," she snapped. "You need to get desensitized. You're too weak."

Nate shot over a glare. "I won't let you hurt her."

Grace closed her eyes and pulled on her hair for a few seconds. She stared at Nate, unblinking. "I know you're not stupid enough to believe you can actually stop me. You seem to care about what happens to this girl. If that's the case, you'd better get that amulet, and I have some information that will help you. Now sit down, shut up, and listen."

ANISE FLOATED UP THE STAIRS TO her third floor apartment, dancing, twisting, and twirling slowly like smoke from a flame. Humming, she thought about every moment of her evening with Nate that she'd like to sketch. She opened the door, and her smile dropped like softball-sized hail.

Brian sat on the couch, beer in hand. His eyes were

hazy, and his speech was slurred. "Who the fuck was that guy you were kissing?" he demanded.

"What the hell are you still doing here?" she demanded in return, setting her bag down by the door.

"I asked you a question!" He downed the last of his beer, crushed the can, and threw it on the floor.

"And I told you to leave. Get the hell out!" Her heart pounded.

"You said you were going out with the girls." His face was red and his eyes full of hate.

"And I did. But what I did after that is none of your damn business."

"You're cheating on me!" Brian slurred.

"No, I'm not. We broke up."

He got up from the couch, and his clenched fist punched a hole in the nearest wall.

"Brian, you need to calm down!" Her heart raced even faster, and she took a few steps backward.

"You're a cheating cunt!" In his rage, he took a swing at her face. She leaned back, and the moving fist found nothing but air. His own momentum caused him to stumble and land hard on his hands and knees. "You tripped me!"

"I did not; I'm too far away for that, and you know it."

Brian pushed himself to his feet. "How long have you been seeing him?" he growled.

"I'm going to call Corinne to come get you. You need to leave!"

"I'm not leaving! Don't you dare call my sister!"

"You can't stay here, Brian. You just tried to punch me! I want you out *now*! You and I are through!"

"You can't break up with me!" Brian shouted, his hands forming fists again.

Anise stepped backward again, her pounding heart echoing in her ears. Brian had been violent in the past and had been known to break things, and this wasn't the first time he put his fist through the wall, but he had never been violent toward *her* before. *How far would he go?* Not wanting to find out, she darted toward the door to leave. In her hurry, she slipped on some crushed beer cans and fell backward, landing hard in a seated position.

Brian grabbed the table lamp and yanked it out of the wall. Anise looked up just in time to see the lamp flying directly toward her head. She had no time to duck—but just enough to know that the lamp was going to hit her. Involuntarily, she cringed and braced herself. At the last moment, the lamp changed its trajectory in the air and flew back in the direction from which it came. It landed about five feet in front of her, closer to Brian's feet than her own. Anise looked at the lamp, which was lying innocently on the floor, its shade askew. She hadn't touched it; what happened?

Brian's eyes were as wide as saucers, and his jaw fell so hard, Anise thought that if it had hit the floor it might have left a dent. He started a panicked ramble. "What the hell? How did that happen? Why is your necklace glowing? What kind of black magic bullshit is this?"

Anise scrambled to her feet. "Get out, Brian!"

Brian stared at the lamp for a moment, his eyes and mouth still wide open. "I must be really wasted." He went into the bedroom and locked the door behind him.

Too exhausted to consider the lamp's behavior, and still trembling from fear, Anise looked down at her chest and noticed that Brian had been right. Her amulet was indeed glowing a soft light from under her shirt. It seemed to radiate from the black center stone. She wanted to ponder the possible explanations for that, but more importantly, she needed to get away from Brian. She grabbed her bag and headed a block away to Vanessa's place.

Part 2
TOXIC SLUDGE

Chapter 8

Tuesday, June 5, 2012

Brian awoke the next morning to the sound of Anise entering the apartment. He belched when he rolled over which made him nauseated, and there was a jackhammering in his head. Various blurred pieces of memories of the night before began running through his mind. They'd both been angry and he remembered hearing her slam the door on her way out. *Shit.* Things had gotten way out of hand. He looked over at her pillow. They hadn't slept next to each other in a few nights, and he missed her. He needed to make everything right again.

Brian got up and walked into the living room in his boxers. "Hey, I'm really sorry about last night. I was really drunk, and I don't remember everything that happened exactly, but...I'm sorry. I promise I won't drink that much again. You were right; I need to cut back on the beer."

She looked at him. "I hope you mean that. Now put on some pants."

"I do. I promise. What do I need pants for?" Brian only then saw Vanessa sitting at their kitchen table staring at him with disgust. He left to put on a pair of

sweatpants and a t-shirt and sat through an uncomfortable silence while Anise walked around the apartment
grabbing clean clothes and a few other personal items.
Vanessa wouldn't stop glaring at him. "Can you give us a
minute to talk?" Brian asked Vanessa.

"No." Vanessa stayed put and continued glaring at
him.

He glared back and wondered how he was going
to smooth things over with Anise. Being ganged up on
made it harder to think. "So, what do you have going on
today?" he asked Anise, not knowing what else to say.

"Survey work in the morning and working at Doreen's
this afternoon," she replied without looking at him.

"Cool." He looked at the amulet around her neck and
faintly remembered it glowing when he tried to throw
the lamp at her. But that couldn't be right. It was made
of metal and stones. It must've just been reflecting the
light from the ceiling.

"Why are you staring at the amulet?" Anise demanded.

"That thing really creeps me out. And we've been
fighting ever since you brought it home. It's weird. You
need to sell that thing."

"We've been fighting since long before I brought
home my amulet. And for the last and final time, it is
NOT for sale. GOT IT?" She took the last few bites of the
breakfast sandwich she'd been eating and zipped up her
tote bag.

"Well, at least get it appraised," Brian said. "If not for
me, then for you. Aren't you curious about how much it's
worth and where it came from?" He hoped she'd take the
bait. If those gemstones were real, maybe he could ask a
lot more for it than just a few hundred.

"The only reason I'm here right now is to get some
clothes for work and to see what you remember about
last night." She went into the bedroom and grabbed a
pair of shoes.

"I apologized," he said, following her around the

apartment. "What are you still mad about?"

"Seriously?" Her eyes shot daggers at him. "You punched a hole in the wall and then tried to punch me!"

"I was drunk. I said I was sorry."

Anise scoffed at him. "Plus, I broke up with you last night. Twice. And you're still here."

He raised an eyebrow at her. "I don't remember that."

She rolled her eyes. "Why am I not surprised? But yes, I did."

"You didn't mean that. You were just pissed."

"I've never meant anything more."

"Bullshit." Brian laughed and went to grab a beer from the refrigerator. When he saw the anger on Anise's face, he shook his head. "Fine. You leave if you want to. You can't kick me out. This is my apartment as much as it is yours."

She put a hand on her hip. "Really? Because the last time I checked, my name was the only one on the lease. I lived here before you ever did."

He cracked open his beer and took a sip. "We decided to live together. That makes this my place too."

"We decided nothing! You moved all your stuff in here when your lease ran out without even asking me first." Her eyes narrowed at him.

"Would you have said no if I had asked?"

"I don't know, Brian," she said, sounding annoyed. "I wasn't sure if I was ready to live with you yet. Or at all."

"Whatever," he said, taking a swig of his beer. "We were going to end up living together eventually, so what's the problem?"

"The problem is that your behavior was disrespectful. You should've asked."

Brian sighed. Why was she making a scene when they both knew she'd forgive him anyway? All this fighting was unnecessary and exhausting. "You're making too much of this whole thing. Stop being a fucking princess."

"Grow up, Brian!" Vanessa exploded at him. "Since

you don't take responsibility for your actions, you have to at least accept the consequences. Anise doesn't want you anymore, so be a man and get the fuck out of her place." She stood up from the kitchen table. "Are you ready to go?" she asked Anise.

"Yes," Anise replied and picked up her bag. She turned to Brian. "We broke up. I'm going to work, and by the time I get back, you better be gone."

The girls left, and Brian sat on the couch staring at his beer. Anise seemed serious about wanting to break up, but he wasn't convinced it was over. Maybe he'd call his sister. Corinne might have some ideas on how to get Anise to forgive him.

ANISE STOOD IN THE MALL WITH her clipboard, watching potential respondents walk by, wanting to be anywhere but there at that moment. Her mind kept replaying the lamp suddenly switching directions in the air. She knew it hadn't been her imagination because Brian saw it too. Did the lamp have a weight in the bottom that somehow made it have a backspin mid-flight? Or maybe the cord got caught on something that caused the lamp to get pulled back? It must've been something like that. Satisfied with these possible explanations, Anise's musings turned darker. Brian had tried to punch her and throw something at her. She'd never seen him be violent toward her before. What if he tried to hurt her again? She couldn't go home alone until she had the locks changed.

"Anise."

She gasped and jumped, startled by the voice that came out of nowhere. She turned to find its origin. "Nate!"

"Sorry, I didn't mean to scare you."

She shook her head. "It's okay. My mind was somewhere else." But now her mind was on him, and she was happy to see him. He'd said he'd be here, and he'd kept his promise. That made her smile.

"What's troubling you?"

Her smile turned into a frown and she sighed. "Brian saw us through the window last night. He saw us kissing. He was really pissed."

"Oh, shit. What happened?"

She didn't want to tell him about the violence. "He was drunk. We fought." She shrugged and looked at the ground.

He looked confused. "I thought you got rid of the toxic sludge."

"So did I. I broke up with him yesterday, but he didn't remember because he was too drunk. So I reminded him this morning and ordered him out."

"Great, so you're free to go out with me tonight."

"No," she started, shaking her head. "I have to make sure he and all his crap are gone when I get home. I have to get the locks changed."

"I can help you do that tomorrow. Let's have some fun tonight. You deserve it."

"I do want to see you again," she told him. "But not tonight. I'm really not in the mood to go out."

"Not even to the Concert in the Park?" He reached into his pocket and held up two tickets.

"What?! Are you serious?" Anise exclaimed, a feeling of awe overwhelming her. "How did you do that? They were all sold out!"

He grinned at her. "I have my ways."

"You're not going to tell me?" she asked coyly.

"I hear that mysterious guys are sexier, so no," he teased.

She beamed at him. "Well, whatever your ways are, they're impressive."

"So is that a yes?" he asked, his hopeful eyes beckoning her.

She could feel her delight overtaking her face. He'd

listened to what she'd said about wanting to see the concert, took care to remember, and went through a great effort, great expense, or both to plan a thoughtful date. Her mood of not wanting to go out had changed into excited anticipation of that evening. "Yes!"

"WHY ARE YOU SO SMILEY TODAY?" Doreen asked Anise later that afternoon, about two hours into her shift.

"What? I'm not smiley," Anise replied, denying the fact that she was smiling at that very moment.

Doreen gave her an amused look. "You've had a grin on your face ever since you got here; now what gives?"

Anise laughed. "Nothing, I'm just in a good mood." She didn't want to tell Doreen that her upcoming date with Nate was the reason for her happiness. That would lead to her having to explain about Brian, and she didn't want to think about him at the moment.

By the way she looked at Anise, Doreen didn't seem to buy it but let it go. Not long afterward, she let Anise leave work at the thrift shop a couple hours early. "It's dead in here today," Doreen said. "Go enjoy the beautiful summer weather, and have some fun."

Anise thought about Brian's suggestion of getting the amulet appraised. Maybe it wasn't a bad idea. She didn't care about the value since she'd never sell it, but she was curious about its history. Anise hopped on her bicycle and headed a few blocks away to Casley Antiques, a small shop that had been in town for as long as she could remember. An older man who wore a nametag that said 'Robert', greeted her from behind a glass counter when she walked in. "Good afternoon, Miss. How can I help you?"

Anise walked past the old paintings, jewelry, dishes, and other vintage treasures to greet him. "I was given this as a gift," she said, putting the amulet on the counter, "and was hoping you might be able to tell me who made it or what time period it's from."

"Let me put on my glasses and take a look," said Robert, reaching underneath his navy blue cardigan and into his shirt pocket for his reading glasses. He picked up the amulet, stared at it, flipped it over, and studied the chain and gemstones. "My, this is certainly unique. I've never seen anything quite like it before. And you don't know anything about it?"

"No, not a thing," Anise responded. "Just that my friend found it at a thrift store."

Robert looked at it a few minutes more. "Well, I have to admit you've stumped me, young lady. I have no idea what time period this is from. It seems old—very old, based on the wearing on the edges, but that doesn't help us much. He ran a finger over the black center stone and looked thoughtful. "If you're looking for an appraisal, I could give you an estimated value based on the stones and metal, but it wouldn't be accurate. There's always more than that to be considered. I suggest you take it to the museum over on Walker Street and talk to my nephew Jonathan Casley. He's one of the curators there. I could give him a call now to see if he's available to talk with you this afternoon if you'd like."

"That would be great, thank you!" said Anise.

While Robert was on the phone, Anise enjoyed a short moment of peace and quiet. It felt good to relax and not give in to her mind's constant worry about dealing with Brian or finding a better job.

Robert hung up the phone and walked back to Anise. "Jonathan said to come on over. He has no meetings today and is excited to see your necklace," he said.

"Thank you so much for your help," Anise replied. "I'll head over there right away." She rode her bike to the museum and walked briskly down a long hallway of offices until she found a door with a nameplate that read

'Jonathan Casley.' She knocked. A few seconds later, the door opened.

A man in his mid-twenties was on the other side. His white button-down shirt was a size too large, and his tie had been loosened. Although his goatee had been recently groomed, his light brown hair was in need of a trim and threatened to fall in his light green eyes. Despite his mildly disheveled wardrobe and hairstyle choices, he had a friendly face and nice smile, and Anise thought he looked scholarly but cute with his dark rimmed glasses.

He hadn't said anything yet and his face looked frozen as he stared at her.

"Hello," she greeted him.

"Uh...hi," he stammered in reply, his cheeks turning red. "You must be the one my uncle sent over?"

"Yes, I'm Anise Viston. Thanks for agreeing to see me."

"Sure thing. I'm Jonathan Casley. My uncle described your necklace to me. I'm really excited to see it." He waved her into his small, windowless office and they sat at a tiny conference table in the corner of the room. "Can I get you anything? Coffee? Water?"

"No, thank you, I'm fine." Anise removed her necklace and handed it to him. "My friend who runs a thrift store gave it to me," she explained. "She found it in one of the donation bags. To me, it looks like an amulet from the Middle Ages or something, but it's probably not as romantic as all that. I'm just curious as to who made it or where it's from."

"Wow," said Jonathan. He was silent for a few moments and gingerly held the jewelry in both hands as he inspected it. "This is...wow. It's amazing. And you don't know anything about where it came from or who donated it?"

"No, not a thing," she replied.

"It can't be what I think it is. It's in such great shape. But if it is...wow!" Jonathan leaned back in his chair and continued to study the necklace.

He looked so lost in thought that Anise wondered if he'd forgotten she was there. As a gentle reminder of her presence, she asked him, "What do you think it is?"

A look of wonder was plastered on his face. "I can't believe it. It looks just like the Armor Jewelry of the ancient Mallandian warriors."

"Armor Jewelry?" she asked, intrigued. "And...Mallandian warriors?"

Jonathan finally turned to look at her and spoke with the excitement of a child on Christmas morning. "Mallandia was a small kingdom in Bronze Age Europe, in what's now northern Germany. The people who lived there created jewelry that, according to legend, acted as very efficient armor and made them extremely powerful warriors. You're right to call it an amulet because that's exactly what it is. Your amulet looks just like the one that's described in the legend!" His voice became more and more excited as he spoke. "I just can't believe that it's lasted this long..." He turned it over in his hands again, unable to take his eyes off of it.

"How long would that be?"

"Supposedly, the Jewelry was first used in a war in or around the year 2300 BCE."

"This amulet is over 4,000 years old?" she asked incredulously.

He nodded, his hair flopping over the lenses of his glasses. "Hard to believe, isn't it? It looks like it's maybe just a few hundred years old, if that. If you were at my uncle's store to find out about its value, and if it *is* that Armor Jewelry, I can tell you right now that it's priceless. But before I get your hopes up, we have to consider the possibility that it could be a replica. If it is, it's really well done. The copper alloy metal looks exactly right, and this looks like a polished black agate stone in the center."

"A copper alloy," said Anise. "I was wondering what metal that was. And what are the stripy orange and white stones surrounding the black agate?"

"Those are sardonyx." Jonathan turned the amulet over to look at the back and grabbed his magnifying glass from his desk. "And the inscription is there, too. If it *is* a replica, someone knew what they were doing. It's still just barely visible; did you notice it?"

"No, there's an inscription?"

He handed her the amulet and magnifying glass.

She searched for letters on the back of the amulet, but only saw faint, worn symbols that looked like waves and swirls. While she continued looking, he explained, "Each piece of Jewelry was inscribed with the same incantation. It was said that's what helped to make them so powerful."

She looked at him with curiosity. "How powerful were they said to be? And how can jewelry act as armor?"

"My supervisor Dr. Smithton is an expert on Mallandia. He'd be able to answer your questions a lot better than I can. Unfortunately, he's not here right now. I think he's in meetings all afternoon. But there's a very old text in the museum library that talks about all of this. Would you like to walk down there with me? I think you'd find it very interesting!" He was smiling, and his green eyes sparkled with anticipation.

"I'd love to!" exclaimed Anise. Jonathan's excitement was contagious.

"Great, let's go!" He got up, held the door open for her, and followed her out. His hand gestured forward. "We'll be following this hallway here and going down the stairs to the basement. I should warn you, it's chilly down there. It helps preserve the books."

"That's okay, I have a jacket," Anise replied, pulling her oversized sweat jacket out of her tote. "So how long have you been a curator?" She was finding this experience to be like an adventure and was wondering if she should have perhaps majored in ancient history or archeology instead of marketing.

"I got my master's a year ago, and this is a one-year

internship for me. In the fall I'll go back to school for my doctorate."

"Wow. I guess I don't have to ask if you like it. I can see your passion for it."

"I honestly can't imagine ever doing anything else. Are you interested in ancient history and artifacts?"

"I've never really given it much thought until right now. But what I'm learning from you is nothing short of fascinating." *How wonderful it must be to love your job,* thought Anise.

They reached the library, and Jonathan led her into a dark and dusty corner. He asked her to have a seat at the nearby table, found a pair of white gloves for each of them, and handed one pair to her. She put them on, and he went through a door in the corner, telling her he'd be right back. Shortly, he brought over a thick text, fragile from age. "Because this book is *so* old, the cool basement air isn't enough. We have to keep it in a climate-controlled room when it's not in use," he explained. Jonathan opened the book, checked the table of contents, and turned to the page he wanted.

"Here it is!" he exclaimed, his excitement bubbling up once again. "The Legend of the Armor Jewelry! This book is an English translation of the original," Jonathan explained, "and it's a little hard to read because the printing press hadn't been invented yet at the time this translation was written. Originally, the legend probably would have been told in the language of Mallandia, which has been dead since the fall of the kingdom. They had their own alphabet of sorts which is incredible because it was previously thought there were no written languages in the area at the time!"

"So the wavy and swirly symbols I saw on the back of my amulet was their written language?" Anise asked.

"Yes! We call them Curly symbols for lack of a better term. That's what was used to write the incantation."

"The incantation," Anise repeated. "Is that like a

magic spell?"

"Basically, yes, that's what it was. The spell, together with the energy of the gemstones, is supposedly what gave the Jewelry its powers."

"What does the incantation say?" she inquired.

"I wish I knew," sighed Jonathan wistfully. "I've looked for that answer in this book before but never found it. There seems to be a missing page near the end of this section. Maybe that's where the answer is. But that's something I can ask Dr. Smithton later, and I can let you know if you'd like."

"That would be great; I'd love to know!" she replied, smiling at him.

"So would I," he said, smiling back at her. His cheeks flushed, and his gaze quickly turned back to the old book. "So moving on to the legend—your amulet is part of a set of Jewelry that was developed for the Mallandian war-riors. It says that each warrior got a complete set. And see, on this page, it shows a drawing of the amulet that came with the set."

Anise moved her chair closer to Jonathan and looked at the black and white drawing. "It really does look exactly like my amulet!" she exclaimed. It had a square shape with bulging edges and rounded corners, a large striped center stone, and five striped smaller stones evenly spaced in a circle closely surrounding the center stone, just like the one Anise held in her hand.

"The metal is an alloy of gold, silver, and copper," continued Jonathan, summarizing what he was reading in the book. "The black and white stone is a black agate, and the smaller stones are sardonyx, like I mentioned before. Black agate and sardonyx are both said to protect against evil. The amulet was used for protection against others who intended to do the wearer of the amulet harm. It really stresses that intention is important."

Anise took a thoughtful pause. "So if it was a non-in-tentional *accident*, they could still be harmed while wearing the amulet?"

Jonathan nodded. "That's what it sounds like to me."

"Interesting. Does it say what would happen if some-one tried to harm them while they wore the amulet?"

"Yes! According to the legend, enemy weapons were either unable to penetrate any protective gear that was worn or they would just miss their target altogether. So, for example, if the enemy swung a battle-ax at a warrior who was wearing the amulet, even if his aim was perfect, and the warrior didn't move out of the way, the ax would just miss. In fact, the amulet as armor was said to be so effective, the warriors stopped wearing their regular body armor of metal scales."

"Oh my god..." said Anise, loosely covering her mouth with her hand. She had a flashback of Brian throwing the lamp at her and how strange it had been that it had missed hitting her. Although she'd come up with logical explanations for what might have happened, she was now beginning to doubt them. She'd bought that cheap lamp at the thrift store for a dollar. It was light and was easily tipped over. Given how fast the lamp had been thrown and the short distance it had to travel to get to her, backspin from a weighted base was unlikely. And she recalled the cord on the floor—it hadn't gotten caught on anything. She put her hand back in her lap. But of course, a magical protective amulet wasn't the reason the lamp had missed hitting her either. It was just a very strange coincidence.

"I know—a pretty big claim, right?" laughed Jonathan. "This is the ring the warriors wore," he continued, point-ing out another drawing in the book. The setting of the ring was in the shape of a rounded rectangle and boasted a rectangular stone. "The ring is said to be a weapon. It was used when a warrior was in close proximity to an enemy and didn't have access to his usual weapon for whatever reason. Since it was used defensively, it was still considered to be armor as well as a weapon. What you normally see is the carnelian stone, which would be a reddish-orange color, but if you turn the setting counter-clockwise ninety degrees, the stone is flipped over to reveal a mix of the minerals carnelian, cinnabar, and orpiment. So on the reverse side, you'd see the carnelian with bands of red and yellow running through it. The last two are very toxic, containing mercury and arsenic. According to this, the cinnabar and orpiment would deliver poisons into the victim through the skin, while the carnelian would calm him, maybe to keep him from fighting back. The poison would make the victim so sick, they'd be worthless as a warrior for about twelve hours."

"Wow, that's a scary ring," Anise commented.

"For sure," agreed Jonathan.

He turned the page in the book and showed her another drawing. She saw a pair of hoop earrings with a rounded bar through the middle, bisecting the circular shape. The bar on each earring also ran through a stone. "These are the earrings. The stones you see on the bars in the middle are made out of chalcedony which is a light blue stone, and the settings and the bar are the same alloy as the other pieces of Jewelry. Chalcedony is said to increase vigor, stamina, and vitality. The earrings were armor against weakness, injury, and disease. If a warrior wore the earrings, he'd have the energy and strength of five men, be very resistant to illness, and need very little sleep. He'd be able to outlast anyone in a battle. If he was injured, it would be unlikely that he'd develop an infection."

"So if a warrior was wearing all three, he'd be pretty much unstoppable and indestructible."

"Yes," Jonathan told her, "but even more so than you'd think. The Jewelry was meant to work together, so if a warrior was wearing multiple pieces, the abilities granted by the Jewelry to the wearer would be increased. The example in the book says that if a warrior was wearing all three pieces, he'd fight like fifty men, never become ill, wouldn't age, wouldn't need sleep, couldn't be injured in any way, and the poison he'd deliver from the ring would be fatal."

"Had this actually been true," Anise speculated, "then Mallandia would have easily become a world power."

Jonathan shrugged. "Apparently, good things don't last. I don't know much about stones and minerals. But according to the book, it seems that if a stone is used often in highly charged situations, like war for example, it runs out of energy and become useless over time."

"My friend Erin uses gemstones for healing purposes," interjected Anise. "She's told me something like that. I think she said that you have to clear the toxic energy from them and recharge them every now and then."

"These warriors would have killed for that information," said Jonathan, turning the page. "They didn't know their stones could be cleared and used again. Once the Jewelry stopped working for them, they just dropped it on the battlefield and left it there. It wasn't until much later that people discovered the stones could be cleared of their energy by placing them in or under running water, and that what recharges the stones is sunlight."

Anise nodded. "That's how Erin takes care of her gemstones too. So what did they do when their Jewelry stopped working?"

"They kept remaking the Jewelry," Jonathan answered. "The problem with that plan is that the gemstones they used for the Jewelry weren't native to their area. They came from places like Egypt and Mesopotamia, which is incredible because it's proof that they traded with other civilizations! But when these other civilizations realized how powerful the Mallandians were becoming with their new way of fighting wars, all trade stopped. So once the Mallandians ran out of gemstones completely, and they were no longer more powerful than anyone else, they had to go back to traditional fighting methods."

"What happened then?" Anise asked, completely drawn in to Jonathan's story.

"Mallandia didn't have the weaponry or advanced technologies of other major civilizations at the time, and their army was slaughtered in a battle. An archeologist named Dr. Frederick Dromly discovered the battlefield sixty or so years ago. He believes that ironically, Mallandia fell largely in part *because* of the Jewelry. After the major loss of that battle, the people that were left became farmers and started using irrigation in order to grow their crops. Once they started planting on the former battlefields, the rings that were left behind were washed when it rained and then recharged in the sunlight. They started leaking the poison into the soil, which ruined the soil for planting and poisoned the plants that were growing there. To prevent further poisoning, the Mallandians destroyed all the Jewelry they could find."

"*All* of it?" asked Anise. "So this *is* a replica?"

"Well, I don't know," admitted Jonathan. "It's very possible that some of the Jewelry survived and was discovered at some point. Do you mind if I take some pictures of your amulet to show to Dr. Smithton?"

"Not at all! I'd love to know as much as you and Dr. Smithton are able to tell me."

"I can't wait to learn more, too!" said Jonathan excitedly. "Would you like me to call you with what I find out?"

"I'd really appreciate that!" said Anise. She wrote down her phone number and handed it to him. She considered what she had learned for a few moments as Jonathan laid the amulet on the table and took pictures of it with his cell phone camera.

"You really shouldn't wear your amulet," Jonathan told her. "If it *is* the real thing, it's priceless and needs to be protected. You should keep it in a safe."

"Okay," she said, putting it back around her neck and wondering how much a safe might cost.

He walked her up the stairs, down the hallway, and

to the front doors of the museum. As they walked, they engaged in polite conversation. Anise enjoyed his friendly nature and how easy it was to talk to him.

"It was such a pleasure to meet you, Anise. Thanks for bringing in your amulet; I really enjoyed talking with you about it."

"Thank *you* for all the fascinating information!" she replied.

"I'll be in touch very soon," he said, flashing his nice smile at her again and holding out his hand.

"I look forward to it," she replied as she shook his hand.

Checking the time on her phone as she left the museum, she felt a spark of excitement when she realized it was late afternoon. And Tuesday! Time to teach her kickboxing fitness class! Just like she had on Saturday, Anise put on her disguise of a cap, sunglasses, and oversized jacket, rode her bike a few blocks past the market, and coasted down the hill. After looking around her to make sure the coast was clear, she wheeled it into the alleyway and chained it on the large metal pipe.

She hoped Brian would be completely moved out by the time she got home. The thought of him being out of her life for good gave her a sense of relief. She went in the side door and down the narrow hallway. Excitement sparked again as she thought about Nate and how she'd get to see him soon.

She changed into sneakers, gathered her hair into a ponytail, and put on some music. "Okay!" she said brightly to her class as soon as the clock read four-thirty. "Let's get started!" Simply looking around the room during the warm-up exercises gave her a charge. This small gym was one of her favorite places in the world. She never felt more powerful than when she was here. She felt lucky no one she knew had ever seen her coming here. If they did, everything good about this place would be ruined.

Chapter 9

After texting her friends about some of the interesting history of her amulet that she'd learned, as well as how excited she was to see Nate again that evening, Anise stood in front of her closet trying to decide what to wear to the concert.

Brian wasn't there, but his clothes and video games were still in the apartment. Maybe he had gone to get boxes?

It was going to be an unseasonably warm evening for early June, so she chose a long, flowy tank top, skinny jeans, and wedge sandals, topped with the amulet. Until a safe could be afforded, she'd have to keep it with her at all times. She tucked it underneath her top. From what she found out this afternoon, it was worth a lot more she'd ever have imagined, and it would be nice to not be bothered by any more strangers wanting to buy it from her.

As she touched up her makeup, Anise put on some upbeat pop music and danced around to help expel some nervous energy. The excitement to see Nate again was so strong she could barely stand it. With him, the feeling of being so alive was almost overwhelming—in the most marvelous way possible. She loved how he could make her laugh. His confidence was so inspirational and sexy, and all the attention he paid her made Anise feel so desirable. He listened and remembered what she said, and never in her life had she been pursued so hard. Her strong feelings for him were almost a little frightening, as she had only known him for a few days, but it was a good frightening. There was something very special about him.

She turned off her thoughts before her head started spinning and left the apartment. During the walk toward the park to meet Nate, Anise thought about the amulet and all she learned about it that day. It seemed more likely to her that she was in possession of a replica and not an actual 4,000-year-old piece of jewelry. However, that example Jonathan gave about the battle-ax missing its mark sounded exactly like what had happened with the lamp the night before. It came right at her, and she hadn't moved. Yet somehow, it changed direction and started moving in the opposite way. *But that's ridiculous*, she told herself. *There's no such thing as a magical piece of jewelry. Magic spells are not real.* Suddenly, she remembered washing the amulet under the running faucet in her bathroom and setting it in the sunny window afterward. *That's how the Mallandian warriors should've cleansed and recharged their gemstones,* Anise thought, slightly embarrassed for even considering the possibility of the amulet having any of the power Jonathan had described earlier.

She got to the park about fifteen minutes before their scheduled meeting time, having left her apartment early to make sure she'd avoid seeing Brian. She couldn't wait until she could have her place all to herself again. All thoughts of Brian were forgotten as she fantasized about what might happen when Nate came over. Her daydream was interrupted when she heard the roar of Nate's motorcycle. She watched him park and walk over the grass to meet her.

She waved and gave him a hug in greeting. "Hi!"

"Hi, honey. You look beautiful tonight," he whispered in her ear as he returned her embrace.

Honey. He said it again! Her smile reflected her delight.

As they stood in line to enter the section of the park that had the stage, he put his arms around her from behind. She leaned into him and felt like nothing else had ever been so right.

They found a place to sit on the grass and spread a blanket on the ground that Nate had brought in a backpack. Anise sat next to him with her legs curled up beside her and leaned against the side of his chest. She looked up at him, and he moved some of her bangs out of her eyes. The concert started forty-five minutes late, but neither one of them noticed.

"So which band tonight is your favorite?" Anise asked him, looking at the line up on the program.

"Bent Razors, definitely."

"Really? Me too! I love their "Secret Garden" song!" She sang part of the chorus.

"You have a nice voice," Nate told her.

Anise made a face. "No, I was so pitchy."

"You're right, it was awful," he teased.

She gave him a mock glare and smacked him on the arm.

He grinned at her. "I think my ears are bleeding."

"Nate!" she protested, laughing.

He laughed with her. "Seriously though, I didn't hear any pitch problems. You sounded good."

"Well, thank you." She looked at him with an embarrassing burning in her cheeks. Receiving compliments had always felt awkward for her, but she still enjoyed hearing them, especially when they came from Nate. She put her hand on his thigh. "And thank you for getting the tickets. I don't know how you managed it. I was told they sold out early last week. You're amazing," she said with a flirtatious smile, wanting to pay him a compliment in return.

Nate tilted Anise's chin up toward him and kissed her until her desire made her dizzy and breathless.

*** *** ***

AS THEY GOT READY TO LEAVE after the last band had played, Anise checked her phone—two missed calls and three texts from Brian. Rolling her eyes at the screen, she deleted all the messages without reading or listening to them.

"Do you want to get a drink or something to eat?" Nate asked her.

"I'd love to!" she agreed, excited to expand her evening with him. "Are you okay with The Blue Pineapple? It's my favorite bar. They have an amazing cocktail menu, and the food is to die for. It's actually good and not just gross bar food."

"Of course. Let's go." He grabbed the blanket and backpack and they headed toward his bike.

Anise chirped happily about the performances they'd just seen, but when she looked up at his face, Nate seemed to be far away. She wondered what he was thinking and if he'd heard her. He'd always been completely present with her, and his distant stare felt strange.

"You're awfully quiet over there," Anise said, grabbing his helmet from off the rearview mirror on his bike and putting it on. "Is everything okay?" She hoped he was having as good a time as she was and that his silence meant nothing more than he was a good listener. Her eyes caught and held his as she touched his hand, caressing a couple of his fingers.

"Yeah," he replied with a grin. "I was just thinking..." He grabbed the chin of the helmet she wore and wiggled it. "This is a little big for you."

"I should get my own," Anise agreed. "Maybe a purple one! Then we could go on longer rides together." She imagined a romantic ride through the mountains to see the fields of wildflowers and hoped he'd be up for something like that. "You know, if you want."

Nate shook his head. "Don't do that."

"Why not?" Her excitement faded quickly, and she let go of his hand to twist her garnet ring rapidly around her finger. *Does he not want to see me again?*

"Because I'd like to get it for you."

She couldn't help but smile at him and promised herself she'd stop feeling so insecure. This date was going great, and she should relax and enjoy it. He looked away and ran a hand through his almost-black hair before getting on his bike. She climbed on behind him and wrapped her arms around his waist. The loud roar of the motorcycle rang musically in her ears, and she enjoyed the sights and sounds of the downtown streets as well having Nate between her arms. Her hands were tempted to wander over his chest at the red lights, but she kept them clasped firmly together.

As soon as they were seated at a table at The Blue Pineapple, Nate asked the server for a dessert menu.

"Do you have a sweet tooth?" Anise asked him.

"Not really," he replied. "But whenever I eat out, I always have dessert first."

She grinned at him. "I love that idea!"

"Try it," he encouraged her and handed her the menu.

"The desserts here are huge. Maybe we could split something?" she suggested.

"Sure. What looks good?"

Anise let her eyes wander over his face and arms for a moment before looking at the menu. She searched for something without chocolate since he didn't like it. "How about the strawberry cheesecake?"

"Sounds great," he confirmed. "One strawberry cheesecake, two forks," he added to the server.

"So what's the story with eating dessert first?" Anise

wanted to know.

Nate shrugged. "Just an idiosyncrasy left over from childhood. Nothing interesting."

"I think it's interesting. Is this something fun your family used to do? Like a tradition?"

"No, nothing like that." His face grimaced slightly. "Forget about it."

She reached across the table and took his hand, intertwining her fingers with his. "Tell me. Please?" she requested, looking forward to learning more about his past.

His face turned hard and flat, and he looked at her as if he were trying to decide if he wanted to leave.

Was he acting strange and distant again, or did she say something awful? "Sorry," she said, taking her hand back. She twisted her garnet ring around her finger and stared at it. "I didn't mean to pry or make you uncomfortable."

"No," he said, his expression softening. He held out his hand. "Come back." Once her hand was back in his, he lifted her fingers to his lips. "I'm sorry. It's just not exactly a good memory." Nate rested the back of his hand on the table while still holding hers. "When I was a kid, I was really good at annoying the adults at the dinner table. More often than not, I'd get sent to my room before dinner was over."

Their cheesecake was set in front of them, and they placed their dinner and drink orders. They each grabbed a fork.

"So you never got dessert then," Anise concluded once the server had left. She took a small bite of the creamy cake and let it melt like heaven in her mouth. "What did you do that got you in so much trouble? Did you throw things or..."

He shook his head. "No. They didn't like things I said. I talked back a lot."

"That seems harsh. You were just a kid. Did you at

least get to finish your dinner before they sent you away?" She looked up and was surprised to see that Nate had almost finished his half of the slice of cake.

"Not usually," he replied. "Which is probably why I eat really fast, too."

"That's terrible," Anise said softly as her heart broke for him. "I'm sorry that happened to you."

Nate was quiet. Anise was about to change the subject when he spoke again. "I know eating too fast is an unhealthy habit. Maybe you can help remind me to slow down."

"Happy to help. What should our signal be? I could say something, or I could squeeze your hand or your arm..."

"You squeeze whatever you want, honey," he told her with a slight smirk.

"Okay." She let out a soft laugh. "Our dinners together are going to be fun," she promised him boldly.

Their food came and Anise dug in. After watching Nate take three large bites in a row without chewing, she squeezed his knee under the table.

"Oh, shit," he mumbled and rested his fork on his plate. After swallowing, he thanked her. "I don't realize when it's happening."

"Or you just wanted me to squeeze you," Anise teased.

"No, but that *is* a bonus," he said.

"If you like it that much, I don't think it'll help you stop," she said decidedly.

"We can't know that for sure unless we try it anyway."

Anise laughed. "I can't argue with that."

"So, being an artist, have you heard about the art fair in Lundville this weekend?" he asked.

"Yes! My friends are taking me there as a graduation gift," Anise said excitedly. She then wondered if Nate had been simply making conversation by asking her that question or if he'd been planning to ask her to go with him. If the latter, it would've been a very thoughtful date idea.

"Are you getting a booth?" he asked. "Selling some of your work?"

"Oh, god no. I'm not ready for that. The artists there are professionals. We're just going for fun."

"Maybe someday in the future?"

"Maybe. That would be the dream."

He asked her more about her art, and she happily answered his questions, but feeling her passion for her art as she spoke made her more and more disappointed with herself for not having gone to art school when she'd had the chance. The fire his questions were lighting under her to change that made her feel excited for her future—something she hadn't felt for some time. She mentally made a plan to find a better job so she could start saving up for tuition.

After their meal and participating in trivia night, they danced off the calories until closing time.

"I should get you home, honey," said Nate, as he held the door open for her. "It's getting late."

"Yeah, I guess," Anise agreed reluctantly.

Nate stopped his motorcycle a few blocks away from her apartment.

"You didn't have to do that," Anise told him. "I asked Brian to move out, so he's not there to hear us this time."

"I'm glad," Nate said. "But this way I'll be able to spend a few more minutes with you."

Hand in hand, they walked together the rest of the way.

"Thank you for tonight, Nate. I can't remember the last time I've had so much fun!" Anise exclaimed, smiling up at him.

"Me either," he said. "We have so much in common, and you're so easy to talk to. Not to mention fucking gorgeous." He flashed a devilish grin at her, and she felt her cheeks flush.

"Aw," she replied, "thanks! You're okay-looking, too."

She playfully bumped her shoulder against his arm.

"Just okay-looking?" he asked, doubtfully, holding his hands out in mock confusion. They were nearing her apartment building.

"That's right," she answered, and giggled at her attempt to tease him.

"What happened to the hottest guy you've ever seen?" he asked, as he picked her up and carried her around the side of her building. She shrieked and laughed as she wrapped her arms around the back of his neck to hold on. He carefully set her down so her back was against the wall, and he stood in front of her, so close they were almost touching. He gazed at her intensely—in a way that made her long to know what he'd do next.

"You're never gonna let me live that down, are you?" Anise asked him with excited anticipation.

"Never," he confirmed with a smirk.

"Well then, I have a confession to make. You're fuck-ing gorgeous, too."

They stood in the shadows of the building while he slowly leaned in and kissed her. For a moment, he paused and ran his fingers through her hair. As his fin-gers glided softly over her neck, they slipped under the amulet's chain. "What's this necklace you're wearing?" he asked.

She started to tell him that her friend Doreen had given the amulet to her and that she had taken it to a curator at the museum that day. But she stopped talking to concentrate on how good his finger felt as it was trac-ing her skin where the chain lay against her. He started at her neck and moved down over her décolletage, onto her cleavage, and under her top. As his finger moved lower, her breath quickened. She bit her lower lip as she looked up at him to let him know she was loving it and wanted more.

His eyes never left hers until he pulled the amulet out and looked at it. "This is really unique. Let me see this closer," he said and attempted to remove it from around her neck.

"No, don't take it off," she said, grabbing the chain. She blinked when the center stone flashed a quick light into her eye. Maybe it was reflecting the moonlight. "I'm a little overprotective of it because I—"

Nate let out a cry of pain, dropped the amulet, and grabbed his arm.

"Are you okay?" she asked him, touching his arm.

"Yeah, I am now," he replied. "That was weird. I got a burning pain in my arm."

"Does that happen often?" she asked him, worried.

"No, never happened before."

"That *is* weird."

He rubbed his arm and straightened up. "It's fine now. Anyway, let me see it," he said.

She held up the amulet for him to take a look but kept the chain around her neck.

"Wow. I've never seen anything like it."

"I know, right?"

"But it's kind of hard to see in the dark," he told her. He held out his hand. "Can I take it under the street lamp so I can see it better?"

"I don't want to take it off," she repeated, looking up at him coyly. "But you can look at it. You'll just have to search for it again." She felt her face flush again as she dropped it underneath her top.

He let out a quiet laugh. "With pleasure," he replied. He kissed her neck as his hand slowly traced her cleavage once more. His fingers slipped under her top, and she let out a quick, subtle moan of pleasure as he softly caressed her breasts through her thin, lacy bra. One strap of her tank top fell off her shoulder. Her eyes closed when his lips touched hers, and she pressed herself against his growing arousal.

"Let's go upstairs," Nate suggested.

Anise was tempted to say yes. Undressing for him

and finding out what he'd do about it had kept her awake every night since she'd met him. But this was their first real date, and what she felt for him went so much deeper than a physical attraction alone. She could see this being long term, and she didn't want to send him the wrong signal and make him think sex was all she wanted from him. Building more emotional intimacy first felt like the right thing to do. "Not tonight. It's too soon."

He gently lifted her fallen tank top's strap back on her shoulder. "Okay, honey." He kissed her again, and they began walking hand-in-hand toward the door of Anise's apartment building. "Tonight was fun."

"Yes, it was!" she agreed, beaming at him. "Call me tomorrow?"

"Absolutely." He paused and looked like he was thinking about something. "You know, I never did get a good look at your amulet."

"Oh, right!" she laughed. "I forgot all about it." She led him to the light of the street lamp, pulled it out from under her shirt, and showed it to him.

Nate grabbed it and tried to take it off her in a way that was almost forceful. Surprised by his behavior, she grasped the chain again. "Don't," she said. The center stone reflected a flash of the light from the street lamp.

For the second time, he doubled over grasping his arm.

"What is going on with you?" Anise demanded in confusion. "I already told you twice I don't want to take it off. You've been acting strangely on and off all night. What gives?"

"Honey," Nate said, his eyes squinting with pain, "I need you to trust me, and give me the amulet."

Anise felt her jaw fall open with surprise. She'd been right—something strange *was* going on with him. She couldn't believe that yet another person was trying to take her amulet away from her. And why was that person Nate, the man she'd been falling for just a moment earlier? She felt her stomach churn and her heart begin to pound. "And I need you to leave me alone!" she said with her voice raised. She backed away from him.

"Anise, please, just trust me, and hand it over. It's for your own good." He reached for the amulet and once again doubled over with a grunt of pain.

She saw his eyes open wide when the amulet seemed to glow too brightly to be a reflection. "Don't you dare threaten me!" she yelled at him, as she pushed him away and ran.

Nate recovered quickly and ran after her. She raced up the steps and into the building as fast as she could. Rounding the corner, she fled up the stairwell to her third-floor apartment. She was fast, even in her wedge sandals, but he was faster. His echoing footsteps in the stairwell were growing louder, and she looked at him over her shoulder. She screamed as she saw him gaining on her as he took the stairs three at a time. Anise flew down the hallway while fishing for her keys in her purse. She unlocked her door in record time and went inside, attempting to close the door behind her, but Nate had caught up with her and shoved his way into her apartment.

"Give me the amulet," he demanded, his tone sounding almost desperate. "Give it to me or they'll kill you." The creak of a floorboard made them both look over just in time to see a fist flying at Nate's face.

BRIAN FELT A TESTOSTERONE-FILLED RUSH AS his knuckles landed on his target's eye. Knocked out with one punch, the dark-haired guy that'd followed Anise into the apartment fell to the floor, his blood pooling under his face.

Brian looked at Anise as she gasped and held her hands over her mouth. She was breathing heavily and her entire body shook. His attention then turned to the guy on the floor. He was the same one Anise had been making out with the night before. The one she'd grabbed by the jacket and pulled in for more, as if his lips were like crack to her. Brian thought back on his entire relationship with her but couldn't remember an instance when Anise had ever done that with him or anything like it. Not even close. What did this guy have that he didn't? With one swift jerk of the foot, Brian kicked him in the face and watched his head snap back.

"Brian, stop! Don't kill him!"

"I'll be right back," he told her. "I have to take out the trash." He grabbed the unconscious body and swung it over his shoulder. He walked down the stairs, out the door, and to the dumpster used by the residents of the apartment building. He grabbed the guy's wallet from his pocket and pulled out the cash. Throwing the guy inside the open dumpster, Brian spit on him, stuffed the corner of his wallet in his mouth, and slammed the lid. As he climbed the stairs, it took everything in him not to punch a hole in the stairwell wall. His mind couldn't even form rational thoughts as it was consumed with a fantasy of setting the dumpster on fire. Back in the apartment, he found Anise sitting on their couch, her face in her hands.

She looked up at him. "Thank you," she said, a few tears making their way down her cheeks.

"So that's the guy you think is better than me?" he said in a harsh but calm voice. He hadn't had a drink all day in hopes of spending some quality time with Anise that evening. He was planning on having a real conversation with her about their relationship. Upon getting more advice from Corinne, he thought about what he wanted to say and how to say it in a way that wouldn't sound accusatory. He had even gone to the grocery store to buy ingredients for a dinner he planned to cook for her. For hours, he had waited for her to come home and had no idea where she'd been. He'd been really worried and was so disappointed in how the evening turned out. Well, except for punching that dick weasel in the face. That was fun.

"Why are you here?" Anise demanded. She was still shaking.

Brian wanted to go to her and comfort her so badly. He wanted to hold her and tell her everything would be all right, that *they* would be all right. But he couldn't tell her that if he didn't believe it himself. *Where did we go so wrong?* he wondered. The more he looked at Anise shaking, the angrier he got. *This is all her fault. She's a fucking cheat,* he thought. He could hear Corinne in his head telling him that he's a cheat, too, but he felt the two scenarios were entirely different. He didn't care about Hailey at all—he was just using her. Anise must have really liked this guy to have gone out with him two nights in a row. Still, he felt guilty, and he hated that feeling. He was angry at Anise for pushing him away and driving him toward another woman. *This is all her fault,* he repeated to himself. And it wasn't just her cheating. She'd been dishonest about other things, too. "Why are you lying to me about everything?"

"What are you talking about? I'm not!"

"Bullshit! I've followed you when you thought I was at home. You put on a hat and a big jacket like no one would recognize you, and you go to some gym. And when you get home, you lie about it."

The surprise was prominent on her face as her eyes opened wide and her jaw fell.

"Yeah, I know about that. I'm not stupid, Anise. Either you're a goddamn hypocrite spending money we don't have or you went there to meet up with *him*."

"What difference does that make anymore? We broke up. Why didn't you move out?" Anise asked again.

Brian ignored her questions. "I heard him say he wants the amulet. Why?! That piece of shit necklace has been nothing but trouble for us ever since you got it. It's time that thing went into the trash where it belongs—right next to your boyfriend." He started walking toward her.

"He's not my boyfriend," insisted Anise, wiping her eyes. "And leave my amulet alone!" She clutched the amulet tightly as he got nearer.

Brian tried to grab it but got a burning sensation in his arm. As he swore from the pain, he noticed Anise looking down at the amulet she still clutched in her hands. The creepy thing was glowing again.

"This is no replica," she mumbled and started walking toward the front door.

"What does that mean?" he yelled at her. "And where the hell are you going? It's the middle of the night!"

"Anywhere but here!" she answered back. "I'm so sick of fighting with you!"

In his rage, he roared, "Good idea! Go crawl in the dumpster with your boyfriend where you belong, you trash whore!"

"I want you out of my apartment!" she screamed back at him.

"I'm never moving out!" he boomed.

After he heard her slam the door, he reached into the cupboard above the refrigerator and pulled out a bottle of Jim Beam. Beer just wouldn't cut it at this moment.

Chapter 10

Wednesday, June 6, 2012

Nate woke with a start as he spit out whatever was in his mouth. He couldn't see in the pitch blackness, and when he turned his head, something covered his face, and he couldn't breathe. Whatever it was, it clung to his mouth and nose. He pulled at it as he tried to sit up. It felt like thin plastic. He tried to stand on the foul-smelling surface, but his feet sunk in between the lumps and his head hit the very low ceiling.

What the hell?

Groggily he reached his arms up to the ceiling and found that it moved when he touched it. Giving it a big push, the ceiling opened up to the night sky, and he saw the stars twinkling at him. The nearby street lamp shone on his humiliation like a spotlight, and his splitting headache made him wonder if whatever had happened to him had caused him a concussion. He saw his wallet resting on the bags of trash and shoved it back in his pocket.

Nate climbed out of the dumpster and found himself standing in the alley next to Anise's apartment building. He still didn't quite recall what had happened but slowly started remembering on the tedious walk out of the alley toward the street. His jaw hurt, his head pounded, his left eye was swollen shut, and there was dried blood on his shirt.

Nate sat on the curb in the cool night air with his head in his hands trying to will away his headache. His mind went through the events of the evening to refresh his still-fuzzy memory. He pictured Anise standing with him in the alley, teasing him by dropping the amulet under her top and daring him to fetch it. He hadn't been able to help letting out a little laugh at her behavior. *So fucking cute.*

And how she'd leaned her head on his shoulder at the concert. How her hips had beckoned him when they were dancing at the bar. The way she'd pressed into him when he kissed her... For a blissful little while, he let himself remember all the best parts of the evening. But as his memory came back in full, reality snuck up behind him and sunk its unyielding fingers into his throat. He swallowed.

His mind turned to the amulet. When he'd tried to take it, he'd been stunned for a moment as he watched the amulet start glowing like Grace warned him it might do if he wasn't careful. He hadn't believed her. Now he found himself wishing he had so he could've come up with a better plan. When Anise had realized he'd betrayed her, the hurt in her expression had made him feel like a monster.

He wished she'd allowed him to come upstairs. Then she might've take the amulet off, put it down somewhere, and he could've walked away with it without scaring her. Maybe she wouldn't have noticed it missing right away, and she might've thought it was the loser ex-boyfriend who took it for revenge. If that happened, maybe they could've still seen each other...but it was useless to think that way now. Plus, it wouldn't have worked anyway, not with her ex still in the apartment.

If only Anise hadn't been wearing the amulet. Things

might have been different. They could've had their incredible date and then he could've easily broken into her apartment while she was sleeping to take it. His head raised from his hands. Maybe that could still happen. He rose from his seat on the sidewalk and groaned. Everything hurt, but he had to try. He walked up the stairs slowly, thinking about what Grace would do to Anise if he didn't get the amulet tonight. If he failed again, Anise would end up dead.

Finally reaching the third floor, Nate fished his lock pick out of his jacket pocket. He listened carefully at the door. Hearing nothing, he first tried the door handle. It turned, and the door opened. He frowned as he wondered why she hadn't locked the door after having been chased. He knew he'd scared her, so why wouldn't she have taken precautions to protect herself? He started worrying about her. Had the loser boyfriend done something to her?

Nate put his lock pick back in his pocket and slowly opened the door, peaking inside. He saw the loser passed out on the couch, snoring loudly. Nate looked at the behemoth, surprised that a punch from someone that large hadn't done more damage. He was grateful he didn't have any broken bones. Walking silently through the apartment, he looked in the tiny kitchen, the bathroom, and the bedroom, but Anise was nowhere. He searched the entire place for the amulet, but it wasn't there. Of course Anise would have it with her, wherever she was.

He cursed himself for failing to protect her. Now Grace would go after her. Not knowing where Anise or the amulet was, he was unable to come up with another plan, so he left the apartment quietly and rode home, hoping he'd happen to see Anise on the street so he could explain. No such luck.

Nate had never been so happy to open the door to his condo. He wanted a hot shower, ibuprofen, and to sleep off the evening's consequences. In the morning, he'd figure out a better way to get the amulet before Grace came to find him. He could still get the amulet; he could still keep Anise safe.

He switched on the light and discovered that he wasn't alone. His groan was involuntary. "What the fuck?! Why are you people always here when I get home?"

"What happened to your face?" asked Dan, stepping toward him. As soon as he got close, he backed away. "And why do you smell like garbage?"

"More importantly, did you get the amulet?" Grace asked him expectantly as she leaned forward from her seat on his sofa.

Nate groaned again and held his hand up to his aching head. "No."

Dan grimaced while Grace became enraged. "What do you mean, no?" she shrieked, and pulled on her white hair. "What happened?"

"She was wearing it tonight, and I tried to take it off her, but I kept getting these pains in my arm. You didn't tell me that would happen. She ran, and I chased her into her apartment, where her boyfriend knocked me out," Nate explained. His pride wouldn't allow him to mention the dumpster.

"How is it possible," Grace began, "that you completely screwed this up? I told you enough of what you needed to know. I don't understand how you could let this happen."

"You actually expected me to take what you said seriously? To believe that she has a magic necklace?" Nate shot back.

"Yes, because it's true!" Grace insisted.

"I know that now," Nate replied with annoyance, rubbing his aching head.

"If you had trusted me and followed my instructions more closely, you could've gotten the amulet!" Grace screeched.

Nate almost laughed. "I will never trust you as long

as I live."

Grace gave him a look of disgust. "You should see yourself now; you look so weak and helpless with your face all mangled. It's pathetic. You've been nothing but worthless to us in this whole venture. All these days wasted!" She sighed dramatically and leaned back on his couch with an exasperated look.

Nate knew better than to protest or fight back. It wouldn't do any good. *You can't reason with the illogical,* he often reminded himself. She always needed someone to blame everything on because nothing was ever her fault, and he'd been her scapegoat for as long as he could remember. It didn't matter that she had also made failed attempts at getting the amulet. The only thing that mattered to her was that *Nate* had failed, and she would appease her ego by reminding him of that.

Grace looked at Dan expectantly.

Dan sat up straight. "I'm really disappointed in you," he told Nate, as he shook his head in disdain. "I thought you were smarter than that."

"He's too much like his mother," Grace snapped.

Dan hung his head.

"I wouldn't know," snarled Nate. "When are you going to tell me what you did to her, Grace?"

"Stop being so sensitive; it's emasculating. And don't change the subject!" she yelled at him, even though she was the one who had brought it up. She turned to Dan again. "You haven't been a big help either! You only do something when I ask you to. Why can't you take the initiative once in a while? Why do I have to do everything by myself? You're just as weak and worthless as he is!"

"Every time I've done that, Mother, you've stopped me and told me that everything I did was wrong and that I should just wait to take directions from you!" Dan yelled back at her. His face turned as red as his hair.

"Oh, sure," she answered, her voice dripping with sarcasm. "Now it's *my* fault you can't do anything right!"

she wailed, pulling on her hair. "Everyone always blames the mother!"

In the midst of this drama, Nate had a flashback to a happy childhood day where his mother was playing with him in the sandbox at the park where he had taken Anise the night before. He was very young, maybe only four or five years old. She'd always called him her little prince. They were building a sandcastle together, and she told him something about this being his royal castle, and that he was a strong, smart, and good prince, and not to believe anyone that ever told him any differently. That was the last time he'd ever seen her, and neither Grace nor Dan had ever answered his questions about what had happened to her. *If she only knew what I've done to appease these two trolls,* he thought to himself, *she might have to retract that statement.*

"It's a sad day when you're an old woman and can't rely on anyone for help," Grace continued with a pathetic sigh. "Dan, Nate is obviously not capable of handling even the simplest task. We'll just have to take care of this ourselves, with or without initiative from you. Let's go." Grace got up and headed toward the door, and Dan followed.

"Hold on," said Nate, stepping between them and his door. "What are you going to do? This is getting way out of hand. I don't want to see anyone else get killed over this."

"I knew we shouldn't have brought you with us last time," sneered Grace.

"You're the one who begged me for my help!" Nate shot back.

"Yes, for your *help,* which you failed to provide! You were completely worthless. You just stood there and did nothing. And if I'd known you'd grow up to be too weak to do what needed to be done, I'd have—"

"Stop, Mother!" Dan pleaded with her.

Grace's eyes narrowed as she stared at Nate.

"You'd have what?" Nate demanded, even though he already knew the answer.

Grace's eyes got large and she cringed, waving a hand in front of her face.

"Uh oh." Dan's eyes locked on Grace with concern. "She might be having an episode."

Grace started to scream. "Bees! Bees!"

"Does she have to do this in my apartment?" Nate groaned.

Dan glared at him. "You know she can't help it!"

"If it were anyone else in the world, I'd care," Nate said. "But you need to get *her* the hell out of here."

"Why do you hate her so much?" Dan demanded.

"Are you fucking kidding me?!" Nate cried. "Do you not remember all the shit she did to me?"

Grace's arms flew violently back and forth in an attempt to swat away the insects that weren't actually there. She waved her arms around Nate's face as he stepped back in annoyance. "Kill him before he kills you, Gracie," she whispered under her breath.

Nate rolled his eyes. Not this again.

"Mother!" Dan shouted with a horrified expression. He put an arm around her to steady her. "Take one of your pills!" He rummaged through her purse and grabbed a pill bottle.

Grace pulled hard on her hair until some came out in her hand.

"It's not real, Mother. It's just another hallucination." Dan shoved a pill in her mouth.

She dropped her fistful of hair on Nate's floor and spit out the pill in Dan's face. "I know that! Leave me alone! I don't need pills!"

"Yeah, that looked perfectly normal to me," Nate chimed in.

She glared at him. "Nate, if you don't want to see anyone get killed, then by all means stay home and out of my way. I'll figure out what to do with you when we get back." Grace tried to walk around him to the door.

Nate stopped her by grabbing her arm. "Don't threaten me," he warned her. "You remember what happened the last time you tried that."

"Yes, you tried to have me committed. And how did that work out for you?" She laughed heartily, holding her belly and throwing back her head. "I'm shaking in my boots."

"I'm all too happy to try again. I won't fail this time." He tightened his grip on her.

"Let go of me," she told him through gritted teeth.

"You're going to fail, too," he said, still squeezing her arm. "The protective power of that amulet is really strong. I felt the effects firsthand. As long as she's wearing it, there's no way you'll succeed."

"Don't get fresh with me, you arrogant little shit," she said to Nate, shaking off his grip from her arm. "What you've forgotten is that I have the ring." She took a ring out of her purse and slipped it onto her finger.

Grace showed it to him, and Nate recognized it as the carnelian ring they'd stolen from Richard and Marilyn Woods one week earlier. His mind replayed Grace shooting the Woods couple to death in their bedroom, and his hatred for the old hag grew. No way would he let her do the same thing to Anise or anyone else. "I will not let you hurt her! And neither will the amulet!"

Grace rolled her eyes at him. "I know the protective power of the amulet. Do you know the power of the poison ring?" She twisted the top of the ring ninety degrees counter-clockwise, which mechanically flipped the stone over. She grabbed Nate's arm and pushed the stone of the ring onto his skin, leaving it there for about a second before letting him go. He'd felt a warm sensation where the ring touched him and then something sharp, almost like a pin prick. A few seconds after she let his arm go, he began shivering and sweating profusely at the same time. His legs felt weak and gave way under him. He fell to the ground convulsing mildly, but he felt strangely calm and peaceful at the same time. His vision became blurry and his limbs tingly, and the room began to spin.

"You're going to be very sick in a few minutes," Grace told Nate. "You're going to have one hell of a mess to clean up tomorrow," she added with her nose crinkled in disgust. "Too bad, this rug looks really expensive." She bent down to feel his gray and white hand knotted wool rug that sat under his maple coffee table.

"Hang on," Dan said to Nate. "I'll get you to the bathroom." Dan was shorter than Nate and not strong enough to lift him completely. He tried to pull Nate to a standing position but dropped him.

Nate groaned when his body hit the floor. His stomach started churning.

"Let's go, Dan!" Grace commanded. "I have no desire to watch him upchuck everywhere."

"You promised me you wouldn't poison him! So gimme a minute!" Dan said, sounding irritated.

"Relax!" came Grace's huffed reply. "By tomorrow afternoon he'll be completely fine."

Ignoring her, Dan grabbed Nate's arms and hurriedly dragged him across the hardwood floor to the bathroom. He dropped him between the shower and the toilet.

Nate's head hit the cold tiles. "Get me a pillow. Please," Nate begged in a mumble.

"No, I have to go." Dan's face looked nervous, and Nate knew it was because he'd dared to talk back to Grace. *Fucking coward.*

Grace poked her head into the bathroom. "As miserable as you're about to be, you should consider yourself lucky, Nate," she said to him. "If I were in possession of the amulet and earrings as well, you wouldn't just be sick, you'd be dead by now."

Part 3

WHEN YOU KNOW WHAT THE RIGHT THING TO DO IS, DO YOU REALLY HAVE ANY OTHER CHOICE?

Chapter 11

Wednesday, June 6, 2012

Y ou are not allowed to carry a drink with you when you're out in the field talking to potential respondents," Dawn had reminded Anise and her co-workers. "It doesn't look professional." Today, Anise didn't care. She bought an extra-large coffee and held it behind her clipboard so Dawn wouldn't notice. She hadn't slept a wink last night, despite how soft and comfortable Vanessa's couch had been. Her head had been swimming in a multitude of thoughts and worries. She replayed how angry Brian had been and wondered if she'd be able to go home after work. Nate was on her mind, too, as well as his sudden personality change. Why did he go from being her dream man one minute to a nightmare the next? What exactly did he know about the amulet? And what about the amulet itself? How could it be true that under the influence of an ancient magical spell, it was protecting her? And what was she supposed to do about all this?

She pulled out the affirmation card that she'd shoved in her pocket earlier that morning and read it. *When you don't know what to do, do nothing. The answer will be revealed with time.*

Anise had read somewhere that being in the sun helped with jet lag, so she figured it might help her feel better from her sleepless night, too. On her lunch break, she bought a soft pretzel and a Coke and stepped out into the parking lot to soak up some rays. The warm sun felt so good on her face that she looked upward and closed her eyes. She felt her phone vibrate in her bag and looked at it. Brian again. He'd already left some voicemails earlier that morning that she didn't want to hear. Putting the phone on mute, she took another bite of her pretzel. As soon as she finished her lunch, she heard someone come up behind her.

"Anise."

She turned around. "Nate." Her heart started beating quickly with anxiety, but she felt safe with the amulet around her neck. "You look like shit," she told him.

"I know," he replied quietly. He had a black eye that was almost swollen shut, and he walked slowly, carefully, and a little hunched over, as if he were in a lot of pain. His hands were on his stomach, and he swallowed as if trying to fight off nausea. It made Anise wonder how hard Brian had hit and kicked him.

She frowned at him. "Go away, Nate. Stay away from me."

"I tried calling instead," he said, "but you weren't answering your phone. Is your boyfriend okay?"

"What's that supposed to mean?" she asked him angrily. "You're the one who got hurt, not Brian."

Nate looked like he was about to fall over, and he sat down on the curb. His hand rubbed his forehead. "That's not what I mean. You apparently weren't home last night when they were looking for you. Did they kill him?"

"What the hell are you talking about?" Her heart started pounding and her mouth went dry. *Kill?* "He just tried to call me; he's fine. Why would someone want to kill Brian?"

"They want your amulet. They were looking for you

last night but didn't find you. I figured they found your boyfriend instead. I'm glad he's okay."

"And how did you know I left home again last night? Were you following me, you creepy-ass weirdo?" She glared at him.

He appeared to stifle a laugh and then swallowed again. He took a deep breath before speaking. "I deserve that. But no, honey, I wasn't following you. They told me you weren't there."

Anise felt a panic attack coming on and tried to calm herself by taking deep breaths. She paced back and forth in front of him, trying to get out the nervous energy. "Don't ever call me 'honey' again!" she yelled at Nate. "Who the hell are you, and what's going on? Why were you pretending to like me? Who are 'they'? And what do you know about this?" she asked him, holding up her amulet by its chain that was around her neck.

Nate shook his head slowly. "None of that matters right now. What does matter is they won't stop until they get what they want. Be smart, Anise, and give me the amulet now before something happens to you."

"Fuck off!" she told him with a glare. "And don't you dare threaten me again!"

Squealing tires could be heard coming from the other side of the parking lot. Gripping on to a nearby trash can and pulling himself up with a slight groan, Nate stood, and they both saw a car barreling toward them.

"Shit. That's them," he said to Anise with alarm in his voice. "They must've followed me here."

The fear she'd heard in his statement was undeniable, and for a second, she froze and stared at him, unable to move or think.

"They *will* kill you," he added. "*Run.*"

Anise had no idea why she trusted Nate at that particular moment, after he'd pretended to be something he wasn't, but she turned and ran back into the mall. She didn't want to bring attention to herself, so she slowed to a brisk walk. She quickly stepped down the escalator and hid behind a kiosk where the employee there was trying to sell sunglasses to an elderly couple. Turning slowly, she looked around the side of the kiosk. She saw two people run into the mall from the door upstairs where she had just entered. They were a middle-aged, red-haired man and an older woman with unkempt white hair. Anise couldn't help but gasp when she saw them. She recognized the man as the person Brian had brought home from the dispensary who wanted to buy her amulet. The woman was the elderly lady who had fought her at Doreen's when she wouldn't sell it. She started hyperventilating and looking around for an escape. *What the hell am I going to do?*

Much to Anise's horror, the woman spotted her and pointed in her direction. *Oh, god! Now what?* With her heart beating out of her chest, Anise turned and fled out a different set of doors, which luckily weren't but fifty feet from her. Once outside though, she realized she needed another plan. Her bicycle was on the other side of the mall, not that she could outrun their car on her bike. She turned to her right and saw tired shoppers boarding the city bus. As fast as she could go, she ran toward the bus, which had loaded its last passenger and was pulling away from the curb. As her feet pounded the sidewalk, she was glad she'd decided to wear flats today instead of heels. "Stop! Wait!" she yelled, waving her arms and screaming at the bus. It rounded the corner and then stopped. She saw the tail end of it sticking out from the side of a department store. In a few seconds, she reached the bus and climbed aboard. She sat down near the back of the bus and turned to look out the window. She saw the man and older woman running toward the bus as well. Breathing heavily, she turned to see if the bus driver was going to wait for them, too. "Go! Please!" she mouthed desperately to the driver who was looking at her in the rear-view mirror. The woman driving the bus gave her a slight nod.

As the bus pulled out onto the highway, her pursuers faded into the distance. The old woman, shaking her fist, disappeared completely when the bus rounded a curve. Anise slid down in the seat and closed her eyes with relief. Her mind began swirling. She felt so foolish for falling for Nate's lies. He'd never wanted her; he'd just wanted her amulet all along. He was working with the man and woman who were now chasing her in order to get it. But if he was working with them, why would he warn her that they would kill her? Maybe he was trying to get it first? Or maybe he was just trying to scare her into handing it over. She couldn't guess the answers to these questions, but she figured they all must know something about her amulet's power.

Her thoughts turned to Brian when she remembered Nate asking if he was okay. Anise knew he was alive, but she grew worried anyway and grabbed her phone to check her voicemails. The first was from Brian at about 5:30 a.m. His words were slurred, and she had to listen very carefully to understand his message. He said something about getting up to take a piss and finding two masked criminals in the bathroom rooting through the drawers. One of them pricked him with something sharp, and he collapsed, hitting his head on the toilet on his way down, and knocking himself out. A few minutes ago, he woke up and called the police. There was a short pause, and then Brian said that he had to go, as he thought he was going to be sick. The next voicemail was from Nate at 9:00 a.m., asking her to call him back, please. His tone almost sounded like begging. At 10:15 a.m., another voicemail from Brian asking her to bring some medicine for a stomachache as he'd been sicker than a dog all morning, and he could barely move. Also, he had said, the police didn't do anything but take a report because nothing had been stolen. The last notification on her phone was a missed call from Brian while she had been standing outside in the sun.

Nate looked like he was feeling sick, too, she recalled, trying to find the connection, if there was any. Her heart was still pounding as she desperately tried to think of what to do. She couldn't go to the police. What would she tell them? That even though she had no proof, there were unknown people chasing her, breaking into her apartment, and threatening her life because she wouldn't give them her magical amulet? That sounded ludicrous. Who would believe her? And what could they do even if they did believe? She covered her face with her hands and took a deep breath. Pulling the affirmation card out of her pocket, she read it again. *When you don't know what to do, do nothing. The answer will be revealed with time.*

Letting the advice from the card calm her, she settled in her seat and closed her eyes, letting her body relax. Suddenly, she knew which bus stop she needed. Her eyes flew open. She would go to the one person she knew who might actually believe her and be able to help her.

"Hon, are you okay? Do you need any help?" the driver asked Anise as she was about to deboard the bus.

"No, I'm okay, thanks," Anise replied, trying not to be rude in her hurry. She quickly stepped off the bus and started running down the sidewalk.

ANISE BOUNDED UP THE STEPS IN the museum and pounded on Jonathan Casley's office door. She was trembling and gasping for air.

"Anise! Hi!" he exclaimed when he opened the door. His look of surprise quickly turned to one of concern. "Are you okay?"

She was so out of breath, all she could do was shake her head *no*.

"Come in," he told her. "Sit here." He helped her to his desk chair. "Have you been running?"

She sat. "I need to talk to you," she said quietly to Jonathan between gasps. She jumped when she looked up and saw another person in the room. "In private, please," she added. She noticed the alarm on the elderly man's long face from her dramatic entrance and hoped he'd forgive her for her rudeness.

He rose out of his seat and touched Jonathan on the shoulder. "Is there anything I can do?" he asked with concern in his voice. He eyed Anise who hadn't yet caught her breath.

"Just give us a few minutes, Dr. Smithton," Jonathan replied, honoring Anise's request for privacy.

Dr. Smithton nodded. "I'll be in my office if you need me." He looked back at Anise as he left the room. "And straighten your tie," he tried to whisper to Jonathan, but Anise heard every word. "There's a lady present."

"I'll get you some water," Jonathan told Anise and stepped into the hallway. Upon his return, he handed her a paper cup full of cold water, and she took it gratefully. She noticed his tie had been straightened.

"So what's going on?" he asked. His worry could be seen in every wrinkle of his brow.

Sipping on the water, Anise tried to explain her predicament to him. "The amulet," she began, speaking very quickly, "is real. This is no replica. It's real, and it protects me. I didn't get hit by the lamp, and people are chasing me. Who else knows about this?" A pause to breathe made her realize how panicked she was, and the look on Jonathan's face told her that she wasn't making much sense. "Please don't look at me like that. I'm just really freaking out here!"

Jonathan gave her a warm smile. "It's okay," he told her. "You're safe here. Now slow down, and tell me who's chasing you." He grabbed another chair from the tiny conference table in the corner of his office and pulled it next to her.

"I don't know," she replied, wringing her hands nervously and twisting her garnet ring around her finger. "But I think they're going to kill me."

"Can you describe them?" he asked.

His voice sounded kind and full of concern. Anise let herself start to relax. She told him about the old woman, middle-aged, red-haired man, and Nate and how they all tried to take her amulet. "I ran away from all of them and luckily lost them. I don't know how or if they're all connected." She put her face in her hands. Too many emotions were flowing through her. She was scared for her life and was shaking. She was embarrassed for her frantic behavior in front of Jonathan. She was humiliated at having been fooled by Nate so easily and so angry at herself for being heartbroken by his betrayal. A few tears ran down her cheeks.

"Okay, well, I promise you're safe here," Jonathan repeated. He grabbed a box of tissues from his desk and held it out to her.

She took one and dabbed her eyes. "I know it's unbelievable, but it really does work," she continued emphatically. "I had washed it under the bathroom tap at home and put it in a sunny window. Later that night, my boyfriend, well, my ex-boyfriend now, threw a lamp at my head and—"

Jonathan interrupted her. "Is that what you meant when you said you didn't get hit by a lamp? Did he hurt you? Are you okay?"

"Yes, I'm fine," Anise said, holding up her hand to signal that she wasn't done telling her story. "What I wanted to tell you is that the lamp was flying right at my head, and at the last second it changed direction and missed me. It was just like your battle-ax example in that old book. His aim was perfect, and I didn't move, but it still missed me. The amulet protects me, and it glows when it does."

Jonathan let out the breath he was holding in. "Do you have somewhere safe you can stay?" he asked her.

"I'm not worried about Brian right now," she said, slightly annoyed that he wasn't understanding. "I'm worried about the people who are after me because of this," she continued, touching her fingers to the amulet. Jonathan was looking at her like she should be in a padded cell. "Okay, I know how it sounds, and I can tell you don't believe me. I don't blame you, but I can prove it to you."

"You don't have to do that, Anise," Jonathan said. "Is there anyone I can call for you?"

"No!" she exclaimed in frustration. "Here," she said, getting up and handing him the paperweight from his desk. "Throw this at my head and you'll see."

"I would never throw anything at you. No one should ever be throwing anything at you." His words were adamant, and the concern in his expression grew.

"Fine," she said. "I'll do it myself." She tossed the paperweight into the air and stood right underneath it. It hit her square on the head. "Ow! What the hell?" she complained loudly, rubbing her head.

Jonathan quickly picked up the paperweight and kept it in his hand. "Please don't do that again," he said. "Are you okay?"

"I think so," she mumbled, rubbing her head. "Why didn't it work? Am I forgetting something about the legend?"

He paused, seemingly trying to figure out the right thing to say.

"Please, Jonathan. Humor me."

He frowned but submitted to her wishes. "According to the legend, the amulet only protects you from those who have an intention to do you harm. Your intention was to prove something to me, not hurt yourself."

"Oh, that's right." She'd forgotten about that part. Her fingers felt a lump forming under her hair.

"What can I do to help? Can I drive you to a friend's house? Or buy you lunch in the cafeteria downstairs?"

"No, all I need is for you to humor me again, just for a few minutes. If you don't want to throw the paperweight, then fine. How about the box of tissues? And please, have the intention to hit me with it."

He frowned and paused for a moment. "All right," he agreed, holding his hands up in defeat. "I will be a gentleman and throw this box of tissues at you."

She laughed at his joke. "Thank you. I'm ready." She faced him and waited.

He raised his arm to throw the box and lowered it again. "Are you sure...?"

"Throw it!" she demanded.

He tossed the box of tissues gently. It headed straight for her nose, but right before it reached her, it turned, hitting the wall to her left. It fell to the ground and bounced once before landing on its side.

"What the...?" Jonathan looked surprised. "It must have been the way I threw it. Let's try it again."

Anise handed him the tissue box and said nothing. She figured it would take several tries before he'd believe it.

He threw it again, a little harder this time, and wore a look of concentration. Again, it headed straight for Anise's nose. Just before it would have collided with her face, it turned and started flying in the exact opposite direction, back toward Jonathan. It landed on the floor right in front of his foot. He stood still with his mouth gaped open.

"Did you notice it's glowing?" Anise asked. "It's a soft glow, especially in the light."

Jonathan switched off the overhead lights to better see the glow of the amulet. "Holy shit!" he exclaimed. "That's amazing!" He threw other various office supplies at her that wouldn't make too much noise upon landing and got more and more excited with each test they conducted.

"Anise, I'm sorry I didn't believe you earlier," he apologized when their testing was complete. He looked so genuinely sorry that she forgave him instantly.

"As long as you believe me now," she replied, relieved.

"I do," he said. "And I promise I'll help you figure out who's chasing you and how they know about the amulet."

Chapter 12

Nate hadn't budged from the curb where he'd sat down to talk to Anise several minutes prior. Although much improved from the night before, he still felt sick from the poison and didn't want to move. Being in the sun and sitting still was helping slightly. He'd attempted to stand and slow his two cohorts down, but the world had started spinning, and they'd pushed right past him to run after Anise. If he hadn't stayed seated, he would've passed out. Slowly, he sipped on the water he'd brought in his backpack to rehydrate.

Looking through the glass doors of the mall, it had been funny to watch the old hag and her evil spawn try to run after Anise who was much younger and in better shape than either of them. Or at least it would've been if the situation weren't so grievous. When they were out of Nate's line of vision, he put his head in his hands and tried to will himself to feel better. He wouldn't be able to do much to help Anise in this condition.

As much as he didn't want to see either of them just then, Nate waited for them to return and tell him what happened. They came out of the mall and stopped at the curb where he sat.

"What are you doing here?" Dan asked.

Nate looked up at him. "I was making one more

attempt to get the amulet," he replied. "But obviously, that didn't work. What happened with you? Did you catch her?"

"No!" screeched Grace. "Thanks to this candy-ass, the girl escaped on a bus!"

"How is that my fault, Mother?" demanded Dan. The two argued back and forth about the appropriate way to assign blame, while Nate fantasized about the bus running over the both of them.

"Well, now what are we going to do?" yelled Grace, as she pulled on her hair. "Someone better help me come up with a good plan and quick!" Her eyes were narrowed and dripping with venom when she looked at Nate.

Nate began hatching a plan of his own. He knew that if he didn't do something that pleased the old hag soon, she would have no qualms about getting rid of him. If he wanted to stop Grace from killing anyone else, the first needless death he had to prevent was his own. "I just want to apologize to the both of you," he said, getting up from the curb slowly and reaching out to grab the nearby trash can for balance. "I know that I failed you both in this mission. You were right, Grace; I was weak and let you do all the dirty work. I screwed up. I don't deserve another chance, but I want to prove myself to you, if you'll let me. I think I know where Anise went."

She let out a snort. "Why are you so humble all of a sudden? Do you think that makes you sound more sincere, you lying sack of shit?"

Nate sighed. "Fine, I was laying it on thick. But I really am taking responsibility for my failures, and I wanted you to know."

She gave him a look that said she didn't believe him.

Nate continued. "I've spent enough time with Anise to know where she went. Let me prove myself to you. Unless you have a better plan."

Grace glared at Nate. To Dan she said, "Go get the car."

✳✳✳

"So, HOW DO YOU THINK WE should start?" Anise asked Jonathan.

"The man who was in my office when you first got here was my supervisor I told you about before. His name is Dr. Smithton. He's the expert on ancient artifacts from Mallandia. We were actually about to start discussing your amulet when you knocked on the door. I think we should get him back in here and find out everything we can about it."

"Okay," agreed Anise. "Let's do it."

Jonathan stepped out of his office to see if his supervisor would still be available for their meeting. Anise looked around the small room while she waited for Jonathan to return. His office walls were completely bare and the only source of light was the fluorescent fixture above her head. The tiny conference table sat in the corner. On one side of his desk was a picture of Jonathan with three people who resembled him greatly. Judging by their ages, Anise assumed they were his parents and sister. On the other side was a wire pencil holder in the shape of a guitar. The middle had stacks of papers, a laptop, and measuring tape.

After a few minutes, Jonathan and the older man that Anise had seen when she first arrived walked into the office. The older man wore an expertly tailored, light gray pinstripe suit, a lavender tie with small white polka-dots, and a pocket square to match. His full, white hair sat in perfect waves on his head. He was far past the average age of retirement and boasted an impressive height. Anise noticed he was almost as tall as Brian. He towered over Jonathan who wore a brown button down shirt, again too large for him, and a forest green tie that had fraying edges. Jonathan was probably a couple inches shorter than Nate. Anise rubbed her brow in an attempt to get Nate out of her head.

"This is Dr. Morty Smithton," Jonathan said, introducing them. "Dr. S., this is Anise Viston. She's the owner of the amulet I told you about."

"Well, hello, Anise," said Dr. Smithton in a kind voice. "It's a pleasure to meet you, young lady."

"Hello, Dr. Smithton," replied Anise. "It's very nice to meet you, too."

"I do hope you're feeling better," Dr. Smithton added, as his light gray eyes looked at her with concern.

"Yes," she answered him. "I am. Thank you. I am *so* sorry for interrupting your meeting earlier. But it really was an emergency."

"No apologies necessary," he responded, his kind eyes giving her a warm smile.

"I showed Dr. Smithton the pictures I took of the amulet," Jonathan said to Anise.

"Yes," the older man agreed, "but they were a little hard to see, as they came out too dark. May I see the actual amulet?"

"Of course," replied Anise. She removed the amulet from around her neck and handed it to him.

Dr. Smithton put on his glasses and took the amulet. He carefully examined the metal, stones, and the incantation on the back. "It's faint, but it's definitely there," he mumbled to himself. "Amazing!" he said out loud and stared at the amulet, his gaze growing distant as if his mind was elsewhere. "This is authentic," he said a few moments later as he handed it back to Anise. "How on earth did you come to possess it?"

She explained to him about it being her graduation present from a family friend who found it in a thrift store donation bag.

"Well, how fortuitous for you," he commented.

"Dr. S.," interjected Jonathan, "could you tell us what you were going to tell me earlier? More about the amulet and the legend itself?"

"And, if possible, who else might know about the legend?" piped up Anise.

"Oh, certainly. I believe Jonathan told you the basics? About how each set came with a ring, amulet, and earrings, and what power each gave to the wearer?"

"Yes," replied Anise. "The amulet offers protection, the ring poisons the enemy, and the earrings provide strength."

"That's correct," continued Dr. Smithton. "And do you know how Mallandia fell?"

"Yes, we discussed that too," replied Jonathan.

"Wonderful, let's continue on with the legend from there," said Dr. Smithton. His speech was slow and deliberate. "It took them awhile, but after the Mallandians discovered that the rings were poisoning the land, all the Armor Jewelry was collected and destroyed. But one set of Jewelry was kept by an ancient ruler who believed that the kind of power possessed by the Jewelry shouldn't be so quickly dismissed. It was passed down through the generations of the ruler's descendants. The set was at some point broken up for reasons we don't know.

"Also passed down was the legend itself. Do you remember games of Telephone from when you were young children? One person would whisper a sentence into the next person's ear, that person would whisper it to the next, and so on down the line. By the time it got to the last person, the sentence was often frightfully different from how it began."

Both Anise and Jonathan nodded.

"Good. Then you know, when retold by several different people, how much a story can change over time. This one, for the most part, has been forgotten as it's so old. Only those with access to a few very old texts have heard of this legend in the present day. And I know of no one who's taught it in their classes in any university. They typically prefer to stick to teaching just the facts, you see. The text the two of you looked at yesterday is the only one of its kind in existence, to my knowledge anyway. I've read the other texts that had information about the legend when I was a much younger man, but it seems that they have been lost since then. Such a shame.

"Because of that, I would venture to guess that only my research team and my professor from when I was a young graduate student would know about this legend, and all but two of them have passed on. They may have mentioned the legend to family members, but it's likely their families wouldn't have done anything with the knowledge."

"Who are the two people who know about the Jewelry?" Anise asked, desperately wanting to know more about who could be chasing her.

"The only one still alive from my research group is a woman I'd known since my first day of college. She had the same major as I did, and we were in several classes together. Sharper than anyone I'd ever met before. Extraordinarily brilliant." Dr. Smithton paused, and his face looked distant, as if his thoughts were carrying him into the past. "Her name was Grace. She was simply lovely—until you got to know her. Then she became quite the shrew! I had much less contact with her after...well. That's an entirely different story. But she at least had an admirable passion for ancient artifacts.

"The other person with knowledge of the Armor Jewelry was my professor, Frederick Dromly."

"Wait, what? Are you talking about *the* Dr. Frederick Dromly?" Jonathan asked excitedly. "The famous archeologist?"

"Yes, that would be him," Dr. Smithton said. "Wait here." He got up and left the room.

"Wow!" Jonathan exclaimed. "This is amazing! I mentioned Dr. Dromly to you yesterday, right?"

Anise nodded. "Yes. You said he's the one who discovered the ancient Mallandian battlefield."

Jonathan's face was beaming. "How cool is that? I've

watched all his talks and appearances that I could find online. I have all of his books!"

"You're a big fan," Anise concluded, unable to stop smiling at Jonathan's excitement.

"I can't believe Dr. S. knew him personally!"

Dr. Smithton entered the room and handed a framed picture to Jonathan. "This is me with Dr. Dromly at Springfield University."

Anise peered over and saw a young Dr. Smithton standing next to another man. Dr. Dromly's appearance surprised her. With his fame and knowledge, she'd imagined a large body to accompany his large life. However, Dr. Dromly looked like he was almost a foot shorter than Dr. Smithton and was very slender. He appeared oblivious to his small stature though. He had a cape draped over his shoulders like a superhero, and the confidence in his countenance and stance made it seem like he considered himself to be ten feet tall. The photograph had been signed and said, "Go forth, Morty! Write your own story. – Frederick Dromly"

Write your own story. That was what Anise was trying to do ever since she'd stood on her mother's stoop after finding out about Les, vowing to change her life. She made a mental reminder to write that on a note card later. She was beginning to become a fan of Dr. Dromly herself. "Why is he wearing a cape?" she couldn't stop herself from asking.

Dr. Smithton shook his head. "Great question. He's worn a cape since the first time I saw him in class. No one knows why."

"Where is he now?" she wondered.

"He's in his mid-80s and enjoying his retirement in Destin. So, besides Professor Dromly, Grace, myself, my protégé Jonathan, and now you, Anise, I don't believe anyone else would know about the Jewelry, at least not to the extent that we do."

"What about the people you've worked with for a long

time here at the museum?" Jonathan asked. "You never talked with them about the Jewelry like you have with me?"

"Not to the same extent. They were focused on other pursuits. Besides, they've all long since retired and have other interests now."

"Are they though?" Jonathan wondered out loud. "It seems every time someone retires from the museum, they head to Florida to work on a secret project. It's kind of strange. What's going on over there?"

"I'm not entirely sure, but it's nothing to do with the Jewelry," Dr. Smithton said. "And a retirement in Florida certainly isn't an oddity."

"Could we get back to the old textbook you mentioned, Dr. Smithton?" Anise asked gently.

"Yes, good idea, let's focus. My team and I pored over that book, especially the section about the legend. We became quite enthralled with it, really, and had dreams that we might actually uncover the entire last surviving Jewelry set. We traced the lineage of the ruler as best we could and contacted his living descendants. It was a lot of work, but we were able to track down the owners of the earrings and of the ring. The earrings were in Egypt with an elderly man who had no family. Grace, the others, and I had visited him to see the earrings and make sure they were the actual artifact we were looking for. They were authentic and spectacular! An exquisite chalcedony stone so pale blue they were almost white. Just before he passed away several years ago, he donated the earrings to the Malawi National Museum in Egypt. They've been part of a traveling exhibit about Mallandia and have been all over the world. I've been trying to get them to come to our museum, but they're in such high demand it'll be at least a year before that can happen. However, they are currently at the history museum in Springfield.

"The ring," he continued, "belonged to a man by the name of Richard Woods up in Canada. Grace and I, along with our teammates, visited him many years ago. He has since passed on and the ring had been given to his nephew by the same name. I have recently been trying to convince this younger Richard Woods to loan the ring to the museum to add to the traveling exhibit, but he was very hesitant. Kept saying his mother wouldn't have approved of that. I actually called again just a few days ago, and his stepdaughter informed me of his and his wife's passing. Apparently, they were both murdered in their home just a few days prior. It was very sad. It was a break in, but it didn't look like much was taken. I'll need to wait for a more appropriate time to inquire about the fate of the ring.

"The amulet was never found," continued Dr. Smithton, looking at Anise, "until now." His smile showed his excitement. "I never thought I'd actually get to see it! Perhaps you might loan it to the traveling exhibit? I could make some calls and have it delivered with a courier service I use often for the transport of valuable items."

"Maybe..." Anise said. She thought about how the amulet had protected her from Nate and Brian. She felt safe when she was wearing it, especially now that people were chasing her. "It was a gift though, and I'm not sure I want to part with it."

"Certainly. You think on it," Dr. Smithton encouraged her.

"What does Grace look like?" Anise asked him. "Do you have a picture of her?"

"I'm afraid I don't," replied Dr. Smithton. "When she was a young graduate student, she had red hair and was considered quite the beauty. However, I don't know what she looks like today; I haven't seen the woman in years. Why do you ask?"

"Oh, just curious," Anise mumbled.

"Yesterday we were wondering what the incantation says," spoke up Jonathan.

"Well, I believe you know that there's a page missing from the text," replied Smithton. "The text mentions the incantation, so it's possible the actual meaning of it would be on the missing page. Although I wish I could answer that question, I just don't know. That page has been missing since the first time I laid eyes on that book."

"Dr. Smithton," began Anise, carefully. "What would happen if someone had broken into the Woods' home to steal the ring and then came after me for the amulet?"

"I'm not sure what you're asking me," replied Dr. Smithton.

"I guess what I want to know is...if it came down to the ring versus the amulet in a fight, which would win? The ring delivers poison, but the amulet is protective. Which is stronger?"

"That's an interesting question," Dr. Smithton said, "and one I've thought about many times before. The pieces were meant to work together, not against each other. And according to the legend, no one piece is stronger than another."

"Okay..." Anise said. "So then, what do you *think* would happen?"

"That's a little like asking the age old question of what happens when an unstoppable force meets an immovable object. But let's see if the three of us can figure something out together. Jonathan, what do you think?"

Jonathan wrinkled his brow in thought. "If it is like an unstoppable force meeting an immovable object... that's an impossible scenario. So, something would have to happen to stop them from meeting, or in this case, working against each other. Maybe they would each cancel out the power of the other. So if Anise wore the amulet and I wore the ring and tried to use it to poison her, nothing would happen."

"Yes, but it wouldn't be 'nothing', exactly," said Dr. Smithton. "If the ring was rendered ineffective, then that would mean the amulet was working. Both of their powers would have to be canceled out, like you said. So during the moment you try to poison her with the ring, the ring would be ineffective as would the amulet."

"So does that mean during that moment I would be vulnerable to being harmed in another way?" asked Anise.

"Precisely," said Smithton. "But only in that moment. It stands to reason that as soon as the pieces retreat to their own corners, if you will, their powers return. Of course, it seems there's another way that would stop the pieces from working against each other."

"What's that?" asked Anise immediately, wide-eyed, and hanging on to Dr. Smithton's every word.

"Well, I'm no physicist," he began, "but if the pieces don't simply shut down when used against one another, the opposing energies could very well destroy each other simultaneously."

"Would that happen right away or take some time?" Anise asked him. "And how destructive would the opposing energies be? Would they only destroy each other—or the people and things around them, too?"

Dr. Smithton laughed and held up his hands in a shrug. "I imagine that you could pit them against each other for a short period without worry. A good length of time, though, would likely end in destruction. As for your other questions, your guess is as good as mine. Thank goodness it's just a legend and nothing we'll ever have to worry about."

Anise looked at the ground.

"I think we should tell him," Jonathan said to her, touching her shoulder. "We could use his advice."

She nodded. "Dr. Smithton, when I came here earlier, I was being chased by people who want my amulet. Last night, they broke into my apartment when I wasn't home to look for it. My ex-boyfriend Brian was there, and he was really sick all night, for seemingly no reason. Because of that, I think they also have the ring and poisoned him with it."

"My dear, this is only a legend. The Jewelry doesn't actually possess any power. Even if these people who broke into your home have the ring, they couldn't possibly have poisoned your ex-boyfriend with it." Dr. Smithton looked at her the same way Jonathan had when he didn't believe her at first.

Jonathan and Anise exchanged a look.

"We need to show you something, Dr. S.," said Jonathan. He closed his office door as Anise handed him the paperweight.

Chapter 13

Nate sat on the steps just outside the Museum of Ancient History. The nausea had finally subsided, but his body was still weak. His jaw still hurt, too, although the swelling had gone down significantly. He watched as Dan walked away to scope out any other possible exit doors from the museum.

"Are you sure she came here?" Grace asked Nate as she scowled at him.

"Yes," he replied. "Last night she was telling me how she came here to talk to one of the curators about the amulet. She must have learned about the legend attached to it and has probably figured out by now that it's been protecting her. She probably wants more information about the legend."

"Damn it!" mumbled Grace.

"Why does that upset you?" Nate asked. "What don't you want her to find out?"

She ignored his questions. "When she comes out, we need to be ready for her."

"Do you have a plan?" asked Nate. "She has the amulet. What can you do?"

"We have the ring," Grace replied with annoyance in her voice. "Remember, I told you that it'll negate the protection of the amulet when I press the ring to her skin.

Then we can use this." Out of her purse, she pulled just enough of a gun to show him.

"What the hell? You can't just shoot her here on the street!" he hissed.

"Keep your voice down, you little shit," whispered Grace harshly. "Of course not here! We'll force her into the car, drive to the forest outside of town, and kill her there."

It felt like a gut punch to Nate. "If the amulet won't work because of the ring, why can't we just take it from her? I tried everything I could to get the amulet from her so you wouldn't hurt her. Why do you want to kill her now?"

"I don't need her trying to fight back or calling the cops! Besides, if she's learned about the legend, then she knows too much."

Nate didn't know what to do. There was so much more he wanted to say, but he felt the mental and emotional numbness wash over him as it always did when things got too overwhelming, and words wouldn't come out.

Dan returned from his mission of finding alternative exits. "There's a door on the side," he said, "and the parking garage is in the back of the building."

"Okay," said Grace. "I'll stay here at the main entrance. You two go make yourselves useful and man the other exits."

The two men walked around the side of the building. Nate claimed the parking garage as his post, and Dan manned the side door. In the alley right next to the parking garage entrance and exit, Nate sat on the ground and leaned against the side of the museum with his head in his hands. The alley smelled like urine and trash, which was bringing back the nausea Nate thought was over. He hoped he was right in thinking Anise would come out that way. She was scared, and it was doubtful she'd leave out the front. He thought about the last time he visited the museum and was pretty sure he recalled the side door being just an emergency exit, not one to be used otherwise, or else an alarm would go off. She would do best to come out the garage. And when she did, well, he didn't quite know what he'd say to her yet.

In his mind, Nate berated himself for leading Grace directly to Anise. He'd hoped that by finding Anise and taking the amulet once and for all, Grace would finally be happy, and neither he nor Anise would have to worry about their lives being in jeopardy. If he'd known Grace had a gun with plans to kill her anyway, he would've led them on a wild goose chase to another city, another state, another country. But of course Grace would have a gun with her; why didn't he think of that? He wasn't normally so careless. The ring's poison must've done something to his head. Since his plan hadn't worked out so far, he would have to come up with another idea and fast.

ANISE WATCHED DR. SMITHTON'S EYES GROW wide as he looked rapidly from Jonathan to Anise and back again, clutching his heart. "Are you trying to give an old man a heart attack?" he asked. "I can't believe it! The legend is true?" He stood up and sat back down again, as if he didn't know what to do with himself. "I can't believe what I just saw!" He laughed out loud.

When Jonathan had raised his arm to throw the paperweight at her, Anise almost laughed at Dr. Smithton's reaction which was something between a yell and a gasp. When the paperweight was on its way toward her face, she didn't flinch. Even though Jonathan had thrown it straight and with very good aim, it had simply turned at the last second as if something had physically pushed it off course. They had demonstrated the power of the amulet to Dr. Smithton a few more times and had let him throw something at Anise, too. Each time, the result was the same. She was never touched. "Amazing!" he exclaimed.

"Dr. Smithton," began Anise, "I'm really convinced that the older woman and the red-haired man have the ring. My ex-boyfriend Brian was very sick last night, and it looked like my...well, the younger man that tried to take the amulet—Nate—he looked like he might've been sick, too. And he, the other man, and the older woman have tried to take the amulet. They have to know about the power this Jewelry holds."

Dr. Smithton leaned back in his chair and crossed his arms. "I'd bet my life that the woman is Grace."

"The former classmate you told us about?" Jonathan asked. "The one from your grad school research group who knows about the legend?"

"Yes," confirmed Dr. Smithton. "And the red-headed man is almost assuredly her son Dan."

"We have to do something about this," said Jonathan. "If they have the ring, that means they were willing to kill Richard Woods and his wife for it. We can't let the Jewelry fall into the wrong hands. Who knows what they'd do with that kind of power? Plus, the artifacts themselves have existed for four thousand years, and someone needs to make sure they're protected."

Anise smiled at Jonathan gratefully. When she'd raced to the museum that day, the most she had hoped for was some further knowledge about the ring and amulet in order to help her make a decision on what to do next. She never expected to receive this much help from him or anyone.

"There's only one way to stop them," said Dr. Smithton. "We must become more powerful than they are by possessing the earrings. However, like I said, the earrings are not likely to be in this museum until next year, and since they're chasing you now, we can't possibly wait that long anyway. So, you must go to Springfield where the earrings are currently on display."

"Go to Springfield?" asked Anise, incredulously. "And do what—steal the earrings from the museum?" She laughed at the idea.

"Borrow them for an undetermined length of time," insisted Dr. Smithton. "For a *very* good cause. Imagine what will happen if you don't."

A pit started forming in Anise's stomach when she realized he was serious. "How would I know what's going to happen? I don't know them or what they're planning to do."

"Think about it," Dr. Smithton said. "They wouldn't sleep. They wouldn't age. They'd have super strength. They'd never get ill. They could do anything they wanted and go anywhere they wanted and couldn't be captured or harmed. They'd have a deadly weapon that couldn't be stopped."

"But we can stop them before it starts, Anise," Jonathan said. "I'm going to Springfield to get the earrings. As the owner of the amulet, and as someone who at least somewhat knows the people we're dealing with, I could really use your help."

Anise stared at them in disbelief. "The two of you can't possibly be serious!" she told the men. "If you think they'll be after the earrings next, then call the Springfield museum to warn them. Call the Springfield police department. Or call the local police or the Canadian authorities and tell them you believe they murdered Richard Woods for the ring. Wouldn't that be a better plan of action than risking our lives and committing illegal acts?"

"Not if you want to stay alive," Dr. Smithton told her.

"What do you mean?" The pit in her stomach grew larger, and a wave of dizziness hit her. She rubbed her forehead to help orient herself.

"Like I said, the few people who know the legend besides Grace are in this room. She'd know who called the authorities on her, and she'd have no problem killing anyone who got in her way. No, the best thing to do is to beat her at her own game."

"No!" Anise cried. Earlier, the amulet had made her feel safe. Now that she knew the ring could negate the amulet's protection and that her pursuers had the ring, keeping the amulet actually made her less safe. They'd find her, be able to take the amulet from her, and then what? Nate had told her they'd kill her, and Dr. Smithton just confirmed it. She took off the amulet and handed it to Jonathan. "I can't take this anymore! I'm tired of being chased by murderers! I'm done with this whole thing. I wish you the best of luck, Jonathan, Dr. Smithton. The amulet is yours now. I hope it protects you in Springfield." She turned on her heel and flew out of the room. Walking quickly down the hall, Anise felt a panic attack coming on. Seeing a restroom, she darted in and splashed some cold water on her face.

She pulled her stack of alphabetized affirmation cards out of her bag and quickly found the one she wanted. "I inhale tranquility," she said, clutching the card and taking in a breath. She let it out. "I exhale anxiety." Slowly, she repeated it a few times. It didn't help as much as she'd hoped, and she wanted another way to try to clear her mind. Reaching into her tote bag, she grabbed her sketchbook. Flipping through it to find an empty page, she saw her drawing of Les in the hospital room. Her thoughts turned to what he had said right before collapsing in front of her mother's house. "Ancient jewelry that has healing powers, that protects you..." she repeated, remembering his words. "He was talking about the Armor Jewelry! What was he trying to tell me?" she asked her reflection in the mirror. "Is it a coincidence that my brother knows about this Jewelry, or does my family have some sort of connection to it?" She paced back and forth in front of the stalls trying to ponder this new revelation. *Healing powers...* Stopping in her tracks, she thought about his desire to find a treatment for whatever it was that making him lose consciousness. She whispered to herself, "Could this Jewelry give him back the life he once had? Could it prevent his early death?"

She took a deep breath. If she ran away from this, she'd be making a decision out of fear and self-doubt, just like she used to do. But she was different now. She'd made the decision to change her life and she intended to see it through. Her reflection stared at her, asking an important question. *Who do I want to be in this situation?*

The answer came quickly. Reaching into her tote, she rooted through her affirmation cards again and pulled out the perfect one. "I can do this." She left the restroom and headed back to Jonathan's office. "I can do this. I can do this," she repeated down the hallway. Although her stomach churned and her arms felt numb, her steps were confident, and nothing would stop her.

She burst back into Jonathan's office where she found him and Dr. Smithton in a deep discussion. "I'm sorry," she said to them both. "I changed my mind. I'm in."

"Wonderful!" Dr. Smithton exclaimed.

Jonathan handed back her amulet. "What made you change your mind?"

Anise paused a moment and looked at the floor. She could tell them about Les, but she barely knew them. She'd already told Nate about him and wished she hadn't. Nate hadn't been who she'd thought, and she couldn't trust him with anything, much less her most personal life details. "It's a long story," was all she said.

"Okay," Jonathan said. "I'm grateful for your help."

Anise thought about Les's words again. *Ancient jewelry that has healing powers, that protects you...* Anise couldn't remember Jonathan saying anything about healing powers when they'd been looking at the old text in the museum library. "Dr. Smithton, does the Jewelry have healing powers?"

He gave her a surprised look. "What makes you ask that?"

She shrugged. "I was just wondering...you know, it's so powerful and all."

"It's interesting you should say that," Dr. Smithton said. "There is a part of the legend that mentions healing abilities, but as of yet, I've found no specifics."

"So you don't know which piece would be the one with healing powers?"

"I unfortunately don't," he replied. "Perhaps the earrings would make the most sense, although there could be an argument for the amulet as well. But for our purposes today, that's neither here nor there. Let's come up with a plan. Follow me. I think we'll be more comfortable in my office." After a quick walk down the hall, Dr. Smithton opened his door and waved Anise and Jonathan through.

Anise sat in one of the large, leather chairs at the conference table and looked around. Unlike Jonathan's tiny, bare office, Dr. Smithton's seemed comfortable and homey. A leather sofa had been placed next to the filing cabinet. He had a mini fridge and a coffee maker in the corner. Potted plants stood by the large window, and paintings of philosophers hung on the wall. She swiveled the chair around and lifted a few of the slats of the closed blinds to look out of the second-story window. "Oh my god!" she exclaimed. "That woman on the steps down there. She's one of the people who've been chasing me!"

"That little old lady?" asked Jonathan, as he looked out the window. "She seems so small and harmless."

"How does she know I'm here?" Another panic attack started and got worse with every passing second. Her heart beat faster, her palms started sweating, and she began to feel nauseated. "She's waiting for me to come out!"

"It's okay," Jonathan told her. "Take some deep breaths. I'll get you more water." He grabbed her cup and returned quickly.

Dr. Smithton looked out the window at the woman Anise had pointed out. He took a sharp breath in. "Grace!" he exclaimed. He sat down at the table with a look of dread on his face. "The two of you best be leaving for Springfield now. Grace is a very shrewd and determined woman. I have no doubt that her plan is to steal the earrings as soon as she has your amulet. You must understand that she knows as much about the Jewelry as we do, and she might even already have a plan to break into the Springfield Museum. Time is of the essence. You must get there before she does."

"Wait, you're not coming with us?" Anise asked him.

"I wish I could," Dr. Smithton said, "more than you know. But I have a respiratory condition that requires me to bring a tank of oxygen when I fly. There's no time for me to get what I need. The two of you need to leave immediately."

"But how am I going to leave?" asked Anise. She got up and started pacing. "Grace is waiting for me out front, and I bet Nate and the red-haired man—Dan, was it?—are probably waiting at different exits." Her breathing was rapid, and she felt faint from hyperventilating.

Jonathan led her to a chair and had her sit. "Don't worry," he said. "I'm parked in the parking garage below the museum. I'll walk out to the car to make sure no one is there. Then I'll come back and get you, and we'll drive out together. You can duck down in the seat. No one will see you." He had his hand on her shoulder, and his light green eyes looked at her reassuringly. Her anxiety started to dissipate, and she felt grateful for Jonathan's calming presence.

"Before you leave, I have something for you," Dr. Smithton said. "I've worked at other museums in my life, and the Springfield Museum is one of them. That was many years before now, but I visited about five years ago and the structure of the building had not changed. I still have a map of the layout in my files."

He rummaged through an overstuffed filing cabinet. "Here it is!" Dr. Smithton exclaimed. He unfolded the map and spread it out on the table. "Here's the front door," he explained, pointing to the map, "and over here is where they keep the rotating exhibits. The Mallandia exhibit should be in this large room in the back."

"Thanks, Dr. S.," said Jonathan. "This'll be a great help." To Anise he said, "Are you ready?"

"As ready as I'll ever be," she replied, still feeling anxious.

Jonathan's face suddenly dropped as he looked at Dr. Smithton who was sitting in his desk chair with his head in his hands. "Are you okay, Dr. S.?" Jonathan asked his mentor.

"This is wrong," Dr. Smithton said. "I can't ask you to do this. Either one of you."

"I want to," Jonathan replied.

"I do, too," said Anise.

"What you two don't realize is how dangerous Grace is. You were right, Anise, this idea is horrible. I can't ask either of you to risk your lives. I'm sorry I told you about the legend."

"No, Dr. Smithton, *you* were right. My life is *already* in danger," Anise reminded him. "Nate said that Grace won't stop until she has my amulet, and from what you've told me about her, I have to believe him. But you bring up a good point. There's no sense in putting both of our lives at risk. Jonathan can stay here while I go to Springfield."

"Absolutely not!" protested Jonathan. "Anise, there's no way I'd let you do this by yourself."

Anise looked at Jonathan with gratitude.

"Very well," Dr. Smithton said, with some reluctance still in his voice. "Remember, *do not* allow Grace to possess the earrings. Bring them back with you, and I will help you defeat her so she no longer comes after you."

They nodded at him. "We will," Anise assured him.

"And Jonathan...Godspeed."

DR. SMITHTON CLOSED HIS OFFICE DOOR after the young people left. Sighing, he wondered how their adventure would turn out and if he did the right thing by letting them go. Jonathan and Anise had no idea what they were up against. Grace was the most dangerous person he'd ever met.

Raising a slat of the blinds, he peeked through his second story window. There she was, sitting on the concrete stairs that led up to the museum doors. It'd been so long since he'd last seen her. She'd cut her formerly red hair into a shoulder-length style. It glimmered a shining white in the sun. Her lovely blouse looked expensive as did her shoes. She sat with her back straight and her head alert, turning every so often to take in the sights and people that surrounded her. She stood to stretch and looked straight at the museum doors with a scowl. Even the ugliest of expressions, however, couldn't change the radiance of her face. She was still beautiful. But like Belladonna or Oleander, she followed an undeniable rule of nature—the more beautiful something is, the more deadly.

JONATHAN LED ANISE TO A BACK elevator, and they took it down to the parking garage. Jonathan stuck his head out when the doors opened to make sure no one was around. They both stepped out into the garage. "Wait here," Jonathan told her.

Anise watched him walk to his car a few rows over, close to the opening of the garage that led to the alley and out to the street. He stepped slowly there and back, looking around him the entire time. "Okay, it looks clear to me. Come on."

They walked briskly to his older model black Honda Accord. He held the door for Anise on the passenger's side. She got in; he closed the door and got in on the driver's side. "Push the seat all the way back," he said, "so you can duck down on the floor." She did as he suggested, and he covered her with a blanket that he grabbed from the backseat. "Sorry it has dog hair on it. I'll have to call my parents when I get a chance and ask them to take care of Max tonight."

Jonathan started the car and backed out of his parking spot. Anise's heart started beating rapidly again, and she felt like she was suffocating under the hairy blanket. *I can do this,* she told herself.

"We're driving up the ramp that leads out of here now," he told her. "I don't see anyone at all," he continued, once they were out of the garage. "Let me drive just a few more blocks away, and then you can come out from hiding." After a minute, he lifted the blanket. "Okay, Anise, come on out."

She threw off the blanket and plopped into the front passenger seat. "I'm so relieved we made it! That seems like it was entirely too easy!"

"Doing okay?" he asked her.

"Yeah!" she replied, calming down now that they were out of immediate danger. She sighed and leaned back in the seat. Her text notification sounded, and she grabbed her phone. One message from Brian.

Brian: Where are u? Come home. I need that stomachache medicine.

She uttered a grunt of disgust at her phone. Why was he still in the apartment? They had broken up. What would be the best response? *Who do I want to be in this situation?* She wanted to never talk to him again or at least tell him that where she was and what she was doing was none of his business. On the other hand, if she told him that or ignored his text, he'd explode again, possibly sell more of her things, or leave the apartment in complete shambles, which she would have to pay for. And with what money? She didn't want to concoct a lie, but it seemed like the easiest way out for now. Joy had once told her that the best lies are mostly truths.

> **Anise: Being sent on a business trip. Hope you're feeling better. Not sure why you're still at my apartment. Please call Corinne and Ray and have them help you move.**

There. Only two words were a lie. One if you didn't include "trip." Hopefully, he would buy it. She was about to put her phone away when the text notification sounded again.

Brian: *Where r u going*

Anise sighed. If she didn't tell him, he'd check her banking information and be able to figure it out for himself. It wouldn't be the first time he'd spied on her.

> **Anise: Springfield.**

Jonathan looked over and saw she had her phone out. "Could you go to the airport's website and see if they have any flights leaving for Springfield soon?"

After searching, she told him, "They've got one that leaves in two hours."

"Perfect. Let's make sure we're on it."

Chapter 14

Several hours later, it was closing time for the museum. Nate sighed with relief as he checked his watch. Anise was safe—at least for the moment. He also didn't feel sick anymore, but his body was still a little weak and he wanted to stay sitting down. He closed his eyes and leaned his head and back against the brick wall. From his position by the parking garage, he could hear Grace storming around the side of the building, her heavy, stomping footsteps echoing in the alleyway. The footsteps stopped for a moment. "The museum is closed!" she yelled, presumably at Dan near the side door, so angry she was sputtering. The footsteps resumed. When they stopped again, Nate opened his eyes to see Grace and Dan glaring down at him. "The museum is closed!" she said again to him.

"Yeah, I heard you the first time you said it. Wanna keep your voice down?"

"I thought you said she was in there!"

"I'm sure she was. She must have slipped by us."

Grace groaned with exasperation. "So you saw nothing? Heard nothing?"

"Nothing," Nate lied. A few hours prior, he had heard a man say, "Wait here." Nate had peered into the parking garage and saw Anise pressed up against the wall by the elevators, shaking like a mouse in a trap. He'd moved to the other side of the dumpster, so they wouldn't see him when they drove off. The man must have been the curator she'd mentioned before. Nate hoped for her sake that they had a good plan.

"Well," continued Grace with a huff. "I know she didn't come out my door. I didn't take my eyes off it all day. And she couldn't have come out Dan's door. It's just one small side door. She would have had to push her way past him to get out." She glared at Nate, shaking her head. He looked back at her without reacting, waiting for the inevitable explosion. Both of her fists grabbed her hair by the roots and pulled. "I can't believe you screwed up everything again!" There it was. As Grace berated Nate, he thought about Anise and wondered what she was going to do next. "Are you even listening to me, Nate?" Grace asked him.

"Yup."

"What did I just say?"

"What matters more is what are we going to do next?"

"Oh, sure," Grace said sarcastically. "Always leave everything up to me. We brought you in to help! You're really losing your touch, Nate!"

"I think I have an idea, Mother," Dan chimed in. "I still have her boyfriend's phone number from when I was trying to buy the amulet from him. Maybe he knows where she is. Let me borrow your prepaid phone so he doesn't recognize my number. Nate, what's the name of the company Anise works for? It's a market research survey company, right?" Dan asked.

"None of your business. You both need to drop this shit. It's gotten way out of hand. The Jewelry is powerful, I get it, but what are you actually going to use it for? Is everything we've done worth it? If you know about it, I'm sure others do, too, and eventually, one of them will take you down."

Dan stood there with a look of contemplation. "He's

got a point, Mother. What *is* your intention for the Jewelry? Stealing artifacts from museums is one thing. But now...we've killed people."

"Lorelei would be ashamed of you," Nate told him, trying to capitalize on Dan's hesitation.

Dan nodded, his eyes threatening to spill over.

Grace sighed with an eye roll. "Are you really that boneheaded?" she asked her son while pulling on her hair again. "He's manipulating you! Don't be such a pathetic candy-ass, Dan! Take some authority, and handle this! My god, sometimes I think you're just as weak as he is! Come on, do something—you're embarrassing me and yourself!"

Dan opened his mouth to respond, but before he got a word out, Grace began screaming. "It's a cast iron pan!" she yelled. "Put it down! Put it down!" She covered her head, ducked, and screamed again. "No!" She began crawling away on her hands and knees.

Nate groaned in exasperation. Her hallucinations were ridiculous. Always with the insects or a cast iron pan.

"Mother!" Dan grabbed a pill from her purse and pushed it in her mouth. "Don't spit it out this time!"

Breathing heavily, Grace spit out the pill and stood up. "I don't need a pill, you candy-ass!" She firmly pulled on her hair as she winced. "What I need is for you to take care of him and find Anise," she said, pointing a finger at Nate who was still sitting on the ground. "You know my hallucinations are worse when I'm stressed, and he's making everything worse! Are you going to be a man, or do I have to take care of everything?"

Dan's face turned red and his brown eyes narrowed. He looked from his mother to Nate and back to Grace. He turned and kicked Nate in the gut. "Tell me where Anise works, you little shit!" Dan kicked him again. "Tell me, now, before I fucking kill you!"

Nate covered his aching gut with his hands as he

doubled over. He knew these two were happily violent, but even he was surprised with the number of death threats he'd received from them over the last few days. He'd gone on several heists at museums with them in the past, however, he hadn't been prepared for what occurred at the Woods residence, never in his life thinking that any of these artifacts were worth killing another human being over. If Grace killed Anise too, he'd never forgive himself. He hadn't felt guilty about any of the other crimes he'd committed, but he felt sick about the deaths of the Woods couple he'd witnessed and sorry for how he'd hurt and scared Anise.

Until now, his only relationships with women had been either sexual or out of obligation, so he found it strange how easy it was to care about Anise. He'd continued with his attempts to obtain the amulet both to keep Anise alive and for the information he'd been promised, but he was beginning to rethink the importance of holding on to a past that was gone for good. Would that information they promised really help him?

Anise had treated him with kindness and respect. She'd even been moved by and understood the value of the park he'd saved unlike anyone else he'd tried to share it with. She had a heart with a rare purity. Never in his life had he met a woman with an innocence so beautiful that it made him want to be the one to protect it.

As he looked up at Dan's angry face and thought about his cohorts' obsession over the Jewelry, he knew that neither Dan nor Grace would ever have any interest in the perpetuation of anything beautiful—and that any information they offered him would probably be a lie anyway. He was angry that he'd let his desperation dull his intelligence. They had to be stopped.

Slowly, Nate stood, his hands forming fists. "I may be weak from the poison," he told Dan. "But I can still kick your ass. Do you remember what happened last time? Your face won't be recognizable when I'm through with you."

The fear in Dan's eyes grew as Nate stepped toward him. He started sweating and looked around. Dan darted behind Grace and held on to her shoulders. "I know you wouldn't hit a woman," he said.

"This is what you call being a man?" she screeched at her son. "Get the hell off me you candy-ass!" she cried, brushing his hands off her shoulders. "While you two candy-asses were exchanging pathetic threats, I found out where Anise works." She held up her phone. "It's the only market research survey company in town. Bradley Field Services. And you," she said, turning to Nate. In one swift motion, she removed the gun from her purse, cocked it, and reached up to press the barrel against his forehead. "Are you with me or against me?"

Nate held up his hands to indicate his surrender. "With you," he lied to save his life.

"I'm holding you to that," she told him. "If you cross me or refuse to help, you won't live another day."

Dan sheepishly took her phone when Grace handed it to him and dialed Brian's number. "It's ringing," he told Grace.

"I want to hear!" Grace hissed.

Dan put the speaker on.

"This is Brian."

"Brian, hello," said Dan. "This is Mike; I'm the manager at Bradley Field Services. This call is about Anise. She listed you as an emergency contact."

"Is she okay?"

"Well, that's what I'd like to know. You see, Anise left for lunch today and never came back to work. I was hoping you might know where she went and if she's all right. I can't seem to reach her on her phone."

"She told me she was going to Springfield on a business trip." Brian paused. "It seems to me that if you're really her manager, you would've known that."

Dan hung up.

"Springfield?" said Grace. Suddenly, her eyes opened wide. "Do you know what's in Springfield?"

Dan shook his head. Nate was leaning against the brick wall of the museum still holding his abdomen.

"The earrings! They're on display in the Springfield Museum right now. She's one step ahead of us!"

Even with as much pain as he was in, Nate had to laugh at Grace's displeasure.

"Shut up! SHUT UP!" she screamed at him. "You just wait and see if there's anything to laugh about once I get what I want!"

Nate wanted to tell her, "Yeah, good luck with that," but he knew better. Grace would see that as a threat, which it would have been. He had to keep humoring her just a little while longer.

"Let's get to the airport," suggested Dan. "Anise doesn't know what she's doing; she'll never get the earrings before we do."

BRIAN SAT ON THE COUCH, UTTERLY confused. He didn't know what to believe. Who was lying to him—Anise? Or the man on the phone? That phone call was very suspicious. Why would her supervisor not know where she is *after* sending her on a business trip? He must be the one who was lying. On the other hand, why would a company that's paying only slightly more than minimum wage send a brand-new employee out of town on a business trip at the last minute? He picked up his phone and called the number of the person who had said he was Mike from Anise's work. It went to a voicemail system that repeated the number and requested that a message be left. He hung up and looked online for the phone number of Bradley Field Services. He dialed the number, hoping someone would still be there to pick up. After three rings, someone answered.

"Bradley Field Services, this is Dawn."

"Hi Dawn, my name is Brian, and I'm Anise Viston's boyfriend. I just got a call from Mike at your office, and he said that he was worried because Anise never came back from lunch. Anise told me she was being sent on a business trip to Springfield. So, I don't know what's going on, and I'm really worried. Can you clear things up for me?"

"Well, Brian, it's true that Anise never came back from lunch. Honestly, we thought she decided to quit without giving notice. It happens a lot in our office; this job is not for everyone. But we don't send our mall employees on business trips. And we don't have a Mike working in our office, so I'm not sure who called you. I've been the only one here for the last couple of hours."

Brian was silent. Something was very wrong.

"Brian," Dawn continued, "I really like Anise. If she needs anything, I'm more than happy to help in any way I can. Please have her call me, so we can straighten out what happened today."

"Thanks for your help," Brian said, and hung up the phone. He stayed still on the couch and tried to figure out what was happening. *So Anise is going somewhere and lying to me about it,* he thought to himself. *And some guy is looking for her, but he didn't sound like the guy I punched out last night. So who the hell is this guy, and why is he trying to find her?*

He decided to text her.

Brian: Some guy Mike called me from your work looking 4 u

Anise: There is no Mike at my work.

Brian: Then who the hell was he

Anise: No idea. What did you tell him?

Brian: That u r going 2 Springfield

Anise: Why would you tell a stranger that?!

Brian: He seemed 2 know u. R u fucking him 2?

Anise: I'm about to get on the plane. I don't have time for this. Move out. I'm texting Corinne so she can help you.

Brian threw his phone down on the couch next to him in disgust. How many guys was she cheating on him with? He grabbed one of the paintings she'd made off the wall and smashed it over the end table. He threw the cracked frame and both halves of the painting on the carpet. "Fuck this, I'm done with her games," he said out loud to himself. His stomach was finally feeling better, so he headed to the kitchen to get a beer. He got to the fridge but paused when he touched the door handle. *What if she's in some kind of trouble? Maybe that guy who called is chasing her for some reason, and I just gave away her location. Maybe she's being forced to lie to me by someone who's kidnapped her.* He pressed his lips together, thinking how unlikely that scenario would be. *Or maybe she lied because she's going on a trip with that Nate guy. Maybe she forgave him for being a dick last night. Maybe Dawn at the survey place just didn't want to give me any information because she doesn't know who I am. Or maybe Anise asked her to lie if I called the office. Dawn said she liked her; maybe they're friends.*

Brian took his hand away from the refrigerator and walked into their bedroom. Sifting through Anise's folder marked "Important" in the filing cabinet, he found her list of accounts and online usernames and passwords. Grabbing his phone, he logged on to her account at the local bank and correctly answered the security questions that popped up. He clicked on debit card transactions. This bank advertised that they post transactions made with a debit card within a few minutes of the occurrence—and that would come in very handy right now. He saw that she had made a purchase at The Airport Café and bought a plane ticket to Springfield from the discount airline. So she wasn't lying about that. But if she really was going for work, then her company would have paid for the ticket. If she was kidnapped, then her abductor probably wouldn't use her debit card to buy a ticket for her, as that could easily be traced, obviously. It was looking more and more like she was going voluntarily for some reason. *I bet she's with him*, Brian thought, picturing Nate. He could feel his face getting hot with humiliation and anger.

He sat still for a few minutes, trying to decide what he wanted to do. He could forget about it and grab a beer, as had been his first reaction. That would calm him down, and he could call Hailey. For a while now he'd been fantasizing about having the apartment to himself so he could invite her over. Her roommate was always home when he went to her place, and the roommate knew Anise from a class they had together a year or two ago. Brian was always very nice to the roommate out of fear she'd tell Anise everything. She always looked at him in a very judgmental way whenever he was over there. It would be nice to have the extra privacy. *What Anise is doing is very different from what I'm doing*, Brian told himself again to ease his guilty conscience. *For me, it's just sex. For her, it's more than that. She really likes this asshole.* Brian pictured Anise with Nate again, unable to get how she'd kissed him out of his head.

He tried to forget about it, or at least calm down, as Corinne always tried to get him to do. He picked up the phone to call Hailey but put it back down again. Hailey couldn't help him right now, and he wasn't much in the mood to see her anyway. He couldn't get Anise out of his mind. The thought that she might be with someone else tortured him so much that he started pacing the floor and could hardly breathe from the rage.

It would serve Anise right if Hailey came over tonight, Brian told himself in an attempt to think about something else and calm down. He grabbed his phone and dialed her number. To his surprise, a man answered.

"Yeah?"

"Who is this?" demanded Brian.

"You called me, dude. Who the hell are you?"

"This is Hailey's phone. Where is she?" Brian asked.

At that moment, he heard Hailey calling to the man on her phone. "Hey, are you coming back to bed?" she giggled. "Wait, is that *my* phone? Who is it?"

"I'll be right there, babe," the man said to her.

He then turned his attention back to Brian. "Hailey's busy," he said before hanging up.

Stunned, Brian sat and stared at his phone for a few seconds before the anger kicked back in. "What the hell?" he yelled. "Is every woman I know a goddamn whore?" In his rage, he stood up and put his fist through the wall.

His thoughts turned back to Anise and how she might be with Nate at that moment. Not knowing for sure was the hardest part for him. He felt his rage growing exponentially, and it prompted him to take action. Brian went back into the bedroom and opened Anise's jewelry box. Lifting up the felt-covered ring holder, he grabbed the cash she kept there for emergencies.

"Only $250?" he said. She once told him she'd put $500 aside for emergencies. "Oh, right," he mumbled, remembering he'd taken the other $250 out of the jewelry box the week before. His workman's comp checks had stopped, and he didn't want Anise to know and start giving him shit about getting a job again.

He checked the website of the discount airline and saw that the next plane to Springfield didn't leave until 6 o'clock the next morning. Brian didn't want to wait that long and couldn't afford to buy a plane ticket anyway—he had about $5 in his wallet and maybe $25 in his savings account. He'd stolen about $300 out of Nate's wallet before tossing him in the dumpster, but he'd already spent it on a new video game, a few cases of beer, and the more expensive weed at the dispensary. However, he did have Anise's $250 in emergency cash, and as far as he was concerned, this constituted an emergency. She might still be in trouble of some kind, and if she was, he wanted to help her. But if she was with *him*, he *had* to know right away. That money should buy him just enough gas to get to Springfield and back; his car got very good gas mileage. He'd keep checking her account online to see where she was using her debit card, and when he saw what hotel she checked into, he'd know where to go. But he needed to start out now, as Springfield was a fourteen-hour drive away. That way, he'd get there by morning and could surprise or confront her in the lobby of the hotel when she came down to leave for the day.

He was almost out the door when his cell phone rang. He answered it without first looking at the caller ID. "What?" he demanded of the person on the other line.

"Brian? It's Corinne. Are you okay?"

"Yeah, it's just not a good time right now. I'm on my way out. I have to take care of something."

"You sound angry. Can you do me a favor, please, and sit down for a few minutes?"

Brian knew exactly what Corinne was thinking. She knew what Brian was capable of when he let his anger get the better of him. When he became obsessed with a thought, it would completely take over his mind and behavior, and he wouldn't be capable of thinking of anything else. As children, she had witnessed him get out of control to the point of becoming violent. The aggression was never directed toward her, and she was the only one who could ever get him to calm down. However, he'd thrown things, put his fist through walls, and gotten into fights at school or in the neighborhood.

As he got older, he had grown out of it at least somewhat, and his violent behavior lessened once he got into high school. But when something extremely important to him went wrong, he could easily still feel the uncontrollable rage that had been more common in his earlier years. He knew the alcohol he drank helped him and calmed him down, but she kept nagging him about it, telling him it actually made things worse. She'd been working with him on his anger since she received her degree and had been so proud of him when he told her of the progress he'd been making. There had been times recently where he looked his anger triggers in the face and remained calm. Tonight though, there was no way that was going to happen.

Still, he loved his sister and knew she was just trying to help him. He complied with her request. "Okay, I'm sitting."

"Thank you. Now what's going on? Is it Anise? She texted me and said you two broke up."

"We didn't. She's just mad. You can't take her seriously when she gets like that."

"She seemed serious to me. She said you weren't listening to her and asked if I could make sure you get all your stuff out and leave your key on the counter. Ray and I are happy to help you move, Brian. And you can stay with us as long as you need to."

"It's not a good time, Corinne; I have to get on the road."

"If you're going to drive, you need to be calm. Where are you going?"

"It's a long story that I don't have time for."

"Give me the condensed version."

"Fine." Brian spoke quickly, and he heard the trembling in his own voice. He was sure Corinne would think that he was on the verge of a meltdown. "Anise is flying to Springfield tonight. She said it was for work, but her boss doesn't know anything about it or why she left work early today without telling anyone. Last night I caught her on a date with some guy, and I punched him out. Some other guy just called trying to find her and said he was her boss, but he's not. She's lying to me, that guy is lying to me, and I don't know what's going on."

"Oh, sweetie, I'm so sorry she's seeing someone else. Did you try talking to her about it?"

"No, I can barely look at her! She ran away last night, and I haven't seen her since. Then I get this text from her that she's going to Springfield."

"What do you mean she ran away? Why would she do that?"

Brian was silent, not wanting to relive it.

"Brian? Were you acting violent?"

Another pause. "Yeah."

"Okay, well, maybe she's just afraid to come home, and this is her made-up excuse to not see you for a couple days. So, what was your plan for tonight?"

Brian could hear the concern in her voice. "I'm going to drive there. If I leave now, I can get there by morning."

"And what are you going to do once you get there? Have you thought this through?"

"Yes. I'm going to wait for her in the lobby of her hotel so I can find out once and for all what the hell is going on."

"Brian, I've gotten to know Anise pretty well, and we both know that she has a really good heart. I know that the two of you have been experiencing some relationship distress lately, but I really don't think she would just run away with another man. If she's seeing someone else, that's unfortunate, and probably a result of the lack of communication between the two of you, which is the reason you're seeing Hailey. But we both know she isn't the type to do anything so extreme as to take an impromptu vacation, nor would she leave work early without telling anyone. I don't know for sure what's going on, but it sounds like she just needs some space."

Brian knew his sister's take on what was happening made sense and was probably true, but he didn't want to hear it. He had a knot in his stomach the size of a basketball, and it was urging him to go find Anise.

"I don't care!" he shouted. "I have to know what she's doing!"

"Sweetie, let me come over; we'll talk some more."

"No! I'm going. I love you, but I have to do this. Goodbye."

"I love you too, but Bri, please don't go—"

He hung up on her and walked out the door.

Chapter 15

Right after the flight attendant served her a Coke, Anise spilled it all over the tray table. "I'm so sorry!" she apologized. "I tend to spill things when I'm nervous," she giggled awkwardly as her cheeks burned. The flight attendant gave her an unamused stare and handed her several napkins and another Coke before serving Jonathan his cranberry juice.

Jonathan helped Anise mop up the carbonated mess. "Are you okay?" he asked her.

"No," she told him, still embarrassed at her clumsiness. She was glad they had the row of three seats to themselves so no one else had to see her like that. "My ex-boyfriend, Brian, texted me just before we boarded the plane. He told me some guy named Mike from my work called him asking for me, and Brian told him that I'm going to Springfield."

"Okay. So what?"

"So, there's no one named Mike where I work. Who was he?"

"You think Brian just gave your location to one of the men chasing you?"

"I hope not." Her stomach ached with frantic butterflies.

"Okay, well, tell me what you know about these people that might be following us to Springfield. We have to come up with a plan to get the earrings, and if we're going to have competition, I'd like to know what we're up against."

Anise twisted her garnet ring around her finger. "Grace, who Dr. Smithton knows, is the older woman who came into the thrift shop where I work and tried to buy the amulet from me. When I told her no, she started yelling and pulling on her hair. She had to be escorted from the shop. The middle-aged man, who Dr. Smithton said is Grace's son Dan, was the one who tried to buy the amulet from Brian in our apartment. And Nate is..." She paused, uncomfortably thinking of how to describe him.

"Nate is the guy you're dating? The one who told you to give the amulet to him, so Grace and Dan wouldn't kill you?"

"Right," Anise said, her cheeks burning again. "And I know Brian's still in my apartment, and I thought I made it clear that we're over, but I guess I must not have, and—"

"You don't have to explain," Jonathan interrupted her. The tone of his voice was kind and comforting. "No judgment here."

She smiled at him gratefully. "I should have gotten a Sprite or ginger ale," she said. "This caffeine isn't going to help my anxiety."

"Do you want my cranberry juice instead?" he asked her.

"That's kind of you, but no," she said. "I get an upset stomach when I get nervous, and soda is the only thing that helps."

"Maybe it'll help you to know that I'm just as nervous as you are," Jonathan told her.

"Really? You don't look nervous at all." She paused. "Can I ask you a question?"

"Of course," he replied.

"If we don't do this the right way, we're looking at prison time. The way you decided so quickly that you wanted to go to Springfield for the earrings was amazing to me. How can you make a decision like that so easily?"

"You know how powerful the Jewelry is," began Jonathan. "Think of what someone with bad intentions could do if they had super strength, couldn't be hurt, and were poisonous to the touch. You can't allow power like that to get into the hands of the wrong people. And when you know what the right thing to do is, do you really have any other choice?"

Anise looked at Jonathan with great admiration. "That has to be the most selfless and courageous thing I've ever heard anyone say," she told him, with complete sincerity. "You're truly amazing."

"And you're right here next to me, making the same decision," Jonathan said. "That makes you just as amazing."

Anise looked down at her fidgeting hands. She certainly didn't feel amazing. She was terrified of committing a crime—even if it was for a good reason, even more frightened of going to prison and losing her freedom, and the thought of a possible confrontation with Nate, Grace, and Dan made her want to run in the other direction. "Do you have any ideas on how to pull this off?" she asked Jonathan.

"I do," he replied. "But let's not talk about it on the plane. When we land, the museum will be closed for the day, but that's just as well, since we'll need time to make a plan. So, let's stop off at a drugstore for toothpaste and whatever else we'll need tonight, grab some take-out, and then we'll come up with ideas at the hotel."

Anise nodded her agreement and stared out the window. She couldn't stop the nervous energy that was surging through her like tumultuous waves crashing against a rocky cliff. She leaned her seat back and closed her eyes, but that didn't help. She couldn't think of an affirmation card with powerful enough words to make her feel better either. Maybe drawing would be enough of a distraction. Reaching into her tote bag, she grabbed her sketchbook.

"Are you cold?" Jonathan asked her. "You're shaking."

"No," she replied, wishing she could crawl into a hole to hide. "I'm just having anxiety."

"Maybe talking will help get your mind off things," Jonathan suggested. "Why don't you tell me a little more about yourself? I hardly know anything about you."

"Okay," she agreed, resting the sketchbook in her lap. "Like what?"

"Tell me about your job at the thrift store."

"I absolutely love it!" She felt her body relax as she pictured herself at Doreen's shop. "The old treasures hold such an energy of romance. I love to look at each piece and imagine its story. Who owned it, what it's been though, what it might tell me if it could talk. And many of the customers come in looking for a piece that reminds them of a time long ago. One that can bring back the beautiful memories of their youth. It makes me wonder what I might miss about this time period when I'm older, and what beautiful future memories I have yet to build and with whom." She stopped talking and instantly regretted her words. Her head hung low as she remembered a time she walked in on Brian and her mother looking through her journal, laughing and making fun of her and her "childish romantic notions" as they had called it.

"I like that," Jonathan told her. "That's really poetic."

She looked up at him, pleasantly surprised. "I've been working there for my friend Doreen since high school. But it's only part-time, so I recently got another part-time job, too."

"Doing what?"

Anise groaned. "I don't want to tell you. It's too embarrassing."

"Embarrassing?" He flashed a teasing smile. "Okay, let me see if I can guess. Are you a circus clown?"

"No," she replied with a smirk.

"Porta Potty cleaner?"

"Ew, no!"

"Okay, I've got it. You dance at busy intersections while twirling advertisement signs."

She let out a little laugh. "No!"

"All right, hmmm, I'm out of ideas."

"I conduct market research surveys at the mall."

"Oh. There's no reason to be embarrassed about that. I'm guessing you don't like it?"

"I hate it. I'm terrible at approaching people. I wish I could just work at the thrift store. But it doesn't pay the bills, and since I have my marketing degree, I wanted to use it. Well, not that I need a degree to conduct surveys. I'm hoping I can move up in a marketing company and do something more important." She looked at him, about to apologize for rambling, but saw that Jonathan was looking at her with interest. "And I hope I still have a job to come home to," she added. "The people who are chasing me showed up at the mall on my lunch break, and I panicked and ran. I haven't called my boss to explain why I left; I wouldn't even begin to know what to say."

"I'm sure we'll be back home by tomorrow night," Jonathan said in a reassuring voice. "You can go in on Friday and let your boss know you had an emergency."

"Yeah..." Anise agreed, not sure if that would work. She'd never gotten into any trouble at a job before. Dawn would have to be a very understanding boss if Anise had any chance of not getting fired.

"I know we left in a hurry," Jonathan said with a worried look. "I should've offered you more time to take care of things. Is everything else squared away? Pets? Kids?"

"I don't have either," Anise told him. "Anything else can wait until I get back. You?"

"Just my dog Max. I texted my parents, and they're going to go pick him up from my place. He's the family dog and mostly stays with them anyway. Someday I'll buy a house with a yard and then I can keep him full time.

As far as work, Dr. S. knows where I am, so I'm all set."

"Good." Anise wondered what kind of emergency she'd have to make up if her boss wanted more details.

"So, what marketing position do you eventually want?" Jonathan asked, interrupting her thoughts.

"I'm not sure yet. Maybe something to do with product promotions or campaigns. I want to do something where I can be creative and artistic."

"Nice. Do you do anything now that's creative and artistic?" he asked, eyeing the sketchbook in her lap.

"I like to paint. And I draw all the time," she said, holding up her sketchbook. "I don't know how good I am, but I really enjoy it."

"Can I see?"

She usually never let anyone else look at it, but his eyes had lit up, and he seemed genuinely interested. She handed him her sketchbook and watched him flip through it.

Each page had its own sketch in black and white with careful shadowing. A saying or single words accompanied each drawing in a geometric shape around the picture, off to the side, or weaving through the drawing.

"Wow, these are amazing! Hey, it's the amulet," he said, pointing. It had a caption that read, "Magic exists for those who seek it."

Anise watched him smile.

He turned another page. "Your faces have so much detail." He continued perusing. "It looks like you have a muse. This face has shown up a few times." The captions for the face read, "When falling feels like flying," and "Right now, no one else, nothing else, matters."

Anise looked at her lap. "Yeah," she said quietly. She didn't want to tell Jonathan that it was Nate.

"This must be why you have a pencil behind your ear. Is it specifically for sketching?"

"No," she replied, removing the pencil from behind her ear. "This one I keep there in case I get inspired and need to write something down. Sometimes I'll draw with it, but I have a box of various pencils in my bag specifically for sketching."

"So are your captions inspired by your drawings or is it the other way around?"

"It can be either or. But I feel like I always want words with my sketches."

Jonathan looked at her with interest. "Why is that?"

"They say a picture's worth a thousand words, but I think exactly *which* thousand words depends on who's looking at it. I love that about art, especially when I'm painting. But for some reason when I'm drawing, I want specific emotions to come through. And the great thing about words is that just of few of them can change someone's perspective. Take this drawing for example." She turned a few pages in her sketchbook until Jonathan was looking at Les in the hospital bed. "When you just look at the picture, you feel sad for the sick man. But now read the caption."

"Someone who loves you is rushing to be by your side for when you wake," Jonathan read. "I see what you mean. You still feel sad for him, but also hopeful that he'll wake up and glad that he won't be alone."

"Exactly! Just a few words but a lot more depth of emotion."

"You have talent. I'm impressed."

"Thanks." She felt her cheeks grow warm from the compliment as he handed back her drawings. "So what do you do besides work at the museum?"

"When school starts again, I won't have time for anything but studying. In the meantime, though, I've been playing Frisbee golf in the park with my buddies a lot lately. Skiing in the winter. And I front a band, so we play in the bars most weekends."

"Really? That's awesome! Have I heard you? What's your band's name?"

"Even Fury. It was inspired by our drummer who

always has the exact same even expression on his face when he plays. He's really just concentrating, but he looks pissed." Jonathan imitated his drummer's face, which made Anise laugh.

"Wait, your band played at the Concert in the Park last night! I was there. You were incredible!"

"Thanks! Yeah, it was the first time we were invited to play there. We loved it!"

"It seems I'm not the only one here who's creative and artistic," she said. "Were you the one wearing the metal-studded shirt?"

"Yeah." His light green eyes sparkled just like they did when he discussed ancient history. "That was me."

"I thought you looked familiar, but I wasn't sure because you looked so different. I absolutely love that shirt!"

Shyness overtook his expression as he looked down and his cheeks turned red. "Thanks! I like clothes shopping when I'm looking for things I can wear on a stage. Work clothes I have a harder time with, as you probably can tell." He looked a little embarrassed as he removed his tie. "I hate these things. And stiff, starchy button-down shirts are the worst. Especially when they're brown."

"They don't really seem like you," Anise agreed.

Jonathan shook his head. "They're not. I'm very much a jeans and t-shirt kind of guy."

"Maybe if you got different colors? Or shirts that... um..."

Jonathan laughed. "Fit me properly?" he finished for her. "I know. Dr. S. has already informed me that I don't look as sharp as I could. He even bought me a gift card to an upscale store for my birthday last month."

"And you haven't used it yet?" Anise said, almost horrified. "When your boss buys you a gift card for work clothes, he's saying something!"

Jonathan blushed. "You're right. The thing is, I'm not sure what looks good. My grandmother bought me these clothes. She obviously thinks I'm bigger than I am. I'm grateful to her though. I don't think I could do any better."

"I'd be happy to help you shop sometime," Anise offered. She then shrugged. "If you want."

"Yes! Please!" he answered emphatically. "I need all the help I can get."

"It sounds like you're close with your grandmother?" she asked.

"Yes," he confirmed. "With my whole family. My parents are here in town, and my grandparents live next door. I see them all the time. My sister Jamie's down in Santa Fe. She visits several times a year with her husband and my nieces. Some of my cousins still live in town. And you met my uncle Robert when you asked him to appraise your amulet in his shop."

"That must be nice to have such a close knit family," Anise said wistfully.

"Tell me about yours," Jonathan said.

"My father lives in New York. My mother's in town. We're not close."

"What about friends? My bandmates are like brothers to me."

Anise happily thought about Erin, Joy, and Vanessa. "I have three best friends that I've known since grade school!" She didn't realize how relaxed she'd become from their conversation until they were interrupted by the captain's voice, telling them they'd be on the ground shortly and that flight attendants were to prepare the cabin for landing. Being brought back into the present meant the return of her anxiety as well. Practicing some relaxing breathing exercises Erin had taught her, Anise watched out the window until the plane gently touched the earth.

✳✳✳

AFTER SHOPPING AT A DRUGSTORE IN Springfield, they stopped at a Chinese restaurant and ordered egg rolls, chicken chow mein, and beef with broccoli to-go. Jonathan drove them to a small hotel in their rental car. They stepped into the modest lobby, and Jonathan checked them in while Anise held their food and drug store purchases.

"Here's your room key," he said, handing it to her. "You're 206. I'm 204, right next door."

"Thanks for charging my room, too. I don't have a credit card right now, and there's probably not enough in my account to use my debit card since I bought the plane ticket."

"No problem."

"I can pay you back with cash though." Anise reached into her tote bag and opened her wallet. She pulled out one of the hundreds that she'd won with Nate at the dance contest. Looking at it made her sad and angry at the same time. She handed it to Jonathan. "Will this cover what I owe you?"

"Yeah, thanks."

Anise took a few minutes to get settled in her room and then lightly tapped on Jonathan's door. They opened their cartons of Chinese food and rice and spread open the map of the Springfield Museum Dr. Smithton had given them on one of the beds.

"Are you sure we shouldn't break in tonight while no one's there?" Anise asked Jonathan.

"I'm sure," he answered her. "It's pretty difficult to break into a museum, even a smaller one, like the Springfield Museum or the one back home. Every door and window has an alarm on it. It'll be far easier to go there tomorrow, pay our admission, and find a place to hide right before closing."

"I guess we should hide somewhere near the earrings," Anise speculated, "so we have more time—won't they have motion sensors that'll see us as soon as we move?"

"There's a time right after museums close when they don't yet have their motion sensors on," Jonathan explained. "The public is gone, but the staff is still there, as well as a cleaning crew. We won't have the risk of being detected by moving at that point. What we'll have to worry about most of all is being caught by staff and breaking into whatever display case the earrings are in. We'll have to make sure to be able to break into it quickly because all the display cases will have glass-break alarms and probably shock sensors that go off if the case gets bumped or moved. So, once we break into the case and grab the earrings, two different alarms will go off, and we'll have to get out of there as soon as possible. Tomorrow, when we check out the place, we'll have to locate the nearest door or window for our escape before breaking into the display case. Maybe one of these," he said, pointing at the map. "We'll have to see them in person to know which would be best."

Anise began to feel nervous spasms in her stomach and took a sip of her Coke. She watched as Jonathan started folding the map.

"Wait, so that's it? That's the whole plan? What about the guards? What about the security cameras?"

"We'll finalize those details tomorrow when we're there," he told her. "We're going to spend all day there getting very familiar with the layout. We'll have to identify where all the security cameras and motion detectors are, and we can mark them on the map. We have to find a concealed hiding place to wait for closing. We'll have to find emergency hiding places near the earrings just in case a staff member walks by. And we'll need to figure out the best way to break into the display case."

"Should we wear masks or something because of the cameras?" asked Anise, as she grabbed an egg roll.

"Not necessarily. This is a smaller museum like ours back home. We only have security cameras by each of the doors. There's no money in the budget for cameras in the galleries as well. My best guess is that the Springfield Museum is the same way. But that is a good point, and we'll make sure to locate all the cameras tomorrow. Now that I think about it, we should also probably leave through a window. If we leave through any door, we'll most likely be on camera."

"And how are we going to break into the display case? Can we carry in anything that could be used to smash the glass?"

"No," he answered. "They'll have security looking through bags and purses at the door. But I imagine the museum may have wall-mounted fire extinguishers in the hallways. The one back home does. That would definitely be heavy enough to break glass. If not, we'll have to figure something else out."

"That's a good idea," she told him, pointing her index finger at him. "What about fingerprints?"

"No worries, I bought a box of latex gloves for us at the drugstore."

"What will security think when they find a pair of latex gloves in my bag?"

"I can keep them in my back pockets."

"Okay." Jonathan had a few good ideas, but there were also a lot of unknowns. Anise frowned slightly. This flimsy plan was a little unsettling. "We'll be on camera for sure when we walk into the museum. Couldn't they tell that we walked in but never came back out?"

Jonathan took a thoughtful pause. "Yeah, good point. Let's go buy some baseball caps tonight. Tomorrow, make sure that you wear your hair up under the cap. If we find that there are no cameras inside the museum, you can take it off. The caps won't hide our faces completely, but it should help at least a little. I hope."

"Okay, that sounds good," she replied.

Jonathan crunched into an egg roll. "You asked really good questions. I'm glad you're here with me. If I forget anything, I have no doubt you'll think of it."

Now that they talked things over, Anise was feeling slightly better about what they had to do. Even though he didn't seem very prepared, Jonathan appeared to know enough about museum security so that they at least had a chance at success. She wondered where Nate was and what he was doing, not to mention Grace and Dan.

"It's only seven o'clock," Jonathan said, glancing at the clock on the nightstand. "Would you like to go do something besides just buy ski masks and baseball caps?"

"Like what?" Anise asked.

"I have my gift card with me," Jonathan said.

"You want to shop for clothes *now*?" Anise said with a laugh.

"If that's okay with you. Honestly, I'm really nervous about tomorrow, and I need a distraction. Besides, if we get arrested, I don't want to be wearing this ugly shirt in my mugshot."

Anise laughed. "Okay, let's go! I'm really nervous, too, and a distraction sounds great. And it would be nice to have something else to wear besides my work clothes. But please, no more jokes about getting arrested."

Jonathan shrugged. "Hey, you laughed."

Chapter 16

At an altitude of thirty thousand feet, Nate got comfortable in his aisle seat and opened his laptop, grateful that the poison was completely out of his system so he could finally feel normal again. The middle and window seats to his left were occupied by an older couple who'd already fallen asleep. Grace and Dan sat directly behind him, but the white noise of the plane drowned out Grace's usual complaints of how dry her skin felt and how much she detested the noise of the crying babies. For the next two hours or so, he'd have a little peace and some time to come up with a plan. He ignored his laptop for a moment to give his eyes a rest. In his mind, he carefully went over the conversation he'd had with Grace and Dan in the car on the way to the airport.

"So, what's your plan for the alarms?" Grace had asked Nate from the backseat of the car. "You won't have all your tools with you this time, and we won't have time to find everything we need once we're there."

"I know," replied Nate. "We're going to have to go about it a little differently this time. We have no chance of breaking in without my tools after hours, so after we scope out the place, let's plan on breaking into the warehouse in the back of the museum just before closing. It should be empty, the alarms won't be on yet, and we can plan on blacking out the camera before it sees us—just long enough for us to break in."

"Okay," said Dan. "That should work."

"Yeah," Nate began, "but not having my tools creates another problem. We need something to open the display case, and since these are high security items, we won't be able to smash it open and go. I know we're short on time, but we'll need something to open it."

"We'll just have to make time to pick something up," Grace told him.

"I could pick the lock on the display case," offered Dan.

Grace shook her head. "Once you touch that lock, the vibration sensor alarm will go off. That'll give the guards a head start. Plus, there could be multiple locks which would take too long to pick open. We need a faster way. We could cut into it."

"No. Nothing I know of that cuts will be quiet enough," Nate said, thinking out loud. "A hand saw will be too loud and set off the vibration sensors. A laser or plasma cutter won't set off the sensors but will also be too loud. I'll have to pry it open with something. Even though that'll trigger the alarm switches, it'll be fast. To do it that way, we'd have to get a crowbar."

"Then we'll do that," Grace said decidedly.

"We'll have to be quick," Dan concluded, "and get the hell out of there before the guards come running."

"Easier said than done," Nate replied. "How quick we can be is going to depend on where we plan to exit the museum, which is another problem. When we leave, any door or window we open will trigger another alarm because I don't have my magnets, and we'll be caught on camera because I don't have my EMI device."

"There has to be a better way to do this!" exclaimed Grace.

"I agree." Nate paused for a moment to think. "Tell me what you think of this," he said. "Since I won't be *able to deactivate the individual alarms on the display case or our way out of the museum, we break into the central control room and deactivate all the alarms."*

"Yes!" agreed Grace. "Dan, you have your pen, right?"

"Always," Dan replied. His "pen" was actually an electric lock pick set that folded up into what looked like a pen, perfect for traveling. "But we'll need to find a different way to get in. The locks are probably digital."

"So you steal a badge from a guard," Nate told him.

"Great, so Dan will get us into the central control room. But we don't want to be seen; how will we get the guards out?" Grace asked Nate.

"Yeah, so first I'll need you to set off an internal alarm across the museum, so the guards will leave the room," he told Grace. "Then you," he said to Dan, "get us into central control. That'll give me the opportunity to deactivate the alarms."

"How?" Dan asked. "By cutting the phone cords? That'll just trigger another alarm. And you don't have your cell jammer for any back up phone systems."

A cocky laugh escaped Nate's lips as he reached into his travel bag and grabbed his laptop. "You underestimate me."

One of the flight attendants interrupted Nate's thoughts. "Sir, would you like something to drink?" she asked.

"Just water," he replied.

She handed him a bottled water and cup of ice before doing a double take. "Oh my god, your eye is almost swollen shut!"

"It's fine," he told her, not wanting to think about the humiliating sucker punch from Anise's beast of an ex.

"No, it's not. I've got just a few more rows to serve, but then I'll be right back with an ice pack." She smiled at him. "I'm Carlie, by the way."

About ten minutes later, Carlie returned to him with a zipper storage bag full of ice, wrapped in several paper towels. She'd brought a couple of her female co-workers with her.

DAN WAS SITTING IN AN AISLE seat behind Nate, with Grace next to him, snoring. He nudged her until she moved her head and was quiet. Now that he could hear what was being said, he sat back and watched as the ladies made a fuss over Nate, fantasizing that the same thing would happen to him if he were the one with a black eye. They stood clogging up the aisle next to Nate's seat, their fingers caressing near his eye. Each of them was young with flawless make-up and pinned-up hair. They were wearing white, shimmering blouses, scarves tied around their necks featuring the airline's logo, and navy skirts that skimmed their curves from their hips to their knees. Under the skirts was pantyhose that Dan imagined would be fun to peel off slowly.

"See how bad it is?" Carlie told her co-workers with a look of concern on her face. She handed Nate the ice pack she'd brought and said, "Here, hold this on your eye. It should help with the swelling."

"This is arnica cream," one of Carlie's co-workers explained to Nate. "It helps get rid of bruises faster. Hold still, I'll put some on you."

"How did that happen?" another one asked.

"I got into a fight," Nate responded.

"It looks painful!"

"Yeah," he admitted with a grin, "but you should see the other guy."

Dan rolled his eyes when the ladies actually giggled at that tired phrase. *Unbelievable.* He kicked the back of Nate's seat and slumped down with his arms crossed.

∗∗∗

SEVERAL HOURS INTO HIS DRIVE, BRIAN pulled off the freeway to fill up his gas tank and buy some snacks. Once he had a full tank and the beef jerky and Mountain Dew he craved, he checked Anise's debit card transactions on his phone before pulling back out on the road. A few hours ago, she'd spent $26.71 at a Chinese restaurant in Springfield. That was a lot of money to spend for just one person. The knot in his stomach grew. There was also a charge for $14.36 at a drug store. Probably just for the necessities like a toothbrush and some make-up. Although, it was also enough for a box of condoms and breath mints. She had also gone shopping at some clothing stores she liked. Why hadn't she checked into a hotel yet? It was already 11:30 at night. Maybe she was out at a bar somewhere partying with *him*.

Brian pulled away from the gas station and back onto the freeway. His phone had been ringing every half hour or so, and it had been Corinne every time. He didn't want to talk to her and hear about how wrong he was. What about what Anise had done to him? He knew Corinne didn't like to see him so angry, but it was Anise who had made him this way, and she needed to be held accountable. He wasn't sure what he'd say to her when he finally found her. That would depend upon the situation.

Brian shifted in his seat, getting uncomfortable as he considered the possible outcomes. If he waited for her in her hotel lobby, he might catch her with *him*. If that happened, he would blacken Nate's other eye, yell at Anise until she cried, and force her to beg him for forgiveness. He could complain that the drive made his lower back hurt even though he felt fine. He could milk his injury for all its worth, especially since it seemed like Anise had lost respect for him. All she talked about anymore was him contributing to their finances. A gold-digging bitch like that *should* be forced to pay for everything for a while; it would serve her right for being so selfish.

Or maybe he'd leave her to purposely break her heart and live with Corinne for a while until he found a job. He had the best sister in the world. He'd have to apologize to her when he got home.

Or maybe Anise went alone, or with a friend, just to get away from him, like Corinne thought. If so, he'd tell her that he was worried because she was lying, and he wanted to see for himself that she was all right. That might even win him some points with her.

Checking Anise's debit card history again made him yell out loud, "What the fuck?" She still hadn't checked into a hotel—or had she? That Nate guy must have paid for it.

About two hours outside of Springfield, it was still dark out, and Brian was so focused on his thoughts, he didn't see the large object in the road in front of him. With a loud bang, he ran into it and rolled over it. He pulled into the shoulder and stopped the car. Grabbing his flashlight, he got out to assess the damage. His right front bumper was completely pushed in, and his right front tire was flat. Shouting all the expletives he could think of, he opened his trunk, only to recall that he had sold his spare tire for some extra cash. It was pitch black out and everything would be closed this time of night.

Now what?

Chapter 17

Thursday, June 7, 2012

The next morning, Dan, Nate, and Grace ate breakfast in Dan's hotel room. Grace had claimed the
desk, while the men each sat on one of the two
queen-sized beds.

"Are you both clear on what you're supposed to do?"
asked Grace, hoping the two candy-asses would live up
to her expectations.

"Absolutely," said Dan. "Not much longer now, Mother,
and you'll have what your heart desires."

She ignored him and turned to Nate. "You'd better
not screw everything up again."

"Do you want my help or not?" said Nate with annoyance.

The brat. She wanted to slap his face like she used to.
"Of course, we need you. You seem to have a plan in mind,
and it better work!"

"Then how about a little gratitude?"

"Gratitude?" Grace snorted. "For not getting the amulet when you said you would? For letting that girl get away?
For turning your back on me and not having contact with
us for the last nine years? For being disrespectful toward

me every chance you get? For trying to have me committed? For almost killing me?"

"Have you forgotten how many heists we've been on that were successful only because of me?" Nate reminded her.

"I remember very well." A memory flashed through her mind of when Nate got past a heat sensing motion detector by walking with a large piece of Styrofoam in front of him that he'd found in the dumpster of whatever museum they had broken into. She and Dan had been ready to find a different museum to rob, one that would be easier to move around in, but they ended up getting away with some very valuable artifacts thanks to Nate. That was just one of the many times his ingenuity had greatly impressed her. His skills were exceptional. "But you've been screwing up these last few days, and it better not happen again. Don't think I don't know what's going on."

"What the hell are you talking about?" Nate narrowed his eyes.

Grace got up, put her face near his, and hissed, "Anise. You're turning against us for the benefit of *her*. I can tell you have feelings for that girl."

"What? You're ridiculous!" Nate turned away from Grace.

She knew he hated when she got too close to him, so she took a step closer. "Don't let a pretty face distract you from what you need to do, Nate. Dan made that mistake once, and it cost us plenty."

Dan shifted uncomfortably in his chair.

"You *will* get us in that museum, and you *will* remain loyal to us," warned Grace. "Or else. Understand?" No way would she let Nate or anyone else get in her way. Not when she was so close to getting everything she'd wanted for decades.

*** * * ***

AFTER BREAKFAST, ANISE AND JONATHAN WALKED across the green grass in Springfield City Park toward the museum across the street. She made sure her hair was still neatly tucked underneath her cap and nervously twisted the garnet ring around her finger as she thought about their unfinished plan to steal the earrings.

"Oh, look," Anise said, pointing to a sign that had distracted her from her worries. "Springfield has a Concert in the Park, too, and it's tonight!"

"I think I know someone who's playing here," said Jonathan, stopping to look at the sign. He pointed to a name of one of the bands that was listed to play. "Yeah! That's my buddy Ivan's band."

"You know someone here?"

His face brightened. "In high school I belonged to a club called Music America. Every summer we'd travel to a new place and learn about that city's musical history. We then got to form bands with other students and try playing some of that city's style of music. Ivan was in the same club at his high school, so I saw him every year. He was really good, so I always made sure I joined his band at the end of the trip."

"That sounds fun!"

"It really was! I met some great people, too. I'm still in touch with a lot of them. I have friends from that club in almost every state."

Anise didn't doubt it. With Jonathan's personality, he probably made a friend wherever he went.

As they walked up the steps of the Springfield Museum, she noticed Jonathan glancing over at her. When she returned his gaze, he laughed. "Don't look so scared," he said. "Remember, we're happy tourists just hanging out at the museum today."

"Right," she agreed, her fingers touching the outline

of the amulet that was still around her neck and tucked under her t-shirt that she'd bought the night before. "Happy tourists." Her nerves had tightened her throat so much that she'd barely been able to choke down her scrambled eggs that morning. However, she'd sipped on a Coke in the car on the way to the museum, so her stomach was quiet. At the moment though, she was thinking about the two thin ski masks at the bottom of her tote bag. They had purchased them while they were at the mall just in case there were security cameras in the galleries after all. Jonathan had assured her that the guards would think they were a regular hat, or maybe even a sweater, and that they wouldn't look that closely. Just in case, Anise had taken a handful of feminine products from the hotel lobby's restroom and placed them over the ski masks, hoping for a male security guard at the door.

When they got to the front door, she saw that she was in luck. The guard checking bags was a man. He was digging quite thoroughly through the visitors' bags ahead of her. When it was her turn, Anise handed him her tote and watched him open it. He peered inside and handed her bag back to her immediately. "You're good to go, Miss." She thanked him and stepped into the museum.

Jonathan followed her inside. "I told you they don't look that closely," he whispered. She smiled at him, not mentioning the secret insurance policy she had used in case he'd been wrong. "Did you see the security camera out front?" he went on to ask her.

"Oh, shit! I was so nervous, I forgot to look!" she replied, ashamed for already screwing up.

"That's okay. I saw it. It covers the entire lobby. But look around and tell me if you see any other cameras."

As they walked, her eyes scanned the walls, ceilings, and corners, but she didn't see any cameras in the hallway or in the first gallery. "I don't," she said, "but there was a fire extinguisher in the hallway."

"Great," he said. "Let's scope out this room, then find the earrings."

The first gallery had Native American artifacts local to the region. Tools, blankets, skins, and clothes were prominently displayed in their cases.

"There's a motion detector in the corner near the ceiling," Jonathan whispered to her. "Are you ready to move on? I'd like to check out the room that should have the Mallandia exhibit, according to the map."

She nodded. Together, they walked the long hallway of white tile to the last gallery at the end of the hall, looking at old black and white pictures of Springfield that hung on the walls along the way. Once inside, they circled the entire gallery clockwise, peering carefully into each display case. They saw some artifacts from Bronze Age Greece on display, and as they rounded the corner, Mesopotamian artifacts were featured. Jonathan smiled each time Anise asked him a question about an artifact, and his face beamed when he answered her.

"This looks like a game!" she exclaimed, pointing to one of the artifacts, her finger tapping the glass that protected it. The item she saw looked like two board games connected by a bridge. The entire board had beautifully painted squares upon which players would place round tokens that had five dots each painted on them. There were also three pyramid-shaped dice made out of bones.

"Wow," said Jonathan. "I wasn't expecting to see this here. This is The Royal Game of Ur. The Sumerians played it. It's thought to be similar to backgammon."

"Oh, look!" exclaimed Anise, moving on to the next case. "Clay tablets with ancient writing!"

"Yes," he agreed. "Cuneiform writing from Mesopotamia. The tablets were baked to preserve them."

They walked through ancient Egyptian displays and rounded a corner, finally getting to understand the layout of the room. The front half of the gallery was being used to display the artifacts from Bronze Age Greece and all the items on loan from other museums relating to Mallandia. The back half had artifacts from both ancient Mesopotamia and Egypt, and they were divided from the Mallandia and Greek sections by a stand-alone wall, which stopped several yards before it reached each end of the room.

"We're getting into the Mallandia section, finally," Anise commented as they walked back into the front half of the gallery, reading the description with the artifacts in the next display case. When Jonathan was silent, Anise lifted her eyes to check on him. She saw him looking around with a worried expression on his face. "Is everything okay?" she asked him.

"These artifacts are extremely old and famous. The Springfield Museum must have spent a lot of money to purchase new and better security for this gallery in order for other museums to even consider loaning out these objects to them."

"What does that mean for us?" she whispered.

"I don't know," he replied. "Hopefully all will still go to plan." He looked around at the perimeter of the ceiling.

Anise looked too. Still no security cameras, but several motion detectors. She continued to look in each display case while Jonathan followed her.

JONATHAN WIPED THE SWEAT FROM HIS brow. They still hadn't found the earrings, didn't know the first thing about museum theft, and would probably be arrested tonight if this didn't go perfectly. After several minutes of worrying and wondering if they should abort their plan and go home, Jonathan felt Anise grabbing his arm. "The earrings," she whispered. "I think I found them." She pointed to a display case attached to the wall.

He peered inside. There they were—the pale, sky

blue stones, each with a metal bar running through them. The bars bisected circular hoops and looked exactly like the drawing in the old book he'd shown Anise.

"The metal is the same as my amulet," she stated. "These have to be the right ones."

Jonathan nodded. "That's them," he confirmed.

"Chalcedony Earrings," Anise said, reading the sign next to the earrings. "That's not much of a description."

"Like Dr. S said," replied Jonathan, "no one else knows the story behind them anymore."

Both Jonathan and Anise stared at them for several minutes. "They're beautiful," remarked Anise. She leaned her face in close to the top of the display case. "The hoops have the same curly symbols that are on the back of my amulet."

Jonathan took a closer look as well. "Yeah, the incantation." He squatted to pretend he was taking a better look but was actually searching for alarms. He was able to see two magnetic switches glued to the underside of the wood trim next to the access door inside the display case, and he figured there were probably more that he couldn't see, like the vibration sensors. There was no getting around those. He'd just have to smash the case, grab the earrings, and run. But where would they go? He stood up and looked around again. The gallery was completely windowless. Jonathan looked up at the ceiling and let out a nervous breath. *I have absolutely no idea what I'm doing,* he thought.

"What's the matter?" Anise whispered to him.

"There are no windows in this room," he told her.

"Let's check the nearby rooms," she suggested.

They walked out of the gallery and noticed that each window in the hallway had bars. Jonathan sighed in nervous frustration. To their right, the restrooms in the hallway were the nearest rooms to the Mallandia-themed gallery. They communicated their shared idea with just a nod, and each walked through their respective restroom doors. Jonathan was relieved to see a bar-free window near the ceiling that would be easy to open. The windows weren't large but would be just big enough for them to fit through. He checked the stalls; no one else was in the room. Jonathan carried the trash can to the end of the restroom and placed it just beneath the window. He climbed on top of it and looked out the window. He saw that it was about a twelve-foot drop to the ground below. There were also trees and bushes in the vicinity, so they would be hidden for a short time until they made a mad dash for the strip mall that was on the other side of the park across the street. They had purposely parked their rental car behind the strip mall instead of in the museum parking lot. His thought was that it was close enough to get to quickly, but far enough away to remain hidden and not be seen fleeing the scene of a crime.

He waited for Anise on a bench in the hallway. Neither the butterflies in his stomach nor his racing mind would leave him alone. The plan they had so far was shit. They were playing a dangerous and serious game, and he wanted to be more prepared. They had to solidify their plan and quick. Time was of the essence. Anise had put her trust in him, and he didn't want to let her down. He'd been so impressed with her intelligence, bravery, and ability to think of things that he'd missed, and he wanted to impress her, too. He took a deep breath in and let it out slowly through pursed lips, trying to clear his mind and focus. Even with her admitted issue with anxiety, she seemed to be handling this situation better than he was. Aside from her occasionally fidgety hands, she hadn't looked nervous all day.

He thought back to the first time he'd seen her. She'd stood there on the other side of his office door in an outfit straight from a fashion magazine, making him intensely regret the clothes he'd chosen to wear that morning. Her face had been flawless, even under the harsh fluorescent lights in the hallway, and her side-parted brown hair waved over her left eye like one of those 1940's movie sirens. The small pencil perched behind her ear, ready for use at any given second, had told him she must be efficient and often inspired which had made him long to know more. Cherry-stained lips had smiled at him, and his mind had already started composing a song about her.

She stepped out of the restroom and said hello to a stranger while holding open the door. As she walked toward him, Jonathan watched her soft, graceful steps and enjoyed seeing her pretty face when she sat next to him. "There was a window in the men's room that we can fit through," he whispered. "I think we should use it as our escape route. Unless there was one in the ladies' room by chance? It's closer to the gallery."

She nodded. "Yes, there was. We'll leave from there. And I think I found our hiding spot!" she whispered back.

"Where?" he asked, eager to hear her thoughts. He'd been wracking his brain on where the best place to hide would be but had come up with nothing.

"When I was washing my hands, I noticed there was a very large duct cover on the wall above my head to the left where the last mirror ended. I waited until the other woman in the room left and then climbed up onto the counter that connects the sinks. I peered into the duct and saw just how large it really was. It was square-shaped and definitely big enough for a person to crawl into. The screws holding it in place were loose when I touched them, and I know I'd be able to pull myself inside if I stood on the sinks or even the trash can."

"That's perfect," Jonathan told her, his nervous butterflies finally starting to settle down. "Now that you mention it, there's one in the men's room too. I think we should hide separately. If one of us gets caught, at least the other one will still have a chance at the earrings. Near closing time, there shouldn't be anyone in the restrooms. We'll be able to crawl in our ducts without being seen.

Plus, the louvers in the cover looked like they might be spaced far enough apart for our arms to fit through. Let's not forget to swipe some knives from the museum cafeteria when we have lunch. That way we can reattach the cover from the inside, using the knives as screwdrivers. You know, just in case someone comes in. As long as the knives are steel anyway. Plastic knives wouldn't work."

"I would never have thought of reattaching the cover if you hadn't said anything," Anise said, grimacing at her oversight. "I'm so glad I'm not doing this alone."

"Me too," he said. "I wouldn't have thought of hiding in the ducts. We make a great team." He gave her a nod even though he was considering asking her to leave the museum to wait for him somewhere. He felt responsible for coming up with the best possible plan he could, and his earlier realization of how little prepared he was scared him. He felt he had pressured her into coming here by making his decision so quickly and talked her into the idea of this being "the right thing to do." However, was it right of him to place her in a risky situation of his choosing, especially when he himself was not ready for it? He didn't even give her a chance to make up her own mind about what's right for her.

Anise nodded back at him. "Let's grab some lunch."

When she stood up, he pulled her back down. "Wait a minute. You should go wait for me at a coffee shop or something. I'll take care of this and meet you there. It wasn't fair of me to push you into this situation. It was my idea, and it should be my responsibility."

She looked at him with surprise. "No way! I came to you for information, but you gave me so much more. I never expected you to offer this much help. You're the one who doesn't need to be here. I'm not going anywhere."

He smiled at her. "Neither am I."

She smiled back. "It's settled then. We're in this together. Now, lunchtime."

The museum's café didn't have an extensive menu,

but the cheeseburger sounded good to both of them. A shared basket of onion rings rounded off their meal. They chose a table in the back corner so they could review their plan in private.

Jonathan rolled out the map of the museum on their table. "Thirty minutes before closing time, 5:30 p.m., we each go into our respective restrooms," began Jonathan, pointing at the map. "We'll have the steel knives with us to reattach the air duct covers. We'll wait until 6:10 and then come out of the bathrooms and meet in the gallery by the earrings. We'll need a way to communicate while we're in the bathrooms, just in case something goes wrong."

"We'll text," said Anise. "Just make sure your phone is on mute."

"Yes, I'll do that now." He pulled out his phone and muted it, and Anise followed suit. He had a thought about an article he had once read regarding law enforcement being able to read their texts that were still on their phones without a warrant. It wasn't a great idea, but they needed a way to communicate, so he figured they'd have to take the chance.

"Just make sure that the moment you send or receive a text, you delete it from your phone," Jonathan told Anise.

"I will," Anise promised. "Now, what if we're in the gallery and hear someone coming? We didn't find emergency hiding spots in there yet," Anise told him.

"You're right; we'll do that right after lunch. Oh, and let's back up for a minute. We'll need to grab the fire extinguisher on our way to the gallery."

"Right," agreed Anise. "So once we're in the gallery, we'll smash open the display case with the fire extinguisher, grab the earrings, and climb out of the window in one of the restrooms."

"Yes," said Jonathan. "If all goes as planned, by the time they respond to the alarms, we should be long gone.

What we really need to watch out for is staff walking the halls, but there's nothing we can do to prevent that. I'll need you to make sure the hallways are clear the moment I break open the display case." He thought for a moment. "When we go into the restrooms at 5:30, we need to make sure to unlock the windows before getting into the ducts. Every second counts."

"Then we run across the street and the park to the car and go where?" asked Anise.

"Straight to the airport to return the car and fly home."

They stared at each other, trying to determine if they had missed any pertinent detail. The nervousness in Anise's eyes was apparent now, and Jonathan saw her put a hand to her stomach.

"I'm going to get a refill on this Coke," she said, "and I'll grab the knives while I'm at it."

After they finished their lunch, they walked back into the Mallandia exhibition. It was filled with nothing but enclosed cases. There was no real place to hide that Jonathan saw, should the necessity present itself. He looked up when he heard Anise calling to him from the Egyptian corner of the room. He followed her voice and looked at the sarcophagus she'd found. It was pushed up against the wall with just enough room to hide behind it. "Perfect."

Chapter 18

Brian wanted to either punch his steering wheel or rest his head on it and take a nap. Instead, he drowsily stared out the windshield and let the gentle motion of the car settle the volcanic rage inside him. The glare from the late afternoon sun bouncing off the chrome bumper of the truck in front of him was annoying, and if the night before hadn't been one of the worst in his life, he would've longed for the soothing cover of a starry, black sky. But he never wanted to think about that night again. Trying to hitchhike in the dark had been futile, and once dawn came, his luck still didn't change. After several infuriating hours, he was finally picked up by a trucker, who took him into the next town and dropped him off on the side of the road with directions on how to get to the nearest tire store. Brian had walked two and a half miles, purchased a tire with a credit card that he knew he couldn't pay off, and after telling everyone in the tire store about his unfortunate circumstances, had hoped for an act of kindness from one of the strangers. No one seemed to care, however, and he walked the two-and-a-half miles back to the freeway with his tire. After sticking out his thumb for an hour, another good-natured trucker brought him back to his car where he put on his new tire, hoping that the cars zooming by him would see him and be careful. Now that he was back on the road, he had only two more hours to go before reaching Springfield.

With his eyes darting back and forth between the road and his phone, he checked Anise's debit card transaction list and saw that she'd bought a ticket to the Springfield Museum first thing in the morning and some lunch at the museum café in the afternoon. He had no other leads, so his plan was to head for the museum and hope that she was still there by the time he arrived. It was obvious she was in Springfield to have fun and get away from him. He was sorry he'd thrown the lamp at her and understood she may be afraid of him right now, but she didn't have to lie. She better not be with *him*. With his eyes narrowed and a knot in his stomach, he typed the museum's address into his road maps app on his phone and sped the rest of the way into town.

"IT'S 5:30, ARE YOU READY?" JONATHAN asked Anise.

Her head was spinning with anxiety, but she wanted to be brave. "As ready as I'll ever be." She gave him a quick hug. "Good luck."

"Good luck," he replied, hugging her back. "And remember, once you put on your gloves, don't take them off until we're out of the museum."

"I won't."

"Oh, and one more thing. Turn off the GPS on your phone, just in case."

"I'll do it right now," she said, grabbing her phone from her bag.

They waited a few moments for the hallway to clear and then darted into the bathrooms without being seen. Anise went straight to the window and after putting on her latex gloves, moved the trash can underneath the window, stepped on it, and opened the two locks before jumping back to the floor. She moved the trash can so it was underneath the duct, hopped onto the sink counter, and leaning toward the duct, removed the screws from the air duct cover using the museum café's knife as a screwdriver. She removed the cover and while looking around for a place to put it, decided that it should be kept with her so she could reach it. She put the cover diagonally through the opening into the air duct, pushing it as far back as she could reach. She carefully climbed onto the trash can again and pulled herself up into the duct, bumping her knees on the wall along the way.

Her nose wrinkled in disgust. *Holy shit, it's dusty in here,* she thought, doing her best not to inhale deeply. She could already feel her throat getting irritated. Completely inside the duct, she grabbed the cover in front of her along with the screws and knife. Realizing the duct wasn't as wide as she'd thought, she started hyperventilating. *Shit! I can't turn around!* There was no way she'd be able to replace the cover without turning around. What if someone came in and found her like this? *I have to replace this cover!* Her heart started pounding as she wondered what she should do. Quickly, she crawled forward. She felt her hair and her jacket touching the top of the duct— no doubt doing a great job of cleaning off the dust. She wondered how Jonathan was doing and if he was having the same problems. She tried hard to not let her knees and shoes clunk on the metal. "I can do this," she whispered, taking slow, deep breaths so as to not let her anxiety turn into panic.

Once she reached where the duct turned, she noticed that it also turned the other direction. She had a choice of going right or left. Relieved, she turned left, backed up, and then turned left again to go in the direction from which she came. Reaching the entrance, she held the cover with one hand and reached through the widely spaced louvers with the other to reinsert the screw. Her arm barely fit. It took her an entire minute to find the hole for the screw because she couldn't see what she was doing. Her arm began aching from holding it up in the awkward position. She tightened the screw with her fingers and then heard the bathroom door open. Quickly, she retracted her arm back into the duct, lay down on her stomach, and as quietly as possible, pushed herself backward. She watched from inside the wall as a woman went into a stall.

Her heart pounded in her ears as she recognized the woman. *Grace?! Oh, shit!*

Anise covered her mouth and nose with her hand and then realized that her hand was covered in thick dust and dirt. *Ew!* She quietly wiped the dust from her mouth onto the inside of her jacket, the only part of her outerwear that was still clean. She looked on in horror as Grace washed her hands and left the restroom. *Was she planning the same thing – to stay past closing and grab the earrings? Were Nate and Dan here too? Where were they going to hide? How long were they going to wait before going after the earrings?* The last thing she wanted was to run into them. They would kill her—and Jonathan, too.

Heart racing, Anise grabbed her phone out of her tote bag to text Jonathan and noticed he had already sent her a text about five minutes earlier.

Jonathan: *I'm in. Are you ok?*

Anise: *I'm ok. Grace came in the bathroom after I reattached the cover. Didn't notice me, luckily.*

Jonathan: *Shit. She must have same plan we do.*

Anise: What should we do?

Jonathan: Let's move up the time we leave the bathrooms to 6:05. They don't know we're here. The faster we move, the better.

Anise: Ok. Did you have probs moving in duct? And reattaching cover?

Jonathan: Yes. Had to turn around where duct turns. Couldn't attach cover. Arm too big. Just kept it inside duct with me. Good enough.

Anise decided to not reattach the other screw on the cover. It seemed to be holding just fine with one, and removing only one loose screw would make it faster for her to leave when it came time. She pressed her tongue to the roof of her mouth and held her breath to keep from sneezing. Her muscles felt tight and her stomach began churning, making her wish that she had a soda.

Anise: Even more terrified now that Grace is here. I'm so nervous I hope I don't puke in this duct.

Jonathan: It'll all be ok and over before you know it. Think happy and undusty thoughts.

She suppressed a giggle.

Anise: Don't make me laugh!

Her cell phone clock read 5:53. *Only twelve more minutes and I can get out of this dusty hell hole,* she thought. She felt something on top of her head that she brushed off quickly. *Please don't be a spider.* She checked her phone again and was annoyed to see it was still only 5:53.

She texted Jonathan again.

Anise: I think time moves slower inside ducts.

Jonathan: I think you're right. It's hard to breathe in here too. I wonder if this is how my sister felt when she got stuck in a drain.

Anise: I want to hear the rest of that story.

Jonathan: Will do, once we're outta here.

Anise was looking forward to learning more about her new friend. Wondering about him and his story was a welcome distraction.

GRACE HAD CRAWLED INTO A CORNER under several large display cases on the second floor and was waiting for a text message signal from Nate or Dan. On that signal, she was to make it look like a small statue had fallen on one of the cases and rattled it, thus setting off the vibration sensor. She would then run quickly to the room next door and hide there until the guards went back to their post. This location was the farthest point in the museum from the central control room, which would give Nate as much time as possible to work his magic. She didn't like being so far away from the action and drummed her leather-gloved fingers impatiently on the floor. How could she make sure everything went to plan from under a display case? *This will get me closer to what I need*, she thought. *They better not screw up if they know what's good for them.*

For a moment, she let herself daydream about how things could be. There'd been a time when things were better. She'd been happy—but that was a long time ago. However, everything she'd lost could be found again, if only this plan worked. She wouldn't have to suffer from the intense migraines that were only helped by pulling on her hair. And her hair could be beautiful again if she stopped pulling on it. The hallucinations that seemed so real—real enough to frighten the hell out of her every time—would stop too. She could heal herself from the past. She could love again.

But this girl, Anise...she could ruin everything. Grace couldn't let that happen. She hung her head, ashamed that for a moment she'd felt a twinge of insecurity. *Don't be weak!* she scolded herself. *Anise doesn't know who she's dealing with. And she'll be dead soon enough.*

NATE CHECKED HIS WATCH. SIX O'CLOCK. Closing time for the museum. He and Dan were in the museum's small warehouse off a restricted hallway, very close to the central control room where the two guards would be sitting. The guards would monitor the video from the cameras outside the building, as well as the one in the lobby, and were required to immediately respond in person should any internal alarm sound. That was what Nate's entire plan relied upon.

Dan was sitting on a forklift, pretending to drive it. Nate was pacing back and forth, holding a crowbar, wondering how the evening would turn out. If Grace was right in thinking Anise was going to Springfield to steal the earrings, it would mean Anise was probably in the building hiding somewhere right now, scared and alone. Nate hated the thought.

He turned his attention to his plans—not the plans Grace and Dan knew about, but his own. Grace would never stop until she got what she wanted. If all went smoothly, Grace could leave with the earrings and amulet and stop terrorizing Anise. But Grace didn't like to leave witnesses and had already expressed a desire to kill her. Nate let out a nervous breath he hadn't realized he'd been holding. How was he going to pull this off?

Nate knew he could physically overpower Grace and Dan, but not when Grace also had the ring. Simply overpowering her wouldn't be enough. Grace would either have to be killed or locked up for this to end. But if he called the cops, Anise would be locked up too. He couldn't do that to her.

In that case, who would do the honors of offing the old hag? He looked at the crowbar he held in his hand and then at the red-headed idiot in the forklift. Dan would never kill Grace. And Nate knew himself enough to know he wouldn't either. Of that, he was sure. If Grace were in his shoes, she'd have no problems killing her enemy, and Nate wanted to be nothing like her.

Nate ran a hand through his hair in frustration. If he and Dan didn't kill Grace, the only one left to do it was Anise. And that was out of the question. Anise was innocent; she shouldn't have to do it. She shouldn't even be here. So Grace would live. Although, if she were about to kill Anise, and he had no other choice...

"Did that stewardess give you her number?" Dan asked, interrupting Nate's musings.

"Flight attendant," Nate corrected him, hoping Dan didn't want to start a waste-of-time conversation now. There were more important things to think about.

"Whatever! Did she?" Dan asked.

"They always do," Nate said arrogantly just to piss Dan off, hoping that would shut him up. No such luck.

"Lucky son of a bitch. Even with your fucked up face." Dan's shoulders slumped and his mouth formed a pout. He pressed some of the buttons on the forklift's dashboard. "Are you gonna call her?"

"No," Nate responded. He continued pacing.

"Why not? Let me live through you."

"You're a fucking jack-ass." Nate shook his head.

"What?" Dan held out his hands questioningly. "What did I say wrong?"

"In case you haven't noticed, I'm kinda busy doing something more important," Nate snapped. He couldn't make any plans if Dan wouldn't keep quiet.

Dan slumped down in the forklift's seat. "I didn't mean now. When we're done. Later tonight." When Nate didn't respond, Dan continued. "Or is there some other chick you'd rather be with?"

Nate was still silent, desperate for a better plan and trying to ignore Dan who wouldn't stop talking.

"Come on, give me something!" Dan begged.

Nate finally gave up and answered him. "Yeah. There's someone else."

"Nice! Is she even hotter than the stewardess?"

"Shut up!" Nate said with annoyance. There was no solution. What was he going to do? He checked his watch again. "It's time. Text the old hag."

THE TEXT GRACE RECEIVED FROM DAN had one word— *now.*

Finally, she thought, as she carefully crawled out from under the display case. She quickly stepped over to the wooden totem statue and pushed it, making sure it would land directly on the nearby case with a solid blow. As soon as it hit, she raced through the gallery as fast as her tired, old legs would take her. The vibration sensor in the display case started sounding from the impact. Rounding the corner into the next gallery, she hid behind a large tapestry that hung from the ceiling and waited.

JONATHAN: READY?

His text came in at 6:05. She happily texted him back.

Anise: Yes!

She crawled forward, so grateful she'd be out of the dust bunny cave in just a few more seconds. She reached her hand through the duct cover and carefully twisted the lone screw holding the cover on while gripping the cover with her other hand. Finally, once the screw was removed, she stuck her head out of the duct and took a deep breath of clean air. *I probably should climb out backward,* she thought, looking down, *so I don't land on my face.* Just then, she heard the bathroom door open. Heart pounding, she quickly backed into the duct again, bringing the cover inside as Jonathan said he had done.

A loud voice traveled throughout the ladies' room. "And he was, like, 'Crystal, just 'cause we have a kid doesn't mean I can't go out', and I was, like, 'If going out to you means being gone till four in the morning and coming home shit-faced, then yeah, you can't go out.'"

From her place in the duct, Anise saw two young female cleaning crew members coming in, wheeling their supply cart behind them. She backed further into the duct and accidentally kicked the side of it with her shoe in her hurry.

"Oh my god, Heidi, what was that?" asked Crystal.

"It came from that vent," replied Heidi. "Go check it out."

"I don't wanna check it out. What if it's an animal or something?"

"Just look inside. An animal can't hurt you from in there, chicken shit."

Shit! thought Anise. *They're going to see me for sure.* She scurried backward as fast as she could go until she was around the corner, not caring about the noise she made any longer.

"Eeewww, did you hear that? Something's in there!" exclaimed Crystal. "I am so not looking in there. That's all you," she said to Heidi.

"Whatever," said Heidi with annoyance. A light shined into the duct, and Anise guessed it must be coming from Heidi's cell phone.

"The cover looks messed up," Heidi commented, "but I don't see anything in there at all."

Anise tried her best not to breathe heavily, for every sound made in the metal duct echoed, so she held the clean inside of her jacket against her nose and mouth.

"Something *was* in there," Heidi continued. "You can tell because a lot of the dust is wiped away. But whatever it was left. I don't see or hear anything."

"Thank god," remarked Crystal. "Now let's get cleaning the crappers over with."

Anise pulled out her phone and texted Jonathan.

Anise: Almost got caught by cleaning crew. Still in duct. Where r u?

Jonathan: Been waiting for you by bathroom door. Will go back in duct until you text me they're gone, he responded.

Anise: Good idea. They might come in your bathroom next.

MITCHELL AND TED, THE MUSEUM SECURITY guards, were looking forward to another peaceful night of drinking coffee and playing cards.

"Evening, Ted," Mitchell said as he walked into the

central control room where Ted had just arrived a minute earlier.

"Mitchell," greeted Ted.

Mitchell sat down with a groan. "This chair isn't good for my back."

"Yeah, they're uncomfortable," Ted agreed.

"It's not just that. Wait till you get to be my age, kid. Everything hurts."

"Are you going to piss and moan all night again? Why don't you retire, old man?" Ted asked. He didn't particularly care to be reminded that life would suck more and more the older you get.

"Make better investments than I did," Mitchell replied. "Wait. What the..."

"What's going on?" Ted asked, rummaging through his backpack for the turkey sandwich his wife had made for him before he left for work.

Mitchell pointed to a flashing light on his screen. "An alarm's going off in the Makason Gallery upstairs."

"Shit." Ted put his turkey on rye back into his backpack. "Let's go." They left the central control room, and the door shut behind them, locking itself. The administrative and docent staffs as well as the curators were on their way out of the museum, and Ted felt their eyes follow him as he and Mitchell ran down the hallway and huffed and puffed their way up the stairs to the second floor.

∗∗∗

"LET'S DO IT," SAID NATE. HE and Dan checked the hallway to make sure it was clear and then ran the short distance to the central control room. Dan had the badge he'd stolen, and they were inside within seconds. Nate put on a pair of thin leather gloves he had in his jacket pocket and sat down in front of the computer-based system of alarm and camera monitoring and access control. He pulled out a flash drive from his pocket and inserted it into a USB port on the side of the computer. A program immediately started downloading.

"What's that?" Dan asked him.

"All my code writing classes finally being put to good use," Nate told him.

"So that's what you were working on in the car and on the plane?"

"And most of last night. Yeah." The message of download completion flashed on the screen, and Nate removed the flash drive and put it back in his pocket. "No need to worry about any alarms you hear now. Just watch out for the guards and staff," he told Dan. "You go find the old bat. I'll flush this flash drive and get the earrings. Meet me in that back gallery where the earrings are now, and we'll all leave from there."

"THERE IN THE BACK," SAID TED. He and Mitchell made their way through the Makason gallery and over to where Ted was pointing. "The wooden statue fell and must have set off the shock sensor when it hit the display case."

Mitchell helped Ted lift the wooden totem to a standing position. "The base is a little shaky and uneven," he noticed. "It must've fallen on its own. Nothing else seems to be out of place, and that was the only alarm going off."

"Stay put, mother fucker," Ted told the totem. "I've got a sandwich to get back to. No more interruptions."

HEIDI AND CRYSTAL, WORKING QUICKLY, FINISHED cleaning the ladies' room in about seven minutes and left.

Anise waited impatiently in the dusty duct. After what seemed like forever, Anise received a text from Jonathan that everything was clear. This time, she started backing out toward the opening of the duct. Reaching behind her while on her knees, she grabbed the cover and moved it away from the opening of the duct. She kicked her legs out and pushed the rest of her body out with her hands, landing with her feet on the floor. She placed her tote bag under the window. She wouldn't need it in the gallery, and she could grab it on her way out. As she passed by the mirrors over the sinks, she was horrified. Never in her life had she been that filthy. Dust and grime covered her hair and created dark splotches on her face and clothes. There was no time to clean up, however—Jonathan was waiting for her. She peeked out of the ladies' room door and saw no one but Jonathan, his dusty head poking out of the men's room door. At the same time, they joined each other in the hallway and walked briskly toward the gallery. Jonathan quietly removed the fire extinguisher from its place on the wall. They made their way to the display case with the earrings and peered in once more.

"I'll smash the case and grab the earrings," Jonathan whispered. "You keep watch down the hallway to make sure no one is around. Then run as fast as you can, and I'll be right behind you. The ladies' room is closer, and from the men's room window it looked like it would be a shorter drop as well."

Anise nodded, her heart beating out of her chest. She felt dizzy and short of breath, but they were almost done now. They just had to grab the earrings and then they could leave and go home. Jonathan looked at her, and she gave him a thumbs up to signal that the coast was clear.

***

TED AND MITCHELL GOT BACK TO central control and flopped down in their uncomfortable chairs.

"That's more than enough exercise for me for one night," remarked Mitchell. Ted grunted his agreement with a mouthful of turkey.

"Shit!"

"What now?" asked Ted.

"Another goddamn alarm is going off. It's in the front gallery now."

Ted threw down his sandwich on a napkin. They left the control room and ran down the hallway toward the front gallery.

JONATHAN LIFTED THE FIRE EXTINGUISHER. HE figured the glass would be quite thick and that he'd need to hit it with all his strength in order to break through it properly the first time. He focused, and brought the extinguisher down with more force than he knew he had. His shoulders definitely felt the blow, but the glass did not. There wasn't even a crack. No vibration alarm was sounding either, for that matter. *What the hell?* he thought. *This is not glass.*

He felt his arm being pulled by Anise. "Jonathan, come on," she whispered. "I saw guards running in the hallway." They ran to the other side of the room and behind the sarcophagus as planned, in case of emergency. Jonathan felt Anise grab his hand and squeeze. He squeezed back. They heard footsteps in the gallery. The footsteps lead up to the sarcophagus and stopped. Jonathan began sweating so much that his glasses slid partway down his nose. Not daring to move and push them back in place, he sat frozen. His hand ached as he felt Anise squeezing it in a death grip.

✳✳✳

MITCHELL AND TED REACHED THE FRONT gallery near the lobby and looked around. They walked the perimeter of the room to see what might've happened, scoping out all the Native American displays. Everything appeared to be as it should.

"I don't see a damn thing," complained Ted. "Which alarm was it?"

"It was a shock sensor," replied Mitchell, "but everything looks fine to me. Let's head back."

ANISE'S GRIP ON JONATHAN'S HAND HADN'T loosened at all. She was starting to cut off his circulation a little, but he couldn't very well tell her that now. He knew how afraid she must be, as he had never been this scared in his life. Even so, he couldn't help but wonder why he hadn't noticed the display cases weren't made of glass. They had spent enough time looking through them at the earrings and other treasures all day. Maybe it was because all the display cases at the museum back home were all older and made of glass. There had never been a good enough reason to buy new ones. But here at the Springfield Museum, it made sense that new, stronger materials would be used, now that such rare, priceless artifacts were on display. He felt so embarrassed. *How the hell are we going to get the earrings now?*

To his great relief, the footsteps started moving again, this time away from them. A few seconds later, they heard the footsteps stop again, followed by a loud cracking sound. Footsteps again, then, nothing.

After waiting a minute or two, Jonathan reclaimed his hand, wiggled his fingers to encourage blood to start flowing again, and peered out from the protection of the sarcophagus. He saw nothing. He motioned for Anise to follow him, and they made their way back to the display case that held the earrings and looked inside.

"Jonathan!" she whispered. It had been pried open.

"I know," he whispered back. The earrings were gone.

Out of the corner of his eye, Jonathan saw a shadow move from behind a display not far from them.

"Looking for these?" a dark haired man with vivid blue eyes asked them, holding up the earrings.

"Nate," Anise said softly in a wavering voice.

Chapter 19

Exhausted, Mitchell and Ted dragged themselves back to central control. They were still taking gasping breaths from their unexpected running, not to mention the adrenaline from the most active night they'd ever seen at the museum.

Ted felt his stomach rumbling. He had his sandwich halfway to his mouth when Mitchell said, "You're not going to believe this."

"You gotta be kidding me! Son of a bitch!"

"In the basement this time."

"We're gonna spend all night writing incident reports." Ted threw down his sandwich again, then thought better of it and picked it back up. "I'm not leaving you behind anymore," he said.

Mitchell, Ted, and the turkey on rye went through the hall, down the stairwell, and into the exhibit hall in the basement.

Ted walked the hall quickly, flashlight in one hand, sandwich in the other. Mitchell went slowly, looking into every case.

"I see nothing," grumbled Ted, not bothering to hide the irritation in his voice.

"Me either. Let's head back. *Again.*"

As soon as they reached the control room, they saw

the flashing red light on the computer screen.

"What the hell is going on?" said Ted. "Just turn it off, Mitchell; it's another false alarm. I'm not running all over hell and creation all night long."

"You're not getting out of it, Ted. We're going. Second floor."

Ted mumbled under his breath through a mouthful of turkey but followed Mitchell out the door again. They were too out of breath to say anything to each other, so they trotted along in silence. When they were almost at the stairwell, an elderly woman and a ginger-haired man stepped off the stairs into the hallway.

"Hold it right there!" shouted Mitchell, as he and Ted pointed their guns at the two intruders.

"On your knees!" yelled Ted. "Hands where I can see them!"

The ginger complied right away. The old woman did too, but not until after she fidgeted with her ring. Ted watched as Mitchell grabbed the woman by the arm and she grabbed his.

Ted had no idea what happened, but a few seconds later, Mitchell was lying on the floor, shivering, sweating, and convulsing. "Mitchell!" Out of surprise, Ted turned his back to the intruders to attend to his co-worker. He felt the old woman grab his arm as well, and after a warm sensation and a sharp poking near his elbow, Ted found himself in the same predicament as Mitchell.

The old woman grabbed Mitchell's gun as the ginger grabbed Ted's. She aimed and shot Mitchell point blank in the chest. She looked over at the ginger, who hadn't pulled the trigger, but was still aiming the gun at Ted with a shaky hand.

"Well, what are you waiting for?" she demanded.

Ted had never felt so sick and knew he should be more afraid, but he'd never felt so calm either.

The ginger looked at the old woman with wide eyes and sweat running down his brow. He looked like he might pass out.

"You took care of Lorelei, didn't you?" she hissed at him, with her hand grabbing a fistful of her white hair. She then motioned to Ted. "This is a stranger! It should be easy in comparison! Be the man I raised and do what needs to be done! Or are you just another worthless, weak loser?" She pointed her gun in the ginger's face. "DO IT!"

He swallowed, took a deep breath, and aimed the gun at Ted's chest.

Ted tried to get up to run but barely managed to crawl. He let out a cry when he felt the bullet in his back. He collapsed on the white tiles and watched them turn red.

"Shove them in that closet and wipe up the blood," Ted heard the old woman say.

"Why?" asked the ginger.

"We don't know when their shift change is! If a new guard comes in, he'll see the bodies right away. If he doesn't immediately notice anything out of the ordinary, it'll buy us some time."

The old woman's voice faded further and further away before Ted lost consciousness.

JONATHAN WONDERED WHERE HE'D SEEN NATE before as he watched him put on the earrings.

"How do I look?" Nate asked Anise. "I just had my ears pierced for the occasion." The way he'd said it sounded like he was trying to joke around with her. Jonathan glared at him. Who in their right mind would make a joke right now? Was this guy some kind of psychopath? Jonathan then realized where he'd seen Nate's face before. He was one Anise had drawn over and over in her sketch book. Jonathan hated him instantly.

Anise remained silent as Jonathan tried to decide

what to do next. Before he could come up with a plan, gun shots rang out from somewhere inside the museum, and he and Anise looked at each other in horror. Jonathan wondered who was being shot and if they would be next.

"Honey, I'm sorry," Nate continued, bringing their attention back to him. He pointed at the amulet that was still around her neck. "I'm going to have to take that. Then you two need to get the hell out of here. If I give it to Grace, there's still a chance she'll be satisfied enough to let you live."

"Give it up, Nate," Anise snarled at him. "I know you're just trying to scare me! You're not getting my amulet because you want to gain whatever control they're after first! And I told you not to call me that anymore!"

"Do you two not understand that Grace and Dan will kill you?" He started walking toward her when Jonathan stepped in front of his path.

"Stay away from her," Jonathan warned, glaring at him.

Nate returned his glare with disdain and annoyance. Jonathan let out a "Hey!" and stumbled to the side when Nate pushed him out of the way.

Nate's hand reached for the amulet around Anise's neck, but before he could touch it, he let out a yelp of pain and rubbed his arm. "What the hell?" he said. "I thought the earrings were supposed to make you stronger?"

"Looks like you didn't do your homework," Jonathan told him with as much snark as he could conjure up. "The earrings haven't been cleared and charged in a few millennia." He gathered his courage and took a swing at Nate. It was too late when he realized that had he swung with the other hand, it would have landed square on the black eye of his opponent. Nate's one non-swollen eye must've seen Jonathan's south-paw punch coming, giving him time to duck and deliver a hook of his own. Jonathan was on the ground with his glasses sliding across the floor before he knew what had happened.

"Stop it!" Anise begged them both. "The guards are going to hear us for sure. They're probably already on their way because you pried into that display case," she snarled at Nate as she kneeled next to Jonathan. Her fingers gently touched his throbbing face, and the song he'd started composing in his head the moment he'd met her continued with the second verse.

"No, they aren't," Nate assured her.

"How is that possible?" she snapped at him. A look of horror washed over her face. "What did you do to them?"

Jonathan was surprised when Nate's expression was one of hurt feelings. But that couldn't be right. Psychopaths don't have feelings.

"Nothing!" Nate insisted. "Last night, I stayed up writing a computer virus, and I just installed it on the alarm control PC. All the alarms have been shut down. Also, every so often, it gives a fake alarm warning for a random location in the museum, with the exception of this room. The guards will be running around all night trying to figure out what's going on." He then looked at Jonathan. "By the way, for future reference, you can't break polycarbonate with a fire extinguisher," Nate told him with an amused grin.

Humiliated and livid, Jonathan got up and attacked Nate with everything he had. He heard Anise let out a shriek. Nate was strong and quick, and Jonathan took a few punches before he barely managed to deliver one of his own. The next blow he took easily knocked him to the ground. Jonathan saw stars, and it took him a moment to get his bearings.

"Get out of here!" Nate demanded. "Both of you!"

Jonathan held a hand to his forehead to try to stop the spinning. "We're not leaving without the earrings!" He stood up and walked toward Nate, his hands clenched into tight, angry fists.

"Just stop. You can't win against me," Nate said matter-of-factly.

Jonathan took a swing that Nate blocked. Before he knew it, Jonathan was back on the ground holding the side of his face. He'd never wanted to hurt anyone before, but words couldn't express how much he wanted to bring Nate to his knees. But how was he going to manage that? He started scrambling backward when Nate took a step toward him.

"Don't hurt him!" Anise told Nate, giving him a shove. "I'm warning you!" She shoved him again.

He grabbed her forearms and held them up by her shoulders. "Stop," he told her in a tone so gentle it surprised Jonathan again. Anise's feet stumbled over each other as Nate carefully but firmly moved her to the side, and set his sights on Jonathan again.

To Jonathan's complete shock, Anise fiercely moved her arms in a swift, downward motion to break Nate's grip. She grabbed him by the arms and kneed him in the groin as if she were trying to move through him. When he doubled over, her forearm came down on the back of his neck with the force of her entire body, and he fell face first to the ground. With one knee on his back, she grabbed his head, pulled it up, and rammed it onto the tile floor.

Nate's body was still. Jonathan looked up to see Anise standing over him, handing back his glasses. "Whoa," was all he was able to say as he put his glasses back on. *What the hell just happened?* He stared in awe at her beautiful face for a moment, then quickly regained his wits. Kneeling in front of the unconscious criminal, he removed the earrings from Nate's ears and handed them to Anise. "Let's get out of here," he said. Anise nodded and made a mad dash toward the ladies' room. Jonathan got up to run too but fell again when a hand caught his ankle.

"Where's Anise?" asked Nate, groggily.

"Gone," replied Jonathan, kicking Nate in his black

eye to free his leg. He started after Anise again only to be stopped at the opening to the hallway by Grace and Dan.

WHAT HAPPENED TO JONATHAN? ANISE WONDERED, thinking he'd been right behind her. Her heart started pounding. She opened the bathroom door a crack just in time to see Grace and Dan confronting him. She immediately closed the door and started to have a panic attack. With her heart racing, hands sweating, and stomach churning, she tried to come up with a plan. She took a deep breath and realized that she was literally holding the answer in the palm of her hand. The earrings paired with the amulet were supposed to make her more powerful than Grace with just the ring. Gently, she washed the earrings under the tap in one of the sinks, and then she used the trash can as a step to be able to reach up and set them in the restroom window, where a few rays of sun were shining through the trees. She wondered how much sun the stones needed to become recharged. If only she had thought to ask Dr. Smithton that question when she'd had the chance.

Trying to distract herself from the anxiety, she paced the floor of the restroom and took a few minutes to wash the dust from her hair, face, and tote bag in one of the sinks. She brushed as much dust as she could off her clothes. Her only chance at helping Jonathan was to wait until the earrings charged. She hoped he would be okay until then.

DAN AND GRACE GRABBED JONATHAN BY the arms and ushered him back into the gallery. "Let me go!" Jonathan shouted as he struggled against them. What was he going to do now? He hoped that Anise had escaped the museum with the earrings. She could call the cops and this whole thing could end soon. Right?

"Who is this?" Grace asked Nate.

"I have no idea," Nate responded. He held a hand to his head where it had hit the floor and looked like he might fall over, but he came to assist Dan with keeping Jonathan immobilized.

They sat Jonathan in a chair against the wall next to a display of Grecian urns, and as Dan and Nate pinned him down, Grace pulled a thin rope from her pocket and tied his wrists and ankles to the chair, while he resisted with everything he had. His efforts were futile, however, and he soon found himself unable to move his arms or legs. The rope was tight and his wrists were hurting already.

"Who are you?" Grace demanded.

Jonathan wasn't about to offer his name. "I'm a museum curator from—"

"Oh, now I get it," she said, interrupting him. "Morty Smithton sent you to do his dirty work."

"Well, he thinks highly of you, too, Grace," snarled Jonathan.

"Who's Morty Smithton?" Dan asked Grace.

She ignored him. "He always did like to delegate the undesirable jobs to a pawn, the candy-ass," she said, with a sneer at Jonathan.

"I volunteered," protested Jonathan, "to preserve and protect the artifacts, per the Curators' Code of Ethics. Perhaps you've heard of it?" he asked Grace, his question dripping with sarcasm.

Dan snickered at Jonathan's indignant statement while Grace rolled her eyes.

"That's very honorable, Boy Scout," said Nate with an obnoxious grin. "But you have to realize that all the ethics in the world won't help you defeat two lunatics with delusional aspirations of world domination."

Grace glared at him.

"You're right, psychopath," shot back Jonathan, although he was a little confused by Nate's statement. Why would he call his partners in crime 'lunatics' and 'delusional' in front of the enemy? "And all the delusional aspirations in the world won't bring you domination. If I can't defeat you, someone else will."

Nate laughed out loud. "Does that sound familiar at all?" he asked his two partners.

"Enough of this already," Grace said to Nate. "Stop wasting my time with this ridiculous banter! You have the earrings, right? Let's get out of here right after I end him." She pointed her gun at Jonathan.

"No," said Nate, after touching his earlobes. He let out a quiet groan that Jonathan barely heard.

"What?" Grace shrieked. "You screwed up again, you worthless little shit?! What did I ever do to deserve such incompetence around me?" She searched Jonathan's pockets for the earrings but found nothing. Grace looked around. "The girl, she came with you, didn't she? She must be around here, too. Where is she?"

"Don't do anything with him until I get back," Nate demanded, pointing at Jonathan. He ran out into the hallway.

Jonathan presumed Nate was going to look for Anise. She must've escaped out the window by now so she should be safe. Jonathan remained silent, staring Grace right in the eyes. If his life ended tonight, at least he knew he'd done everything he could to help Anise and to protect precious artifacts.

"WHERE IS THE GIRL?" Grace screamed in his face.

"Gone," he told her. "She took the earrings and ran. She's long gone by now."

"Liar!" she yelled at him.

Her ear-piercing shriek and wild, unkempt white hair on which she kept pulling made Jonathan think of her as half Banshee, half Medusa. As frightened as he was, he couldn't help but think: *doesn't this woman own a comb?*

Grace held the ring in front of his face and twisted it to expose the poisonous side. "You know what I can do to you with this ring, right? Tell me where she is," she threatened him.

Chapter 20

After what seemed like the longest and most frustrating road trip ever, Brian finally made it to the Springfield Museum. It was already evening; he hoped Anise was still there, although that was unlikely. If not, he'd have to drive around to nearby hotels to look for her. Corinne was still calling him every so often, but he'd talk to her later. Finding Anise was his number one priority right now.

He hadn't slept in 36 hours, hadn't eaten since his beef jerky in the car the night before, and couldn't get Anise and Nate out of his mind. He'd spent money on that goddamn tire that would have to cut into his beer savings. He was humiliated, angry, and exhausted. If one more thing went wrong, he felt like he could definitely hurt somebody.

Brian found free parking on the street. The stairs that lead up to the museum seemed never-ending, but he dragged himself along. He grabbed the door handle and pulled, but the door didn't move. His eyes moved to the sign on the door that stated museum hours were nine to six daily. *Closed*. *Shit*. He hit his head on the glass door and felt like an idiot. All this way for nothing, and Corinne had warned him, too. He should've listened to her.

Just then, he saw something move in his peripheral vision. He looked up. *Was that Nate?* He ran to the window next to the front door and peered in to see who it was. The man had dark hair and had the same build as Nate. Brian hadn't seen his face, but it very possibly could be *him*. He was running along the hallway, ducking into galleries as he went and then coming back out, as if he was looking for someone or something. Angry that his suspicions had possibly just been proven right, Brian tried the window even though it had bars on it, but it was locked as well. He walked around the museum trying every window he could reach, not caring if anyone saw him.

THE SUN HAD MOVED AND WAS no longer shining in the window of the ladies' room. Anise picked up the earrings and walked over to one of the mirrors above the sinks to put them on. The posts of the earrings were larger than she was used to, and she had to work them into her piercings slowly by pushing them in tiny increments. She felt her piercings being stretched, and it made her earlobes throb with a small amount of pain.

Once in, she admired their beauty. She stood looking at the chalcedony hoops in the mirror for a few seconds, not knowing what to expect. She didn't feel any different. According to the legend, the earrings were supposed to provide the wearer with strength, endurance, health, and vitality and that both the earrings' and the amulet's power would be intensified by each other. She really didn't feel any more energetic and had no idea how to test for vitality. And she certainly didn't have time to expose herself to someone with a cold to test for health or attempt a marathon to test for endurance. But strength—that was something she could test here in the ladies' room. There wasn't anything freestanding and heavy for her to try lifting, so she grabbed the edges of the counter that held the sinks, closed her eyes, and pulled. To her surprise, she heard a loud tearing sound. She opened her eyes and saw that the entire counter was disconnected from the wall. *Holy shit! I barely touched it!* she thought, as she placed the counter on the floor. In the mirror's reflection, she noticed the chalcedony gemstones sparkling by her face and looked at them in wonder. *Does that mean they're working? Kind of like when the amulet glows? Or perhaps the sink counter was already really loose, and my feat of strength was a fluke?* She decided to try another test before confronting Grace.

She looked at the metal dividers of the bathroom stalls. They seemed to be screwed into the wall and floor, and everything looked pretty sturdy. She grabbed the side wall of the stall from the bottom which was about a foot above the floor, braced herself, and pulled hard. In a split second, she had fallen backward into a seated position from the intensity of her pull, and she was holding the entire stall in her hands, two walls and a door, which had come out of the wall and broken away from the second stall. Her arms were still above her head from falling backward, and she felt like she was holding nothing heavier than perhaps a paperback book. The strength tests definitely worked! She turned her head toward the mirrors and saw the earrings once again were sparkling. An idea popped in her head as a way to test her endurance as well. She kept her arms above her head while still holding the entire stall for about a minute, and they never started to feel tired or heavy. "Okay, it's time to go back out there and help Jonathan," she told herself in a shaking voice, trying to ignore the nauseating fear. "I can do this."

✳ ✳ ✳

NATE HURRIED BACK TO THE GALLERY. "I didn't find her," he announced.

"As if you could find your nose on your face," Grace snapped at him. "And what were those loud sounds I heard?"

Nate had heard the unusual sounds coming from the ladies' room. He hoped Anise had charged the earrings and was testing out her new strength. "They sounded like they were coming from the basement," he lied.

Grace was hovering over their captive curator, threatening him with the ring. Boy Scout was struggling against his ropes, his glasses were falling off his face, and he looked like he might piss himself at any moment. *Shit.* "If you poison him, he's probably going to pass out for a while like I did," Nate told Grace. "Not a good idea if you want information from him."

Grace glared at Nate. "Dan, you get him to tell you where the girl is," she said, pointing to Boy Scout. "In the meantime, *I'm* going to go look for her since Nate is so incompetent. I'm positive she wouldn't just leave this candy-ass behind. She's got to be somewhere in the museum." She grabbed Dan's and Nate's sleeves and pulled their ears close to her mouth. "Listen carefully! If you see her before I do, I want you to strike this deal with her. Tell her if she gives you some of her blood, you'll let her live."

"What the hell are you talking about?" Nate demanded. "Why?"

"You don't have to understand it, just do it!" Grace snarled at him. "Once she agrees to the deal, and *only* then, make sure you put some of her blood in this bag. I'll need it for something very important later."

"Then we let her go?" asked Dan. "As per the deal?"

"No. Then you kill her anyway." She put a freezer bag in Dan's shirt pocket and then turned and quickly walked away.

"What the fuck?!" Nate asked Dan in a panicked

whisper. "Blood?! What does she want that for? And why does she want us to strike that fucked up deal?"

Dan shook his head. "How the hell should I know? But if it's what Mother wants..."

"So you're going to do it?"

Dan laughed nervously. "Oh, no, I'm not going to do it. That's your job." He shoved the freezer bag in Nate's hand and headed back to Boy Scout.

Nate dropped the freezer bag on the floor and followed him.

Dan bent over, and from under his pant leg, he pulled out a gun.

"Where'd you get that?" Nate asked him.

"The security guard didn't need it anymore." Dan checked to see how many bullets the gun had while Boy Scout watched and turned pale. "We both know you're lying," Dan said to Boy Scout in a calm voice. "You know exactly where Anise went, don't you? Why don't you tell me where she's hiding, and once we find her, we'll let you go. Hell, we'll even let her go, too. All we want is the Jewelry."

Boy Scout looked Dan in the eye. "If you think I'm going to believe that bullshit, you're a lot more vacuous than you look."

"What does vacuous mean?" Dan hissed to Nate.

Nate ignored him. Now that he knew there was no way Grace was going to let Anise live, Nate had to make a decision on how to stop the old hag. "I'm going to help Grace look," he announced to Dan and headed out of the gallery. Except he wouldn't look for Anise, he'd look for Grace. And once he found her...he wasn't sure what would happen. But he'd stop her. Somehow.

AFTER HAVING WALKED AROUND TO THE other side of the

museum, Brian climbed onto a low tree branch and finally found a window that was unlocked. He pulled himself up through the window and found himself to be in a men's restroom. Hoping there weren't guards walking around in the hallway, he opened the door and looked out. He heard people talking in the gallery to his left but couldn't understand what they were saying. Brian stepped out into the hallway, figuring that they were probably museum staff setting up a new exhibit. He would have to avoid them and be quiet. He turned to his right and started quickly down the hall.

He walked through every gallery and then headed upstairs. "Nate must be around here somewhere," Brian mumbled to himself. No one at all was to be found on the second floor, so he came back down the stairs and continued on to the basement. Again, no one was to be found there either. He started heading back toward the one gallery he didn't check, the one with the voices coming from it. Maybe Nate and Anise were with the museum staff after hours? But why? None of this was making any sense to him. He hoped he could peek into the gallery and see who was in there without being seen. He tiptoed over to the open doors of the gallery and very carefully looked inside. It was difficult to tell exactly who he saw, as there were display cases in the way, but he saw two men. A red-haired man had his back to Brian. Another man that Brian didn't recognize had glasses and was sitting on a chair against the wall. He could only see the head of that man, as there was a display case in front of him. The one that could have been Nate wasn't there, and there was no sign of Anise, either.

Suddenly, his phone began to vibrate. It was Corinne calling, yet again. Brian ducked under a nearby set of stairs and took the call. He knew his sister must be worried sick.

"Corinne, I'm fine, but I can't talk right now. I'll call you later, okay?" Brian whispered.

"No, Brian, it's not okay! Where the hell are you, and what are you doing?"

"I thought I saw the guy Anise is dating running around the halls of the Springfield Museum, so I broke in, and I'm trying to find him. I thought Anise would be with him."

"Brian, do you realize how paranoid you sound right now?"

"Yeah, okay, but it's true."

"So, did you find Anise?"

"No," he replied, feeling embarrassed. "I walked around the entire museum and looked in every gallery, and she was nowhere."

"And were you able to confirm the man you saw as the one Anise is seeing?"

He sighed. "No. I only saw the back of his head through a window. He probably works at the museum."

"You didn't find him and confront him?"

"Of course not, Corinne; I don't want to get caught breaking and entering. That's the last thing I need after what I've been through today."

"So you drove all night, broke into a museum, and didn't find anything at all. Don't you think you overreacted?"

Feeling embarrassed, Brian saw how unlikely it would be that the dark haired man was Nate. Anise wasn't there either, and why would she be? The museum was closed. "Yeah, okay." He hung his head in shame.

"Come back home, Brian," his sister encouraged.

"I'm on my way." They said their goodbyes and hung up. Although there still were plenty of unanswered questions, such as why she was in Springfield and who paid for her lodging last night, they could wait to be answered. He didn't need to risk jail time. Anise was afraid of him right now, and he couldn't blame her. She was probably here with one of her friends to feel safe for a while. He felt like an idiot for overreacting and guilty for wanting to hurt her. After listening for footsteps and carefully looking around, he came out from behind the stairs and started walking back toward the men's room where he had entered the museum. He'd start driving back tonight and pull over into a rest stop when he was too tired to drive anymore.

He tiptoed back toward the restroom, but when he reached out a hand to push the door open, he heard what sounded like a low, quiet groan coming from inside a closet to his left. He stepped over to the closet door and listened for a few seconds. Nothing.

He started to walk away when he heard it again. He grasped the knob and opened the door, cringing in disgust at what he saw. Two security guards were on the floor of the closet. The older one was staring up at the ceiling with wide-open, unblinking eyes. "Holy shit," Brian said, under his breath. The other one was groaning softly. Every bodily fluid Brian could think of was on the floor of the closet. He almost gagged from the sight and the smell and had to look away to take in a breath and compose himself. "What the hell happened?" he asked the younger one, but the guard couldn't speak. "I'll call for help," Brian told him, closing the closet door again so he wouldn't get sick from the stench. He took his cell phone out of his pocket and dialed 9-1-1. An operator picked up after one ring.

"9-1-1, what's your emergency?"

"I'm at the Springfield Museum, and..." Brian hung up the phone when he happened to glance down the hall. A brown-haired woman had just poked her head out of the women's restroom about twenty-five yards away from him. When her head swiveled in his direction, she saw him, and she gave him a look of shock.

"Brian?!" came her familiar voice.

"Anise!" He couldn't believe he'd decided to give her the benefit of the doubt when he'd been right all along. She was a lying, cheating slut, and he felt all his rage coming back in triplicate.

"Brian, what are you doing here?" she asked in a loud whisper as she briskly walked toward him.

He started toward her as well. "You better answer me that question first!" he yelled at her.

"Shhh!" she hushed him. "Keep your voice down! We're not alone—"

He interrupted her, his voice still booming. "You're obviously not on a business trip, so why are you here? What happened to those guards in the closet? And why are you here with *him?* You better start explaining, and it better be good!"

She looked like she wanted to bolt, so he reached out and tried to grab her. A sudden burning sensation shot through his arm, and as he rubbed it, he saw her amulet start to glow. The eerie, unnatural light that seemed to come from the center stone caused him to shiver and made him want to grab it and smash it into a million pieces on the floor. The last time he'd seen the amulet glow, he'd told himself it was just the reflection of the overhead lights. He reminded himself of that and his explanation made him feel a little less disturbed by the weird glow that got stronger the closer he was to her. He ignored the amulet, got in Anise's face, and thundered at her, "Tell me what the fuck is going on!" He enjoyed seeing the frightened look on her lying face.

"Go away Brian!" Anise yelled back.

"Start talking now or you'll regret it," Brian gruffly snarled at her. He almost jumped when Nate stepped in front of him. He'd hadn't even heard Nate approaching. So she *was* here with *him.*

"Leave her alone," Nate demanded.

"I don't need your help, Nate," Anise told him as she took a few steps away from him.

"That's not what it looks like to me," he responded. He took a step closer to Brian and looked at him, expressionless. "Here's how it's going to be. You're going to apologize to her and go home, or I'm going to make you wish you had."

Brian didn't like the way Nate's freakishly blue eyes looked dead when they stared at him, especially the eye with the shiner. It was creepy and intimidating and made him want to back away, but he forced himself to maintain his position. "Fuck you!" Brian shouted. "Stay away from my girlfriend!" He took a swing at Nate.

Nate dodged Brian's flying fist and landed three swift punches in a row.

"Stop! Both of you!" Anise yelled at them.

Brian touched his aching nose and felt blood. Surprised that Nate hadn't fallen as easily as the last time he'd seen him, Brian let a few expletives fly in Nate's direction. He couldn't let this asshole win. Anise was watching. Or was she? Brian saw her turn and head toward the gallery behind her. "Where the hell do you think you're going?"

"Go home, Brian! And not to *my* apartment!" she shot back.

He darted after her and tried to grab her again. Her amulet began to glow and a shot of pain surged up his arm. "What is that?" he demanded, pointing at the amulet. "It's like it's protecting you!"

"It is!" she yelled back. "It glows every time you intend to hurt me!"

Brian opened his mouth to yell at her but didn't know what to say. "Bullshit! Stop lying!"

"It's true," she insisted and turned to leave again.

He knew at that moment that he'd lost her. Not only was she still lying and cheating, she was insulting his intelligence. Watching the love of his life humiliate him and then walk away like she was glad to be rid of him made him need to break something, and for a moment, he wanted that something to be her long, thin neck. As soon as he imagined his hands around her throat and took a couple steps toward her, she turned around to face him, and the amulet began to glow again. "What the...?!"

"You were planning to hurt me again, weren't you?" she said, motioning to the amulet.

"Okay, let's say it's true," Brian snarled. He didn't know how she was reading his mind or making the amulet glow, but he wasn't going to be bested by a goddamn necklace, especially not in front of Anise and her new boyfriend. He enjoyed the look of fear in her eyes as he stepped closer to her. "You have to take it off sometime, bitch, and when you do, I'm going to—" Brian didn't get to finish his sentence. Before he knew what was happening, he was flat on his back, his head slamming on the cold, tile floor. His eyes opened wide to see that Nate had tackled him.

"Don't fucking threaten her again!" Nate's fists rained blows of fury on Brian's face.

After a short struggle on the museum floor, Brian shoved Nate off of him and they both jumped to their feet.

"You're dead, mother fucker!" Brian spit out some blood as his hands tightly turned into fists.

"You're almost right," said another voice. A tiny old woman stepped out from a small gallery off the hallway and positioned herself between Brian and Nate. While Brian tried to make sense of her presence, she raised her arm and he found himself staring down the barrel of her gun. Before he could react, there was a loud ring and a bright light. Everything that came next seemed to happen in slow motion. Brian felt a terrible headache, and he felt himself falling as everything went black. He never felt his body hit the ground.

Chapter 21

Anise let out the loudest scream of her life. She tried to move, but her limbs were frozen for a moment. Brian's lifeless body lay on the floor of the museum hallway in a crumpled, unnatural way. His blood had splattered on the ground, on the wall, and on the hanging photograph of downtown Springfield in 1912. In horror, she mindlessly ran toward Brian and then stopped. Creeping forward the last couple of feet, she approached Brian's body. Kneeling on the ground next to him, she looked at his face. The expression that had been so angry just thirty seconds before was now emotionless. There was a hole in his forehead, and his eyes looked at her without seeing. She covered her mouth with her hand and screamed into her palm.

Faintly, she heard voices in the background. They got louder as her initial shock began to wear off.

"What the fuck, Grace?!" Nate's voice was saying. "I had the situation handled!"

"We don't have time for you to fight some goliath!" came Grace's retort. "Show off on your own time! Besides, we can't leave a witness alive, and you're not man enough to kill anyone!"

Anise's panic attack came on quickly, and she wasn't sure if she'd faint or get sick. She didn't have time to do either. Grace was standing next to her and pressing a gun to the back of her neck with one hand and the poison-exposed part of the ring to her head with the other. Anise knew that by using the ring on her, Grace was trying to cancel out the powers of the amulet. While hyperventilating, Anise brought her elbow back forcefully onto whatever part of Grace she could reach in an attempt to make her lose her balance. Anise was surprised when Grace flew several feet backward before she hit the floor.

It must be the strength from the earrings!

Grace got up and ran toward Anise. The Armor ring on Grace's finger still had the poisonous side exposed, and her gun was pointed at Anise's head as she ran.

With surprising speed, Nate tackled Grace and reached for the gun. From her place on the ground, Grace pressed on his shoulder, causing him to yell out and roll off of her. As he winced and held his shoulder, she put a bullet in his thigh.

Anise flinched at the sound of the gunshot and looked up to see Grace aiming the gun at her again. Turning away from Grace, Anise ran toward the gallery. She could hear Grace's footsteps behind her. Her fear caused her to look at Grace over her shoulder, and she tripped, falling flat on her face.

Grace caught up to her, knelt on her back, pressed the ring to her skin, and held the gun to the back of her head again. "This is too easy!" Grace laughed. Her laughter stopped quickly, however. "What's going on?" Grace yelled at the gun. "The goddamn trigger's stuck!"

Anise knew that wearing both the amulet and the earrings was increasing both her protection and her strength, and Grace wouldn't be able to cancel out the amulet's power because Grace had only one piece of Armor Jewelry where Anise had two. She wondered how long it would take Grace to figure out that she was wearing the earrings.

Thrashing herself to the side with all her might,

Anise rolled Grace off her back and got up to run again. She glanced behind her to see Grace aiming the gun at her back, trying to shoot over and over.

Anise heard Grace planting a couple bullets in the photographs on the wall in the hallway. Glass exploded and rained onto the tile floor. Moving as fast as she could, Anise was amazed at how the earrings made her feel like she was bounding instead of running, almost like she was flying between steps. The earrings made her move differently, and she knew she'd have to be mindful about what she was doing or she might accidentally hurt herself or someone else. She darted through the gallery doors but stopped, frantically turning one way and then the other to look around for Jonathan. Finally, she caught sight of him tied up in a chair in the ancient Greece section.

Grace had followed her and ran at her with a raised arm, her fist grasping the gun's barrel as if she wanted to hit Anise over the head with the end of the gun, but it was ripped from her hand by a force so strong it took her glove off as well. Both the gun and glove went flying to the Mallandia side of the gallery. She screamed and pulled on her hair while her face crinkled up as if she were in pain.

Grace ran toward the gun that had landed near a display of Mallandian beads but stopped in her tracks. "Ants! And beetles!" Grace yelled. Anise watched her frantically brushing off her clothes and tongue. "The ceiling! It's caving in!" Grace ducked and covered her head. She looked up and screamed. "Not the cast iron pan!"

Even though Anise was still shaking from everything she'd just witnessed, she'd now had enough of the emotional trauma and was ready to put an end to things any way she could. She would not let Grace get away with murder. Reminding herself that she had both the amulet and the earrings now, she felt a little stronger and more confident. Ignoring Grace, she turned back toward Jonathan who was staring at her with sweat running down his face. She'd left him alone entirely too long, and she hoped they hadn't hurt him. She heard Grace running toward her from the other side of the room, her huffing and puffing getting louder.

Dan was threatening Jonathan with a gun. "Don't touch him!" Anise yelled, as she walked straight toward Dan and Jonathan, her eyes glued to Dan's face.

Dan aimed the gun at her legs and pulled the trigger. He was close to point blank range, but Anise was not hit. The bullet whizzed around her and left a hole in the wall to her left. Anise kept walking confidently toward him, never missing a stride. She grabbed his gun, and although Dan held on tightly, she easily pulled it from his grip. She didn't know anything about guns and hadn't the slightest idea how to remove the bullets, so she simply grasped the barrel with both hands and with all her might, bent it until it was in the shape of a "U." She flung it across the room, and everyone watched as it crashed through the drywall.

Grace's eyes narrowed. "I know what's going on now. The way you were running, and your strength...you're wearing the earrings, aren't you? You charged them with running water and a sunny window! You were in the bathroom! The one place I didn't look!"

Feeling powerful, Anise flipped her hair over her shoulder so Grace could catch a glimpse of an earring. She wanted to say something that would let them all know that *she* was in charge now. But she noticed some of Brian's blood was on her hand, and the realization of what had happened in the hallway hit Anise like a bus with no breaks. She blinked back tears as visions of Brian's death assaulted her mind, and she felt sick with guilt. The guilt rapidly turned to anger that she carried in her clenched jaw. She saw Dan looking at her with wide, frightened eyes, and she shoved him away with all her might. Her force lifted him off the ground as he flew backward into a display case of Greek goddess statues, knocking it over.

Anise turned on her heel and headed toward Grace, who was watching her from near the entryway to the gallery.

"Why?" Anise shouted at Grace. "Why did you have to kill him?" She placed a hand over the glowing amulet and tried to sound as confident as possible but heard her voice wavering. Through the doors of the gallery, she could see Brian's body in the hallway. Angry tears threatened to spill over. If only she'd been more honest with Brian, maybe he wouldn't have come looking for her and still be alive.

"Get out of my way!" Grace snarled at her while walking around her, bumping into her shoulder as she passed. "I've had enough of this! End him!" she shouted to Dan while pointing at Jonathan. "And then she'll be next!"

"Hey!" Anise shouted at her. "We're not done here!" She picked up Grace's small, frail body and threw her into a chair twenty feet away. Grace landed hard, her head banging against a case of Mallandian sword hilts as she fell on the wooden chair on her hip. She winced, eyes closed, holding her hip.

From her place by the gallery doors, Anise's gaze traveled to the Egyptian section of the room when she heard movement, and she caught sight of Nate watching from near the sarcophagus. He had tied his light, cotton jacket around his leg. Blood was soaking through, and it made Anise wonder how he'd managed to hobble back to the gallery. Ignoring him, she walked over to Grace who hadn't moved after crash landing into the chair. "Give me the ring," Anise demanded.

"Never!" shot back Grace with a snarl.

"Give me the ring before I pull your fucking hand off!" Anise forcefully grabbed Grace's arm, ripped the ring off her finger, and put it on her own.

Grace screamed. "You broke my finger!" She held up her hand in front of her face, and Anise saw that Grace's finger was indeed bent the wrong way.

Anise felt sick and backed away from Grace. She

hadn't meant to break Grace's bones, but she hadn't known her own strength. Her anger had made her lose her mindfulness when it came to moving while wearing the earrings. She couldn't let this happen again. This wasn't her. She hated violence. Now that she had all the Jewelry, she was unstoppable. She could untie Jonathan, and they could go home, right?

She turned away and darted toward Jonathan. Dan had recovered from Anise's shove and had made his way back to where Jonathan was tied to the chair. Anise saw Dan pull a knife out of his pocket, as he no longer had his gun.

Jonathan! She should've untied him first before taking her anger out on Grace. She ran faster toward him.

"Stop!" commanded Dan. "Or your friend dies," he added, as he held the knife to Jonathan's throat.

Anise stopped. Jonathan stared at her, sweating and breathing quickly.

"Ha!" came the happy sound of victory from Grace.

Dan's face lit up. "I'm taking the initiative!" he announced proudly to Grace.

Humiliated, Anise couldn't believe that here she was, with all of the Armor Jewelry in her possession, and she still couldn't defeat these people. She picked up a nearby trash can and flung it at Dan out of frustration, hoping it would hit him hard enough to knock him out. Dan dropped the knife and ducked. Unfortunately, her aim was off, and the trash can hit Jonathan in the arm, hard. She covered her mouth and nose with her hands as Jonathan winced.

Grace laughed out loud and Dan joined her. He picked up the knife and again held it to Jonathan's throat.

Anise knew she had to find some way to stop Dan from hurting Jonathan. Out of desperation, she walked over to Nate, shoved him aside, and, with some effort, picked up the stone sarcophagus. Nate slammed into the wall, landing half in, half out of the drywall, and struggled to free himself. Leaving Nate in the wall, Anise threw the sarcophagus in Grace's direction from halfway across the room. Anise didn't want to hurt anyone but was hoping to scare Grace and Dan enough to gain control of the situation.

Grace screamed, but easily managed to jump out of the way of being crushed under the weight of the giant coffin. The stone shattered against the wall, and the mummy, along with large pieces of the stone, fell out on top of Grace, knocking her over. She screamed again, clawing her way free from her corpse captor.

"You finally have a friend your own age to hang out with," Nate called over to her, still trying to free himself from the wall.

"What's wrong with you?" Grace screamed her reply. "Why aren't you helping me?"

Before anyone could say anything else, Anise tore the large display case of Mallandian sword hilts out of the wall. The electrical wires for the lighting in the case tore in half and shot out a few sparks. She held it up over her head, not really wanting to throw it on top of Grace but hoping that the threatening pose might be enough to start a negotiation—Grace's life for Jonathan's. At that moment, she heard Jonathan cry out in pain. Dan had stabbed him in the back with his pocket knife.

"I warned you!" he yelled out. "You hurt Mother, and I'll slit his throat!"

Anise slowly put down the display case. She didn't want to take any chances, as it seemed unlikely Dan would be willing to negotiate. Grace was no longer a threat, but Dan was. How to stop him? She started making her way toward him.

"Stay where you are," Dan warned her. "Or he'll be dead before you get here. Hand over the Jewelry to Mother, and I'll let you and your friend go."

Anise looked at Jonathan, who was squeezing his eyes shut, probably from the pain of the knife wounds in his back. There was a stream of blood running down his back that had soaked through his brand new t-shirt that Anise had helped him pick out the night before.

She felt so helpless, even with all of her new found ability. She turned around and looked at Nate who had just managed to pull himself out of the wall. The jacket around his leg was completely saturated with his blood. He caught her gaze and made a turning motion with one hand over the ring finger of his other hand, while pointing with his eyes at Grace. Was he trying to tell her to poison Grace with the ring? She shook her head at him with a horrified look in her eyes. If she used the ring, Grace would die. Anise knew she could never kill anyone under any circumstances. He then made a motion that told her to take off her amulet first and then use the ring. Why was he trying to help her? *He probably just doesn't want me to hurt him,* she thought, narrowing her eyes. She understood that his suggestion was just to immobilize Grace with the poison, and she was considering it, but her thoughts were interrupted.

"My legs!" Grace was screaming. "I think they're broken! I can't move!"

"Nate, don't just stand there, help her!" said Dan.

Grace was still struggling with the large pieces of the sarcophagus that had her legs trapped. Nate looked at Anise and winked with his one good eye as he limped over to Grace. He tried to pick up the large stone pieces to free her, but he groaned when attempting to budge them.

"They're too heavy," Nate said to Dan. "I need your help. You better hurry; it looks like she's getting crushed. She might lose both her legs," he said in a worried voice. The way he smirked at Anise made her understand that he was lying.

"I can't breathe!" Grace yelled. "Hurry, Dan! Help me!"

Dan began hurrying over to his mother while Anise

started toward Jonathan.

"Don't let her get to him!" Grace commanded. "They'll make off with the Jewelry!"

Dan hurried back to Jonathan and held the knife to his throat again. "Stay away!" he shouted to Anise.

"Help me!" shouted Grace again.

"Well which is it?" Dan cried out in frustration.

Nate smiled at Anise, and when she caught herself smiling back, she looked away. She was grateful to him for turning the tables so quickly, even if the only reason was so he'd have a chance to get the Jewelry first. But she never wanted to see his smile again, and he'd certainly never get to see hers.

"Stay there," Nate told Dan. "I'll get Anise to help me."

"What?!" Anise cried.

"If Dan puts down the knife, will you please help?"

"Okay," Anise agreed. To Dan she said, "Get rid of the knife."

"No!" shouted Grace. "Don't do it, Dan!"

"She's in really bad shape," Nate said to Dan with a slight grin in Anise's direction. "I hope it's not too late."

"Okay," Dan said, dropping the knife to the floor and kicking it across the room.

"No! What are you doing?!" Grace screamed.

Anise came over to Grace to lift the stone pieces off her. As she lifted the first stone, she noticed she was having a lot of trouble. How strange, after having picked up the entire sarcophagus so easily. As she lifted the second stone, her arms started shaking from the weight, and she dropped it right next to Grace. She grabbed the third stone and realized that she didn't have a chance in hell at lifting it anymore. What was happening?

Nate helped her remove the last stone, kneeled behind Grace's head, and pointed at Jonathan with his eyes. "Go," he mouthed at her.

Suddenly, she remembered the window sill in the bathroom and how the rays had been weak through the tree branches. There hadn't been enough sun. The earrings were running out of energy.

Anise got up and made a mad dash toward Jonathan, hoping she still had enough strength to fight Dan.

Immediately afterward, Jonathan let out another cry of pain. "I always carry a spare," Dan told Anise coldly, referring to the second pocket knife that was now cutting into Jonathan's shoulder.

Anise let out an involuntary cry. *Why didn't I at least try to negotiate more?* she asked herself. *I should've asked Dan to untie him, not just throw the knife away. What the hell was I thinking?*

"I've had enough of this!" shouted Dan. "Give Mother the Jewelry, or he's dead. Now!"

"Don't do it, Anise!" Jonathan told her, wincing from another stab. "Then they'll kill us both!"

"I can't let you die," Anise told him, right before he passed out.

Grace snorted in amusement. "She's weak!" she exclaimed with delight. "Just like you," she added callously, looking at Nate.

Carefully, Anise removed the earrings. Grace snatched them from her hand and put them in her own ears. Next, Anise removed the ring, and Grace grabbed it before Anise had it completely off.

"Now the amulet!" demanded Dan.

Anise backed away from Grace. "No," she said. She placed her hand over the amulet, and it glowed as Grace got up and walked toward her. Anise realized that the earrings were making Grace stronger or else she wouldn't have been able to stride so quickly and seemingly without any pain.

"I'll just have to take it then!" said Grace.

She grabbed Anise, and with some of the last remaining energy of the earrings, she managed to pick Anise up and drop her flat on her back. She twisted the ring and held it to Anise's arm while pinning her down. Anise started feeling a little of the poison being injected into her body from the ring. *The earrings must still have a little power left*, she realized, as they emitted a few weak sparkles, *or else I wouldn't feel any of the poison*. If the earrings had completely run out of power, the amulet and ring would be canceling each other out. But since Grace had both the earrings and the ring, even though the earrings were about out of charge, she was stronger than Anise. Anise kicked Grace in the legs, and Grace tried to beat Anise over the head with a piece of the broken sarcophagus.

The earrings had almost stopped sparkling and Anise no longer felt the poison being injected into her system. As soon as the earrings charge died, she and Grace would be on equal ground. She tried to push Grace away with her hands and feet.

"What's going on? Why aren't I stronger from the earrings?" Grace wondered out loud as she struggled against Anise's attempts to fight back. The earrings barely had any sparkles left. Grace hadn't been able to fight Anise into submission but had just enough extra strength from the earrings to push her head down and remove the amulet from around her neck. The two continued struggling. Grace tried to put the amulet on, but when Anise pushed her, she dropped it. Both women reached to grab it, but each held the other off. "Why aren't you helping me?" Grace demanded of Nate who was hobbling toward them. "Grab the amulet! We need to end this!"

"You're right." Nate stepped up to her. "Grace, watch out!" he warned.

Startled, Grace jumped up to look at him. "For what?" she asked him with a confused look on her face.

"This!" Nate's right jab met her face. Grace's head snapped backward, and she went down, hit her head on the ground, and was still.

"What the hell?!" Dan shouted as he started running across the room toward Grace.

Quickly, Nate removed the ring from Grace's finger and the earrings from her lobes, and he handed them to Anise as she picked up the amulet from the floor. "Take them," he said, his intense blue eyes looking at her in a way she remembered all too well. "Run!" he told her.

Anise looked behind her and saw Dan almost upon them. Clutching all the Jewelry tightly in her hand, she ran but wasn't sure of a plan beyond that. It's not like she'd leave Jonathan behind. Maybe if she could find a place to hide and think for a minute she could decide how to get them both out of there. Nate stood and took a swing at Dan who swung back with the knife, slashing Nate's arm.

Anise ran harder but felt a little weak and nauseated from the poison and wasn't quick enough. Dan came speeding up to her and tackled her. She fell face down on the ground and dropped the Jewelry, which scattered across the gallery floor.

Anise, Dan, and Nate all scrambled to get to the Jewelry first. Dan climbed right over Anise, stepping on her back and almost kicking her in the face along the way. Dan reached the ring and slipped it on his finger. Nate and Dan each got one of the earrings, and Anise managed to claim her amulet. Anise found herself wondering if the earrings had any power separately or if they had to be together. She put the amulet around her neck.

Neither man was going to give up possession of the other Jewelry so easily. With no time to put the earrings on, they attacked each other with everything they had. While the boys kept themselves busy, Anise finally got the chance to run over to Jonathan, who had regained consciousness.

"I'm so sorry," Anise apologized as she untied him. "Are you okay?"

"Yeah," he said, even though he looked anything but okay. His face was pale and there was dried blood on his back. "Come on," he said as soon as she freed him from the rope. She followed him through the Greek and Meso-potamian exhibits and over to the ancient Egyptian side of the gallery. Jonathan reached up and took two piri-form maces off the wall, handing one to her. She rested the cone-shaped stone mace head on her shoulder and held on to its handle firmly. They snuck around to the other side of the room where Nate and Dan were still fighting.

"You take Dan; I'll take Nate," Jonathan said, and charged.

"No!" yelled Anise, not wanting any more violence, but then quickly shut her mouth when she realized her yell warned Nate and Dan of their attacker.

Nate and Dan both turned to protect themselves against Jonathan and his mace. Anise hurried over to the three men, wondering how she'd stop the fighting without having to hurt anyone. After taking a swing that missed his target, Jonathan stumbled and fell on his knees. His mace fell to the floor and rolled over by Dan's feet. Nate threw a punch at Dan that landed on his jaw and then got another slice in his arm from Dan's knife.

Dan kicked Jonathan in the face, and he went down. Picking up the mace, Dan hit Nate in the chest and knocked the wind out of him. Nate also went down, wheezing heav-ily.

Scared, Anise backed away. She saw Dan pry the other earring out of Nate's hand and then start walking toward her with the mace. Wanting to distract his mind, Anise darted away and raised her mace over the body of the still unconscious Grace.

"Mother!" yelled Dan, and scurried over to her. He took a swing at Anise, but she jumped out of the way. The amulet glowed. He scowled at her, but it quickly faded as he put on the earrings. Since he wore the ring and there was still a minute amount of energy left in the earrings, he lunged at her and was able to knock her over with another swing of the mace that smacked her in the leg. She went down with a hand on her chest, feeling like she couldn't breathe. Dan removed the amulet forcefully from around her neck. Looking down his nose at her, he put it on. "You wanna piss with the big dogs little girl, you better learn to lift your leg higher than that. Right, Mother?" He looked over at Grace and the disappointment showed in his expression when he realized she hadn't come to yet.

Anise grimaced and grabbed the back of her thigh where Dan had hit her. She turned to look behind her. Relief washed over her when she saw that Jonathan had his eyes open. Nate was still trying to catch his breath from the heavy blow of the mace to his chest.

"Mother," Dan said softly, kneeling down next to Grace. "I did it! We have all the Jewelry. Wake up." He shook her gently, and Grace opened her eyes.

Suddenly, the sound of police sirens filled the air, and they were coming closer.

"Who called the cops?" Nate asked, looking at Anise and Jonathan. "I know the alarms didn't trigger any calls. I made sure of it."

"You have the Jewelry?" Grace asked Dan.

"Yes," Dan confirmed. "And now we have to get out of here before the cops get here."

"Give it to me!" Grace demanded.

"I will, but later, Mother. Right now, we really have to go." He tried to pick her up.

"No! Now!" she yelled at him, and pushed him away. "You'll lose it!"

With a sigh, he took the earrings out of his ears and handed them to her. Then he removed the ring. He held it between his thumb and forefinger as he waited for her to put on the earrings.

Jonathan had crawled so slowly and quietly across the floor that no one had noticed him but Anise. He glanced at her as she made a twisting motion with her fingers. Jonathan nodded, indicating that he knew exactly what she wanted him to do. He snatched the ring from Dan's hand, put it on his finger, twisted it, and held it to Dan's bare forearm.

"Now!" Jonathan shouted.

Dan wore the amulet, so now the ring and amulet were canceling each other out, and Dan was susceptible to being hurt. Anise raised her mace and clocked Dan right in the chest. He fell backward, gasping. Jonathan kept pressing the ring to Dan so Anise could hit him again. As much as she hated it, Anise swung again, her actions controlled by fear and adrenaline. Grace tried to push Anise away from her son, to no avail. As soon as Dan sat up, the mace hit him in the chest, and he fell again, his head hitting the floor.

"He's out!" Jonathan told her.

Anise turned to Grace, who tried to back away from her. Nate had recovered and made his way over to his cohorts. He picked up the mace that was on the floor next to Dan and struck Grace near her clavicle. She fell and hit her head on the floor which knocked her unconscious again.

Jonathan looked at Nate, and Nate looked back at Jonathan. It seemed to Anise that the two of them were trying to decide on whether or not to trust one another. The boys stood on either side of her, each with a puffed out chest, squared shoulders, and a mutual ominous glare at the other. Jonathan's finger that wore the armor ring twitched a little, and he left it with the poisonous side exposed. Nate's grip on the mace he held tightened. Neither moved, but Anise felt the tension thickening with every second.

Chapter 22

As Jonathan and Nate stared each other down, Anise decided to defuse the situation before they did something unnecessarily violent.

"Come on," she said to both of them as the sirens grew louder. "We need to leave before we get caught."

"Here," Nate said, taking the amulet off Dan and handing it to Anise. "Don't forget to take this with you."

"Aren't you coming?" Anise asked him.

"No," said Nate. "Grace will try to make you her scapegoat. Someone has to insist that you two weren't here."

Anise looked at him with both gratitude and confusion, but there was no time to try to figure him out now. "The earrings," Anise said.

"We can take this," Jonathan said, holding up his hand that wore the ring, "but leave the earrings. If anything is missing from the museum display, they'll know someone else had to have been here, and they'll come looking for us. It's not worth the risk; we'll have to find another way to get them later." Carefully, he twisted the ring's setting so the poisonous side flipped over, leaving the non-poisonous side showing.

"Go," Nate told them. "I'll clean up any traces of your blood, Boy Scout. You two were never here."

Jonathan gave Nate a look of disbelief. He then took Anise's hand, and they ran to the restroom and lowered themselves out the window. Jogging across the street, they easily blended into the Concert in the Park that was still going on. Anise placed her jacket over Jonathan's shoulders so no one would see the blood stains. His wounds seemed to have stopped bleeding, to her relief. She quickly brushed some of the dust off his face and hair. Facing each other, they discreetly removed their latex gloves they had promised each other they wouldn't take off until they were out of the museum and headed toward their rental car.

Anise wanted to go directly to the hospital for Jonathan's stab wounds.

"No," he told her. "We can't go to the hospital. They'll be required to report it to the authorities, and being named in two police reports in the same night isn't going to look good."

"You're right," Anise replied. "Let's get rid of the gloves and go to the drug store for hydrogen peroxide to clean you up."

She drove them down a main road in town. During the drive, Jonathan used some anti-bacterial wipes Anise had in her tote bag to clean the remaining dust off his skin, hair, and clothes. After they found a drugstore, Anise went into the restroom and flushed the gloves away. They got supplies to clean Jonathan's wounds, and several bandages. After finding an empty lot to park by, Anise had Jonathan remove his t-shirt so she could clean his back. She noticed that the wounds weren't as deep as she had anticipated. It was almost as if Dan hadn't really wanted to hurt Jonathan. She finished quickly and fished a new t-shirt out of the shopping bags they'd left in the backseat.

He put it on, his expression grateful. "Thanks! Good as new."

Jonathan insisted on going back to the concert to

see his friend so they would have an alibi for where they were that night. As she drove carefully through the unfamiliar streets, he kept talking quickly about what had happened at the museum, and she could tell adrenaline was still pumping through him. Anise felt wired and shaky, but also as if the evening had been nothing but a scary dream. Trying to distract herself from the odd feeling, she asked Jonathan, "When we were in the ducts, you mentioned a story about your sister?"

"Oh, right. I promised you the rest of that story," he said. "Jamie climbed into a sewer drain once when we were kids when some other kid dared her to. She couldn't get out, and all the other kids ran away so they wouldn't get in trouble. I ended up riding my bike to the nearest neighborhood, and when I got there, I was lucky to find some really nice people. I explained what happened, and they called the police and my parents. We finally got Jamie out. I mentioned this in the duct because being in there and looking through the slotted cover made me think of Jamie looking through the slotted cover of the sewer grate."

"So you've always been brave in scary situations. I wish I could be," Anise said. She noticed Jonathan was looking intently at her. "What?" she asked him, smiling.

He gave her a look of awe. "You're kidding, right? You were extremely brave. I couldn't have done it without you. I can't believe how you kicked Nate's ass! That was so incredible! How'd you do it?"

She almost didn't tell him, but after what they'd just been through, she knew she could trust him. "A year or so ago, I was mugged when I was walking home one night. For months afterward, I got panic attacks whenever I left my apartment. So to feel more confident, I secretly started taking self-defense and kickboxing fitness classes. I got really good, and they made me feel so much safer. Now I put on a hat, sunglasses, and an oversized jacket to disguise myself and sneak over to the gym to teach kickboxing fitness a couple times a week. It lets me practice my skills without having to spar with anyone, since I never liked that part."

"That's great!" Jonathan exclaimed. "But why would you keep that a secret?"

"My family is...less than supportive. Same with Brian who was my boyfriend at the time. Plus he would've wanted to spend the extra money I was earning on stuff we don't need instead of putting it toward bills." Thinking of Brian made her voice start wavering. "I thought about telling my friends Erin and Vanessa, but I knew I'd feel bad if I told them and not Joy. I love Joy, but she can't keep a secret no matter how hard she tries, and I didn't want this getting back to my mom or Brian. So I told no one."

"I'm really sorry about Brian," Jonathan said.

Anise nodded, her guilt filling her eyes with tears. She asked Jonathan for a tissue and pointed at her tote bag.

He rummaged through until he found some and handed one to her. "So why wouldn't your mom and Brian support your self-defense classes? It sounds like a really good thing to me."

She shrugged and dabbed her eyes. "They've always been judgmental when it comes to me, even for something that most people would think is good. I don't know why. And for some reason, I let it get to me. When I feel like I might be judged by them or anyone, I get really nervous and I screw up, like at my recent job interviews. They take that as proof that they were right, and they'd tell me so. But when I started taking the classes, I realized that because no one I knew was around to judge me, I could relax and enjoy them. And because I was relaxed, I didn't screw anything up. It was the first thing I really excelled at, and I grew to trust myself and my own instincts a little bit more."

"Well, I think it's great," Jonathan told her. "I promise I won't tell anyone."

"Thank you," she said, giving him an appreciative look. "But it's okay. I don't want to keep it a secret anymore."

"Good. Anyone else in the world besides your mom and Brian would be incredibly supportive and impressed. You took Nate down so quickly when I couldn't land a punch," Jonathan marveled again. "Have you ever had to use your fighting skills before?"

Jonathan's admiration made her mind flash back to earlier that evening when Jonathan's attempts to fight Nate proved futile. She'd impressed herself at how she'd stepped in, and with her self-defense and kickboxing training plus the element of surprise, she'd managed to knock Nate out. "Just once," Anise replied. "Grace came into the thrift shop before I knew who she was. She became violent, and I had to stop her. But that's the only other time I've had to fight someone, and I'm glad. I hated every second of both of those fights. I can't stand violence. I only did it because I didn't see another way out of the situation. But I hope I never have to do that to anyone ever again."

"I get that," Jonathan said. "I don't like fighting either. I had a hard time using the maces tonight and watching the sarcophagus get destroyed. Precious artifacts like that need to be protected, but we didn't have a choice. Unfortunately, compromising our integrity was necessary to stay alive."

Anise kept her eyes on the road. There was so much to think about still. They managed to take down Grace and escape the museum with their lives tonight, but what if they still got arrested for breaking and entering, attempted robbery—

She was grateful when Jonathan's kind words interrupted her fear. "I hope you know that you were amazing back there, Anise. I know you said you don't think you're brave, but I have to disagree."

"I've had issues with anxiety and panic attacks for almost as long as I can remember," she reminded him. "I was terrified. They had you tied to a chair. They could've killed you, but you never told them where I was. You risked your life to help me. Thank you. *You* were the brave one."

"But you didn't run away even though you had the opportunity. You stayed and fought for yourself, me, and the Jewelry. You were incredible. Fear in that situation would be normal for anyone. And there's no bravery without fear, you know?"

There's no bravery without fear. "Thank you," she said, considering his words. "I like that perspective." She'd have to write that on a blank note card later.

✳ ✳ ✳

"HEY!" JONATHAN SHOUTED AS THEY WALKED across the grass, maneuvering their way through the crowd. It seemed like the entire town had gathered for the Concert in the Park. "That's my friend," he added more quietly to Anise.

She looked over at where he was pointing, and her eyes scanned the mass of people until they landed on one man who waved at them. She followed Jonathan over to him.

Jonathan exchanged greetings with him and then turned to look at Anise. "Ivan, this is Anise. We came out here just to see you guys play."

"Hey, it's nice to meet you," said Ivan. His eyes gave Anise the once over from underneath dark curls. "I hope you liked the set."

"Nice to meet you too," she said. "I really liked the second song you did. What's that one called?"

"Oh, that's 'City Diamonds'. Thanks!" replied Ivan with a big grin.

"Did you see us waving to you right before you went on?" Jonathan asked him, nodding as if to answer for him. "What time was that, 7:00?"

"No, we went on about 6:15, man, but yeah, I think I did see you waving. I'm so glad you made it out here!" He slapped Jonathan on the shoulder where he'd been stabbed. Luckily, Anise was the only one who noticed him wince.

"Me too," Jonathan replied.

"Dude, I gotta ask. What happened to your face?" Ivan said, studying Jonathan's face.

"We went mountain biking yesterday. The trail was steeper than I thought it would be."

"It looks awful, right?" Anise added. "I told him not to go that way. He landed on rocks."

"Listen to your girl next time," Ivan told him, his eyes scanning Jonathan's face in disbelief. "You look like hell. It looks like you lost a fight—bad."

"I've never lost a fight in my life!" Jonathan protested, smirking.

"That's 'cause you've never been in a fight in your life," Ivan said with a laugh. "Hey, the band's gonna go out drinking later," he continued. "You guys should come."

"Definitely," Jonathan agreed.

"Awesome!" said Ivan, slapping Jonathan on the shoulder. "I'll come find you when we're ready to go!"

"You were stabbed, Jonathan," Anise whispered to him, once Ivan had gone. "You really need your rest."

"We need the alibi more," he replied. "Especially because my blood is all over that gallery. Maybe we can say that I had a nosebleed while we were there. Although that won't explain why it's on two different knives. Maybe I can say I'm being framed." A worried look crossed his face.

"You don't believe that Nate will clean it up like he said he would?"

Jonathan scoffed. "Of course not, do you?"

She shrugged. "He let us go. He gave me back my amulet."

"Maybe he's not as bad as Grace or Dan, but he's not a good guy, Anise. I don't know why he let us go, but we have to believe he has his own reasons for it."

She shook her head, completely confused as to what Nate's motive might have been. "I don't know what to believe anymore."

Friday, June 8, 2012

EVEN THOUGH BRIAN'S STUFF WAS EVERYWHERE and reminded her of him, Anise had never been happier to be at home. With all the stress, fear, and guilt she carried, her own bed provided the comfort she needed. She and Jonathan had spent half the night drinking with his friends and flew home first thing in the morning. It was now late afternoon, and she'd just woken up from a nap. She stared at her yellow paisley sheets, mentally making a list of things she had to take care of. Check on her mom. Call her friends. Gather Brian's things. Call Corinne. Throw out her painting that Brian destroyed. Fix the holes Brian punched in the wall.

A loud knock on the door startled her, and she walked over to answer it.

"Anise Viston?"

"Yes?" she said to the man and woman on her doorstep.

They showed her their badges. "We're Agents Harms and Linn, FBI. May we come in?"

Part 4

THE RIGHT THING TO DO ISN'T ALWAYS THAT BLACK AND WHITE

Chapter 23

Anise took a deep breath as she walked with the guard down the hallway of the Springfield Correctional Facility. The gray walls were stark and cold. She could almost feel the pain, anger, and agony that they contained within them, and she shuddered. She was escorted into a large room with several tables. It reminded her a little of her high school cafeteria, except instead of students, the room was filled with inmates and their visitors. It was early, and she hadn't slept much the night before, but she was wide awake with anticipation.

"Wait here," she was ordered. Anise sat in the uncomfortable plastic chair next to a table that wobbled when she touched it.

As Anise looked at her surroundings, she saw Nate being escorted into the room. His guard pointed at her, and Nate's eyes opened wide with surprise when he saw her.

She looked him up and down as he walked over to her. His leg must've healed; he wasn't limping anymore. His eye had healed, too, and his face was back to being ridiculously handsome. Even though she was livid with him, she felt a wave of attraction to him, then a wave of annoyance that he could still make her feel that way after everything that had happened. And his jumpsuit looked awful. "Orange isn't your color."

He sat in the chair next to her. "I know. After I get out of here, I'm never wearing orange again."

"We have a lot to discuss," she informed him.

He gave her a slight smile. "I'm glad you think so. How are you?"

"I'm doing okay. Taking it one day at a time. You?"

"Same." After a moment's pause, he continued. "I'm really glad you're here."

"Why is that?" she asked him in a voice that demanded a good answer.

"Because now I get the chance to apologize. I handled everything all wrong."

"Yes, Nate, you did." She sat back in her chair and crossed her arms.

"I'm sorry. I shouldn't have tried to take your amulet. I should have told you what Grace and Dan were up to."

She frowned at him. "I sincerely hope you don't think you're finished with your apology."

"I'm not finished," he assured her. "I should've done more to protect you at the museum and before then, too. I tried, but it wasn't enough. I'm sorry for betraying your trust."

"I'm confused, and I have a lot of questions," Anise told him. She didn't want him to know how much he'd hurt her, but she knew her expression was probably giving her away.

"I'll tell you anything you want to know."

"I hope you mean that."

"I do. I promise."

She leaned forward, resting her arms on the table. A poster on the wall caught her eye that reminded inmates and their visitors that everything said in the room was being recorded, and it warned that whispering was strictly forbidden. She'd have to be careful about what she said. "You've been really inconsistent, and there's a lot I don't understand. Like when we were at the museum, at first you and Jonathan fought, but at the end you helped us leave. And I'm surprised that you want to apologize to me now, as if you care. All you ever wanted since we first met was my amulet, and you had the perfect opportunity to take it right before I left the museum. But you didn't. You gave it back to me. Why?"

He shook his head. "I don't want your amulet or any of the Jewelry. Grace does. She wanted my help in getting the full set of Armor Jewelry."

"What does Grace want with the Jewelry? I mean, I know..." She thought about how to word it. "I know the legends, but what does she want to do with that power?"

Nate shrugged. "I don't know. She wouldn't tell me."

She paused to think of her next question. "I heard Dan call Grace 'Mother' a few times. But who are they to you? And how did you get involved with them in the first place?"

"Unfortunately, they're my father and grandmother," Nate replied.

"Really?" Anise was surprised. "You look nothing like them."

"I know. They tell me I look like my mother, but I was too young to remember what she looked like."

"What happened to her?"

"They won't tell me. I've tried to find out by looking at old newspaper articles, but all they say is that she went missing and was never found. I have my suspicions though." He looked down at the table, and his shoulders slumped.

Even though her anger was strong, Anise started to feel a little sorry for Nate. "That's terrible. What was her name?"

"Lorelei Brevain."

"Do you remember anything about her?"

"All I can remember is that she was a good person. A great mother. That's why I had to save that park by the freeway. One of my only memories of her was our time there."

"So you were raised by Dan then?"

"Both Dan and Grace, yes."

Anise couldn't imagine what it might do to a person to be raised by someone like Grace. After she had once confessed to Corrine how her parents had treated her as a child, Corrine had told her that emotional abuse can sometimes damage a person's sense of reality and identity. She looked at him with a serious expression. Pretending to rub her forehead with both hands to block the view of any possible cameras, she silently mouthed to him, "Have you done criminal things with your family before?"

Nate frowned, and he squirmed in his seat slightly. He nodded and looked down. "Heists," he mouthed silently back. "I got really skilled at being a professional thief." Then aloud he continued, "But that was during my teenage years. As soon as I turned eighteen, and they had no more legal claim on me, I moved out and had nothing more to do with them."

Nate looked at the ground and appeared to be remembering something. Anise was about to ask him another question when he continued. "I remember the day I left like it was yesterday. My hatred for them was the first thing I thought about in the morning and the last thing at night. I needed to find some peace before it ate me alive. But Grace wouldn't let me quit. I was too good at..." He paused and mouthed, "theft." Aloud he continued, "And they needed me. She threatened my life if I ever stopped helping her, and I knew she meant it. So for my eighteenth birthday, I came up with a plan to get Grace to let me leave. It was drastic, and she almost died, but it worked. She had laughed and told me I reminded her of herself. Grace respects those who stand up to her.

Those who don't, she considers weak. From that respect, I got her to agree that we'd leave each other alone. I just wanted a normal life. Since my eighteenth birthday, I hadn't seen Grace or Dan again until a few months ago. That's when they asked for my help in getting the Armor Jewelry."

"If you want nothing to do with them, why did you agree to help?"

"Grace promised me she'd tell me what happened to my mother. I've been wanting to know that ever since she disappeared. All we ever did in the past was..." He paused again to mouth, "Steal from museums..." Aloud he said, "Because Grace used to be a curator, and she knows the value of the artifacts. I never thought anyone would get hurt."

Anise shifted in her chair. "So the couple I heard about who owned the ring..."

Nate leaned forward and whispered very softly, "Grace killed them when they wouldn't sell it. I didn't want the same thing to happen to you or anyone else."

"So you're saying that when you tried to take my amulet from me, you were actually trying to save my life?" Anise asked, her eyebrows raised.

"Yes." His expression was flat and serious.

Anger bubbled up inside her again. "Well, you went about it in a really fucked up way! You should never have been working with Grace and Dan in the first place," Anise scolded.

Nate shook his head. "I won't apologize for that. If I had stayed out of it, they would've killed you for the amulet. But I am sorry that I went about it in a way that hurt you."

"Did Grace and Dan...force you into the family business? Or did you ask to join?"

"At first, I had no choice. I was told I had to earn my keep."

"What about later? You wanted to continue...stealing?" The last word she'd whispered.

He gave a slight shrug. "I started enjoying the thrill of it—a lot. The adrenaline rush I'd get from it was the best feeling I ever had. And it was the easiest way to find peace. Right after a successful...night at the museum, Grace and Dan were happy and congratulated me on a job well done. They were actually proud of me, and I could relax for a few days. Then Grace would go back to her normal self and things were hell again."

Anise took a thoughtful pause. "Did she hurt you?"

Nate was silent a moment. "Not really."

She gave him a look of disbelief. "She shot you in the leg, so I have a hard time believing that. You promised to answer my questions."

He nodded. "Okay. When I was really young, she started teaching me how to pickpocket and fight. She made me pick fights with other kids. She'd smack my face if I didn't do what she wanted. When I was a little older she'd chase me with a cast iron pan if I pissed her off. A few times she tried to run me over with the car." He stopped when tears began streaming down her face. "Should I continue?"

Anise wiped her cheeks with her fingers. "No. I'm sorry. I don't want to make you relive that."

Nate got up and brought her a box of tissues that was sitting on a nearby table.

She took one and dabbed her eyes. "What did you do to try to stop her?"

"I begged Dan for help, but he's terrified of her and always took her side. I tried to have her committed. More than once. But she's really good at playing the charming little old lady and making me look like the bad guy."

"You said you had a drastic plan where she almost died?"

He squirmed in his seat again. "I did what I had to do to get away from her. I could've killed her, but I didn't. I'm not a monster like she is. I just wanted my freedom.

Do you want to hear the details?"

"God, no." She gazed at his sad expression. "What about the scar by your eye? How did you get that?"

"Dirt bike accident when I was a kid."

"How old were you?"

He thought for a moment. "Four, I think."

"So young? Didn't you have a helmet?"

Nate shook his head.

Anise leaned in and whispered, "What did you do with the things you stole?"

He whispered back, "Grace and Dan have always had a big stash of artifacts just waiting for the right buyer. I preferred to get rid of my share right away. I sold them on the black market. I have my cash from the sales hidden in off shore accounts."

She felt it was none of her business, but she didn't care. "You and your family had been doing this for years, right? The things you took must have been worth a lot in order for you to risk so much to get them. You must've made a lot of money. With what you earned, do you still even need to work a real job?"

He hesitated at first but shook his head. "No."

She leaned back in her seat. "So, what you told me about working in finance..."

"That was true," he insisted. "I wanted to try to make a normal life for myself. That included getting a job and doing everything else most people my age do."

"You put in all the work to get a degree in finance then?"

He nodded. "I have two degrees. The other is in computer science."

"Oh." She had a realization and whispered, "That's how you were able to create that computer virus that kept the guards busy that night."

"That's right," he said with a cocky smirk.

"You look awfully proud of yourself for someone who's just been thrown in prison," she told him with a frown.

"I am," he admitted, ignoring her disapproving look. "It was really complicated, and it worked perfectly."

"It...was brilliant," she admitted. "I'm impressed. But it was also dishonest, immoral, and illegal. That's nothing to be proud of. Why wouldn't you use your skills for good instead? Someone I really respect once said that when you know what the right thing to do is, do you really have any other choice?"

"Whoever said that must've grown up in a Norman Rockwell painting," Nate said with a scoff. "The right thing to do isn't always that black and white. Besides, saving your life and your freedom *is* a good thing. I'd do it for you again if you needed me."

She looked at her hands in her lap while her thoughts raced. Could his criminal actions have actually had altruism behind them? By staying in the museum past closing with the intent to steal the earrings, she had also done a criminal act in the name of what's right. She looked into his cobalt eyes. Anise was embarrassed by what she wanted to ask him next and debated with herself on whether or not to do it.

After a period of silence, he said, "I can tell there's more you want to know. Ask away."

She took a deep breath and gathered her courage. "You lied to me, over and over. You made me believe that you liked me. You did it so well, too. I foolishly thought we had something special. We only went out a few times, but I never felt that way about anyone before, like everything about you was so right, and I thought you might be..." She angrily narrowed her eyebrows. "Was it necessary to humiliate me like that?"

He looked at her, and she could see the intensity in his eyes building.

"I thought it was just me," he said.

"What are you talking about?" Anise asked with a glare.

"You need to know what was real and what wasn't," he replied. "I approached you at the club with an intent to take your amulet from you. I had begged Grace to let me try. Like I said, I didn't want there to be any more casualties. I tried to get you to like me so I could get you in a situation where you'd take the amulet off willingly." He had a slight frown and continued in a whisper. "I was hoping to be able to swipe it without you realizing it instead of scaring you by taking it from you forcefully. But when you interviewed me at the mall and we hung out at Johnny's, things started to change for me. I told Grace I wouldn't help her anymore, that I wouldn't steal from you, and that I wanted out. She threatened your life and mine. So I tried to get the amulet from you again. When I failed, she poisoned me with the ring and went looking for you herself. But I—"

"What do you mean 'things changed for you?'" Anise interrupted him. "What made you change your mind?"

"You did." He leaned back in his chair and looked at her seriously for a moment before continuing. "I really liked getting to know you. The way we get along so well—I've never had so much fun with anyone before. Our conversations at the park, at Johnny's, at the concert—that was all real. I couldn't believe what an incredible woman you are. Smart, beautiful, open, trusting. You're kind to everyone you meet. There're things you understand and care about that most people don't. I've thought about you every day since. We did have something special. There's a strong connection between us, and now I know you felt it, too."

That was the last thing she'd expected him to say, and she hated that she liked hearing him say it. "I did. But that was then."

"No," came his confident reply. "My feelings haven't changed. I still feel that connection, and I think you do, too. If you didn't, you wouldn't be here right now asking me all these questions."

She frowned at him and his bold statement. Damn him for seeing right through her. She didn't want to feel that connection with him anymore. While she now believed he had never wanted to hurt her, and her anger was somewhat diminishing, she still felt that trusting him would be the wrong decision. He'd lied and played her for a fool.

When she didn't respond, Nate changed the subject. "I hadn't heard anything about what happened to you," he said.

"There wasn't any evidence to prove that Jonathan and I were at the museum that night," Anise told Nate in a low whisper as she slowly rubbed her face again to hide her moving lips. "The D.A. decided not to prosecute. He only had Grace's and Dan's word to go on. It was their word versus so many others. The security guard never saw me or Jonathan. Jonathan's friend believed that we were at the Concert at the Park across from the museum at 6:15 that night. Brian's sister said Brian called her, and said he never saw me at the museum when he had looked for me. There was no physical evidence of us being there, either. There were no prints, none of Jonathan's blood, and somehow all the security cameras got erased. The security officer blamed it on a faulty system. He said all the security equipment was malfunctioning that night. So, I want to thank you. If you hadn't stayed behind to erase the security camera's footage and cover our tracks, I'd..." She stopped because she didn't want to think about what could have been. She continued in her normal speaking voice. "I have no idea how you managed it, but I'm grateful. And we don't really talk about that night, but I'm sure Jonathan is grateful too."

"You're welcome," Nate replied with a smile which quickly turned into a frown. "You're still hanging out with Boy Scout?"

"Yes, he's my friend."

"Why'd you pick *him* to help you at the museum anyway? He was useless."

"No, he wasn't. He came up with most of the plan we had." She ignored Nate's smirk and continued in a whisper. "He seemed to know a lot about museum security."

Nate laughed and shook his head. He whispered, "He couldn't even break into the display case! He spent most of the night tied to a chair. And I bet he never threw a punch in his life."

"Are you jealous that I'm still hanging out with him?" she challenged him.

Nate's mischievous sideways smile made an appearance. "Do you want me to be jealous?"

She frowned at him but didn't answer his question. "Tell me what happened with you," she continued. "It hasn't been on the news back home at all."

"I was able to cut a deal," Nate replied. "I revealed the location of where Grace and Dan stash their stolen artifacts in exchange for a smaller sentence. I'll be out in four years."

"Okay," Anise said. She leaned back in her chair. "And what happened to Dan and Grace?"

"Dan got 35 years for attempted murder and attempted robbery. His prints were found on a forklift, and they think he used it to try to steal the sarcophagus, breaking it in the process. Grace was pinned for the murders and got life. Her prints were found on the gun that killed Brian and a security guard. They're in higher security facilities not too far from here."

"Good," said Anise. She'd looked down when Nate mentioned the murders. Some days the guilt was almost too overwhelming to handle.

"I'm really sorry about Brian."

She nodded without looking up.

"Listen," he whispered, leaning over to her and keeping his head down, "I think the FBI is working with Canadian officials to try to pin someone for the murders of the people who owned the ring. They were here asking me questions. You can't be caught with that thing, or it'll look really bad. Promise me you'll find a good place to hide it. Preferably not in your apartment. Okay?"

"No whispering!" shouted a guard who was strolling through the room. "Your one and only warning!"

Anise looked back at Nate. "Thank you, and I promise. As soon as I get back home." She noticed Nate was smiling at her. "What are you smiling about?"

"I didn't expect to ever see you again, beautiful," he told her. "When they told me it was you, I didn't believe them."

Anise wrinkled her nose. "Why are you calling me 'beautiful?' I don't like it."

Nate looked confused. "I've called you beautiful before."

"Calling me beautiful—as in the adjective—is one thing. Using 'beautiful' as a pet name is another. I don't like it. It sounds..." Her face cringed. "It sounds phony. What happened to 'honey?' That felt sincere."

"You told me not to call you that anymore."

"Oh, right." She hated to admit it to herself, but she'd missed hearing him say it. She'd missed a lot of things about him. Anise gave him a little smile and a shrug.

He grinned at her. "Good to know."

"You should also know that I understand how much courage it took for you to stand up to Grace and Dan. Not just because they're terrifying, but also because they're your only family. I think it's harder to stand up to family than anyone else. I'm just starting to find that courage in my own life. Plus, I think I believe you when you say you did all this to protect me. It's the only explanation I can think of that would explain your inconsistent behavior."

"Thanks for flying all the way out here and giving me the chance to explain." There was a glint of hope in his eyes.

Anise nodded at him. "So, please know that I'm grateful." As much as she missed him, she was also glad to see him behind bars after what he did to her. "But please also know that I'm still angry, and I still see you as a liar and a criminal. You deserved every bit of that ass kicking I gave you." She frowned, expecting him to tell her that she'd only been able to do it because he was caught off guard, or that he'd held back, not wanting to hurt her.

Instead, he gave her a smile that looked genuine. "That was amazing. I was so proud of you."

His surprising praise made her flustered. She stared at him and couldn't think of anything to say.

"Where'd you learn that?" he asked.

"You don't get to know that about me," she snapped at him. "Things are not back to normal between us by any means. I don't see how they ever could be, no matter how strong our connection was."

He nodded, and his expression was flat. "Understood."

"And before I leave I wanna know just one more thing." It was trivial, but Anise knew she'd wonder if she didn't ask, and she didn't want to wonder about him. She needed to forget him. "Tell me about the tattoo you said you regret," she demanded, looking at the long-sleeved white t-shirt he wore under the orange short-sleeved jumpsuit.

"I got it when I was fifteen," he explained, pushing up the sleeve on his right arm. "One of my friends had an older brother who'd just become a tattoo artist and wanted to practice on someone."

"Scott and Peter?" Anise asked, remembering his two friends she'd met at Johnny's Bar.

"No. Someone I lost touch with a long time ago."

Anise looked at the jumbled mess on his arm. There were letters and pictures, but there was so much going on it was hard to tell what anything was. "What is it?"

"Originally, I'd asked him to tattoo 'Satan's Helper' up my arm. He did it and added flames that reached my wrist and a pitchfork that went halfway up my neck. But it looked like shit. The flames were too pointy and looked like mountains. The pitchfork looked like a regular fork. And he misspelled Satan. It said 'Satin's Helper."

"Satin?" Anise started to laugh but stopped herself. "Sorry, that's not funny."

"No," Nate disagreed, "it's funny. And humiliating. I haven't worn a short-sleeved shirt since."

Anise looked at his arm more carefully. "So it looks like you tried to cover it up with more tattoos?"

"Yeah, I got a motorcycle and some other random shit, but the letters are so big nothing covered them in the way I'd hoped."

"You're right," Anise agreed. "I can still read 'Satin's Helper' if I look closely enough."

"Right. Short of turning the letters into squares and rectangles, nothing's going to cover them well enough. So except for the motorcycle I've slowly been having all of it removed. I got rid of most of the fork on my neck, and now I can roll up my sleeves to my mid forearm with nothing showing except a little scarring. I have a lot left to go though."

"Why 'Satan's Helper?' Why would you want that on your body?"

He shrugged. "The year before I got the tattoo is when I started helping Grace and Dan with their...activities. Every time I entered a museum, those words popped into my head. I don't know why."

Anise felt sadness overwhelm her. "So you literally branded yourself...as something evil."

Nate stared at the table top and said nothing.

Anise continued, "I hope you know that you're not evil. You've done bad things, but you obviously feel guilty about it or you wouldn't think of yourself as Satan's helper."

Nate raised his gaze to meet hers. "I don't feel guilty about the heists. I enjoyed them."

She watched his eyes turn downward again. "Do you

feel bad that you don't have guilt about the heists?"

"I know I *should*. What kind of a person doesn't have guilt when they do something wrong?"

"So you know it's wrong, but you still enjoy it. And you feel bad about not feeling bad about not having guilt. Interesting." She wasn't sure what to make of that. "I bet *Grace* doesn't feel guilty either."

Nate crossed his arms over his chest. "Exactly. That's why I left home and stopped going on heists. I want to be nothing like her."

"What do you mean when you say you enjoyed the heists? Was it the adrenaline rush?" Anise wanted to know.

An uncontrolled grin graced his lips. "Yeah. The high is incredible."

"If it's just adrenaline...don't you get the same feeling from Motocross?"

"In a way. The heists give me more of a charge though."

"Why?"

"I can't explain why. Maybe it's the added risk of getting caught or the challenge of getting into locked, protected buildings."

Anise wondered if it was the positivity he received from Grace and Dan telling him they were proud of him on the heists that gave him the extra charge he didn't get from Motocross. Besides exciting, dare-devil activities, maybe all Nate really needed was some love. Or maybe it actually was just the added risk and challenge like he'd said. Something in her told her it was probably a little of both. Not wanting to think about it anymore, she checked her watch and stood up to leave. "I have to get back to the airport."

Nate stood and opened his arms to her.

"Are we allowed to hug?" she asked him.

"Yeah," he replied, "just not for too long."

She told herself she shouldn't hug a liar and a criminal, that she should just leave and forget he ever existed, but if she denied wanting to hug him good-bye, she'd be lying to herself again. After everything he'd told her, if anyone needed a hug, it was him. Plus, maybe it would bring her some closure. She allowed him to envelope her in his arms, and she squeezed back. For a moment, the world disappeared again, and it was just the two of them that existed. She'd almost forgotten how good he felt and let her body melt onto his, not wanting to let go. *Dammit.* She mentally cursed their strong and undeniable chemistry that wouldn't leave her the fuck alone.

"Good-bye, Nate," she said, after she'd broken the embrace and turned to leave.

"I know you're mad at me, but can I call you sometime?" he asked.

Anise turned back around. She glared in disbelief at his audacity and wanted to deny his request, but when she opened her mouth to tell him off, the words refused to come out.

Nate looked at her with his intense blue stare that still infiltrated her dreams at night and flashed her a confident grin. "It's not a 'no;' I'll take it!"

✳ ✳ ✳

"HIS FAMILY HAS REQUESTED NO OUTSIDE visitors," the nurse told her. "You can try coming back another time to see if they've changed their minds."

"I *am* family," Anise insisted. "And I can't come back another time. I don't live in Philadelphia; I had to take a plane to get here. Please, I need to see him."

"What are *you* doing here?" Les's mother Patricia Wilkins demanded as she stepped out of Les's hospital room. She glared at Anise.

"I know he's my brother, and I want to see him," Anise told her.

"Absolutely not! How did you know we were here?"

Patricia demanded.

"Your neighbors told me," Anise replied. "I just want to see how he's doing. Please. I came all this way."

"No one asked you to come. You're just like your mother, not leaving this alone. No one wants you here. Please leave before I ask the nurse to call security."

"I know you were afraid my mother might try to take him back," Anise said gently. "And I'm sorry that happened. I'm not trying to be like her. But since he tried to visit us, I think he'd appreciate that I'm here. I just want to see him for a few minutes."

"Do you not understand what we're going through as a family?!" Patricia fired at her. "My son is *dying*. All I want is to spend as much time with him as possible. Every time he has an episode, it could mean the end. One of these days he won't wake up again." She burst into tears. "I don't need this extra stress from you! Nurse!"

Anise held up her hands. "I'm sorry, Mrs. Wilkins. I meant no disrespect. I'll go." She turned and walked down the long, stark hallway.

"If that girl tries to come back, I want you to call security and have her thrown out!" Anise heard Patricia say to the nurse.

Rounding the corner, Anise found a small waiting area with chairs. Digging through her tote bag, she pulled out the disguise she'd wear when she was on her way to teach her kickboxing fitness classes. She tucked her hair up under her cap and put on her oversized sweat jacket. Sitting in one of the chairs, she leaned back to wait. Patricia would have to leave at some point.

Not quite an hour later, Patricia walked by her in a daze with her jacket on and stepped onto the elevator. Anise glided down the hall, breezed by the nurses' station, and entered Les's room. He was very still and looked exactly like the drawing she'd made last time she was with him in a hospital. His eyes were closed and the machines attached to him made unsettling beeping noises.

Anise found the carnelian ring in her tote bag. She pulled the amulet out from under her sweater. "Dr. Smithton said the amulet might have healing powers," she told Les, even though she knew he couldn't hear her. "And if it does, the ring will amplify that power. I'm not sure how this is supposed to work, but I have to try." She put the amulet around his neck and the ring on his finger. After several minutes, she took the Jewelry back. Nothing had happened.

Anise thought for a moment and came up with another idea. She put the amulet around her neck, the ring on her finger, and her hand on her brother's arm. "My friend Jonathan said that the Armor Jewelry works by intention. Maybe if I intend to help you, you'll wake up." She closed her eyes and sent healing thoughts to him. After several more minutes, she opened her eyes. Les was still unconscious. A noise by the door made her look over her shoulder to see a security guard entering the room.

"Time to go, Miss."

Sunday, September 16, 2012

Jonathan waved when he saw Anise enter the café. Her cheeks were rosy from walking in the cool, autumn air, and her brown, wavy hair was windblown. She wore a cropped, olive green jacket over a long velvet skirt with tall cognac-colored boots. He thought she looked stunning and hoped he was presentable enough in his faded jeans and a band t-shirt. He got up and pulled out a chair for her.

"Thank you," she said, smiling.

"It's been awhile," he said. "How have you been?"

"A little better," she told him. "Each day is slightly easier. What about you?"

"Getting busy. Classes started a couple weeks ago." He told her about his schedule and how excited he was to be in school again. "How's work?"

"It's good, actually," Anise replied. "Recruiting respondents is a lot easier now. They're going to make me a manager soon."

"Hey, that's great!" It was obvious her confidence in her abilities was growing, and he was so proud of her for that.

"Thank you! And I'm glad you called. I wanted to talk to you about something." She removed her jacket and hung it on the back of her chair. "I just got back from visiting Nate," she began.

"You visited Nate? Why?" Jonathan asked, almost choking on his iced tea.

"Because I wanted to thank him for his help. We'd be in prison right now, too, had Nate not covered our tracks."

Jonathan raised his eyebrows in shock. "Nate may have helped us get away, but he's also a professional criminal who lied to you and allowed his cohorts to threaten your life. It's unforgiveable as far as I'm concerned."

"Yeah, he shouldn't have lied, but at the time I think he felt it was his best option. He'd been in a devastating situation with his family." She told Jonathan about some of the abuse Nate had endured. "As I think about how I could've better handled my situation with Brian, I can understand why someone would resort to dishonesty when they didn't know how to make their abusive situation better."

"What do you mean?" This was the first time she'd mentioned anything like this to him, and he hoped she knew she could confide in him.

"I feel so guilty about Brian's death. If I hadn't lied about my trip to Springfield being a business trip, he wouldn't have gotten suspicious, and maybe he'd still be alive. I lied because I was afraid he'd destroy my apartment. As if that's important at all in the grand scheme of things. My friends tell me I sometimes let fear make my choices for me, and they're right. If I hadn't..."

"Anise, Brian's death is not your fault." Jonathan wished he could think of some way to make her feel better.

She shrugged. "Maybe, maybe not. But that's beside the point. I just meant I kind of understand why Nate did what he did. Not that it makes it okay, but just that I understand it. I really believe he was trying to help me. And not everything he did was bad. Haven't you ever thought about what could've happened had Nate not stayed behind that night to cover for us?"

"No," Jonathan replied.

Anise continued in a soft voice, "I've been thinking about it a lot. He was punched in the eye, poisoned with the ring, beaten up, shot in the leg, thrown through a wall, cut with a knife, and hit in the chest with a mace. Even after all that, he still managed to erase the security footage, make any traces of us disappear, lie to the police for our benefit, and give up four years of his life so you and I wouldn't have to be locked away. I think it's pretty heroic."

Jonathan had plenty to say about it but kept his mouth shut. Nate was a professional criminal, and his life's work was based around being dishonest and hurting others. His disrespect for human rights was disgusting, not to mention his complete and shameful disregard for the preservation of precious ancient artifacts. Jonathan didn't believe for a second that Nate selflessly went to prison for them. A more likely explanation was that Nate wanted to be rid of Grace's and Dan's presence in his life, and in order to take them down, he had to go down with them. Anise was far too loyal and caring toward those who didn't deserve it. However, Jonathan firmly believed it wasn't up to him to decide who her friends should be. Her loving nature was what he liked most about her.

"He also brought up a good point," Anise whispered. "He thinks it's not safe for me to hold on to the ring because of the ongoing investigation into the murders of the Woods couple."

Jonathan nodded. "That's probably true."

"So, do you have any ideas of where I could keep it?" she asked him, her eyes wide with hope.

"Yes, actually, I do," he replied. "Dr. Smithton has a secret wall safe in his office and probably one in his home too. I bet he'd be more than happy to keep it in one of his safes for you. A lot of his life's work was based around that Jewelry. You should let him keep the amulet for you, too, unless you get your own safe. It's far too precious to wear like a regular piece of jewelry," he said, eyeing the amulet that hung around her neck. "Plus, I can tell he really likes you. He's asked about you often. He keeps wanting to know how you are and when you're going to come by and talk to him about what happened in Springfield."

"Really?" Anise said. "I like him, too. Thanks! I'll go visit him at the museum tomorrow and ask him."

When Anise picked up her menu, Jonathan took a deep breath and summoned all his courage. His heart pounded, and his palms began sweating. "He's not the only one who really likes you," he admitted to her. "I know now is not the time to ask you out. But if you decide you're interested, I hope that you'll let me know when you're ready." He felt his cheeks burning.

Anise gave him a look of surprise but rewarded him with a smile. "I will," she said.

Monday, September 17, 2012

Morty Smithton heard a knock on his office door. He opened it, book in hand, and glasses on the end of his nose. "Well, good morning, my dear!" exclaimed Morty, as he widened his door and motioned for Anise to step inside. "Jonathan told me you'd be stopping by."

"Good morning, Dr. Smithton!" she replied. "I assume he also told you why?"

"Yes, he did. Do you have the ring with you?"

Anise reached into her purse, brought out a ring box, and handed it to him.

He opened it and took out the ring, trying not to let his excitement show too much. Carefully, he twisted the setting ninety degrees and watched the orange-red carnelian stone flip over to expose the poisonous side with the bands of orpiment and cinnabar. "Amazing," he said under his breath, and twisted the setting once more so the poisonous side flipped back over. Morty put the ring back in the box, closed it, and turned to Anise. "I am honored by your trust in me. I promise you I will keep the ring secret and safe."

"Are you sure you're comfortable with this?" Anise asked him. "If you're caught with it..."

"Don't worry," he reassured her. "No one will find it here. Perhaps you'd like me to hold on to the amulet for you as well?"

"Thank you, Dr. Smithton," Anise began. "But I've been feeling a little on edge ever since I got back from Springfield. I feel safer when I wear it, so I'd like to keep it with me."

He nodded at her, hiding his disappointment. "I completely understand."

Anise thanked him again.

"You're very welcome. May I pour you a cup of coffee?"

"Thanks, but no. I'm sorry to cut this short, but I need to get to work."

"Not until you promise me you'll visit again soon." He gave her a friendly smile.

"I promise." She smiled back and left his office, closing his door behind her.

Morty went to the far wall of his office and grabbed the corner of a portrait of Thomas More. He pulled it, and it swung away from the wall like he was turning the page of a book. Behind it was his wall safe. He opened it and took out a piece of paper with one frayed side. It showed a very old black-and-white drawing of a cuff bracelet made out of an alloy of copper, silver, and gold. It had three large center lapis lazuli stones and five smaller red jasper stones lining each of the two edges. It was also featured in another drawing further down on the page with the poison ring, earrings, and Anise's amulet.

On top of a stack of very old texts about Mallandia, he placed the ring inside the safe along with the page that—many years ago—he had secretly torn out of the old text in the museum's basement library that contained the legend of the Armor Jewelry. He took out another small box and opened it, running a finger over a cuff bracelet that perfectly matched the drawing at which he had just looked. Morty's eyes narrowed as he smiled. "Two down, two to go. Take that, Grace."

About the Author

Katarina Kyde grew up in southern Illinois where she constantly made up stories using toys, photographs, markers—anything—as characters. She has a degree in psychology from the University of Illinois and fosters a nerdy love of neuroplasticity, herbalism, and anything with a touch of magic. Currently, she lives in Colorado with her husband and enjoys hiking, kickboxing, and reading. *Protection of Beauty* is her first novel and the first book in the Armor Series.

katarinakyde.com

Acknowledgements

I want to express my deepest gratitude to everyone who helped and supported me during my adventures of writing this series. Thank you so very much...

To my husband, Ed, for being my biggest fan and my Jewelry Engineer, your help with the trailer, for always lending an ear, having the best ideas in brainstorming sessions, editing, your help with any and every side project I dreamed up, for being an inspiration, and for your belief in me. I love you forever and beyond.

To my best friend, Tyler, for editing, seeing the little details I missed, for your never-ending support, for being as excited as I am about all my new writing ideas, for your assistance and how much fun we had with the pictures, videos, and trailer, and for always being someone who'll be honest with me no matter what. Armory House was one of the best decisions I ever made.

To Jude, for the editing, all the time and effort you put in to helping me, for your incredible ideas, your encouragement and friendship, and for just being you.

To Sarah, for all your sage advice, your kind heart, and for helping me wade through a bunch of pages that weren't ready yet to find the potential within.

To Vivian, for your kind words and your help with some very important scenes.

To Gavin, for selflessly sharing your knowledge, expertise, and advice to make my visions for the trailer come to life, and for your kindness, encouragement, and support.

To Catie, for sharing your knowledge and research with me and for always being so supportive and kind to me and every writer you meet.

To Meagan, for being my MLP friend and for generously taking the time to answer my questions about writing and publishing. Oh, so many questions. Thank you for all your thoughtful and helpful responses. I feel so much more prepared because of you.

To Cody, for all the hikes, yoga classes, dinners, and movies, for your part in the trailer, for your advice on romantic scenes, and for listening to me talk incessantly about my books that you hadn't yet read. Thank you for being a friend.

To everyone at Quill & Cup, for giving me a sense of community in the writing world and for sharing your extensive knowledge and experiences. Because of you, I don't feel alone in this anymore. Thank you for welcoming me home.